PRAISE FOR CLARISSA KAE

A hauntingly romantic debut.

— ESTHER HATCH

Eerie. Inspiring. Masterful.

— ADAM BERG

Clarissa Kae entraps readers with her exquisite writing and master storytelling. I couldn't stop reading.

— JESS HEILEMAN

ONCE AND FUTURE WIFE

BOOK ONE

CLARISSA KAE

CARPE VITAM
PRESS LLC

ACKNOWLEDGMENTS

It takes more than a village to raise a child and a book is no different. The labor pains are just as agonizing and the toddler tantrums are just as ugly but the beautiful creation at the end is always worth those sleepless nights.

I am who I am because of Damon and his steady love, his insistence that I am good allows me to put one foot (or rather, one word) in front of the other. His supportive example extends to all three of our daughters who buoy me with laughter when I want to cry. At only fifteen, Kaela has offered insightful comments on my work—and those of other notable authors.

And Ed, whose friendship has been a guiding hand when it got too dark to see. I am forever grateful for your kindness. And Kirk, who is still quoted in our home for helping us rip off a bandaid we never needed.

Justin for reminding me that I cannot sink low enough, I cannot be wrong enough to lose your friendship. Thank you for being both a brother and a friend when I felt I had neither.

As much as I'd like to pretend I'm a lone wolf, writing is anything but lonely. Thank you to Esther Hatch, Jess Heileman, Adam Berg and Connie Williams for your clarity, support—but most important, for listening while I rant about how hard writing is. And Sian Bessey for helping me understand the language, culture and beauty of Wales (any mistakes are my own inadequacies as a student).

Josi Kilpack—who, by the grace of God unwittingly said what I needed to hear at the pivotal point I needed to hear it. Thank you for being a vessel for good.

Kathleen Chatterton and Papa Carlos, for making room to adopt an orphan like me. To our Olson and Davis families who've shown me what a family should be.

—Clarissa

Let us go forth, the tellers of tales,
And seize whatever prey the heart long for,
And have no fear.

Everything exists, everything is true,
And the earth is only a little dust under our feet.
—*W.B. Yeats*

ISLA BELLE THORNE

SACRAMENTO, CALIFORNIA: PRESENT DAY

Twelve hours after my mother was taken kicking and screaming to the hospital, I sat in the waiting room of the psychiatric wing, deliberately staring out the window instead of facing my uncle and cousin. Disinfectant and misery clung to the walls, strangling the tense conversations down to mere grunts. The waiting room slowly quieted with families leaving, promising to return the next morning.

Behind me, my cousin Ty sighed for the millionth time. Without looking I knew my uncle Stephen was skewering him with a glare. Stephen had called the police on my mother but he wasn't to blame. At least he knew where Mom lived. She had kept that little tidbit of information from me. It didn't matter where she lived or who was visiting. The result was always the same—my mother in a hospital, followed by the endless tinkering of medications and counseling sessions. Days would turn to weeks and doctors would remind her that everything she saw and heard wasn't real.

My feet ached from my vigil at the window. The glass was cool and smudged from the excess of cleaning fluid. Windows were often low on the priority list for hospital janitors. I would know. I'd spent my life staring through them.

I'd hoped Stephen and Ty would slip out quietly, but nothing appeared to be easy this time. I could blame it on Christmas being just two months away. Stephen gave an extra dose of worry near the holidays. I settled for the nearest chair. My uncle abruptly left his perch from across the room and sat next me.

I waited for the shoulder squeeze and the clearing of the throat. He'd launch into how none of this was my fault, that Mom's chemical makeup was just a little off. I would nod along and pretend to agree with the lie. Because there was only one glaring difference between my mother and me—I kept my crazy quiet.

"Isla..." Stephen cleared his throat. On cue, he squeezed my shoulder.

"I'm fine." With a faint smile, I turned my gaze back to the window. I had perfected the art of lying in kindergarten. Survival of the fittest was more than a theory—it was a roadmap. The sooner they left, the sooner I could sneak into my mother's room. I needed to know—to see with my own eyes—the severity of her situation, not the dumbed down version doctors tended to give me.

"You're anything but fine." Ty couldn't keep his mouth shut for anything. In the window's reflection, I watched him stretch his long arms and legs. He motioned for his father to switch him places before pointing at me. "My turn with the statue."

Fighting a groan, I rolled my eyes. Ty's smile and future were as golden as the day he was born. His forced happiness was too bright. The false joy in his teasing hurt.

"Not today, Ty." Stephen's raspy voice comforted me. Duty-bound as a brother and uncle, Stephen had never abandoned my mother despite her wild accusations.

The room fell silent with only the three of us. Glancing at the clock, desperation welled. I needed honest answers regarding my mother's care. I was no longer the frightened child but the doctors—including Stephen—would filter the information, my ease their top priority. I didn't need protection. I needed facts. Just like music comforted my mother, facts lulled my racing thoughts, the *what ifs*

2

that pounded in my head. I needed Stephen and Ty to leave, preferably with their good intentions in tow.

My stomach growled loudly. Like a snickering kid at church, Ty burst into laughter too obnoxious to be genuine. Stephen elbowed him. Devoted to the role, Ty shoved a knuckle in his mouth, his shoulders shaking.

"You're ridiculous." Stephen sneered—igniting another round of laughter from his son.

Ty stood, his smile wide. Deep dimples on either side, he was the dark haired version of my mother, bold and beautiful while Stephen's smaller frame and permanent scowl made him appear more like me than Ty. But unlike everyone else in my family, my eyes changed colors, confessing emotions I'd rather stay hidden. Despite his medical background, Stephen believed the phenomenon was a result of my miraculous birth.

Stephen also believed he could save my mother. His faith didn't prove much.

"What are you laughing at?" Stephen leveled his gaze at Ty.

As a child, I feared the narrowing of his eyes and the tightening of his mouth. It wasn't long before I noticed the small uptick of his lip, the constant fighting of a smile. Just like his son, he gathered merriment, although like me, he kept quiet.

"Little Miss Statue is in fact, *not* a statue." Ty wiped at his eyes— his *dry* eyes. He winked at me, trying to force laughter in a humorless situation. "Look, she's cured. She can turn her head again."

Fidgeting in his seat, Stephen *tsked*. "And she can eat. Go make yourself useful."

Donning a semi-serious face, Ty saluted his father and with an overly dramatic goose-step march, left the room.

One down, one to go. "You don't have to stay," I offered gently.

Posters surrounded us, extolling the virtues of the psychiatric wing and calling it the *premier standard in mental health*. The chipped linoleum and dingy walls said otherwise. Stephen would work his magic, leaning heavily on his position with the international Samaritan Exchange, and have my mother transferred to Stanford, our alma mater.

I felt a twinge of homesickness, not for my childhood home but for my university. It'd provided me the stability I craved as a child—that, and not living with my mother had helped heal wounds I didn't know existed. Until today.

Returning to the window, I felt the familiar pull. The once frightening feeling had become an old vice, comforting me like a tattered blanket. The feeling pulled me to a stand and with my back to my uncle, I stared out the window, beyond the broken fountain in the middle of an abandoned courtyard.

With my vision a little hazy, I gripped the windowsill and waited. And then, the flicker, a brief image, not quite a memory but something more, appeared. A man. Blond. Medieval clothes.

A hand on the cold glass, I closed my eyes to escape, blocking out the hospital. Warmth spread over me, like the sun on a cloudy day. I kept the guilt at bay—my mother was in the other room fighting the same demons I now beckoned.

The familiar image of the blond man blossomed, surrounding me. A horse appeared next to the man. And for a moment, life stilled. I stared at him, wishing he—wishing *this* was real. He took my hand, and before I could protest, he boosted me up on his horse. My heart raced. He climbed up behind me. My blood hummed. He wrapped an arm around my waist, pulling my back against his chest.

My pulse beat wildly. His breath on my neck tickled my skin. He covered my hand—the ring on my finger. Warmth filled me, a peace as solid as the floor under me settled in my bones. His lips touched my temple. It felt like home.

"Burritos or jello?" Ty's voice burst through, shattering the moment.

I spun around, my heart pounding. Warmth drained from me, raking my skin and falling to the chipped linoleum floor. The blond man had come and gone, a vision and feeling so strong, so real—just like my mother's voices were to her.

4

"Isla?" Stephen was at my side, his hand supporting my elbow. "Isla Belle?"

"I'm fine." My voice cracked, the loss of the him—the blond— pulled at my heart. "I'm okay."

Stephen and Ty exchanged a look I knew well. I'd shared the same worried expression when speaking about my mother. Except this time I didn't care. Clap me in chains, drug me to oblivion—it didn't matter. The only thing that felt right of late was the man who existed only in my head. I was my mother's child, nothing could change that. Her destiny was mine.

"You are going home." Stephen offered no room for argument. They'd never leave me now. A whimper escaped. He motioned for Ty to join me while he grabbed the folder he'd been working on.

The rough draft of a Samaritan Exchange event flyer slipped from the folder, sliding to my feet. My chest tightened, an all too familiar feeling came over me. Picking up the paper, I froze, halfway between kneeling and standing. On the back of the program featured four headshots, all prominent officers of the organization. My hand trembled. The man in the lower right photo stared back at me. He was the blond man, *my* blond from my dreams, his image just as striking as it was a moment ago in the window. The world stilled. His clothes were wrong, too modern but the worry over my mother melted away. Like he'd done in my visions, the sight of him gave me peace—all would be well.

My thumb caressed his picture; the man I'd dreamed of every day of my life. I knew him like I knew my own name. He was a part of me —as much as my childhood. And mother.

"Isla?" Stephen asked.

I blinked but the image stayed. This wasn't a vision. *No.* I would not believe my visions were real. I was *not* my mother.

"We need to go, Isla. Now." My uncle tried again, sending me back to the cold reality.

I blinked again. The flyer trembled in my hand but the picture never changed. Like fire and ice, I felt both curious and wary. For years, I wished the blond was real and that he was mine. But with a snap, fear washed over me, shoving the peace aside. My mother was down the hall. This couldn't be real, none of it. Her fate was mine.

ISLA BELLE THORNE

SACRAMENTO, CALIFORNIA: PRESENT DAY

I curled into the worn leather of my uncle's town car, the smell of leather conditioner oddly comforting. The driver turned down the radio as the traffic clogged the closer we came to the dreary downtown. Our movement had slowed, congealing like the eggs I couldn't eat this morning.

Stephen narrowed his eyes at the surrounding cars, his irritation with people outside his family growing worse each year. Then again, he'd ignored the fact I was a fully functioning adult—one that graduated a master's program just a few short months ago—and demanded I see a doctor. He'd also ignored the irony in his command; Stephen Cael was a doctor. According to the Samaritan Exchange, where his driver was taking us, he was the *preeminent geneticist of our generation.* I'd been to the headquarters as a child, my uncle taking me for my immunization shots. In middle school I was the first kid to try the shingles vaccine, a disgusting chewable tablet that tasted like battery acid. A grape aftertaste would come a few moments after swallowing and no amount of mouthwash or toothpaste would cut through the flavor.

"I could go to the student health department." It was a desperate attempt but I had to try.

Stephen arched an eyebrow, a frown on his lips. "The Exchange is closer."

"I still have my student ID card." Technically, I wasn't a student but I'd received a letter stating I was covered on the university insurance plan until December.

"You and I both know you're not going to drive to Palo Alto for a check up." Stephen returned to his tablet he was reading, squinting at the screen.

"Says the man who won't wear his bifocals."

A whisper of a smile appeared. "I forgot them."

"Convenient."

He shrugged and handed over the tablet. "Then read for me."

"Please tell me you see the hypocrisy of the situation." I pulled the tablet from his hands and froze—the flyer from last night was front and center. Fighting the temptation to scroll down and see the image of the blond man, I gripped the tablet like a lifeline, the only thing reminding me that this was real. The car. My uncle. This wasn't a vision or a dream. Relaxing my grip, I focused on the screen, hoping the concentration would calm my nerves. *Draft* was typed in a faded gray font diagonally across the image. Keeping my voice steady, I asked, "What is this for?"

"It's a fundraising event coming up." Stephen rubbed the bridge of his nose. "The flyer needs board approval but I can't for the life of me understand why. We have an event coordinator for a reason."

With two fingers, I zoomed in and blew up the pictures, including an outdated image of my uncle. The man next to me was nearly bald; the man in the flyer had thick, curly hair to spare. "How old is this one?"

Stephen didn't bother looking at the tablet. "Not my choice."

"Come on, when was it taken?" A chuckle swallowed half of my sentence. "You should put this on a dating app."

"I'm not the only one with an outdated picture." He ripped the tablet from my hands with a grunt. Using his fingers, he enlarged another photo. "You think Denton still looks like this?"

My pulse raced. The man's thin face and kind eyes were familiar. I fought the urge to ask about the other picture I'd found on the flyer, the one of the blond. The same man from my visions.

"Or Euston?" My uncle hadn't noticed my reaction. He pulled up the image of the famed Dr. Jeffrey Euston. In the picture the doctor looked roughly my age. "The man's career is older than his headshot."

"For being on the edge of medical science, you might want to keep up on technology."

"Photography isn't technology." He growled but the slight upturn of his lips meant he agreed with me. Or at least saw the humor in it. "It's ridiculously hard to get everyone to cooperate."

"They're headshots, not a group picture."

"Tell that to Denton. He's paranoid about pictures." Stephen clicked off the screen just as the driver turned up Main Street, the center of Downtown Sacramento.

Like a protective dragon, the Samaritan Exchange's headquarters towered over the surrounding financial buildings, a behemoth in the midst of giants. For over a century, the Exchange had kept its vigil in the center of the city. The headquarters was an enormous silver rectangle, mirroring the ominous clouds in the sky. California needed rain. My mother needed the Exchange and all that it could offer.

The top floors were once filled with the executive board, according to Stephen. They'd left to some off shore site twenty years ago, leaving my uncle as the only board member in the states. My mother had said Stephen was a lone wolf and loyal to a fault. She regularly criticized him for his tenure at the Exchange. I wondered if she knew his penchant for loyalty had given her the greatest care modern medicine could provide.

Guilt seeped in. I should be at her side in the hospital, not driving to a doctor's appointment. Clasping my hands in my lap, I felt the dread, the wriggling in of doubt. Stephen and Ty had witnessed what they thought was a minor breakdown caused from the stress of my mother's health. The truth was worse. I'd had a vision—and I wanted another. They were a comfort to me when everything else felt shaky. My first available memory was of the blond in my visions. But with Mom in the hospital, I couldn't tell my uncle the truth. For all the glory and grandeur of the Exchange, no one had cured mental illness. Not Stephen, not the board. And until my mother was safely grounded in reality, I would keep my visions a secret.

The driver passed the headquarters, pulling into the underground parking entrance on the corner. Security was posted in the small booth just outside. My uncle handed over his badge to the driver. The security officer took both the driver and my uncle's badges, a hand held scanner beeping with each swipe of the badge.

This was the part that always scared me. The waiting. The *what ifs*. What if we weren't let in, what if they found out I'm crazy...what if they kept me here, forever? Just like every time before, we were let in. There never was a reason for me to be afraid. And yet I always was.

We were dropped off at the sliding doors, the car waiting for us to enter before parking. Stephen held out an arm, waiting for me to enter first.

"Why do I feel like a child being sent to the principal's office?" I hadn't taken a step forward. That would have been the easy thing to do. It was far too tempting to ruffle my uncle's feathers.

"If it quacks like a duck..." Stephen shrugged, the tablet in hand. "Walks like a duck. Maybe it's a duck."

"Maybe it's a parrot that learned to quack."

"Birds of a feather, flock together." He smirked. "If the little guy didn't want to be treated like a duck, he wouldn't act like one."

"You're twisting it." A quick glance at my reflection set me back. My arms were folded and my hip was cocked. I was very much the child.

Stephen followed my gaze, a chuckle escaping. "After you."

The sliding doors opened to the small reception area, a security guard posted on either side of the desk. My heart pounded, banging inside my chest. There was something about this stupid building that had me on edge. I needed to focus on something else. Anything else. Oblivious to my internal struggle, Stephen handed over his badge.

By some miracle, I'd never noticed until now that the image on his ID badge was the same as the flyer. "How did I miss that?"

Stephen followed my gaze to the badge in the woman's hand. "Oh, for heaven's sake. Give it up. I can't control what they use."

"That ID badge that doesn't even look like you." We were drenched in irony. Security cameras dotted the corners and walls—and those were just the visible ones. And yet my uncle used an ID picture from two decades ago. The heaviness in my chest lightened. If there was humor, there was nothing to fear. "I look more like your picture than you do."

Ignoring me, Stephen said, "We're going to the health and wellness floor."

Covering my mouth, I started snickering. Why it was funny, I had no idea.

"What is it now?" He hissed.

"You think something's wrong with me." How could he not see the humor?

"And?"

"And you're taking me to the *health* and *wellness* floor."

Stephen sent an apologetic glance to the receptionist. Keeping his profile to me, he said to the woman, "And she wonders why I'm bringing her."

"Oh, come *on*." The humor was gone. "How is that not funny?"

"I'm consumed in laugher," he said dryly, taking his badge from the woman.

"You might want to tell your face."

He smiled—at least he attempted to but it looked more like Jack Nicholson when he played the insane joker. In one swift expression Stephen killed the humor. The fear was back.

The security guard to our right stepped aside and we entered the elevator behind him. Stephen scanned his badge, the buttons lighting up to give him access. My heart raced. It was stupid, this irrational fear of being in the building.

If I couldn't make Stephen laugh then I'd have to try something else to distract myself.

"Aren't you a doctor?"

He shook his head. "We've been over this."

"But technically, you *are* a doctor."

"I'm a geneticist."

"Pretty sure that's still a doctor." The elevator shifted and began to rise. I clung to the railing.

Stephen sighed and faced me. "Take a deep breath, Isla Belle."

Tucking my chin, I kept my gaze on my shoes. No amount of bickering or laughing could change the color of my eyes. They betrayed me time and time again, showing my true emotions for all to see.

He placed a hand on my shoulder. "You've been under an incredible amount of stress. This is just a check up."

I nodded.

"Isla?"

I lifted my head. Compassion filled his eyes. He squeezed my shoulder.

"I'm fine," I lied.

He smirked. "Tell that to your face."

Rising from the underbelly of the Samaritan Exchange, the glass elevator brightened with daylight. The storm had finally broken through, splattering the ground with California's version of rain. Fall and winter were typically dry. In Wales, a storm could drench a field in less than hour. That was just a million facts I shouldn't know. Like how the field grass in Wales was nothing like California's Bermuda. Bermuda crept along, pulling its offspring from one place to another while Welsh grass grew upwards toward the sky, teasing the sun with a game of hide-n-seek.

"Isla, it's going to be okay," Stephen said just as the elevator beeped, signaling our stop.

In my reflection of the glass, I caught the image of the blond. It wasn't strong enough to be a vision, just enough to offer comfort. My heart stilled. If the man was here, then all would be well.

LADY ISLA BELLE WELLESLEY

WELLESLEY COUNTY, ENGLAND: 1535

*L*ady Isla Belle stood aghast in her mother's room, dumbfounded at how easily her mother had dismissed her. A draft swept into the room, chilling Lady Isla Belle to the bone. The fire flickered, threatening to succumb to the crisp draft. A flame whipped back, casting an ethereal glow on her mother's vacant stare. The morning sonnets from cheerful birds still echoed into the room, the day barely begun. Lady Isla Belle had not yet mounted her practiced argument, a list of all the reasons why she should be outdoors instead of trapped inside with needlework and lessons. The duchess continued to stare blankly out her window, her frown in direct contrast to the hopeful sun rising gently in the sky.

Lady Isla Belle waited, wondering if her mother would change her mind. Or come alive—say or do anything. *Something.* Lady Isla Belle wouldn't be granted freedom this early. Fidgeting, she glanced around the drafty room for clues. Her mother sighed, inviting tension into the otherwise beautiful day. Isla Belle grabbed her skirts, readying for her escape. The rustle of her fabric didn't break her mother's concentration.

Another moment of silence and Isla Belle scurried away. She wasn't sure if her mother had truly meant to release her but Isla Belle was on the verge of bursting, needing to move and speak more than her graceful mother could handle. Isla Belle's temper was forever at war with her mother's plans just as her brother's timid nature thwarted their father's ambitions.

Isla Belle stepped from the suspiciously empty stairs, the hum of the household work missing. The lack of servants could force an early return to her mother's chambers—especially if she ran into the old healer. Leery of drawing attention, Isla Belle quieted her steps. She didn't escape her mother's lessons only to fall prey to the healer's lectures. Not today when the sun was begging her to visit, the birds adding to the allure, beckoning her outside.

If the healer caught her, Isla Belle would be forced to entertain his lists of complaints. Her father, the Duke of Wellesley, provided a roof and small income for the ancient man but had long ago buried his sympathy. The healer would imagine illness in the healthiest and fault in the most generous. If Isla Belle sighed; she was at death's door with the sweating sickness—if her father gave the physician the sweeter cut of meat, the old man believed the food was tainted.

The healer blamed his misfortune on both Lady Isla Belle and Rhys Glyndwr, his onetime apprentice. Orphaned in his native Welsh countryside, Rhys had outgrown the old man—much like the rest of the household. With Isla Belle's penchant for adventure, she was grateful Rhys's gift of healing was as striking as his face. She'd spent more time in both the physicians' care than with her peers.

Isla Belle took the long way to the stables, out and around the main hall. A flash of familiar blond hair turned the corner. Rhys eschewed hats and overgowns indicative of the noble physicians. His ability to choose his dress—or anything else—sparked an envy in Isla Belle. She'd beg on bended knee at her father's feet. *If you were but a man,* the duke would answer.

The inner dining hall held busy servants, bringing a measure of comfort to Isla Belle, at least one area of the estate wasn't affected. She felt a twinge of guilt. Every day she wished for freedom and now that she'd been granted her desire, she felt anxious instead of grateful. She slipped behind two maids carrying oversized baskets and followed their lead to the outer courtyard. The smaller of the two laughed, stopping abruptly in front of her. Isla Belle stumbled, catching herself in time.

They turned and curtseyed low, their gaze on the floor, so unlike their usual greetings. The teasing was gone, not a hint of a jest at Isla Belle's clumsy nature. In unison they murmured, "Milady."

Isla Belle nodded, her eyes searching for the old healer. Something was amiss—even his absence. But there, at the edge of the corridor, the ancient man shuffled between a small group of groomsmen. The old physician narrowed his gaze. Relief washed over her—not everything had changed. Isla Belle ducked behind the nearest pillar. Taking a quick breath, she slipped to the outside courtyard, the sun rewarding her with warmth.

"Lost your way, *fy annwyl?*" The affection in Rhys' voice made her pause, the soft lift at the end of his question unveiling his Welsh ancestry.

Fy annwyl. The childhood term of endearment echoed in Lady Isla Belle's mind. *My beloved.* Like an old blanket, his words centered her, righting the strangeness in the castle. She lifted her chin, turning her profile to him. "And where do you think I'm going?"

Eyes lit with mischief, Rhys said, "To make a deal with the devil."

She grinned, falling in step with him. Their friendship was the one blessing her mother never questioned. "Aren't you the devil?"

"Maybe I am." Rhys shrugged, hitching his medical bag to his shoulder. A breeze sent strands of his golden hair across his face, adding a playful charm to his words. "Or maybe I'm here to keep you from the devil."

"You've come to save me?" Isla Belle batted her eyelashes, mirroring the eager ladies she once saw at court.

"I'm here to save the devil." His face sobered in mock solemnity.

She elbowed him. "*You're* the devil, Rhys."

He stared a moment too long at her eyes. She ducked her head, wishing her eyes would be loyal for once. She clasped her hands together, knowing if she were to raise her head, Rhys would know her mood. He'd see violet, the color of pleasure—at least, that's what Isla

Belle hoped. She'd felt something altogether different of late and would rather keep it to herself.

"I'm the devil?" He stepped closer, his voice low. "And what deal would you like to make?"

Isla Belle felt the rush once more. Her skin prickled and her heart quickened. Only Rhys affected her, raising her pulse and stilling her temper. As a child, she'd follow him, scurrying about at his ankles. Several years older than her, Rhys was busy doing the old physician's bidding—attending to Isla Belle's frequent mishaps. With both parents and an older brother required at court for months on end, Rhys was her most constant friend.

"Have you forgotten your wish already?" Rhys took another step closer, his eyes searching hers.

Isla Belle ducked her head again, her wit abandoning her. She might not understand the sudden humming in her heart but she saw the knowing look in Rhys' eye. Her heart and mood were displayed for all to see.

"Has the great tongue of Lady Isla Belle been tamed?" He reached for her hand, his gaze never leaving her face. His words were teasing but his touch was soft.

She opened her mouth, a sharp rebuke at the ready but with her hand in his, her tongue refused to obey.

"Tell me, is the end of time here at last?" Ever closer, Rhys leaned in and cupped her chin. Firm and gentle, he shifted her gaze to him. "Has wickedness been bound?"

She stared at Rhys, the man she'd known her entire life. She drank in the sight of him, the steel blue eyes and perfect face, not a freckle or blemish to be seen. Isla Belle breathed in his scent, sweet grass and harvested lavender. He stood before her now, like he'd done every day but today—her heart stilled and her mind raced.

Rhys was no longer the orphan apprentice. He was a man. And he was touching her.

Isla Belle whispered dumbly, "You are the devil, Rhys."

"I'll grant anything you wish." His gaze flicked to her lips.

Shouts from the courtyard distracted him, allowing Isla Belle to gather herself. "Anything I wish?"

Ignoring her, Rhys straightened, his brow furrowing. Isla Belle followed his gaze to the cloud of dust arriving in the courtyard. With a gentle pull, he guided her to the shadows. The servants scattered to the edges instead of gathering for gossip. Whispers grew as a small band of horses neared but no one teased or joked with her. Whoever was coming had the castle on edge. With Rhys' hand at her back, Isla Belle felt suddenly alone. His protective stance meant he knew something, as did the servants but Isla Belle was completely in the dark. The betrayal stung. She'd hoped her friendship with Rhys was stronger than his loyalty to the duke.

"Who is it?" Isla Belle swallowed the rising fear. The air became thick and the world slowed. Her father's frustrations with the king were an open secret at Wellesley. Isla Belle had inherited his irreverent heart, both rankling under the smallest hint of authority.

"Stay here."

Following, she grabbed his hand. "What are you doing?"

"No, *fy annwyl*. Stay here. Please," he pleaded.

Isla Belle searched the courtyard and the fleeing servants, their gaze on their feet. The air thickened, pregnant with tension.

"Isla Belle." Rhys squeezed her hand. "Please."

She took in the sight of him, the darkened circles under his eyes and his slightly thinner frame. He was Rhys, the healer who would march into any man's house, whatever the illness. He was constant and unafraid—but today, fear was in his eyes.

"Shhh…" He brought her close.

Isla Belle briefly closed her eyes, hating that he could read her. "Go."

Rhys arched an eyebrow, questioning her.

"I'll stay put," she lied. This was her home; she would find answers.

Keeping to the shadows under the courtyard's outlining roof, Rhys snuck closer to the trio of horses arriving. Isla Belle followed, keeping her distance. Tall for a woman, she used her height and peered over the maids' heads.

The rider in the middle directed his companions to dismount. Isla Belle had never seen him before. Relief swept over her. Her brother had left with the last stranger and not returned—that was months ago. Isla Belle stepped forward for a better view.

The rider pulled the reins over the horse's head and faced Rhys, staring, like most men and women did. Rhys' face appeared exactly the same on either side. His every move was steady, his walk a glide.

The leader of the riders motioned toward the castle, his lips moving. "...the king...to wait...now..."

Isla Belle's hands raked the stone walls as she inched closer. Rhys took the reins of the leader's horse, nodding along to whatever directions he was told. The leader must have assumed Rhys was nothing but a groomsmen, not the duke's healer and confidante.

Rhys motioned for two servants to join him, their eyes wary. Despite being a servant, the duke treated Rhys as a peer. When he wasn't with the duke, his few spared moments were spent in town healing those too poor to pay.

The servants hesitated a moment before taking the reins, eyeing each other for approval. Isla Belle fell in line behind them. Without looking, she was aware of Rhys' every move. He led the riders inside.

Isla Belle waited for the servants to leave the stables and gently slid the bridle off each horse, leaving a portion of hay in each stall. The leader's horse sniffed at the hay and pawed at the empty water bucket. The horse threw back its head, nostrils flaring. The tantrum wasn't typical of mild messenger horses. Isla Belle stifled the rising fear. Bribing the gelding with a handful of oats, she ran her hands along the saddle. Her father had forbidden candles in the stable and with the cloudy day, the light inside the stable was dim at best. Isla Belle found the messenger bag tied dutifully to the saddle's horn. With her finger, she untied the knot, sending the bag to her other hand. Her heart skipped a beat. Branded front and center of the leather bag was the royal seal. The riders were sent from the king. Isla Belle froze, her heart in her throat. Pieces slid into place—the silence of the servants, Rhys begging her to stay out of reach. Something was wrong, very wrong.

ISLA BELLE THORNE

SACRAMENTO, CALIFORNIA: PRESENT DAY

*W*ith a soft mechanical swish, the elevator doors opened. The medicinal smells I wish I could forget assaulted me, sending my pulse racing. A million memories came to me, each one jockeying for the lead. All of them involved my mother and Stephen—my hand in his. On cue, like he had for most of my life, Stephen guided me out of the elevator, a hand behind my elbow. Part of me wished he'd reach for my hand. The other part would have argued if he tried.

Following him, I walked into the empty waiting room, ceilings ten or twelve feet high and brightly lit. The floors were wood tiled, offering a facade of warmth. Grecian columns held court in each corner of the office, gold filigree at the top and base of each column. This was nothing like the university's health facility. The office looked more like a business waiting room than a medical unit. The clinic where I was inoculated as a kid had walls painted in cartoon characters and overly friendly nurses. This was something else entirely.

Except the smell. Medical offices had a distinct smell, a mixture of despair and disinfectant. The odor was seared into my brain. I could recognize it anywhere.

Instead of telling the receptionist my name, Stephen grabbed the clipboard from the counter and sat on the navy waiting chairs. They were either new or hardly used. I stood at the door. He arched an eyebrow and motioned for me to sit. He'd been on the other side of the healthcare system too long.

I turned to the receptionist. "I'm Isla Belle Thorne."

"All checked in." The woman didn't look up, offering me only the top of her head as a view.

Dumbly, I sat next to my uncle. "How'd they know?"

Stephen held out his badge. "Believe it or not, they know I'm here —and that the picture is me."

"But that's you, not me."

He scoffed. "You don't think they've put two and two together?"

"You're a Cael."

"Who brought you to get vaccines as a child." He slipped the badge back in his pocket and handed over the clipboard. "Trust me, they know."

"You don't think it's creepy?" There were cameras everywhere, four little dots in each corner of the room. "This whole big brother thing. And the idea that they know everything."

Eyeing me, he smirked. "I *am* the big brother."

"And that just got creepier." I loved my uncle but there were things I didn't want him to know. My visions for one.

"Just fill out the form, Isla."

"Do you think they'll at least say my name right?" Most people pronounced it *Issluh* instead of silencing the *s* like they did for island. "I mean, if they know everything, they should know that."

"I wouldn't count on it."

Pulling the pen trapped at the top of the clipboard, I mumbled, "There's clearly zero benefit then."

He rubbed his temple. "Will you always be this cranky at appointments?"

I'm not cranky, I almost said but even in my head I sounded child-ish. There was something irritating about doctors. And their offices. "I hate hospitals."

Stephen squeezed my shoulder, offering, "I know, kid. I know."

Kid. He wasn't my father but he'd claimed me as his own. He stepped in when my mother couldn't. *Kid.* My heart warmed as I filled out the form. Most of it was correct, except the address was Stephen's, not my soon-to-be-former university address. I doubted if the Exchange ever had my mother's address or if they'd given up with her frequent moves. It'd been seven years since I was a legal adult with my last visit to their vaccine clinic a few years before that. I changed the phone number from Stephen's house phone to my cell.

My pen hovered over where I should put my address. "I can't put my Palo Alto address down. I have to move out at the end of the month."

"Keep my address as primary." Stephen voice was soft. It was an invitation, not a demand.

Tapping the pen against the clipboard, I blinked. I'd hoped to be hearing back from potential employers by now. "What if Mom's not better? What if it takes months? I can't just leave her."

"I still have my home in Palo Alto." He placed a hand over my pen. "And the suite downtown."

"Ty's there."

"All the more reason for you to move in."

"No." I shook my head. "I do not need a babysitter."

"But Ty does."

A giggle escaped. "I'll think about it."

He turned back to his tablet, frowning in concentration. Scanning the papers, I waited a moment to make sure Stephen's attention was fully absorbed before checking off symptoms. *Insomnia,* check. *Exhaustion,* check. *Lack of appetite*—I glanced up at Stephen. This might be the wrong time to be honest. Skipping over the appetite, my pen hovered over *headaches.* When I was little my mother complained of headaches, popping open prescription bottles, one after the other. Over time, *headaches* became a curse word. An excuse for needing something. Drugs, alcohol…men.

"Issluh?" A man's voice burst my thoughts.

My pen slipped, marking *headaches* for me. I clutched the clipboard and jumped to a stand. Stephen following suit.

The man was dressed in light blue scrubs, a tablet tucked under his arm. Lugging around a device must be a Samaritan Exchange thing. His badge was attached to the front pocket—and looked more like him than my uncle's. The medical assistant's name was ordinary, a cool John Taylor, fitting his average height and medium brown hair. He eyed Stephen. "And you are?"

"Stephen Cael."

I pointed to John's badge then back at Stephen. "Don't look at his badge though. You won't recognize him."

Stephen sucked in a breath—his patience was gone. I'd crossed a line.

"Sorry," I whispered and obediently handed over the clipboard to the assistant. My face burned with embarrassment.

"Do you have an appointment, Stephen Cael?" John scrolled through his tablet.

"No, I'm here for her." My uncle's voice held a warning. The poor employee had no idea that Stephen Cael was an executive board member.

"I'm so sorry, sir but you'll have to wait here." The assistant didn't look apologetic in the slightest. "It's against HIPPA guidelines."

"What?" Stephen looked as though he was going to burst. "I've been there for every shot she's ever had."

"I'm sure you're Father of the Year, sir, but I can't let you into her appointment." John motioned for me to walk ahead of him. "We've been cited and have to tighten restrictions to adhere to HIPPA, compliments of the good ol' U.S. of A."

I stood there, glancing between them. Never—not once—in my entire life had Stephen Cael not had his way. He clenched his jaw and glared at the assistant. Motioning to me, Stephen said, "I'll be right here. Waiting." He nearly spat the word *waiting*.

I mouthed, *sorry*.

He relaxed, ever so slightly, and sat back on the chair. Only when his attention went back to the tablet did I walk down the hall. Stephen had no idea the amount of times I'd gone to the university health clinic. He'd always been a tad overprotective but this was new.

The assistant closed the exam room door. Climbing onto the medical chair, the paper crinkled and slid underneath me. John stared at me—and then I realized I'd completely missed whatever he was saying.

He shook his head and took my temperature, then my blood pressure. He pulled the clipboard from my hand, saying, "I'll take that."

"Thanks," I mumbled, trying to show I wasn't a complete idiot.

"How long have you had headaches?"

I winced. "Awhile."

"On a scale of one to ten, how bad are they?" He tapped away on his tablet.

"Four. Maybe five."

More tapping. "And how often? Daily? Weekly?"

"Sometimes daily."

Leaving the tablet on the counter, John clipped a pulse reader on my finger. "Sometimes?"

"Depends on how badly I slept." Holding my head in one hand, I was relieved Stephen wasn't here.

"How many hours are you sleeping, on average?" The man took off the pulse reader and wiped it with disinfectant wipes.

"Depends." I held my breath, waiting for the smell to dissipate.

Laying the tablet back on the counter, the assistant faced me and crossed his arms. "You've had headaches for awhile but sometimes daily, depending on how badly you sleep but you don't know just how badly you sleep."

"Yes?"

"Before I go get the doctor, mind telling me why you're here?" His gaze flicked to my stomach.

"I'm not pregnant."

"Didn't think you were." He smirked and I realized he was about my age. Or maybe my cousin's. But that was the end of their similarities. Everything about John Taylor screamed average while my cousin had the *it* factor, a characteristic he shared with my mother.

I nodded and mumbled, "Thanks. I think."

"Now that I've got your attention, mind helping me out?"

I glanced over my shoulder in the direction of the waiting room. "It's confidential."

"You don't know my uncle." I waved my hands in front of me, as if it could erase what I'd said. "That sounded bad."

He shrugged. "I've heard worse."

"I get headaches."

He arched an eyebrow as if to say, *and?*

"And sometimes I wonder if I'm…" *hallucinating.* I swallowed hard. "…going crazy."

He glanced down at his tablet, tapping away. "Why do you think you're going crazy?"

"I'm sure it's in my file." I motioned to him. "My mother's not exactly the pinnacle of health."

"But why do *you* feel crazy?"

Wringing my hands in my lap, I whispered, "I have horrible headaches. I've always had them. And I can't sleep. Not more than a few hours at a time."

"How long?" He tapped again on his tablet.

"Forever." Shaking my head, I offered, "Really, though. I can't remember not having them. But they feel worse of lately. More intense." *Like the visions.*

"Has anything changed in your life that could trigger an increase of the headaches?"

"My mother is in the hospital." My voice cracked. "But that isn't a new thing."

"Normally, I'd send you downstairs to get bloodwork." He held up a hand when I shook my head. "But I'm going to ask the doctor if we can do it in here. Keep things confidential."

"Thanks, I think."

He walked toward the door and stopped. He placed a hand on my arm. "You probably already know this but it's a good thing—" He nodded toward the waiting room. "To have someone who cares."

ISLA BELLE THORNE

SACRAMENTO, CALIFORNIA: PRESENT DAY

*O*nly after I promised to stay with Ty at their downtown suite, did Stephen let me out of his sights. He had peppered me with questions until I gave up, offering only one syllable answers. He'd found fault with every part of the appointment. The medical assistant had drawn my blood and the doctor had come into the exam —asking the same questions as the assistant, offering zero explanations as to why I had the headaches. Stephen had hoped for answers but refused to tell me what he'd wanted out of the exam. His frustration became my salvation, allowing me to skip on our family lunch— granted, I'd escaped to my mother's apartment, not exactly high on the list of nefarious acts.

Nestled on the southern tip of an abandoned park, sat rows of one bedroom houses, if they could be classified as a house at all. Each home shared its walls with a neighbor, the number spray painted on the wall above a pitiful front window. The door to my mother's home was crooked and hung on its hinges for dear life. I'd never been to this part of Sacramento, and from the not so subtle smell of cat urine, I knew why she'd kept it a secret. It'd taken some skillful snooping at my uncle's house to find her address.

Each move had pushed her closer toward poverty despite her

silver spoon childhood, but for once, this was in my favor. The lock was a simple pin tumbler. The fact that the landlord hadn't bothered to install a deadbolt was a double-edged feeling, leaving half of me grateful and the other half guilty.

When I was a kid, she thought a lock would keep her addiction a secret. Turns out, I was the one with the secret. Not her. A quick push and flick; the lock clicked into the open position. I slipped the rake and hook back into my hoodie's pocket and turned the handle.

"You're getting rusty," Ty blurted.

I jumped, banging my wrist into the door. Turning to face my idiot cousin, I glared. "What are you doing?"

"You do realize you're committing a felony, right?" Ty arched his eyebrow, completely unaware that my heart hammered away in my chest.

"What are you doing *here?*" Forcing myself to take a deep breath—and not kill him—I rubbed my forehead and silently counted to ten.

"Apparently committing a felony." He circled me and pushed the door open.

"You can't just walk into my mother's house."

He tossed a smirk over his shoulder. "Isn't that what you're doing?"

The argument died on my lips. I'd come to find out exactly what triggered her latest breakdown and for some reason that justified my crime. At least, before Ty showed up.

Following my cousin into the dark apartment, the familiar feeling of helplessness grew, settling on my shoulders. There weren't any newspaper clippings or red strings pinned between walls. There weren't ramblings or strange symbols strewn from room to room. Movies lied, every last one of them; the evidence painfully obvious in my mother's nearly empty apartment. Crazy didn't announce itself with dramatic flair and take over. It lurked in the shadows of my mother's mind. Play after play on the bookshelves showed what her brilliance could do, while the dozen pills left in the sink showed the darker side of genius.

Dottie Thorne was born to privilege like her brother Stephen and my cousin Ty. The only difference, she was once a rising star whose voltage maxed out the year she birthed me. My life abruptly ended hers. No amount of shoulder squeezes could remove that stain. Not from my uncle, not from anyone.

Standing in my mother's apartment ignited my own fears. The most consistent person in my life wasn't my uncle or cousin, it was the man from my visions. He'd appeared on my uncle's pamphlet, and try as I might, I couldn't dismiss the coincidence. If my future was going to mirror my mothers, I needed to get ahead of it. I needed to find the cure for her before my visions consumed everything.

Therein lay the problem. The Samaritan Exchange housed the world's greatest medical minds. If there was a cure—they would have it, or be in the process of finding it. I couldn't get near it without Stephen. He'd already told me about finding a position at the head-quarters for me but the visions were becoming more frequent—what if I had one while working? Dread twisted my stomach. I'd have to tell him—that was a bridge I wasn't ready to cross.

Ty shoved me forward with a grin, shouldering past me to the front window. The apartment was too small for a true living room and kitchen. The entire area could be crossed in less than ten steps. In the corner of the sad table was a stack of bills. History told me every last envelope would be a collection notice.

"I'll tackle the fridge." With practiced ease, Ty slid a cardboard box to the fridge.

Part of me wished he'd go to Mom's bedroom with me, part of me was grateful he'd be occupied. Yesterday, the doctors had stopped talking when I entered the room, meaning she wasn't responding to treatment. Her glass-eyed, blank expression resembled a zombie instead of a living, breathing woman. Mom would probably be trans-ferred back to her Stanford doctors soon and I doubted she'd paid rent this month. Everything in her apartment would be seized.

My little break-in wasn't just to find information but to keep her fading legacy safe. If she ever healed, I'd return everything to her. *If*— the word made me pause. I'd given up on *when* she'd get healed and embraced *if*. That's not how a daughter should think, but I couldn't ignore the reality of her situation. She needed more help than just her family and routine doctors. She needed one of the Samaritan Exchange's facilities.

During my undergrad, I worshiped the Samaritan Exchange and all they stood for, bettering human lives worldwide. Myself included. According to Stephen, one of the Samaritan's fertility doctors helped my mother name me. Stephen would know, he'd been on the board longer than I've been alive.

Despite studying veterinary instead of medical science, I followed the Samaritan Exchange's every move until Mom suffered an epic breakdown my junior year of college. The thought of one more lab, one more hospital, or one more syringe made me weak—in the knees and in the heart.

My kind professor put in a good word, and suddenly I was graduating with a master's in communications. It wasn't much of a stretch, going from creating scientific theories to communicating—or defending, depending on how controversial the science—to the public.

Down the short hall, I slowly walked, the floors creaking and the odor changing to a musty mildew smell. Her bedroom, if you could call it that, held only her mattress in the center, directly under a wet bulge in the ceiling. Her roof, like the home I was leaving in Palo Alto, wasn't accustomed to the onslaught of rain, even in the late fall. California skipped from drought to drought, rarely seeing this much water. The dark clouds and smell of dew in the mornings reminded me of another place, another time altogether—one that only existed in my mind.

The crooked shade on a small, flickering lamp cast an eerie shadow on the wall. A cardboard box that had seen better days was the only other item in the room. Even the mattress was naked, void of the lush sheets my mother would have insisted be tucked with perfection when I was a child. Mom's possessions were dwindling faster than her grip on reality. If the living room—or kitchenette, depending on how many steps taken—didn't have the built-in shelves, I doubt my mother would have stored her plays.

The sound of breaking glass echoed through the thin wall between the bedroom and living area. Ty mumbled something followed by another clink of glass. Patience wasn't in our genes.

Kneeling on the mattress, I peered into the cardboard box. Instead of couture apparel, my mother had placed a few pieces of paper and her scrapbook. She'd converted her old wedding album into a baby book after she divorced her ex, the poor guy. He was long before my time, back when she was the darling of every critic.

Dumping the box onto the mattress, I heard a metal ping. A gold band had fallen, rolling in circles next to the lamp's cord. The lack of diamonds or any other type of gemstone meant this ring couldn't be hers—and yet, it looked familiar. Holding it up to the meager light, I felt the rush of warmth despite the cold metal. Thin and tiny, the band had small circles looped together. It was too delicate for a man's finger and the gold looked off, a brass tint instead of the more yellow color. A flicker of an image appeared, the ring on my hand.

"What's that?"

I jumped. The ring dropped. "Stop doing that, Ty."

Ignoring his chuckle, I searched the floor with my hands, my heart racing. Finding the ring, I held it up once more—more for myself than Ty. A part of me wondered if it was real. I believed the dreams of the blond man were just that, figments of my imagination. Not until I saw the Samaritan Exchange flyer with the man's headshot did I wonder if maybe, just maybe it was all true. Or maybe I was finally crazy.

The real truth, the hope that I clung to, was if the people I dreamed about were real—living, breathing people, then I couldn't be going insane. And if I was okay, then my mother stood a chance. She'd written dozens of stories, many of them with a comeback theme. She deserved a happy ending as much as her characters.

Angling for better light, I asked Ty, "Have you seen this before?"

Grabbing the ring, he tossed it into the air, catching it again with the same hand. A chill swept across my body, and I shivered, not from the cold but from the loss of the ring. Fear crept in. And I didn't know why.

"Where was it?" Ty hooked the band on his pinky. He glanced around the dingy room, his eyes filling with pity.

"It was in the box."

"Are you sure it was hers?" He handed it back. I snatched it too quickly. He arched an eyebrow. "Don't go all *precious* on me."

"Hilarious." Except it wasn't. I felt my face flush the instant the metal touched my skin. He could have the Tolkien reference, so long as I could hold the band.

"Are you going to wear it or just stare at it?" Ty rubbed the back of his head and stretched.

"It's not mine."

"But you want to." His eyes had lowered, taking on his serious *I'm-a-lawyer* face.

Shrugging, I motioned to the box. "There's almost nothing left of her."

"In many ways."

My throat went dry. His words were a little too close to the truth. I palmed the ring, not able to decide just yet. With my other hand, I pulled the small lamp from the wall, tossing it into my mother's box. "The scrapbook is the only thing worth packing in here."

Ty gathered the book and motioned for the door. "After you."

Taking one last look around, I wondered if my mother would ever be able to live on her own again.

"You should wear it, *Issla.*"

"Shut it." I swatted his shoulder, or what I could reach of it. He'd started calling me *Issla* after I gave up correcting people. The same peers that could say Catalina Island without the *s* would fail again and again to pronounce Isla the same way.

"Seriously, though." Ty batted the scrapbook at my arm. "You should wear it. Keep a piece of her with you."

"What if it isn't hers?"

"Then I'll bail you out of jail." He bumped me again.

"You'd suck at defense." I slid the ring on my finger. Peace hummed once more, the warmth spreading through my veins. The same feeling came at the start of a vision but the ache, the piercing pain when the images faded was becoming harder to bear.

"Yeah, well, maybe there's a reason I struggled in criminal law."

In just a few steps, we were back in the living area. "The going-to-class part or the actual studying part?"

"I got a solid education." Ty winked. He was the only person I knew who could wink and get away with it.

"On female anatomy, not law." I grabbed stacks of plays and put them in one of the empty boxes left in the kitchen. She couldn't have lived here long.

"Doesn't mean it's useless information." He started on the top shelf, his grin smug.

"Doesn't mean it's useful."

"Keep telling yourself that." With two swipes of his arm, he'd finished removing the last of the plays. "You know you start on Monday, right?"

My stomach flipped. Monday was supposed to be the first day of my new job. A job I hadn't even interviewed for—Stephen had pulled some major strings to make it happen.

The future wasn't something I could think of. Not now. Not when my mother's fate seemed so bleak. Not when I'd found nothing to help me understand what happened. I swallowed hard. "I never said yes."

"You didn't exactly say no, either."

"I don't need his help." Of all the lies, this was the biggest. More than my fear of having a vision at work, there was another sad truth; I wasn't my mother. She could waltz into a job interview and turn the tables, have them begging her to work for them. She towered over most women and turned heads with her fiery hair and creamy complexion. She'd shift from tears to jokes in seconds, anything to create a spotlight on herself. She gathered clichés and compliments by the armful.

Life was very much a game, the world very much her stage. She was everything I wasn't. Guiding her moods and outbursts was a skill I mastered. She'd be up one minute, down the next, waving in the wind like an untethered kite while I was deliberate, determined. Unmovable.

And different.

My eyes mirrored my emotions, a shade of blue for each feeling.

Only the woman in my dreams was cursed with the same phenomenon. My mother used my eyes to her advantage. Bluffing wasn't an option.

My face flushed warm. Mom once held the world in her palm, dancing and twirling it to her liking while I wished for another place altogether.

With as much confidence as I could fake, I said, "I can find my own job."

Ty placed a hand over mine. "He's trying to help."

"He wants to keep an eye on me." My uncle had a bad habit of saving his family, performing a flat out miracle with this Samaritan Exchange position. With my undergrad in animal science, I was in no way qualified. The Samaritan Exchange dealt with human health care, not veterinary. But more than that, I'd given up on any and all science the day I found my mother listless in the bathtub. How I still graduated was beyond me—then again, I'm sure Stephen had something to do with that as well.

"And?" Ty held out his arms as if to say, *so what?*

"I don't need to be babysat."

"What if you're the babysitter and I'm the baby?" He must have talked to Stephen. Ty stacked the two boxes, the bottom filled with whatever he'd salvaged from the fridge, the top with Mom's plays.

"You being the baby was never a question."

"And there you have it." He nodded to the front door. "Let's go."

"I'm serious, Ty." Twisting the ring on my finger, I struggled to find the words. "Mom...she never really..."

"Hey." He shook his head. "You're not your mom."

"I didn't say that. I'm just saying..."

He shifted the boxes. "You're playing the *what if* game. What if my dad hadn't bailed her out, would that have changed things? What if she never had you—what if she'd kicked her leg three times every time she opened the door—or touched her nose like the witched—"

"Bewitched." It was my uncle's favorite show. Ty and I never understood Stephen's taste in television.

"Whatever." He smiled, his dimples reminding me of my mother. "You know what I mean. The job is a gift, take it."

"I don't know."

"Then work at the Exchange until you figure it out." With that, he nodded again at the door. "Open the door or I'm introducing you as *Issla* to your future coworkers."

"You do, and I will murder you in your sleep." Pinching his back, I circled around to the door.

"Despite what you just said..." he paused and lowered his voice. "You're not crazy, Isla Belle."

I tucked my head and waited for Ty to pass through. The door swung open, sending a shaft of light across the room. In the small window above the sink, I saw a reflection. A few steps closer, I saw a red-haired woman with alabaster skin instead of my black hair and olive complexion. The hairs on my neck stood on end. I blinked. And then she was gone—replaced with a woman, tall and blonde. Ty was wrong. I was absolutely crazy.

LADY ISLA BELLE WELLESLEY

WELLESLEY COUNTY, ENGLAND: 1535

*L*ady Isla Belle stomped her mud soaked boots against the stone covered courtyard. The sun had tucked behind the horizon and the birds had quieted down, inviting the hush of night. She'd ignored Rhys' orders to stay hidden and instead, followed the horses to the stables. To conceal her disobedience, she had quietly circled around the stables, directly through the muddy and unkept garden. Entering the dining hall, she took smaller steps to hide her boots under the hem of her dress.

Servants moved about the table wordlessly, filling the cups of the riders and Isla Belle's parents. The duchess sat straight, her graceful neck more rigid than regal. With delicate gold earrings and heavy gold chains, she sparkled from her flaxen hair to her gilded shoes, but her eyes harbored fury.

"Sit, Isla Belle," her father, the Duke of Wellesley whispered, affection in his voice. Rhys wasn't sitting to the right of him. Nor was Rhys at the table. Or the hall.

Isla Belle's throat went dry, fear and tension welling inside her. She'd hoped Rhys would be here to give her a clue, give some answer to the sudden secrecy.

The leader of the riders stood and with a wave of his hand offered the empty chair next to him. "Milady."

Isla Belle curtseyed and slowly made her way to the table. She tried to catch her father's eye but his gaze remained on his plate, food untouched. Forcing a smile, Isla Belle sat next to the tall, thin leader, his beard speckled with grey—unlike the typical youthful messenger, this man was seasoned. Isla Belle's skin prickled at the thought. Aside from Rhys, Wellesley gave the most serious tasks to his oldest, most trusted servants.

Food was eaten and plates clicked but no one spoke. Taut smiles. Polite nods. With each passing moment, tension filled the room. Her father kept his chin tucked. This was a man who once helped King Henry annul his first marriage. The Duke of Wellesley cowed to no one. Yet his hunched shoulders showed an entirely different father than the one who'd raised Isla Belle.

Her hands gripped the chair. She searched once more for Rhys and blurted to the rider at her left, "What brings you here?" She felt the weight of her mother's stare. It wasn't Isla's place to ask but Rhys' absence and her father's strange behavior set her on edge.

Her father stood abruptly. "I'll make ready."

"For what?" Isla kept her voice light.

"Isla Belle," her mother chided, her tired eyes framed with the faint beginnings of wrinkles. Her mother lifted her head, her profile more Roman than English. Born to Welsh royalty and schooled in France with Anne Boleyn, the king's current wife. The duchess once held the king's ear and the duke's heart but from the tremor in her hands, the woman seemed to hold nothing but fear.

Isla Belle willed her father to look at her. "Are you going to court?"

The duchess shifted in her chair, her head swiveling between Wellesley and their daughter. Lady Wellesley was both a duchess and daughter of a powerful Marcher Lord. Until today, Lady Isla Belle's mother did what she pleased, much like her close friend, Queen Anne. While Anne was petite and bold, the duchess was calm, and regal— except around her spirited daughter, Isla Belle.

"Excuse us, my lord." The leader bowed, a frown etched on his severe features.

Her mother waited for them to leave before saying, "Isla Belle, you cannot—"

"Yes," Wellesley answered, facing his daughter. "I've been summoned to court."

The duchess narrowed her gaze. "This doesn't—"

A wave silenced his wife, Wellesley focusing once more on Isla Belle. "You and I have been summoned." His face softened. "But your physician does not believe you're well enough to travel."

It'd been weeks since Isla Belle was last injured, a miracle according to Rhys. Isla Belle opened her mouth to argue but stopped when her mother leaned forward, hiding her face in her hands. In a rare show of affection, the duke came to her side and stroked his wife's cheek.

Fear sank into Isla's heart. "What has happened?"

The duke shifted his weight. "King Henry has tired of his wife. He's needing a few of his men to help him."

"Help with what?" Isla Belle stood abruptly, her calves hitting the legs of the chair.

"She's to be tried." Her father sighed. "And he's searching for a new wife."

Despite the fire, the room went cold. Isla Belle stared at the table, her stomach twisting and turning. There was only one thing that could strike fear in her father. "He's asked for me hasn't he?"

Her parents exchanged a knowing glance, the duchess' face darkening. Isla Belle had heard the whispers of the king. It wasn't a secret that he coveted his wife's ladies in waiting; it was the very reason Wellesley kept his daughter away from court.

"Tell me," Isla Belle closed her eyes for a brief moment. There was more, she could feel it with every unspoken word. The king needing a wife wouldn't cause this much strife. Not in this home. Not at Wellesley.

"I'm not certain…" Wellesley tapped the back of the chair with his knuckle. The vein on his neck ticked—he was lying. "Until I know, you will stay here."

Stay here. Rhys had given the same command earlier when the riders had come. He'd known as well. Surrounded by her parents, Isla Belle was very much alone. The clenching of her father's jaw and the despair in her mother's posture; there was still more to the sudden arrival.

Isla Belle motioned to the riders' empty chairs. "They've seen me. They'll know I'm not ill."

"You will retire and send for Rhys." Her father glanced at the duchess, his eyes dimming. "He'll tell me you are ill. Or injured."

"That won't work." The words left Isla Belle's mouth before she could stop herself.

"We have to try." The duke looked from his wife to his daughter. "Promise me you will be obedient."

Her mother folded her hands in her lap, her lips taut. "Please."

Isla Belle came to her mother's side. She reached for her, only to withdraw. Whatever they feared, Isla Belle would face it. "I'll go to court."

Her father offered a sad smile. "No, Isla Belle."

Her heart sank. She tried once more, "I've been summoned. I will go."

"It should be me. I should go with you." Her mother covered her father's hand. She'd watched King Henry wither from a respected king to the spoiled child he'd become. "The queen could use a friend."

"That is why you will not." Wellesley shook his head. "You are under suspicion as well."

The color drained from the duchess' face. Her back straightened and with a firm nod, gave her obedience. Circling the table, Wellesley approached Isla Belle with hands outstretched. "Promise me, you'll do as I say?"

Isla Belle gathered as much charm as she could muster. "Please. Let me try. Whatever this is, I can help. Take me with you."

Her father placed a hand on each of her shoulders. "You could talk a snake into submission." He sighed, his arms sliding back down. "If you were but a man."

The duchess touched her necklace adorned with the delicate Celtic symbols of her family, the piece of jewelry that once offered protection. With a frown on her delicate lips, she said softly, "This is not the future I had painted for us."

The duke's face fell, filling Isla Belle's chest with panic. He cupped his daughter's chin.

"It's time." Rhys entered the dining hall. His eyes, once soft and blue, now held a dark quality, his gaze cold like the wind from the north. When he looked at Isla Belle, she trembled. The world she'd known was shifting, and the men she trusted most kept her in the dark.

"Why me?" Isla Belle lifted her chin from her father's touch. "Why us?"

Her mother cleared her throat. "I am a daughter of a Marcher Lord. A man once beloved by our king's father. He, like every other Welshman, kept the borderlands in order. His great grandfather was rewarded for his loyalty and became a beloved Marcher lord. My father followed in the legacy. But now..." The duchess flicked her wrist in Rhys' direction. Had Isla Belle not been watching, she would have missed it. "King Henry fears them and their myths. He's forgotten that men like my father could help."

"What does this mean?" Isla Belle fought the chill that swept across her neck. "Speak plainly."

"There is nothing plain or simple to say." The duchess straightened her posture. "My family was given borderlands to rule as he saw fit. The land and titles were rewards for loyalty by an English king. My grandfather was fair and firm. He was English but slowly earned the trust of the Welsh. My father grew up with love for the country and married a Welsh woman. That is the beginning and end of the plainness."

Isla Belle opened her mouth to speak but with a sad shake of her mother's head, she stopped.

"Not every Marcher lord was fair. Or kind. The Welsh don't trust most of them. The Marcher lords don't trust the native Welsh. And both don't trust a king whose mood changes with the wind." The duchess let out a small whimper. "I don't understand how this could happen. My family put King Henry's father on the throne yet he's now handing out threats—and to the Welsh? Why? He's already attacked the church. Denied the pope—"

Wellesley squeezed his wife's shoulders. "Understanding the king's motives won't change anything."

The duchess shook her head, a wild look in her eye. In the soft glow of the fire, she looked scared, like captured prey. "We helped the king secure a younger wife, one that should have provided England with an heir. All it did was give him more power." She ran a graceful hand along her skirt, her focus back. She pivoted Queen Anne's changing temper as well as the king's. She would not submit.

Wellesley added, "All we need is an heir. That would put the king and both Wales and England at ease. Our country can't handle another war."

"Our family can't handle another loss," the duchess whispered.

"Another loss?" When neither parent spoke, Isla Belle raised her voice, "What loss?"

"Isla." Rhys guided her toward the stairs.

She spun around, her hands clenched at her side. "Tell me."

"Not now, *fy annwyl.*"

His words softened her and she allowed Rhys to guide her to the stairs. She saw him take in her clothing, the jagged, torn piece of her skirt. Her mother wouldn't notice because of the dark mud but Rhys and his critical eye missed nothing. Isla Belle shifted her shoes underneath, her face burning with embarrassment. She'd been caught.

Waiting for a maid to pass them on the stairs, Isla Belle asked, "When does he leave?"

"We leave tomorrow."

"We?" Isla Belle's steps faltered. She grabbed Rhys, forcing him to look at her. His gaze flicked to her hand on his arm. She snatched her hand back. "Why are you going?"

"Your father needs me." He spoke in the measured voice, the same tone he'd use when speaking to the duchess. He was hiding something —just like her father.

"Why? He isn't ill. There is no need for you to accompany him."

Rhys wasn't recognized with the same favor at court like he was at the castle. Ignoring her, Rhys took another step. This couldn't be her childhood friend, the boy who waited for her to catch up. Nor was he the man who'd sung to her, keeping her mind off the stitching of her wounds.

"Answer me." Isla Belle fought the shiver, a rift had happened and she didn't know why. "Rhys Glyndwr, you will answer me."

When he took another step, she plunged ahead, her boot catching on the ancient stone. She slipped, her ankle and knee hitting the step with a loud smack. She hissed in pain.

In an instant, Rhys' arms were around her. "Easy, *fy annwyl.*"

"Don't." Isla Belle recoiled at his touch. "I am not a child."

"You need help."

"I need the truth," she snapped.

Rhys' gaze slid over her, over all of her, and she knew he did not miss the way her boot caved at her ankle or the tear at her knee. He saw—he *knew* everything.

"Lady Isla Belle," he said to her, helping her to a stand.

"*Lady* Isla Belle?" Her proper name was a slap to her face.

With one word, Rhys had dug a ditch between them. A rush of heat shot up her neck, her cheeks flushing. Rhys' stoic expression betrayed nothing. He held out his hand, cupping her arm.

"Do not touch me." Isla Belle retreated from him, angry that his touch warmed her.

"You're hurt." His tone was firm, impatient.

She wanted to snap, to lash out but her throbbing leg muted her temper.

His brow furrowed, his gaze intent. She dipped her head, not allowing him to see the color of her eyes.

"How long will you pout?" Again, his voice came hard. "How long till I can get you off that foot?"

"I can manage on my own."

"I believe you just did." He motioned to her injured ankle. "Thanks to you, I won't need to lie."

Isla Belle tried to pull from his grasp. "I can still ride."

Rhys wiped a hand down his face and sighed. "For once in your life, Isla Belle, just do as you're told."

The frustration should have angered Isla Belle. She should push against him and demand him to leave. But the whisper of despair in his voice, the hollow look in his eye, held her tongue.

"I need to be alone," Isla Belle said softly. Her heart clenched with the impending loss—even though she didn't fully understand it all. Bracing herself on the wall, she climbed a step.

"Isla Belle," Rhys' harsh whisper brushed over her as he grabbed her arm.

She flinched in response, shrinking from him. His scent surrounded her, the smell of grass and herbs.

"I said, leave me be." She jerked her arm free and continued up the stairs. Her ankle and knee pulsed. From the pain, she knew her leg was swelling. Peering up, she counted twelve more steps. She stifled a groan and tackled another.

Rhys' footsteps thundered after her, her stomach twisting with nerves. Aside from her family, most men and women feared him. They gossiped about the River Wye myths, his ancestral lands. The duchess said superstitions were weapons used on weak minds. It was the one thing Isla Belle and her mother agreed on.

Rhys cut in front of Isla and wrapped his arms around her, gathering her against his chest. "I am sorry, *fy annwyl.*"

She clenched her fists at the old term of endearment. "Stop."

Rhys let her slide from him, keeping her arms in his hands. "I am sorry."

She bit her lip and looked away.

He lifted her chin with a finger, a weak smile forming on his face. "Promise me, you'll do as you're told."

Before Isla Belle could answer, he gathered her once more,

cradling her against him. Her heart struggled to swim in the stormy waters. Rhys caressed her face, halting her thoughts.

His chest rumbled in her ear as he spoke, repeating, "Promise me, *fy annwyl*."

ISLA BELLE THORNE

SACRAMENTO, CALIFORNIA: PRESENT DAY

*A*gainst my better judgement, I drove my beast of a truck, an old '73 Chevy truck to Downtown Sacramento for my follow up doctor's appointment. The call had come while I was gathering boxes for my impending move from Palo Alto. College had been good to me. Having a goal and a steady idea of what the future—from what the week would look like to what my classes would be—had kept me grounded. Maybe that's why the visions were coming more often. I couldn't map out the next few months or years. For the first time in years, I was untethered. A growing restlessness had settled in me, starting the moment I graduated and now, with my mother's health not improving, it had stalled—as if my own ambitions were now frozen. My internal compass was broken, no longer bothering to look ahead for direction.

The steady rumble of the old engine canceled out the traffic noise, both on the freeway and in my head. The reluctant morning sun rose as I turned off the exit, entering the thin streets of downtown. The drive from Palo Alto was just over two hours without traffic, up to four with traffic. Ty thought the motivation for getting a morning appointment was to avoid the unseasonably warm day. My truck's air conditioning was decades past its prime. But truthfully, sleep wasn't my friend, not with my mother unable to communicate and the visions becoming more intense.

Rolling the window down a crack, I let the cool morning air wash the tired from my face. Despite the early hour, the streets were clogged with honking cars and rushed pedestrians, heels and brief-cases galore. Most of the cars carried only one driver, each lost in his or her own small world of tin and wheels. It was oddly comforting, being alone and surrounded. It shouldn't offer relief nor should I crave the solitude.

Instinctively, I touched the ring on my necklace, twisting the band I'd found in my mother's apartment between my thumb and forefin-ger. I'd never seen the ring before then. It didn't resemble my mother's expensive, more sparkly taste, but it gave comfort. And warmth. It felt familiar, like an old friend whose name I'd forgotten.

A headache began uncurling itself in my head, stretching and readying for another day of pain. Its timing was impeccable. I could truthfully tell John Taylor, medical assistant extraordinaire, that I did have a headache. He could tap away, entering the symptoms on his tablet. Rubbing my temple, I knew if I didn't get some serious sleep tonight, it'd grow to a migraine by tomorrow. My old roommate, a dedicated psychology major, blamed the headaches on the stress of my mother, as did my cousin. But I hadn't slept, truly slept, for more than a few hours in years.

Things happened in my sleep. Things that didn't make sense.

Without my uncle, I didn't have the luxury of parking in the underground garage. This was the first time I'd ever come to the Exchange without him. He was consumed in some sort of public rela-tion nightmare, an experiment gone wrong or something to that effect. He'd mumbled, which meant whatever the Exchange was dealing with was serious. Stephen rarely mumbled or murmured when dealing with family. There should have been a thrill in coming alone but Stephen had protected me when my own mother hadn't. He was overprotective—no argument there—but his frown was tempered by his good intentions.

At an excruciatingly slow pace, I found a parking lot just a few blocks from the Samaritan Exchange. Motorcycles lined the front with an empty spot on the end, room enough for my behemoth of a vehicle. I turned off the ignition and my truck sighed in response.

Checking the time, I relaxed, twenty minutes to spare. The hair on my neck stood on end. A feeling of being watched hit me. I glanced around the parking lot. No one. Tucking my phone under my arm, I slid down from the truck and kept my gaze wide. Still no one.

Sleep. I needed massive amounts of sleep.

I locked the truck and fell in line with other pedestrians on the sidewalk, catching the face of a slender man, tan with chiseled features. He gave a nod and tossed a confident smile my way. Stupidly, I stared. He arched an eyebrow and gave me a wide berth. Snagging men was my mother's gift, not mine.

Last year, when Mom was about to be released from another rehab facility, she asked her nurse—a man too young and handsome for her to resist—for a kiss. When he politely refrained, her laugh came hoarse. And for the first time, she looked afraid. Fragile. The bed seemed to swallow her disappearing frame. Her make-up was still on pointe, her nails polished to perfection, but she no longer looked like my mother. I had stood at her side, with unwashed hair and jagged nails and held her hand, watching the life slip from her face, first from her eyes and then from her lips. Year by year, my mother was leaving the world we shared.

The slender man to my left cleared his throat, his gaze straight ahead. He would've been no match for my mother. With a witty remark and tilt of her chin, she would've ensured his devotion.

Turning down Center Street, I felt it again, the eerie sensation of being watched. I climbed the steps to the Samaritan Exchange and turned around. Across the street, I sensed the presence of a man, although I couldn't see through the small copse of trees making up a courtyard. Like a gentle breeze, an urge, tangible and firm, wrapped around me, toying with my hair. The feeling pulled at me, beckoning me to follow.

It'd be another image of the blond man. Plain and striking all at once. Of late, a blue-eyed woman had joined him in the visions.

Sometimes she'd have golden curls, other times she'd have red or black hair. The only consistency was her blue eyes. And her blond companion.

For a moment, the temptation grew. The air stilled and the traffic of downtown muted to near silence. The image blossomed, surrounding me and blocking the people and street.

The screech of a police siren burst through, shattering the image. Warmth drained from me, raking my skin and falling to the sidewalk. The honking of cars and carried conversations came alive as I was once again, alone. The man had come and gone—I should be panicked or shocked. But no, that would be a normal, rational feeling. All I ever felt was an ache, a chasm filled with an unquenchable loss.

I covered my ears, the absence of the man all too clear. The headache, now fully awake, pounded in my skull. The ache in my chest felt too real. It was just another vision, a daydream. Except now, at the footsteps of the Samaritan Exchange, a nagging thought came to light. Why had the blond from my visions appeared on my uncle's pamphlet? The coincidence too glaring to ignore.

One foot in front of the other, I inched toward the Exchange. If I kept moving, I wouldn't feel the grief of the man or my mother. She was technically alive, I tried to remind myself. Even if she still hadn't uttered a word. For a woman determined to be the center of every-thing, her silence was deafening.

The flutter of panic slipped in. My mother's insanity was a shadow, a ghost that I couldn't quite shake. My dreams weren't exactly normal. They were my secret—something I'd never told my cousin or my mother. These dreams had been my companion for longer than I could remember but this vision in broad daylight was new, as were the headaches. They were also the reason I was standing in front of the largest medical organization in the world.

Men and women filed in and out of the building with stoic, bored stares. Catching my reflection of the glass entry door, I had the same resigned face. Forcing a smile, I looked again. The beginnings of dark circles didn't disappear. Some things were beyond control, including the near black color of my eyes. The color of pain, heartache.

Two sets of news camera teams appeared in the reflection behind me, each from a competing broadcast company. Whatever had kept Stephen busy must have hit the news. My mother would have loved the controversy. Gossip was another addiction she couldn't quit. Research was controversial by design but easily enhanced with sprinkles of technology and experiments. Ty, like my mother, thrived on thrills, in any form.

My hand itched to grab my phone and listen to Mom's voice, to have some sort of comfort. The phone would be disconnected soon—I doubted she'd paid any of her bills in months. When I looked in the mirror I couldn't see her, my small frame and dark hair didn't resemble her in the slightest. In less than a week, I struggled to remember what her laugh sounded like.

A security guard held out a plastic bin, a sign behind him listing everything that needed to be scanned. Tossing in my purse, keys and phone—why I never put my keys and phone in the purse was a continual annoyance to Ty—I walked through the body scanner. The security guard handed me the bin, his face expressionless. He'd moved onto the next person before I'd gathered everything. I wondered if my uncle could log into the security feed or if he wasn't allowed to because of the pesky HIPPA guidelines he abhorred.

Four receptionists sat in a semi-circle facing the entry doors, the Exchange's logo, a phoenix clutching the medical staff in its talons, was perched above them. The busy hum of people coming and going was a far cry from my normal visits—no quiet underground parking or executive entryway.

"I can help you." The receptionist on the far right, nodded to me.

"I'm here for an appointment. It's for doctor..." Fishing for the confirmation email, I scrolled through my phone. I'd spent more time with the assistant and couldn't remember the doctor's name, that part of the appointment was mere minutes.

"What's your name?" The receptionist didn't look at me, her fingers poised at the keyboard.

"Isla Belle Thorne."

She nodded and tapped away at the keys. Holding her hand in

front of the monitor, she said, "Take the elevator to the right, level three." The mechanic whirring of a printer began—then ended promptly, producing a barcode the size of a gas station receipt. "Scan this in the elevator. It'll give you access and check you in for your appointment."

Taking the offered barcode, I asked, "Do you remember what the doctor's name is?"

"Sorry." She finally met my gaze, her brown eyes bored and everything but apologetic. "We're not able to see private information on medical appointments. We've been cited—"

"By HIPPA," I finished for her, stifling the chuckle. If only Stephen was with me. He'd be flustered all over again. The receptionist arched an eyebrow before extending her hand to the next in line, signaling her availability.

Following several other people, half of us in professional attire, the other half in street clothes, we filed into the elevator. We each took a turn scanning our barcodes—or badges for those in suits and heels. The third floor was the first stop, my heart racing again. It didn't matter how many times I'd been to the Exchange, my body would always think danger was imminent.

The same receptionist—with all her gusto from the previous week —motioned to the clipboard, never raising her head from her paperwork in front of her. Stephen wasn't here. Neither was Ty. No one to fluster and keep my nerves at bay. I stood at the counter, staring at the clipboard, a pen tucked under the clamp. There wasn't anyone else in the waiting room—such a contrast from the university health facility that crammed so many students in their waiting area, half of us would have to stand.

"Isla Belle." John Taylor winked at me, clearly pleased at himself for saying my name correctly.

"Who told you how to say my name?" My uncle must have gotten to him.

"Not your dad." He shrugged and held out his arm like he'd done the last appointment. "After you."

"He's not my dad."

"Might want to tell him that." John closed the door to the exam room, sliding the tablet on the counter. He took my blood pressure and keeping his eye on the digital read, asked, "How's the headaches?"

"Fun."

He smirked. "Have one now?"

I stiffened. "How do you know?"

"Your blood pressure." His gaze flicked to mine. "Scale of one to ten. How bad?"

"Maybe a five."

"I can't help you if you won't be honest." He arched an eyebrow. I opened my mouth but he stepped back, adding, "Your blood pressure went from low at your last appointment, to a little too high. Just now, right when you said *five*, it spiked even higher."

My phone beeped, signaling a text. I didn't dare answer it with John staring at me. He rolled his eyes and placed my index finger in the plastic pulse reader. His tablet lit up, beeping angrily at him. "Are you kidding me?"

"What?"

He tapped on the device and shook his head. He took off the pulse reader and then replaced it on my other index finger. "Let's try that again."

Once more the tablet beeped at him. He set the tablet back on the counter and slowly turned to me, arms folded. "Your body doesn't lie."

"I've had headaches my entire life." Although never this bad. Or often. When he started toward the door, I grabbed his arm. "I meant what I said. This is only a five. It's not a migraine yet. I can still function."

He offered a sad frown. "Your idea of functioning and your body's idea of functioning are worlds apart."

He disappeared before I could argue. A doctor, this time a woman, came in, a face mask laying limp on her neck. She was young, closer to Ty's age than my uncle. "Good morning, Isla Belle."

"Good morning." A warning flag went off in my head. She was new and entirely too cheerful. There was something wrong but I couldn't put my finger on it.

49

She lifted the tablet John had left. Nodding, she said, "You're showing signs of distress."

"I currently have a headache." The words felt fake. A headache wouldn't result in a change in blood pressure. My background was only veterinary medicine, but even I knew that.

She pursed her lips, her finger scrolling through my file. "Your bloodwork came back relatively normal. At least, for what we've checked."

"What tests did you run?" Dread filled me, twisting my stomach.

"A complete blood panel, CBC, basic metabolic, thyroid…" She cradled the tablet to her chest. "I think we need to run more extensive bloodwork."

That didn't make sense. If my bloodwork came back normal, there was no reason to order more. Maybe I should have waited for Stephen to join me. "You said relatively normal."

"Your pulse and blood pressure don't match your blood panel." Her brow furrowed. "We're missing something."

"I do have a headache," I offered dumbly.

She nodded. "That could account for some."

Twisting the crinkling exam paper, I said, "My mother is in the hospital." *Again,* I almost added.

Her gaze flicked to mine. "That could explain a lot. But I think there's more to it."

Relief came like a splash of cool water. "It's been over a week and no improvement."

The doctor's face softened. "I'm going to order another panel, this time fasting." She gave a little wave. "Just to rule out anything else. It's my job to make sure nothing serious is going on. I am going to prescribe some migraine medication. If taken early enough, they should stop the migraine in its tracks. I'll need you to start tracking a few things for me, the pain level and your diet. Include water intake."

Nodding, I felt oddly uncertain. Everything she had said made perfect sense but my stomach twisted. I was missing something. It'd done the same thing when I was in college and knee deep in research, only to miss something so blatantly obvious—and pointed out by a fellow student.

The doctor made her way to the door, patting my hand as she passed.

I blinked, touched by the gesture. The moment the door closed, dread crept back in. The blood pressure and the pulse could be explained by my mother's hospitalization—even the increased headaches, but nothing justified the visions. Not that I'd disclosed that part.

Leaving the building, I checked my phone.

Stephen had texted, *You start tomorrow. 8 am sharp.*

I groaned. I'd told him I wanted to be interviewed, not just handed the job. *What about the interview?*

He texted back. *Fine. Your "interview" is tomorrow at 8 am sharp.*

I tried—and failed—to come up with a good response on my walk back to my truck. Before I climbed in, I felt the hairs on the back of my neck stand on end. I turned around and for a split second, saw the blond man from my visions staring at me from across the street. His hair was shorter, his clothes more modern but not by much. Cars sped by, blocking the view and then, just as soon as he appeared, he was gone.

ISLA BELLE THORNE

SACRAMENTO, CALIFORNIA: PRESENT DAY

*I*n a suit that cost more than a month's worth of my rent in Palo Alto, Ty folded his arms and leaned against the threshold of the Cael's downtown apartment. "You look like you're going to a funeral."

"Says the man in a black suit." Sliding my resume into the manila folder, I scoffed. Stephen had successfully convinced me to move in. I only agreed to a temporary living situation. Once I knew what my future held, I could better figure out where I was going to live.

"I was talking about your expression, not your clothes." He held out his arms. "For the record, I don't like wearing suits."

"No, you like taking *off* your clothes."

"Someone's in a bad mood." He *tsk*ed and shook his head, not bothering to argue with the truth.

"I am not," I lied and held up a finger. "Okay, maybe I'm not in a good mood but I hate this."

He arched an eyebrow. "You hate being gainfully employed?"

"No." Scowling, I snatched my keys from the counter. "Stephen helping makes it all dirty. Like I couldn't earn it on my own."

"You couldn't."

"Thanks for the vote of confidence."

"It's not an insult." He grabbed his own keys and opened the door. "I wouldn't have worked for the Exchange if I wasn't a Cael."

"Exactly." I followed him to the hallway.

It didn't matter how many times I'd come to this apartment complex, I was always taken back at the sheer magnitude of the place. Surrounded by historical buildings, Stephen's apartment was once the presidential suite of Sacramento's oldest hotel. The first few floors were timeshares with the rest of the building owned by families drowning in old money—like the Caels. When the hotel was refurbished in the late 18th century to owner occupied apartments, the committee took great pains to keep the original, historical charm. To this day, the ornate filigree on the floor boards and bead paneling on the ceiling were replaced with pristine replicas when damaged.

Ty pressed the button for the elevator and smirked in a very Hollywood, James Dean kind of way. "Listen, Stephen's parents were super controlling. They dictated how and when they were going to be."

A neighbor poked his head out of the opposite end of the hallway. He looked both ways and then shook his head, retreating back into his apartment. Ty and I were the youngest occupants by about forty years.

"I get it. Stephen is a thousand times better than his parents but I still would like to accomplish something without his interference." Hitching my purse to my shoulder, I did a mental check, making sure I had my resume, keys, phone and purse. "I'm not like you."

Ty pushed the button for the garage level. "And that means what?"

"I wasn't raised on nepotism."

He chucked. "You realize Stephen shares more of your DNA than I do?"

I froze—he was right. Ty's biological father was some deadbeat, high school boyfriend. Stephen swooped in as the hero—his favorite part to play—when Ty was a toddler. It wasn't an open secret and I doubted Ty even knew the particulars. Even after Ty's parents divorced, Ty went to live with Stephen. He had claimed Ty just like he'd claimed me. "The Exchange offered the job because I'm his niece, not because I'm qualified."

"But you are qualified." Ty tossed his keys in the air, catching them and tossing them again. Restless energy swirled around him. How he ever graduated college, or even law school, was beyond me.

"The position is for media relations." A dull ache began in my head. I hadn't heard back from the doctor's office on when I was doing the next blood panel. The doctor had kept her word, sending in a pain management prescription for the migraines. I'd tucked them in my purse but didn't dare take them in front of Ty.

"Funny, I could have sworn you graduated with a master's in communications."

"That's what I mean." Was he purposely not understanding what I was trying to say? "I have zero, as in nothing, nada—*no* experience. The Samaritan Exchange is, well it's The Samaritan Exchange. You can't reach any higher."

We left the elevator and Ty held out his hand, clicking the fob to unlock his car. "And?"

"Oh, never mind." Throwing my hands in the air, I stalked to my truck.

"Knock 'em dead!" He yelled, his voice echoing in the parking garage.

I gave him a thumbs up but didn't look at him. It was pointless trying to explain my frustration. Two motorcycles parked in the stall next to my truck. I had to shimmy to get to the driver's side. When I tried to reverse, Ty pulled up behind me and rolled down his window, "Check your phone, *Issla.*"

Pulling out my phone, Stephen texted, *Good luck on your interview.*

I leaned out the window. "What does that mean?"

"Be careful what you wish for." Ty's lips stretched to a mischievous grin. He laughed and drove off.

I waited until I was parked down the street at the Exchange to pop two pills in my mouth. Swallowing them without water, I half-ran, half-walked to the front door of the Samaritan Exchange, my pulse racing with Stephen's last text. With a new barcode in hand and another quick elevator ride, I stood inside Suite 701. The receptionist must have just arrived, her coffee still steaming in her hand.

She circled the desk and traded the coffee for a clipboard. "You must be Issla Belle Thorne?"

"The *s* is silent." It was a knee jerk reaction that I couldn't break.

"Oh—so sorry." She wrote a little note on her clipboard.

"No, no." My face flushed. This wasn't the time or place to correct someone. "Sorry, that just came out."

She gave a knowing grin. "Nervous?"

"Completely," I said with relief. It'd be easy to place the blame all on Ty but he was right, I *had* asked for an interview instead of an offer.

The woman held my gaze, her brow furrowing. She was more than likely watching my eyes change from dark to bright blue, having gone from nervous to relaxed. "Have a seat."

"Oh. Yes. Of course." Obediently, I sat only to realize there was no one else. I was the only one to be interviewed. Stephen cast a long shadow.

Because of Stephen, Ty landed the Samaritan Exchange right out of law school without ever applying. I was hoping for a real—an *actual* interview where I could not only prove my worth but ask questions. Instead of venting to Ty, I should have spent the morning asking him questions about the organization.

A door down the hall squawked open, a tall, lanky man with glasses sliding down his nose came forward, a sheepish smile forming. He scratched his head and hesitated, balancing on the balls of his feet. He wore faded khaki pants and a coffee stained polo shirt. My heart sank. He couldn't be the real interviewer. If there was anything real about this interview process at all.

The man leaned against the wall, his brow furrowed. In a crisp English accent, he said with perfect pronunciation, "Isla Belle Thorne?"

He led me to a deceptively large conference room, the table long and narrow. He sat down, a row of several pictures immediately behind him on the wall. Every man wore a suit—including Stephen.

None of the pictures had names attached but one headshot caught my eye. The blond man. *Rhys Staverton*. It was absurd. His real name couldn't be Staverton but Rhys felt right even though I knew it shouldn't. He looked out of place with the formal suit. He didn't look old enough to be next to the silver haired men on either side. Rhys Staverton, if that was his real name, couldn't be more than a year or two older than Ty.

The interviewer offered his hand across the table, a frown on his face. "Dr. Euston."

"Dr. Euston?" I stared, his name echoing in my mind. This man could not be Dr. Euston. He looked nothing like the pictures I'd seen in medical journals. He couldn't be the scientist who pioneered—no, coined the phrase—*genetic healing*. This was a joke. Ty was behind this. "You're Dr. Euston? As in Dr. *Jeffrey* Euston?"

A pink hue crept up his neck. This wasn't a joke. Fumbling to the chair, my face went hot. Dr. Jeffrey Euston wanted to fix our DNA, perfect our roots. No more cancer. No more diseases. No more mental illness. I'd stalked him on the internet like a teen-aged girl obsessed over boy bands.

"Dr. Euston. I can't believe you're—I mean *I'm* here. It's you." The temperature rose. I was an idiot. The room seemed to shrink. Dr. Euston looked at me, eyebrows arched.

"Soooo…" He cleared his throat. "Animal science?"

"Yes." I didn't trust myself to say anything else. We sat silently. A trickle of sweat traveled down my back. Shifting in my seat, I blurted, "I actually wanted to follow in your footsteps. Extend quality of life. But with animals, obviously. I had more freedom working with them, rather than humans." My voice came higher, making me sound more like a high school kid than an educated woman.

He tapped the corner of the paper. "But you got a master's in communications?"

"My mom got sick. I couldn't stand to be in a lab. Or anything that resembled a hospital. Or research." The words just came. Crawling under the desk was tempting. My cheeks felt feverish. Public relations should show finesse, confidence during trouble times, not panic and weakness. I was failing. Miserably.

He folded his hands in his lap and leaned back in the chair. "Isla Belle Thorne, huh."

"Yes?" My name didn't sound appealing at the moment. He'd narrowed his eyes for a split second when saying it. I was missing something but couldn't put my finger on what.

"When were you born?"

"I'm sorry, what?" I coughed awkwardly into my hand. No one, and I mean no one, had ever asked my age. I was fairly certain it wasn't legal. Dr. Euston didn't even look at me when he asked, his eyes glued to the resume. "You want to know when I was born?"

Dr. Euston met my gaze for a moment, and for a half a second, I felt him challenge me. For what, I didn't know. He smiled ruefully and said, "I'd love to have a scientist on the team. I hate meeting with suits telling me why this is bad. Or how this makes us look. It'd be great to have someone who's been on the other side."

There was a *but* to his statement. It hung in the tense air between us.

Dr. Euston leaned back, his entire demeanor shifting. He picked at the fraying hem of his sleeve. "Look, the only reason I'm here is because the powers that be are tired of me whining. I hated the last PR team, and I'll be a pain for the next one."

"You want someone in your corner, not someone telling you what to do. It's what every scientist wants. The public wants to benefit from science without actually seeing the human cost." I had been on both sides of the fence as a student.

"Interesting." Dr. Euston looked more confused than interested. "So you would defend science, no matter the cost?"

Suspicion came fast. Cautiously, I admitted, "It depends."

"Ah, of course it does." He shook his head once, his expression unreadable. He smirked at my resume. "I forgot."

"What am I missing?" I leaned over, wondering what had captured his interest.

He stood and sighed with a flash of irritation. "Please wait here."

"Is it because of my family?" My eyes flicked to Stephen's headshot.

"Your family?" His brow furrowed. "Does Rhys know?"

Rhys. The name sent delicate shivers down my spine. I would not admit my visions to Dr. Euston. Not to him. Not to anyone. Swallowing the panic, I asked a touch too innocently, "Who's Rhys?"

Dr. Euston shook his head and muttered to himself. He left me to marinate in the awkward silence, *Rhys* echoing in my mind.

A few minutes later, the cheerful receptionist poked her head in. "I suppose Dr. Euston forgot to tell you he's done for the day."

Being forgotten in such a short time wasn't how I pictured the interview to go—if it truly was an interview at all. My shoulders sagged. "What happens now?"

She cocked her head to the side, looking more like an eager puppy than the deliverer of bad news. "So sorry. He tends to be an absent-minded professor. I'll find out and give you a call."

"Thank you." When I didn't move she slipped out, her smile fading. I left, each step heavier than the last. Outside, a homeless man started singing. He shook his head at me and then to the sky as I passed.

My phone vibrated. Ty texted, *Congrats.*

He was confused. I'd bombed an interview that was handed to me.

I texted back, *Not quite.*

Have I ever been wrong?

Let me count the ways... Slipping the phone back in my pocket, I lied to myself that it didn't matter. It was one stupid job interview. Mom was rejected several times before she sold her first play. My career would be no different.

LADY ISLA BELLE WELLESLEY

WELLESLEY COUNTY, ENGLAND: 1535

*O*n her injured ankle, Lady Isla Belle Wellesley paced in her room with uneven steps. Her mind imagined the worst of everything. It'd been weeks since the Duke of Wellesley was summoned to court, stealing the healer Rhys with him. With the arrival of her father's last letter, her mother had shut her door. It'd been days since the duchess had spoken. Without Rhys's whispers and explanations, Isla Belle was left alone, her only companion the fear lurking in the shadows.

Leaning into the cold, stone wall, she cursed the rain—but nothing changed. She was as powerless over the weather as she was over her family's fate. The water spilled from the sky, forcing roads to flood and holding the news of her father at bay.

She limped down the stairs from her dim bedroom, her ankle less stable on the descend. Reaching the landing of the dining hall, Lady Isla Belle felt the hush of silence, the servants stilled and bowed their heads. Anger welled inside her. She was abandoned by her own household. Everyone, lord and servant alike worried for their future. A master's fate could bring ruin—or fortune—to them all. When the duchess secured Anne Boleyn as the king's next bride, their status was elevated, as were the servants.

The dining table was dutifully filled with dishes, a plate held for the duke, the duchess and Isla Belle. The sight of the empty chairs added fire to Isla Belle's frustrated heart. With uneven steps, she reached the table, her hand on the back of her father's chair. The fire grew, spreading through her chest. The shuffling of the servants echoed the loneliness. She'd begged to go with her father, remembering the twinkle in the king's smile. Surely, King Henry would still be kind to her. She knew it wasn't true, but she clung to the false hope.

Closing her eyes, she touched her cheek, remembering the pity in Rhys' eyes when she'd asked to accompany them to court. He'd tugged a strand of her hair in teasing and promised in his sing-song accent that all would be well. It was forced. He was no longer the Rhys she knew. Isla Belle didn't know how or why, but he'd changed the day the riders came.

The memory cooled the burgeoning flame. A murmur came from the courtyard. Lady Isla Belle rushed through the hall to the wet cobbled stones. She clung to the corner under the outer roof, safe in the comfort of the shadows.

A head taller than most women, she peered above the laundress maids. Several horses with wet riders climbed the muddy road against the onslaught of rain, none of them carrying an emblem or standard indicating their house. Isla Belle fought the rising panic—the riders could bring hope or despair.

Steadying herself, she gripped the wall and leaned forward on her uninjured foot. The first two horses entering the courtyard were tenant couriers carrying censor scrolls from town. Isla Belle dug her fingers into the wall. Life dared to move on while her fate, and her family's, was frozen, waiting for the king's pardon. Or punishment.

Another rider came. And another. Each without the Wellesley standard.

Isla Belle sank back on her heels. Simmering, her temper grew. Her family had done nothing, only shown kindness to their queen at the behest of the king. They deserved reward, not suspicion.

The last of the riders arrived, no sign of the duke or Rhys. They dismounted, pulling packages from their bags. They were nothing more than summer vendors peddling their wares.

Servants returned to their duties. Her mother, if she still bothered to watch for her husband, would take up pacing once more. Isla Belle refused to move. Her ankle throbbed and her heart ached but without a task or someone to speak with, all she could do was stare at the courtyard. And the empty road beyond.

The setting sun pierced through pregnant clouds, rain still drumming on the roof and cobbled stones. Instead of casting a brilliant rainbow, a thunderous snap lit the sky. Two fir trees guarding the edge of the courtyard burst into flames. Men rushed forward, buckets in hand.

Between the twin fires a man's silhouette appeared. His gait was uncanny, graceful—and familiar. *Rhys.* His back to the flames, Rhys' face was half hidden but Isla Belle knew her friend. It was Rhys. She knew his frame, his walk—she knew him like she knew her own reflection.

Her skin prickled. Something was wrong. He'd arrive without a horse or her father. With shaking limbs, Isla Belle left her corner under the roof and walked toward him, wet curls clinging to her skin and clothes. The tops of the trees collapsed, clapping together before falling to the muddy road. Isla Belle flinched. Rhys was at her side in an instant.

"You're home..." She should feel joy or relief but all she felt was dread. The set of his jaw, the hard line of his mouth made her shrink.

He held a finger to his lips and tucked an arm around her waist. He helped her to the servants' entrance. With practiced care, he fell in sync with her steps and helped her climb the stairs.

"What happened?" Isla Belle whispered.

Rhys didn't answer. Nor did he soothe her with her pet name. A chill wrapped around her neck. He gave a firm shake of his head. Isla Belle tightened her grip, fear filling her. She reached for the door to her room. He grabbed her hand, continuing the climb to her mother's chambers. Each step, the dread grew—and with it, another feeling altogether. The scent of Rhys surrounded Isla Belle. His arm supporting her, she felt every movement, her shoulder against him. His touch had always healed her but this was different, a warmth she'd not felt before.

Leaving her side, Rhys pushed open the duchess' door. Isla Belle shivered from the loss of him. She'd spent her childhood at his side, and yet when she glanced up at his face, he wasn't hers. His face still striking, but he was distant. Whispers had always trailed him, some kind, some suspicious.

Rhys narrowed his gaze, like he'd done hundreds of times before to read her mood. Lady Isla Belle tucked her chin, cutting off his view. Rhys hadn't been home, he'd lost the right to read her moods.

"Rhys." Her mother's voice beckoned them forward. "Isla Belle?"

The room was bathed in grief. Despair was in the withering fire and the stale, hopeless air. The Duchess of Wellesley sat in her chair facing the window, her hair and dress the same as the day before. Her skin was sallow, haunted.

"Mother." Isla Belle circled Rhys, coming to her mother's chair.

Instead of greeting her daughter, the duchess turned to the healer, her back straight with pride. "Tell me."

Rhys took in the room, allowing Isla Belle to do the same. Plates of untouched food were stacked on the desk, several letters scribbled and discarded on the bed.

"Have they taken your tongue as well as my husband?" The duchess asked, her voice barely above a whisper. She turned from Rhys and faced the window. In that moment, the woman seemed to disappear, her body an empty shell. The answer lay in the tightening of Rhys' mouth. Isla's father wasn't coming home.

"Mother?" Isla Belle reached for her hand, recoiling at the cold, clammy skin.

The duchess gave a half-hearted wave. She slumped against the back of the chair, her blonde curls framing her shoulders and face. "It's done, isn't it?"

"What is done?" Isla Belle didn't know who to ask, her mother or Rhys.

Ignoring the question, he went to the window, careful to keep just out of sight. Peering down at the courtyard below, he nodded. "Your father did not help."

Looking from Rhys to her mother, Isla Belle balked, confused at his boldness. "My father—"

"Not *your* father, Isla Belle." Rhys kept his profile to her, his focus on the view below.

Her cheeks flushed. Rhys had cut her off and appeared to know more about her family than she did.

"So the great Marcher Lord visited the almighty king?" The duchess furrowed her brow.

Isla Belle's grandfather was a powerful Welsh nobleman, as volatile as the English king. That was the beginning and end of what she knew.

Rhys gave another nod, his head not turning to either woman. A cool indifference settled on his features. "He reminded King Henry that he, not the English or the French, gave the throne to his father." Rhys smiled ruefully at Isla Belle. "He can't bridle his tongue any more than you."

Isla Belle narrowed her gaze. "I've not spoken to you in weeks, Rhys—"

"What is the price?" The duchess lifted her chin once more, the last of her noble pride.

Rhys turned from the window, his eyes hard. "A Marcher bride."

Isla Belle fidgeted, her gaze shifting between her mother and Rhys. He folded his arms and leaned against the stone wall. His gaze cold like the wind from the north. Her mother had shrunk to a shell of her former self and now Isla Belle's dearest friend, her closest ally had disappeared—replaced with a stranger. She didn't dare ask what a Marcher bride was. His hard gaze flicked to Isla Belle. Looking away, she shivered. The man who'd returned to her was not the gentle Rhys of her childhood.

Isla Belle once danced with him in this very room. The duchess had demanded she learn the proper steps and Rhys be her partner. Cramped in the cold, stone room, Rhys had borne the brunt of Isla Belle's choppy stride and awkward rhythm.

He had finished speaking and lifted his chin but Isla Belle hadn't heard a word. Her world was shifting, and she was struggling to stay upright.

"Say something." Rhys' voice pierced her.

"I've nothing to say." Isla Belle straightened her back. She'd never cowed to him before, she'd not start today. For weeks, she'd weathered the silence and worry alone. She would face whatever was on the horizon, with or without Rhys.

"He wants a *Marcher* bride." He spoke low, emphasizing each word.

Slowly, the realization came. A noose wrapped around Isla Belle's neck. She was unwed and descended from Marcher nobility. She was the bride.

"Who wants the Marcher bride? My father or the king?" From her chair, the duchess gathered her skirts, appearing ready to stand. She pursed her lips and released the fabric, settling back. She closed her eyes for a brief moment. "Anne believes King Henry has already chosen her replacement. Why would he want a Welsh wife?"

"He doesn't." Rhys rubbed the bridge of his nose.

Isla Belle balked. "He's the king—"

"Of a bleeding country," Rhys snapped. Silence filled the room. He'd never spoken to Isla Belle like this. He was the calm, the center while she circled him with questions and teasing—but not today. "He needs an heir. That's all that matters to him."

The bite in his voice sent her pulse racing. She knew what was expected of her, she knew the severity of what was happening. "I've spent weeks worried about my father. My mother." *And you,* she almost confessed. "I've heard nothing. And now, you—"

"Child," the duchess chided, arching a regal eyebrow.

Isla Belle could be wrinkled, gray and nearing death but would always be *child* to the Duchess of Wellesley. Isla Belle's hands clenched into fists before she calmly turned to her mother, feeling the weight of Rhys' gaze. "I'll not stand here in silence. I'll not hide away in this room, pretending—"

"Pretending?" Her mother lifted her head, her profile noble and proud.

"Stop." Isla Belle groaned. "Tell me what is to come."

Ignoring her request, Rhys crossed the room to the tonic cabinet. He'd hauled the medicine into the duchess's chambers before leaving with the duke.

Isla Belle's anger grew at the dismissal. She'd throw the tonic in his face if he dared to offer her a cup. She needed answers, not herbs.

Rhys handed the tonic to her mother, his gaze softening. Isla Belle frowned at the exchange. Both the duke and duchess gave great freedom and respect to the Welsh orphan. It used to endear Rhys to Isla Belle but today, her mother's easy affection pricked Isla Belle's nerves.

The duchess swallowed hard, her face fading to grey. She glanced to the door and then back at Isla Belle. "Tell her."

Isla Belle felt the judgement from Rhys. Loyal to the end, Rhys would protect the duchess. *Tell her.* Whatever was about to be said, Rhys had known—and kept it from her. Isla Belle was very much alone.

Rhys nodded toward Isla Belle. "King Henry will take a Welsh woman, more specifically a Marcher bride and keep his English mistress. Whoever delivers a son will—"

"Be queen," the duchess whispered.

"Will keep her neck," Rhys added darkly. "With Queen Anne in the tower, the king has made his intent clear. Whoever bears the son, he'll marry. England would have an heir, and the woman would have a crown. Her family will be elevated."

"For as long as she is queen," whispered Isla Belle. Her gaze swiveled from the duchess to Rhys. Their stoic, even expressions underlined their decision—they had cowed to the king's demands. "What have you done, Rhys—"

"Do not forget your place, Isla Belle." The duchess' soft voice cut through the air. Isla Belle bit down the retort. Her mother had set a healer servant above her own daughter. "I had hoped my father would help us. But no, he had to force our hand. I will leave in two days."

"*You're* leaving?" Isla Belle looked from her old friend to her mother, sadness in both their eyes. "You said a Marcher bride."

"It won't give you much time." Rhys motioned to the duchess.

"Time for what?" Isla Belle folded her arms, her fingers digging into the fabric.

Her mother looked from Rhys to her, fondness in her gaze. "For you to be kidnapped."

"You've lost your mind." Isla Belle's hands trembled. She froze, unable to breathe. Unable to think. This was not happening. "You cannot do this."

"It is for the best." Strength returned to the duchess, her back straightening.

With his face to the window, Rhys said, "The king will have your head. He'll know you're behind it."

"Better me than her," the duchess said dryly.

"I did not ask you to interfere." Isla hugged herself. There had to be another way. She would not lose both parents. Her father's absence had left its mark. She wasn't safe, not in here. Not in England. "I will be his bride. I can do it."

In an instant, Rhys had Isla Belle sitting on the duchess' bed, his guiding hand at her elbow.

"I would not condemn my daughter to the tower." The duchess lifted her chin, but the rigid posture softened the words. She was a mother protecting her child—at any cost. "This is the only way."

"I would not condemn my mother. For me or anyone else." Isla Belle's voice came low, unsure. She leaned forward, her elbows on her knees—a form that should have invited rebuke from her mother.

"Isla Belle," chided Rhys, handing her a tonic.

Pushing the offered cup away, Lady Isla Belle's cheeks flushed at his reprimand. She wanted to snap, to lash out but found herself leaning into him. "Mother—"

"Do not argue. This is the way it must be." The duchess's words were clipped and cutting.

"And where am I to go—after pretending to be kidnapped?" Isla Belle stared dumbly at the cup in her hand.

Rhys shook his head. "You cannot lie if you do not know."

Isla Belle gripped her cup. "You cannot do this."

"Is there another way? Truly, is there another way to keep you safe?" The duchess threw her arms up in surrender. Her tone came hollow.

"The other way is to send me." Isla Belle couldn't help the growl that escaped. She felt the draft of the outside world the moment her father left. Rhys, her precious friend, was a stranger. And now her mother. She would be utterly alone in only a few days' time.

"We've done what we can." Her mother finally stood, walking slowly to the window.

Not everything. Isla Belle would not let her family suffer.

Rhys caught her gaze and shook his head in warning. He hadn't missed the look in her eye. He mouthed, *no.*

She answered with a glare. Rhys motioned to his left arm; she'd broken her same arm on her last heroic act. The fever had nearly taken her. She'd healed with greater stubbornness than before. The injury was worth it. She'd saved her father's prized filly.

"You will not act the fool. Isla Belle, you must trust us." Rhys rushed to the door, gesturing for her to leave.

"If the king can divorce one wife and condemn another, what makes you safe, Isla Belle?" The duchess tossed a forlorn look before returning back to the window, her gaze on the road leading toward town. "My father is pressuring the king to take you. Henry will resent you; he'll look at you as the enemy, not a wife. Look at Queen Anne. That is your future if you take his hand."

"The king would not cave to your father. You've said it yourself. Your father is a Marcher lord. He's no longer considered English." It was a weak argument but Lady Isla Belle had to try. "If the king takes me, it'll be his own choice, not your father's."

"King Henry fears the Welsh and their myths." Absently, Lady Wellesley touched her necklace adorned with the delicate Celtic symbols of her family.

"And?" Isla Belle tried to pull from Rhys's grasp. "The king is not weak. He'll not fall prey to old stories."

The duchess faced Isla Belle. "It means we are alone. If I go to court, I defy my father. If you go to court, we risk the king's temper. Either way, our fate is sealed."

There was a way out. Isla Belle would use any tool she could find, even superstition. "Having a son cannot be the only thing he desires. Does he fear nothing else?"

"Nothing, Isla Belle." Rhys motioned to the door again, his face blank. "He fears nothing."

Isla Belle's mouth fell open. Her eyes darkened to the color of midnight, filling with hurt. She curtseyed to her mother, her skirt swishing the floor. She left the room and flew down the stairs, her hand on the wall to steady her injured ankle. Her heart clenched with the impending loss. Like she had since she was a child, Isla Belle felt Rhys' presence before she heard him.

"Isla Belle," Rhys' harsh whisper raked against her skin.

She flinched in response, shrinking from his company. His scent surrounded her, the smell of grass and herbs. She had not been this close to him in weeks. An ache crept in. She was losing her childhood, her family. Everything.

"What are you doing?" He scowled. She winced—he softened, and quietly added, "Where are you going?"

"To rest my ankle." She looked away, hoping he couldn't see the color of her mood.

"You lie," Rhys hissed.

It wasn't long ago that he would give praise and patience. Where was the kind man she revered? The king's court had changed him, hardened him into a stranger. Isla Belle had never feared the legends although she wished she could remember the stories. If only she could use them to help her family. She had not given up hope that all would be made right, that her family and Rhys would return to her— until now.

"Stop. Whatever foolish plan you've hatched, stop." Rhys cut in front of her.

"If you will not help me, leave me."

He growled, the sound more animal than human. He wiped his face in his hands. "What do you think I'm doing?"

Isla Belle gripped the stone wall, her other hand on her skirt, unsure what to do. Rhys' temper had simmered from angry to desperate.

"Please." He leaned against the wall, his leg brushing against her skirts. "Trust me, *fy annwyl.*"

"Give me a reason to," she whispered and left him on the stairs.

ISLA BELLE THORNE

SACRAMENTO, CALIFORNIA: PRESENT DAY

*I*nstead of returning to Stephen's suite or my half-packed rental in Palo Alto, I found myself driving to the hospital. This was one aspect of my life where I'd hoped Stephen would interfere—better yet, I had hoped he'd take over my mother's care completely. The few conversations I'd had with the nurses gave me nothing to hold onto.

Entering my mother's room, I saw a nurse leave the neighboring room. "Have you checked on Dorothea Thorne?"

The pity on her face was a direct result of the desperation in my voice. "Sorry, no. But I'll try to find out who did."

Nodding, I braced myself and entered Mom's room. There were two empty chairs, one on each side of my mother's hospital bed. They mirrored her vacant eyes staring at the wall.

Despite trying again, I already knew they'd tell me nothing. I'd cornered her nurse yesterday for information but was given only a head shake. Without a signed consent form from my mother, privacy laws prohibited the staff from telling me anything. I'd already been caught twice trying to look at Mom's charts. It wouldn't be my last attempt, that I knew.

I blamed the silence from the staff and the fact my mother was here at all for my frustration. Both accusations were unfair but I didn't care. Dottie Thorne, the celebrated playwright was physically before me, but the woman I knew was gone. She'd been drowned by the medication pumping in her veins.

"I hate hospitals," I whispered.

A set of quick knocks on the wall set my teeth on edge. Glancing at the clock, I realized it was lunchtime. Ty strutted in, his smile too loud for the room. Ty plopped down in the nearest chair, an ice cream cone in his hand.

"Don't." My voice caught but not from despair. I was angry. No, I was livid. I blinked, frustrated that my vision was blurring. If I cried, Ty would trip over himself to comfort me. I didn't want pity. I wanted facts, even if they hurt. "I don't need ice cream."

Ty twisted the cone in his hand, his face sobering. "It wasn't for you."

"Then eat your ice cream outside." I didn't care about his stupid dessert. He needed to leave. I wanted anything happy or teasing gone. Guilt rushed in—this wasn't his fault.

"It isn't for me, either." Ty's voice came soft, his face fallen. In that moment, he looked like a boy playing dress up. The sight of his dashed hopes swept the rest of my anger aside.

"I'm sorry, Ty."

He stood and wrapped an arm around my shoulders. "Me, too."

The door swung open and a middle aged nurse marched in, her lips pursed. Passing us, she checked my mother's vitals.

"So glad to see you." Charm radiated from Ty. He held out the ice cream. "Plain vanilla in a sugar cone."

The nurse cocked an eyebrow. A slow smile spread across her face. "You remembered."

Only Ty would butter up my mother's nurse. Regret tugged at my heart. A moment ago, I was ready to strangle him for bringing the ice cream into the room. He wasn't making light of my misery. Tyler Cael was definitely Stephen's son, desperately trying to save the day.

"Day shifts are hard." Ty playfully elbowed the woman's arm.

Handing her the ice cream, he added, "My dad used to say his nurses had the hardest jobs."

The woman brightened, playing straight into Ty's hand. His kindness lowered the nurse's guard while gently reminding her of his Cael lineage. "That's nice of you."

Shrugging, he nodded toward my mother. "How's she doing?"

The nurse hesitated. She looked between us. I pretended to be lost in my own thoughts.

Whispering the nurse said, "I'm not sure. Her records are sealed. We're given orders to track the vitals. We're not authorized to adjust or administer new medication."

Ty patted the woman's back. "That must be tough. Doing your job with one hand tied behind your back."

She sighed. "It's impossible. But that's standard care for all Samaritan wards."

Before I could ask what a Samaritan ward was, Ty cocked his head to the side and said, "True. But it doesn't make it any easier."

"Same orders every time." The woman shook her head with a frown. "I suppose she'll be gone soon, the poor woman. She'll be transferred in the next few weeks."

I flinched at *gone*. Her pity didn't sit well with me. Dottie Thorne was an explosion of personality. She could flip from one accent to another and dance from joke to politics without missing a beat. She would heal—she always did. She didn't need anyone's pity.

The nurse smiled at her ice cream cone. "Thank you, for this."

Ty nodded and she left, never once looking my way. He stared at my mother, his brow furrowed. I'd seen this serious side of him on occasion, typically when he was on the verge of making or breaking a case for work. Like my relationship to my mother, he was the very opposite of Stephen. My uncle's joy was beneath the surface, hidden to those not patient enough to look. Ty covered his compassion and responsibility with laughter and teasing. But here, in the stillness of my mother's hospital room, Ty let the Cael façade slip.

"Why is my mother a ward of the Samaritan Exchange?"

Rubbing a thumb along his jaw, Ty leaned back in the chair. "She's been a ward since you were born."

"Why am I just finding this out?" Being kept in the dark on such a monumental secret was beyond a betrayal. I wanted to scream. I wanted to cry. I wanted something—anything to be good for my mom. At least, this once.

"I didn't know. At least, not for sure. I know other cases like hers." Ty frowned, the expression foreign. He motioned to the door. "The nurse just confirmed it."

"Oh." A lump formed in my throat. Until that moment, I hadn't realized how alone I'd felt. "I guess I owe you an apology. And a thanks."

"Don't thank me yet." His hand dropped to the armrest, his fingers tapping the edge. "If she's a ward of the Exchange, you won't have much say in her treatment."

"But Stephen does."

There was an apology in his eyes. "Not quite."

"What do you mean *not quite?*" Panic bubbled in me, my stomach twisting.

"Stephen isn't allowed a say in her welfare anymore." Ty leaned forward, his elbows on his knees. He ran a hand through his hair. "Apparently, she tried to blackmail him but accidentally sent the information to the Exchange. They stepped in and appointed someone else as her guardian."

There was truth in that statement. I felt it in my bones. My mother held a million conspiracies against my uncle and would have no qualms about blackmailing him. I doubted the mistake was a true accident. From the limited experience with the Exchange, they probably already knew that fact before talking to Stephen.

"Why would she need a guardian?" When Ty raised his eyebrows, I blurted, "It doesn't make sense. If she was so bad at taking care of herself, wouldn't I be her guardian? I'm her daughter. And if she was in that bad of shape, a guardian wouldn't have let her live in that disgusting apartment."

"When has Dottie listened to anyone?" Ty asked softly.

"I should have been told." It came out as a pout, but I didn't care.

Ty nodded. "You're right."

His validation felt trite, but I took it all the same. "What can I do?"

"Depends on what your goal is." His ready answer meant he'd been thinking about her—about me.

My throat thickened. Blinking, I looked away, not ready to admit defeat. I wouldn't cry. Not yet.

"She'll probably be transferred to one of the Exchange's affiliated hospitals." Ty went to the window but instead of looking out, he faced me and leaned his back against the wall. His lanky frame reminded me so much of my mother. Even with his frown and the serious look in his eye, he was charming like her. "Stanford, UCLA or Bellevue in New York."

"Stanford's the closest." But she'd been there before and the doctors were already familiar with her case. This should be a good thing but her box had been ticked. She'd been labeled an addict with bipolar tendencies. They would treat the symptoms, not the cause. It wasn't their fault. Dottie might have changed her last name to Thorne but her blood was Cael and Caels clung to their secrets, holding and hiding them from everyone. Doctors would never get to the heart of her issues. She would say the right thing, appease everyone enough to be released once more. And then the cycle would continue.

"This wasn't a binge, Isla Belle." Ty folded his arms and ducked his head.

"She overdosed, Ty. That's exactly—"

"It was too deliberate."

"We don't know that." No one knew that. At least not for sure, I swallowed the thought. For Mom to be suicidal, she'd have to be depressed—depressed enough to think about death. I would have noticed something like that. I'd lived through her highs and lows. No one knew her better than me. Doubt twisted my stomach. No—*no*—I knew my mother better than anyone. "She wouldn't."

He rubbed the back of his neck. "I don't think she necessarily wanted to die."

"What are you saying?" The pause of footsteps out in the hall made me realize just how loud I spoke. "First you say she overdosed on purpose but now you're saying she didn't want to?"

"Stephen let it slip that she has a disorder—"

"She has an addiction problem. She has bipolar tendencies. She's not crazy." The lie echoed between us. My hands shook. I paced at the foot of her bed, the anger pumping in my veins. "You know what I mean."

"She has visions of grandeur," Ty said calmly—too calm. His face was awash in pity.

The anger turned to fear. My mother's visions landed her in this bed. My future appeared just as bleak. "Don't look at me like that. She's fine. It's going to be fine. We're fine."

He took a step toward me, then back again. "You're not crazy, Isla Belle. But you do need to know about your mom."

"How would you know? You didn't even know she was a ward of the Exchange." I spat out the words, knowing full well that he was trying to help. I didn't care.

He nodded, sighing once more. "She's sick, Isla. Can we at least agree on that?"

"I know she's sick, Ty." I wasn't an idiot. The woman was barely above comatose.

He held up his arms in surrender. "And there have been times, I'm not saying all the time but there have been times that she could possibly have been manipulative."

"What's your point?" It felt wrong, accusing her when she couldn't defend herself.

"She needs help. Beyond the scope of what we can do." He groaned. "Not you and I. Not anyone here. She needs Garuda."

"Garuda?" I scoffed. Ty had lost his ever loving mind. Garuda was the original Samaritan Exchange site, founded long before the Exchange came to the states. They'd established themselves on an island a couple hundred miles off the southern coast of California. "Garuda is a laboratory, not a hospital. Look at her, she needs a hospital."

Ty sucked in a breath. The sight of him, steeling himself for this conversation, made me pause. "It's a sovereign territory. The Samaritan Exchange is technically a foreign entity."

"And?"

"There is no FDA process. What's done at Garuda is five to ten, sometimes even twenty years ahead of the rest of us, of the world." He straightened and waited a beat. "If we can get your mom there, I know —I can't say how I know, but I *know* she'll have a fighting chance. Better than anything that can happen here."

His words fell over me, sparking the tiniest bit of hope. There was a possible future for my mother. For me. It helped that I knew—for a fact—that the Exchange employed Dr. Euston. "Tell me what to do."

"You're not going to like it." He tipped his forehead.

"I don't care."

"Plead her case to—"

"You said Stephen can't have—"

"Not Stephen." With a shake of his head, he stepped closer and lowered his voice. "The Exchange has a few fundraising events. They attend to gauge the political temperature. The public, even at the higher rungs of society, can be temperamental with experiments."

"Dr. Euston kind of mentioned it during my so-called interview." The pieces started to fall in line. The two separate news teams outside the Exchange at my doctor's appointment. Euston, or some other doctor, must have fallen out of favor with some influential people. Stephen might have opened the door but my position was truly needed. *I* was needed.

"It's been fun to say the least." Ty gave me a *you have no idea* look, his eyes wide and lips pursed. "It's severe enough that Denton and Staverton have left Garuda to attend the fundraising events."

"Dr. Denton?"

Ty nodded. "Thomas Denton and Rhys Staverton."

"Rhys." My cheeks warmed at the name.

"Their families founded the Exchange on Garuda forever ago." Ty arched an eyebrow before delivering the final blow. "That's who you need to talk to."

Hope fled the room, reality taking its place. "I can't talk to them."

"Can't or won't?"

Holding out my hand, I ticked three fingers. "One, how am I going to ever speak to either one of them? Two, even if I do, they're not going to care about some woman in a hospital. And three, even if I somehow perform the miracle and they say, sure bring your mom to Garuda, how would we get her there?"

"She's not some woman. She's one of their wards." He smiled a touch too bright, confirming his doubt. "And you are going to speak to them."

"Right." I rolled my eyes. "And when is that happening?"

"Tonight." He flicked his wrist, checking the time. "You're my plus one for the gala tonight."

"You're out of your mind."

He shrugged. "Runs in the family."

"It's not going to work, Ty."

He placed both hands on my shoulders. "You can pretend all you want. I know you, *Issla*. You're not giving up that easily. It might not work. But it's worth a shot."

ISLA BELLE THORNE

SACRAMENTO, CALIFORNIA: PRESENT DAY

*T*ugging on the bodice of my dress, I danced and wiggled in front of the mirror. Ty had helped pick a plum color dress for our idiotic plan—*his* plan. Not mine.

I slid my hands down the smooth, strapless bodice. Ty was right; the deep purple complimented my olive skin but it also made my blue eyes appear more striking, and not in a good way. The colors appeared more freakish—Stephen hated that word—than normal.

Even with the four inch heels, the dress skimmed the floor. I practiced walking in the shoes but still felt self-conscious. Ty and I had switched places. In college, I was his wingman but this time, he was technically mine.

"You freaking out yet?" Ty said, knocking loudly. He leaned into the door frame. He fluttered his eyelashes and pretended to wipe away fake tears. "My baby...growing up. You look—"

"I don't know..." Groaning, I headed to the bathroom.

He folded his tuxedo jacket on the chair. "You look great. Let's go."

"There aren't any straps. What if it falls?" Pointing to the corset top, I wriggled my shoulders to prove my point.

"It's too late to change, *Issla*."

"Fine." I grabbed my old, faded purse.

"You can't take that." Ty's eyes went from the purse back to the bed. "Make fun of me all you want, but that purse doesn't go with a ball gown."

He was right. There wouldn't be a need for my purse and with both Ty and Stephen at the gala, there wasn't a need for my phone. I'd already lost touch with my former roommates in the few short months since graduation.

Ty held out his hand. "And the ring."

"Why?" Suspicion crept into the word.

"Because you fiddle with that stupid thing all the time. It's a distraction."

"I do not." Instinctively, my hand hovered over the band on my necklace. "Fine."

I handed it over. He hooked it with his pinky and slipped it into the safe in the closet before jiggling the locked handle.

"Thanks, I think," I mumbled, feeling awkward and naked without it. The weight was both a comfort and a stark reminder of where my mother was.

Two streets from the art gallery, traffic slowed to a crawl, protestors filling the sidewalks. Ty shrank back into the seat, his jaw set. He shook his head, taking in the crowd. His fingers flexed against the leather seat. He didn't crack a joke or even a hint of a smile.

"There's dozens of them." A moment later, I was corrected. The dozens of men and women chanting turned to fifty, maybe even a hundred as we neared the gallery, a several storied building. It was too dark to read their signs and the driver's radio too loud to understand their chants.

Safety officers structured three perimeters, each outlining the other. By the time we reached the steps lined with granite statues and potted plants, we could barely hear the protestors. It didn't sit well, how easily we were separated from their concerns. They shouted on a chilly December night while we were beckoned with glittering chandeliers.

We walked in silence through the foyer, smiles plastered on our faces. I tripped on the last step. Ty steadied me, his arm under mine.

My breath caught as a man to my left morphed to the blond stranger of my dreams, my version of Rhys.

Ty nudged me. "What's wrong?"

The stranger disappeared, evaporating as quickly as he'd come. "Nothing. I'm fine."

"You sure?" He took one look at my eyes and hesitated.

"Okay so I'm not feeling all that great. But I will. This isn't my scene and I kind of have a lot on the line."

It wasn't the whole truth. An ache opened in my heart, as if I missed the stranger in the vision. It scared me, especially when just a few hours before I was in my mother's hospital room. No one dreamed like this, and no one, no *sane* person would pine for a fictional man. But I did. Even now, surrounded by people, I wanted his arms around me, even if it wasn't real.

Ty guided me forward. There was a pull, a flutter in my chest. I clung to his arm and wished with all my might that the stranger would reappear. The man—even if he wasn't real—made me feel safe.

Ty froze, one foot in the air. His mouth fell open, gaping. I followed his gaze to an animated woman shorter than me—a feat in and of itself. Her eyes were large and dark, her hair thick and wavy. She wasn't like the tall beauties Ty normally chased. He dropped my arm and took a step towards her, then back.

"What's her name?" I had to ask.

He didn't move. He kept his gaze on her, his body frozen in place.

"Ty?" I whispered, my hand on his arm.

He shook me off with a warning look. "No one."

"You sure about that?" Grinning, I hooked an arm through his. "You, Tyler Cael, are scared."

"Shut up." He growled and turned his back to the woman. He'd never, in the most literal way possible, *never* growled. Or froze in front of a woman.

"Is she the one that got away?"

"Quit it."

"She turned you down." Being his wingman would never be the same. "Does that even happen? Is that allowed? Can girls reject you?"

"Stop. Talking." He elbowed me and with his gaze fixed on the woman, left me.

"Isla Belle?"

I spun around to see Dr. Euston, his half smile and anxious fidgeting announced his nervousness. I shouldn't have felt smug—but I did. The last time I spoke to him was our awkward interview. "Dr. Euston, how are you?"

"Good. Good." His eyes flitted about.

Ty had abandoned me for his mystery woman. He tugged on her elbow, begging her to talk. The night was turning out to be more entertaining than I ever thought possible.

"Just brilliant." Dr. Euston whined, tugging at his collar.

"Can I help you with something?" I bit back a smile. He was clearly uncomfortable but for some reason his English accent added another level of humor.

"No." He held his breath, allowing his cheeks to puff and slowly deflate. "Not unless you can figure out a way for me to never attend these ghastly events."

"That makes two of us."

Dr. Euston pulled at his collar again. "Have you seen Denton yet?"

My stomach dropped at the name, reminding me of what I'd come to ask. Euston had said it so casually, as if everyone spoke with one of the most celebrated men of science. "Not yet, you?"

He made a face and shook his head. "Yes well. I suppose I'll speak to you later."

This was my chance. Dr. Euston was my way to Denton. "I could help you find him."

"Oh, I don't need to speak to him. I just wondered if he'd arrived yet." He smiled at someone across the room. "I'll take my usual lap around the room before I make my escape."

He took a step from me, taking my sliver of hope with him. I reached for his arm. "Have you decided what to do with me?"

He arched an eyebrow.

"The job."

The realization settled slowly on his face, making me wonder what

81

he thought I meant. He'd approached me as if we held a shared history. I assumed it was because of the interview but he'd clearly forgotten.

"Right." Dr. Euston nodded his head. "Come to the office tomorrow. The project is ready for you to tackle."

"Same office?" It wasn't a conversation with Denton, but it was still a position at the Exchange. Maybe Denton would be there. Or even Rhys.

"Yes." He smiled, a much less awkward than a moment ago. "See you then."

He disappeared in the crowd while Ty made his way back to me. His brow was furrowed. I wanted to tease him about the woman but he murmured, "Here's Denton."

I followed his line of sight and saw a somewhat familiar gray-haired man standing in a crisp tuxedo, his eyes on me. An eerie chill snaked up my neck.

"That's Denton?" I asked, knowing full well the man was the same Dr. Thomas Denton pictured in the Samaritan Exchange's conference room.

The question was swallowed by a hush falling on the crowd. A few dozen black-clad men swarmed silently into the room. Their faces calm, devoid of emotion. The sound of a good-natured argument between two men ended with the crowd erupting into cheerful claps. A circle formed around a blond man who twisted and turned the pegs on an old violin.

"And there's Staverton," Ty whispered.

Ignoring the intensity of Ty's gaze, I rubbed my arms. There he was. Rhys. The man I'd known all my life.

Rhys looked no older than Ty, although more slender and slightly shorter, just an inch or two below six feet. He looked familiar, rooting me to where I stood. His blonde hair fell playfully to his brow. He gently placed the violin in the hollow between his jaw and shoulder. He closed his eyes and slowly swayed before finding his mark, the first note of a spirited rendition of *Flight of the Bumblebee*. His arm stroked back and forth with the dexterity of a sewing needle, tossing his hair while traveling through the music. His lips, upturned with a musician's smile, widened as he switched mid song to *Cantique de Noel, O Holy Night*. His stature straightened. He danced gracefully to the melody, the violin still nestled in his arms.

He turned, facing my section of the circle. He was lithe in frame. His face was odd. Plain but striking—perfectly symmetrical.

Countless hours spent identifying species in my undergrad classes highlighted his strange features. I'd measured the differences in millimeters of thousands of organisms. I had yet to observe anything that was perfectly symmetrical, many scientists believed it impossible. Here was someone who defied that rule, he was physically perfect.

He slowed to a soft melody—one I knew. The surrounding crowd turned to each other asking their friends the name of the tune.

Midnight slumber close surround thee, all through the night. I mouthed the words. *Angels watching e'er around thee, all through the night.*

Every night, a soft tenor had sung those sweet words to me when I dreamed of being the blue-eyed woman.

O'er thy spirit gently stealing, visions of delight revealing. Breathes a pure and holy feeling. All through the night.

I heard Ty's voice but I couldn't tear my eyes away from the violinist. He continued to play, his eyes closing as if remembering a moment of both pain and pleasure.

Though I roam a minstrel lonely, all through the night. My true harp shall praise sing only, all through the night. Love's young dream, alas, is over yet my strains of love shall hover near the presence of my lover.

The gallery faded away. There was only a young man with unkempt hair and simple clothes. I'd fallen from a horse and landed on my back. I stared at the blue sky, knowing he'd come to me. His boyish grin blocked out the sky. He offered a hand and a teasing remark. Into his arms, I laughed, barely able to breathe from our joke. I covered my mouth, a feeble attempt at being dignified.

He disappeared, the vision fading with him.

I whispered, "Earthly dust from off thee shaken, soul immortal shalt thou awaken. With thy last dim journey taken home through the night."

The loss of the vision left a hole. I whimpered. An ache, the pain of happiness leaving. Heat rose from my chest, up through my neck. Shivering, chills swept down my spine.

"Are you okay?" Ty's voice shocked me, ripping me from my mind, forcing me to be here, in the present. "Isla, look at me."

"I'm fine," I lied. *Rhys*. The name rolling around in my head, twisting my thoughts and squeezing my heart.

Ty grabbed my forearm and squatted down to my eye level. "What is going on?"

"It's a migraine." The lie rolled off the tongue. I fished out the prescription bottle, my mind still on the violinist playing. "It's why I've been going to the doctors."

Sighing, he said, "We can do this another night. Let's get you home."

Tossing one last look at Rhys, my heart quickened. I knew him. And so did the woman in my dreams.

RHYS GLYNDWR

WELLESLEY COUNTY, ENGLAND: 1535

*T*he sun had just begun to set, blanketing the country with shadows. Rhys waited just off the path to the River Wye, his gelding tossing its head. He patted the horse's neck. It was growing restless like Rhys. Hours earlier, he'd stayed on the stairs and waited for Isla Belle to enter her room. Rhys needed to know with his own eyes that she was safe. He hated keeping secrets from her but with the king's suspicions, Rhys had to be careful. He'd begun hiding jewels and making plans for their impending journey. He groaned. Rhys needed more time—and Isla Belle needed more patience, a virtue she'd never possessed.

The duke and duchess had always been kind to him but their motives were clear. They knew Rhys' ancestry. Isla Belle knew nothing but had loved him all the same. He knew the signs, the flushed cheeks and unsteady breathing. Her parents had watched, thrilled with her burgeoning affection for someone of Rhys' ilk. But Rhys doubted if she'd love him when she learned the truth.

The wind picked up and the gelding shifted underneath Rhys, its ears flicking toward the castle. Isla Belle would arrive soon; Rhys had known her too long to expect anything less. The path to River Wye was the road she'd take. It would be the braver choice. The castle would search the other paths first as they led toward London instead of Wales. Unaware of the worry she caused, Isla Belle could make a giant circle around Wellesley castle, making her way undetected to King Henry's court.

The horse settled down, as did the wind. Doubt crept in. Rhys had rehearsed Isla Belle's intended plan in his head for most of the afternoon but with the sun dipping below the horizon, Rhys wondered if he knew Isla Belle as well he thought. He knew for certain her lack of obedience. She didn't know, nor would she heed, the whispers of danger.

Rhys felt a deep well of guilt for the duke's dire future. Wellesley was kept in the tower, the duchess joining him soon. The nobleman could have turned Rhys over to the king but for the hopeful future of his daughter, Wellesley never had. Rhys was a Glyndwr, his head was worth more on a spike than on his neck. He was loyal to the Wellesley family since he was a child but now there was an overwhelming responsibility to carry out their wish.

Even risking Isla Belle's ire.

The moment she'd understood her father wasn't returning, her eyes swirled to the dark, near black color of fear. She still didn't know her brother was arrested nor did she know just how bleak her parents' future really was. The blame lay at Rhys' feet. His lineage was a heavy noose around his neck. He believed a part of her knew. And so he stood back, withdrawing himself to the periphery and keeping himself an arms' length away. *For her protection,* was the half truth he told himself.

The horse danced underneath Rhys, its nerves on display. The gelding pulled at the reins, pushing back Rhys's thoughts of Isla Belle's teasing smile—memories of how her vibrant laugh could make a man's heart race. Thoughts of how he was always aware of her presence, and how he felt an undeniable urge to warn her, to protect her, no matter how reckless.

She was the daughter of a duke and in another time, she would have married like the rest of nobility and have golden haired children

—possibly have eyes that shifted in color, matching her mood. She was rash, competitive and alive with the fire inside her. And the mere thought of her, pulled a smile from his lips.

A distant howl of wolves sent a chill down Rhys' back, a foreboding omen. The wolves were the enemy to fear by the River Wye.

The soft whinny of a horse pierced the air. *Isla Belle.* Like Rhys had predicted, she'd snuck out on horseback. Rhys exhaled and shifted his weight in the saddle. The night would be long.

From his hiding spot just off the path, he watched her edge close, almost disbelieving her stubbornness. She wouldn't see him in the deep shadows of the sunset unless his gelding stepped out. Once she rounded the bend, she'd curse him with those blasted eyes.

Isla Belle's posture stiffened as she neared. The dark stallion tossed its head, sending a greeting to Rhys' plain gelding. She'd taken one of her father's two-year-olds. The young fillies and stallions were more apt to run than the older horses; the wiser animals would turn toward home at a moment's notice.

Rhys smiled as her hand went to her waist, her hidden knife. A trick he'd once taught her when an earl tried to take advantage of her innocence. The hidden weapon was supposed to keep her safe, although at the moment, Rhys wished he'd taught her the wisdom of staying indoors instead of securing a knife in her skirt. She loosened her reins, signaling an escape. Before Rhys could stop her, she spurred the stallion into a gallop.

Leaning forward, Rhys clicked to his horse and gave the gelding's haunches freedom to run. He felt the pull to Isla Belle, the odd sensation that never left him. Not since he joined the castle as a boy, twenty years before.

Rhys gave the horse its head, and together they devoured ground, closing the gap. Isla Belle turned the stallion, cutting closer to the trees lining the river bank. Branches raked her cloak. And then, before his eyes, the stallion reared and pawed the air, tossing Isla Belle to the ground. She fell—a loud snap echoed in the night air.

In a blur, Rhys was at her side, his hands searching her head for injuries. Her skin colored pale. Her eyes shifted between the deep blue of pain to the dark, almost black color of fear. Rhys tucked his reprimand in place and whistled, commanding his gelding to stay close.

"Say it." She blinked, her lips taut. "Say I was wrong. Say I never learn."

"And waste my breath?" He should hold his tongue, but his worry flared to frustration. The woman wouldn't stay out of trouble.

Mischief flicked in her eyes, squashing the last of his resolve. With care, he wrapped an arm around her waist and helped her to a tree stump. He searched her head and neck, his face inches from hers. He tried to ignore the blush creeping up her neck, curling around her cheeks. Tipping her chin, he examined her eyes, warming at the touch of her skin. Rhys paused at her torn skirt.

"Do not speak a word of this to my mother." Isla Belle bit her lip, courage in her eyes.

"Tis the brightest thing you've said of late."

"Rhys?" Isla Belle whimpered and gripped his wrist, pain lowering her guard. She was no longer the girl at his heels. She was a lady, one he was sworn to protect.

He squeezed her hand. "I'll be gentle, I promise."

She nodded, her eyes no longer shifting between fear and pain. They'd settled on pain. She rarely cried, rarely complained of her injuries.

Without thinking, he cupped her chin. Isla Belle blinked in obvious shock. He ducked his head, hot with embarrassment. Rhys lifted her ragged skirts and pulled off her slippers and stockings. Her bare ankles were dirty but whole. He touched her feet, counting the bones. He raised the hem further and exposed a swollen shin, a bruise beginning to form. With two gentle fingers, he massaged the sight of the deepest color for a possible break. He felt a divot, his heart sinking.

"Oh." She gripped his hand with an unnatural force.

"Isla Belle," he said, the apology in his throat. He was about to hurt her. Again.

"Just hurry, Rhys." She closed her eyes. This was the second injury to her leg in a matter of weeks.

He retrieved the dwale from the saddle to numb her pain, his horse obediently close. Bringing it to her lips, Rhys offered, "I'll be quick, milady."

Wincing at his *milady,* she begged, "We both know you've seen enough of me to call me by my given name."

He coughed into his fist. She gave a forced laugh and swallowed the soothing dwale, accidentally doubling a normal dose.

Rhys untied his bone-setting bag and waited for the potion to relax her. She began to smile dreamily. He mirrored her look, remembering her words on the last broken bone.

Isla Belle furrowed her brow and cocked her head to the side, almost exactly how she'd done the last time. "Did you know you look different from other men?"

"As you've said." His features were the same on either side. Many of the noble families had commented. Both the duke and duchess knew who or rather, *what* Rhys was.

He eased Isla Belle to the ground, her back against the trunk, her legs straight out in front.

"I miss your laugh," she murmured.

He tucked his head and pushed up the hem of her skirt, wrapping it around her leg to only expose what was necessary. He needed to focus on the task, not the melancholy of her voice. She wasn't the only one who missed their banter.

"You watch me. All the time." She scratched her head and looked at the ends of her hair as if seeing her curls for the first time.

"You need a lot of watching." Rhys kept his voice gruff, hoping it would give her strength. He buckled the end of the bone setter on her ankle, going a bit slower than he should. An honorable man would hurry and take her to the castle in haste. "This will hurt."

She dropped the hair and reached for him, her hand nowhere close. "You would hurt me?"

Rhys stared at the disheveled hair framing her wide-eyed face and heart-shaped mouth. Trust filled her eyes, the color now a vibrant indigo, pleasure instead of pain.

"Never," Rhys lied.

He buckled the top of the bone setter and felt her gaze. Rhys prayed she'd taken enough dwale to dull the pain. He twisted the lever of the bone-setter and kept his hand on the thigh. It tugged and pulled the ankle. He fought to keep her thigh in position. Isla Belle shivered before going limp. Rhys quickly set the bone and felt for the divot. He sighed in relief, feeling the bone aligned. He packed his tools and rubbed vinegar salts on her lip. She woke for only a moment. Rhys tried again, this time with more vinegar. She stiffened with a look of confusion, replaced with pain.

"I'll need your help, Isla Belle."

If Rhys hurried, she would be back at the castle before the rest of the potion left her body. He positioned his horse next to the stump and then guided her up, careful to keep the weight off her injured leg. With great effort, he slid her on top of the saddle, nearly falling himself as he climbed on. Rhys wrapped his arms on either side of her. She leaned back into him, her head tucked under his chin.

"How many is that?" She stared at her hand, holding up three then four fingers. Then back to three. "Three bones? No, four. No. I think three."

Rhys hoped he'd set it properly. He wasn't the physician his mentor was; the older man had never left a patient with a permanent limp.

Isla Belle pulled on Rhys' arms, molding his chest against her back. "I'm cold."

He tightened his grip, squeezing the reins. He kept his hands on the horse and counted the trees in the distance, anything to keep his mind off her warm body. Several years older, he'd watched her grow from a curious girl with golden curls to the willful woman in his arms. Rhys let his guard slip and kissed her softly on the temple.

Isla Belle looked up, confusion swirling in her eyes. "I miss you so."

Guilt pierced his chest. He held her close, saying softly, "Almost there, *fy annwyl.*"

"Beloved." She closed her eyes, appearing to focus on the words instead of her leg. Her mother had stopped speaking the Welsh phrases a few years before and commanded Rhys to do the same. He shouldn't have let it slip nor should he have meant it.

"Fy annwyl," Rhys whispered to himself and shook his head. He twisted a blonde curl around his finger. He was just a boy when Wellesley had taken him in, offering Rhys as a possible healer. This was not the way to repay the kindness.

Isla Belle murmured and leaned into his touch. "My beloved."

ISLA BELLE THORNE

SACRAMENTO, CALIFORNIA: PRESENT DAY

*L*ast night still danced in my mind. Rhys, the man from my visions, played the violin. His hair, his face—he looked exactly like my dreams. I saw him. Ty saw him. He was real —I *wasn't* crazy. *He's real.* The thought changed everything. It didn't explain how or why I dreamed of Rhys but I had hope, like my feet had finally found solid ground. I'd lived with the fear of following my mother but no, Rhys was real.

Excitement hummed under my skin as I made my way to the Exchange. Not even Ty's disappointment last night could dampen the electric buzz coursing through me. Ty hadn't said a word on the way home from the gala last night, his gaze drifting to me repeatedly. He'd sigh and then go back to tapping his knee. The words wouldn't come.

I wasn't ready to admit I'd dreamed of Rhys since I was kid, not with my mother in the hospital. *Rhys.* The name echoed in my mind filling me with a mixture of comfort, fear and wonder. Last night spun my perspective completely around. The guilt for snagging the Exchange job was gone. Although Dr. Euston couldn't have made the conversation more awkward if he tried. I'd never been more grateful that Stephen was my uncle. Dr. Euston was fairly vague at the gallery last night about what I'd be working on but there had to be a way to run into Rhys. Ty had said both he and Denton were in Garuda. Whatever scandal that pulled them from their remote headquarters had Ty running in circles as well. He was up and gone before I left.

I paused—there was a compulsion to find Rhys, to talk to him—but why? He was real but still very much a stranger. He didn't know me anymore than I knew Denton. Doubt wriggled in while hope shook its head. I was missing something.

Flicking my wrist, I checked the time. It'd be another few hours before I could take another dose of pain pills. My head throbbed but even that held a silver lining. Euston was expecting me, that gave me a reason to be in the building. I still hadn't done my blood panel and could use that excuse to wander the halls, pleading ignorance. As a new hire, it'd be understandable if I got lost. This urgency wasn't just about finding Rhys, it had to do with Mom as well. There was a link between us all—even if I didn't understand it.

The receptionist gave a quick nod as a greeting and before I could say anything she motioned to the hall, one hand holding the phone against her, the other with a pen poised to take a message. "He's ready for you in the conference room."

"Thanks," I mumbled, feeling deflated. There would be no exploration today.

Piled along the thin, oval conference table were stacks of research but no sign of Dr. Euston. I avoided looking at the pictures on the wall, I'd spent the night in a weird dream. Both Denton and Rhys were in them, although they were dressed in different clothes and lived in a different place.

Tossing my phone on the table, I reread Dr. Euston's note, *Ideas on how we can call off the dogs?* The words stared at me. My education now seemed trivial. I was completely out of my league. The stupid yellow note sat there, looking innocent. Flipping it over, I paced in front of the door. Nothing in my education had prepped me for this. The research, I assumed, had to do with the protestors last night, but I hadn't paid enough attention.

A beige folder sat between the stacks, a brown smear on the top. I picked it up, the subtle, familiar smell of livestock dung. Smiling, a wave of memories came, the late night reads and hours spent in research. Once upon a time, my days were filled with papers like these. I had to be crazy. Dung doesn't comfort normal people.

I opened the folder and read a scribbled sticky note, *control group gone. Seventeen animals dead.*

This couldn't be right. Dr. Euston didn't study animals. I'd read every one of his publications. Animals were never mentioned, even when comparing human tendencies.

The note was taped to the objective sheet listing the assigned doctors and assistants. Their objective was two-fold. First, identify the longevity gene in a biologically immortal animal, most likely a bacteria. Second, implant the longevity gene into a host animal.

"What do we have here?" Ty asked.

I jumped at his voice. The movement sent my head spinning. The headache had kept me slightly dizzy. "What are you doing?"

"Um, I kind of work here."

"Do you know when Dr. Euston will be in?"

He arched an eyebrow at my reaction, the papers clutched to my chest. "First day and you're already freaking out?"

"I don't know what I'm doing, Ty." I sat down, the papers in my lap.

"How are you feeling?"

"Better." It wasn't a complete lie. "What are you doing—here, I mean. I figured they'd have you busy with the big-wigs."

"I'm up here at the beck and call of the Samaritan Exchange." He loosened his tie and sat opposite me. "And right now, it's dealing with a slew of angry people. What do they have you working on?"

"Not totally sure." I held out the paper for him. He rubbed his forehead with the palm of his hand before shaking his head. I gave up and put it back in my lap. "It's only eight. How in the world are you this tired at eight in the morning?"

"Long day." He held out his hand. "Yes, it can be a long day this early."

He grabbed the paper again, this time leaning back, one foot perched on the chair across the table. "Lovely. Another winner."

"Seventeen animals makes a winner?"

"That's not what I meant." He scowled. It wasn't a natural look for someone stubbornly optimistic. "The science is getting heavier. I'm supposed to understand it *and* defend it."

"There's a lawsuit?"

"Defend is the wrong word." He rubbed his eyes and sighed. "I have a dozen different cases. All like this. I'm in over my head. Way over."

"You're Ty Cael, I don't think you—"

He waved off my comment. "Explain it to me. Pretend I'm five."

"You have a dozen cases and you're asking me to explain this one to you?"

"This one will be added as soon as you determine what went wrong." Ty yanked on his collar again. "Or what could be construed as *wrong.*"

"Or right," I offered. It couldn't all be bad news. "Maybe we did something right."

"If something died, we're in the wrong. Doesn't matter who, why or how. We're in the wrong." He went to the window and leaned his forearm into the glass, his thumb scratching his forehead. "Ask me about a court ruling, got it. Possibilities of a suit, done and done. But this? There's so much gray area."

"Ty, everything with law is gray."

"Apparently science, too."

Especially medical science. Just yesterday we stood in my mother's hospital room. Her mental illness, an ever changing diagnosis, wasn't black or white. Neither was the treatment. "I'll explain but you're ordering lunch."

He chuckled and slowly turned around. "It'll take that long?"

I shrugged. "Depends. How much do you want to learn?"

"I'll take what I can get." He held up his hands in surrender. "I'm sure this will be on my desk by Friday anyway, whether or not you've worked everything out."

"Fantastic." I kicked out the chair next to me, holding the lip of the seat with my toe. "Sit, pretty boy. Sit and learn."

"Don't mind if I do." Ty's dimples all but winked at me, reminding me of Mom. He sat down and let the chair whirl him around before scooting forward to the table. "Ready...go."

"This is just the objective page."

"I'm not an idiot." He tapped on the words *biologically immortal*. "What does that mean?"

He had to be joking. It meant exactly what it said, biologically immortal. If he didn't understand the most basic concepts—

"Stop it." Ty tapped the paper again. "What does it mean to you or what could it mean to a protestor. Not what it means period. I'm not an idiot despite what your face just told me."

"Right." I tucked my head, wondering if it was the color of my eyes that gave me away or if I'd really given him a look. "Biologically immortal is really just that. An organism that can't die on its own."

He raised his eyes. I'd omitted the very thing he'd asked, what it meant to me. The quick answer was I didn't for sure know. When I was doing my undergrad, I'd been too in awe of the idea as a whole. I'd never determined how I felt about it. Biologically immortal was a spectrum, a way to categorize the phenomenon of something living an absurdly long life; not a philosophy.

"Biologically immortal organisms don't age. An outside force has to kill them. Like a predator or trauma." There were pages and pages of information on what organisms they used and why, but none of those would help figure out why it could be controversial. "I remember reading somewhere about using a jellyfish but it changed the sexual reproduction of the animals."

"Slow down, go back, before the sexy jellyfish." He smirked. "This time add in what you think. Because that's what we're going to get crucified for. Opinion is all that matters. Facts only help me if I can make them look pretty."

"Biological immortality or bio-indefinite—"

"You suck at this."

"Fine. *You* tell me what you think."

"I think it's a complete waste of money. And resources." He scoffed but his eyes belied his true interest. "There's a million other vaccines or diseases that could use the Exchange's attention."

"Pretend you're biologically immortal."

Ty's face lit with excitement. He had enough fun for one lifetime. He didn't need any more time than already allotted.

I rolled my eyes. "But I'm ordinary. We are born the same year and with the same health but my hips start hurting at age forty. Then more aches and finally I die of normal, old age. You on the other hand, don't have any aches and pains because your body is regenerating all the cells in your body. There isn't arthritis or illness because your body is its own hospital."

"Got it." He gave a firm nod.

I could almost hear the wheels turning. If our bodies could cure themselves, there'd be no need for vaccines. "But you could still die."

Ty frowned, his eyes dimming. "Keep going."

"You could get hit by a car. Trauma would still kill you. Unless you're truly immortal not biologically immortal. There's a difference."

"Which is?" He pulled the paper from under my hand.

"If you're biologically immortal you do eventually age but not for a couple hundred years. Maybe even a thousand. But if you're immortal, then nothing can kill you. Not even a car."

"Ohhhhh...." He sat back, his eyes wide.

"And true immortality isn't real. Unless you're Hollywood. Biologically immortal however is very real." I underlined the second objective listed on the note. "They wanted to identify the longevity or biologically immortal genes—more important, the exact gene. And it looks like they also wanted to transplant the gene to a large animal."

"Why waste it on an animal? I'll volunteer."

"Did you not read that seventeen animals died?"

Ty stood again, stretching his arms. How he studied for law school was beyond me. The man wouldn't sit still for anything. "Minor detail."

"Yeah, remember, dead anything doesn't look good."

"Immortal means you can't die, period." He pulled out his phone

97

and started typing. "But biologically immortal means you're disease free, right?"

"Yes."

He paused, arching an eyebrow. "This is the part where you tell me your opinion."

"As in, do I believe in it?"

"Is it worth looking into? Or in this case, defending."

I took a deep breath. If we could figure out the fear, the reason protestors hated the project, then we'd have a clearer understanding on how to proceed. "I should say yes. I mean, there's already a cross over. Humans can have late-life mortality plateau—"

"Please tell me you're going to explain that."

"Something that *can* die but only at a much, much older than average age. For people, they're called centenarians."

"People?" He hadn't looked back at his phone, his thumb still poised to keep typing. "So, this does impact people. Not just animals."

"Yes, but organisms that are called biologically immortal live longer than what a centenarian would." There wasn't a computer in the conference room so my phone would have to do. Pulling it out, I searched *centenarians*. "The people live to just over a hundred."

"Sucks for them." He leaned over my shoulder. "Stephen complains about being old every minute of every day."

"Not these people. They *live*. They live like they're thirty with only the beginning of the aches and pains. They age slower. Their knees start giving out after the century mark, not before." Handing him the phone, I said, "But that's not what the study was about, specifically."

"It would stop protestors. Eternal youth, I mean come on. That'll stop critics in their tracks." Ty set the phone down, his brow furrowed. "Unless we started experimenting on the centenarians. That wouldn't help us. Good thing they stuck to alpacas."

"Since when is testing on animals ever acceptable? It's always frowned upon. It doesn't stop experiments, but it does make the scientists more careful. Besides, it's still a hard sell. No one wakes up and says, I can't wait till my hundredth birthday." Mom didn't want to be old. She wanted to sing and dance forever, not stare at a hospital wall.

"Are the centenarians technically immortal. I mean biologically immortal?"

Shrugging, I answered, "It depends on the scientist."

"I'm asking you."

"No. I believe the term should only be used for cells or organism that aren't subject to the Hayflick limit." Not waiting for him to ask, I explained, "The Hayflick limit is the maximum amount of times a cell can regenerate. If there's no limit, the cells keep dividing."

"So they *are* immortal."

"No. They still can die. One bullet to the heart or head. Acute trauma would still kill them. But anything that has to do with getting old or disease, the organism fights. The cells keep dividing—healing. They stay forever young. And I mean forever. Kind of like cancer."

Ty's hand covered mine, forming a lump in my throat. His mother had died from cancer years ago, long before I could remember. "Are you telling me that cancer is considered biologically immortal?"

"Just one of many organisms."

He shook his head. "Why would the Exchange allot time and resources to this?"

"Cancer isn't always a bad thing." Setting my other hand on top of Ty's, I realized just how much he needed my mom to get better. These facts were just snippets from my undergraduate degree, but just like the protestors outside the gallery, the science meant so much more. "Hear me out. Death is inevitable. But what if we could delay it? I mean delay all of it. Every sickness. Every disease. Every ache. All of it. Delay it until the very end and when cancer or whatever illness comes along takes us quickly. But at a hundred years old or who knows, two hundred years old."

Ty swallowed hard. "Cancer is never a good thing."

"You and I. Every normal person, we age. And as we age our little cycle gets shorter. We get sick longer. Easier."

"I heard you the first time, Isla."

"I'm sure the protestors did as well."

The realization came over him. First in the eyes and then in the shoulders. "You think they're trying to cure cancer in this study?"

"Maybe." I squeezed his hand before letting go.

Ty studied my face, reading the color of my eyes. "But it looks like we're just creating another cancer. That's bio terrorism."

"Or maybe they're still just trying to understand the concept. I'm just regurgitating my science degree, not this file."

"I wish they would." His light smile was tainted in grief. "Cure cancer, I mean."

"You're not the first to wish for immortality. Even if it's for someone else."

"Maybe it *is* for me. The world could use an unlimited amount of Ty Cael." His confidence, his easy charisma was so much like Mom. This was Ty at his core, a perpetual ray of sunshine.

"There's a limit, Ty." I hated to do it, but he needed to know everything. Hope wasn't always helpful. "Biological immortality is actually a natural phenomenon. Unless this project shows different, I don't think you can control it. I don't think it's genetic. Every culture from the beginning of time had some sort of myth to explain it. Religions, too. Even today's Bible."

"If Dr. Euston was involved, it's somehow genetic." He turned his attention back to the papers. "He calls it—"

"Genetic healing." I tapped the words *seventeen animals dead*, finally understanding how the project was related to the Samaritan Exchange. "They just accidentally missed the healing part."

He ran his fingers through his hair. "PETA is going to hang us."

"Not if we can prove it was in the animal's favor." I waved away his doubtful look. "Seriously. Euston's thing is destroying all diseases. What if this project was trying to extend the life of the animal? Not end it."

He pointed at me, his smile growing. "And that, ladies and gentlemen, is why I keep you around."

There was pride in words but my stomach did a little flip. I'd spent the morning working on a project in hopes of seeing Rhys. Or Denton. I hadn't checked in at the hospital. My childhood consisted of both Rhys and my mother—my loyalty should lie with her, not the man who was a virtual stranger.

"Is it—if I can defend the project well enough—is it enough of a reason to talk to Denton?" It came out wrong, but I knew from Ty's softened face he knew what I meant.

"It'll get his attention for sure." He nodded to the window, the same direction as my mother's hospital. "Either way, we're not giving up."

ISLA BELLE THORNE

SACRAMENTO, CALIFORNIA: PRESENT DAY

*B*y midmorning Ty was cranky and my brain was fried. Shoving the files aside, I stood, wishing I could change the scenery of the stifling conference room. Dr. Euston had solidified—in his awkward conversation—that I was indeed hired but I'd only been shown the conference room and his little note asking me how to *call off the dogs.* Pacing in front of the window, I tried to find the roof of my mother's hospital. I felt stretched and torn, wanting to get my mother help and wanting to figure out who Rhys was—and now, trying to figure out the mystery of the Exchange's latest experiment gone wrong.

My head ached but now my body felt off as well. There was a heavy feeling in my joints but all of this—according to the few websites I looked up could be attributed to stress. That didn't exactly fit. Not knowing if my mother was coming home or if there was food in the fridge as a young kid, *that* was stressful. Not this. I stopped pacing and placed a hand on the glass. Holding my breath, I fought the guilt and felt the overwhelming relief—my mother being in a hospital, even not knowing her fate, was hard but at least I knew where she was. Her days were predictable.

A thought made it's way in as my finger traced the skyline. Risking a glance over my shoulder, I said to Ty, "When we ran experiments in college, part of the process was figuring out where the hypothesis either failed or succeeded."

"And?" Ty didn't look up from his phone.

"Why isn't Euston here?" Turning around, I leaned my back against the cool glass. "Or a supervisor?"

"It wasn't his experiment."

"I get that, sort of." Professors weren't exactly neck-deep in the student's experiments either but they had to at least keep a pulse on the activity. It was a common stipulation when the university gave approval. "He had to know something about it."

Ty shrugged. "I wouldn't count on it."

"Why not?"

He hesitated, his gaze flicking to the headshots on the wall. "A lot of things are on a *need to know* basis."

"You can't operate a successful experiment with limited information." My skin prickled like it had last night at the fundraising gala. I'd fought the temptation to look at the board's head shots but finally gave in. Stephen and Denton's pictures were clearly decades old but Rhys—or Staverton if you were Ty—only his suit was dated, not his face. My head began pounding and my pulse started to race but a warmth wrapped around my shoulders as I stared. He was a stranger and yet even his picture provided me comfort.

"You'd be surprised at what they accomplish. With or without limited information." Ty's voice pierced the calm, pulling me back to the conference table.

In a rush, I felt torn, as if three masters had come calling, each pulling an appendage. My mother was on one arm, Rhys on another and the Exchange's experiment was wrapping around a leg. The blame was my own doing. No one was forcing me to care about my mother or find Rhys. The Exchange job was given to me but it was still my choice to walk through the door.

Ty rubbed his eyes, pulling my focus back to him. Maybe I had more Cael in me than I'd thought. Stephen didn't have to take care of us. No one forced him to. If anything I'd lashed out, especially during my temperamental teenage years. And yet, he'd never stop. Just like I knew I wouldn't.

A phone rang, piercing the quiet. Ty stood in a snap, answering, "I'm downstairs. I'll be there in a minute." He gave me a nod and disappeared.

The file was scattered in separate piles on the table. It should have pulled me toward it, the information begging to be understood but the temptation to snoop around the building rose with each passing second. Last night I'd been overwhelmed like a silly schoolgirl when Rhys had started playing the violin. I didn't even try to speak to Denton. Or Rhys.

In reality, Denton was the closest thing the medical community had to a god. Speaking with him, let alone begging for a favor sounded crazier than my visions. The idea had more merit when Ty was around. He had a tendency to infuse confidence in even the most bizarre moments.

Another glance at Rhys' head shot made the decision. Maybe crazy was as part of me as Ty and Stephen.

Waiting a moment, I walked down the hall but every door was shut. In every corner glowed the red light of a security camera, sweeping my desire to pick the locks under the rug. I froze—I'd not planned on picking any locks. That would be a fool's errand. I knew better than that. And yet my hand gravitated toward the doorknob. Stephen had already admitted to the all-knowing aspect of the Exchange. Snatching my hand back, I folded my arms, my fingers gripping my sleeves.

Door after door, I read the names. No Euston, Denton or Rhys. Or Staverton. The name didn't sound right. He was Rhys. He'd always been Rhys to me. Retracing my steps back toward the conference room, I heard the muffled voice of the receptionist. I debated on asking her for their schedules or contact information but I couldn't come up with a plausible excuse. I wasn't *that* crazy.

Back in the conference room, I rearranged the files of each alpaca by age. There was an element of pride in figuring out the puzzle but it wasn't because I was trying to be a good employee. Hopefully it would merit a reason to talk to Denton. Or Rhys.

My phone beeped, signaling an email. The Exchange's lab a few floors below me had sent me a barcode for access to the lab and the order for a fasting blood panel. At the bottom, they'd explained what *fasting* meant. My stomach growled. It knew exactly what fasting meant. Ty and I never ordered lunch. It was two in the afternoon, almost six hours since I'd last eaten. If I waited to the eight hour mark, I could run downstairs and do the panel before I took off. My head pounded but I couldn't take another pill without eating.

Two hours. I could handle two hours. Ignoring my stomach, I dived back in and before I knew it, the receptionist was clearing her throat behind me. "I'm off, Miss Thorne."

She waited with keys in hand while I packed the files. Eyeing the security camera in the corner, a chill crept up my neck. Stephen joked with me about the security of the Exchange when he'd accompanied me to the clinic. Without him here, it was infinitely more creepy. With the box in my arms, I followed the receptionist to the elevator.

"Lobby or garage?" She asked, her finger poised.

Settling the box between my feet, I shuffled through the emails for the barcode. "I'm headed to the clinic before I leave."

Her eyes widened a fraction but she said nothing. Pursing her lips, she scanned the barcode from the email for me. Tension filled the silence between us. My appointment bothered her for some reason. I'd thought it would be normal, an employee going to the health clinic in the same building. The flitting of her eyes and the fidgeting of her shoes told me otherwise. The elevator dinged, signaling my floor. She gave me a wide berth as I shuffled past her, files in hand.

An older gentleman with salt and pepper hair greeted me, his lab coat worn. The badge on his lanyard matched him, making me wonder if he was a new hire. My uncle's badge hadn't been updated in decades.

He guided me into a laboratory station, a small television attached to the opposite wall and a cushioned seat on the other. He pushed a stool toward the chair, offering, "You can set your papers there if you'd like."

"How long will I be here?" The medical assistant had drawn my blood before in the office. This lab appeared to be more for comfort than efficiency.

The man squinted at his tablet. "You're just here for a few panels so not long."

"Why the tv?" I still hadn't sat and was now debating the merits of coming.

He glanced up at the television on the wall. "Oh, those are for the longer tests and infusions." He patted his pockets and the counter behind him. "We won't be monitoring you. We're just taking things, not injecting." He grinned. Finding his glasses, he slipped them on.

My confidence fell to the floor. The Samaritan Exchange was the pinnacle of modern medicine and I was going to get my blood drawn by a half-blind, ancient phlebotomist. This couldn't be good.

"Are you feeling alright, dear?" His voice was gentle.

I nodded.

He hesitated and scanned my face. "When's the last time you ate or drank anything besides water?"

"Seven this morning."

Grinning, he said, "Feeling a bit weak in the knees?"

"A bit."

"Would you mind sitting?" There was humor in his voice. "I promise I won't bite."

Gently, I placed the files on the stool and backed into the chair, my heart racing. He soaked a cotton ball with disinfectant—the smell piercing my nose.

I hate hospitals. Clenching my left hand, I counted to three.

"You're not the only one." The phlebotomist winked, wiping the crook of my right elbow.

"Sorry." I winced. "I didn't think I said that out loud."

"If it makes you feel any better, we're not a hospital. Just a lab." He tied a rubber band just above my inner elbow. He placed the needle in against the skin. "It'll be just a pinch."

The walls blurred. His hair faded to a blonde. A rush of warmth came over me. His wrinkles fell away. He tossed a mischievous grin, love in his eyes.

"That wasn't so bad, now was it?" In a snap, the image was ripped away. The gray haired man, eyes full of joy and age, stared at me.

Blinking, I struggled to breathe.

The man cocked his head to the side. "You're a squeamish one. Let me get you some juice before you stand up. You must be sensitive to blood sugar."

With shaking hands, I accepted the small white cup of juice and struggled to thank him. He waved me off and sent me on my way. Leaving the elevator, I caught the image of the blond in my periphery. I turned slowly, the files from the alpaca experiment in my hand. Far in the corner of the lobby, Rhys stood, his dark tailored suit outlining the same man I'd known all my life. He was shaking his head to someone else in a suit, his profile to me. In slow motion, he turned his gaze, our eyes connecting. My heart pounded. I clutched the files, scared I would drop them. His brow furrowed—in anger. I felt the wrath from across the room, shivering from the intensity. He wasn't the man from visions. This was a stranger.

With a heavy heart, I pulled my attention from him and walked to my truck, my hands trembling.

LADY ISLA BELLE WELLESLEY

WELLESLEY COUNTY, ENGLAND: 1535

*L*ady Isla Belle leaned against the window, the morning sun sharing its obnoxious, cheerful rays. There was little light in her room; she hid in plain sight. She shifted her weight on the walking stick and kept her vigil. Last night, long after the castle had gone to bed, Rhys had left, his medical bag attached to the saddle. He had turned, casting a long look at her window, before disappearing from the courtyard.

It was a turn in their usual dance, Isla Belle observing him instead of being watched. Isla Belle was continually aware of his presence, but lately, his gaze, his entire being was more intense. She touched her temple, remembering his lips on her skin. He had kissed her—and she'd thought of little else.

And then, Rhys appeared atop his gelding. He dismounted and led his horse to the stables, his shoulders rounded in exhaustion. He paused—before she could hide—he glanced up to her window. His eyes narrowed; he saw her. He gave a slight nod and continued on his way.

Isla Belle turned, her heart beating wickedly in her chest. With her back against the cool, stone wall, she gripped her walking stick and breathed slowly, her face flushing. She had spoken with titled men, their pockets full of coin and mouths full of boasting, and yet here she stood, cowering.

She gritted her teeth and made her way to the door. Painful—and slow—she inched her way down the stairs, her leg throbbing. Her last step, Isla Belle pivoted and made the mistake of glancing up. She would have to climb each and every step if Rhys ordered her back to bed. He hadn't looked at her when he replaced the larger splint for the smaller, thinner one yesterday. He'd not said a word to her, only gently, silently helped her heal.

With a curt nod, a groomsman opened the outer door for Isla Belle, his disapproval of her being up and about in his taut smile.

"Thank you." Isla Belle's voice trembled, sounding weak instead of commanding. Throwing her shoulders back, she lifted her chin and half-limped, half-walked into the morning air.

Rhys' gelding pawed at the ground, his saddle not removed. Isla Belle's heart sank. Rhys was likely refilling supplies and would be off again. It had been weeks since her mother had left and Isla Belle had injured her leg. Her foolish attempt at running away had given her more than an injured leg. It had stopped her mother's plans to have Isla Belle kidnapped but had propelled her mother's arrival at court. Her brother hadn't yet arrived—and from the blank stares she'd received in return, he never would. She was kept in the dark about her brother, her father and now her mother. She worried about their safety but only to herself, having no one to speak with. Rhys was even more absent than before. She almost craved his surliness to her loneliness.

Isla Belle touched her temple again and closed her eyes, remembering what she shouldn't want—or rather *who*.

"Tell me you were carried down the stairs." Rhys didn't hide his irritation.

Isla Belle opened her eyes with a start. She swallowed a curse. She'd been caught up in the memory and not felt his presence. He folded his arms, lithe and lean. The dark cloak he'd worn last night for another errand was tied just under the saddle. Rhys was leaving and wouldn't be back again tonight.

"I'll take that as a no." His clear, blue eyes didn't soften despite the tender voice.

Isla Belle felt a twinge of envy, his ability to be both gentle and powerful. "I was getting fresh air. That is all..." *your highness.* She almost added.

"What is it?" He nodded toward her window. "What brought you from your bed, down the stairs and out here?"

"It must have been your kindness," she snapped, immediately regretting her tone.

"I'd have come to you, *fy annwyl.*" Rhys' words were like ice and fire on her skin, both competing for the sensation.

Isla Belle groaned in frustration, turning toward the house. She blinked back tears, not knowing what she felt or what she heard. His arm slipped around her waist, lifting her off her injured leg. Rhys placed her arm around his shoulder and carried her walking stick with his free hand.

"No, Rhys." She pulled away. "Leave me be."

The harshness in his features dissolved. He exhaled, his warm breath on her neck. She fought the urge to lean toward him, to breathe in his scent.

"Can I help you, please?" There was an urgency in his plea.

Not trusting her voice, she shook her head. Isla Belle shifted, her leg beginning to throb again.

"What can I do—what can I say?" His arm tightened around her waist before releasing her. He softly whispered, "Isla Belle."

The way he said her name sent a warm shiver along her skin. She met his gaze, the lost tenderness reappeared. Rhys stepped closer, his hand raised to touch her face. She had but to lean in and their faces would touch.

The pounding of hooves stole Rhys' attention. His eyes narrowed, and he leapt back. A tired rider on an exhausted horse galloped into the courtyard, his eyes on Rhys. They exchanged a solemn nod.

She held her breath and prayed it was news of her brother. Or parents.

"They'll be here by week's end. Maybe less." The rider slid from his horse and stuffed parchment and linens into Rhys' bag. Rhys nodded, his hand rubbing his forehead. Not a moment later, the haggard rider galloped back toward the fields.

"Tell me, Rhys." Isla Belle stood tall, ignoring the pain and asked once more, "I need to know."

The debate played out on his face, his perfect, mirrored face. His eyes flitted about nervously as if searching for traitors.

"I can't, Isla Belle."

"Then I will find someone who will."

"You will not." Rhys growled, his face washed in dark fury once more.

"I will." Isla Belle didn't flinch. His guard was down too long, exposing the friend she missed. He marched to his horse and pulled the reins loose. Isla Belle kept her breathing steady, hoping her eyes wouldn't betray her now.

He brought the horse to Isla Belle's side. "We will regret this day."

"I have regretted many days."

Rhys' brow furrowed, his jaw hard and body rigid. "I made a promise."

"To my mother." It wasn't a question. Isla Belle knew where his loyalty lay, not to her, only the duchess. The admission stung all the same.

They stared at each other, both willful. Tension came alive, filling the space once taken by laughter and teasing. Isla Belle's heart pounded, her head full of frustration.

On the verge of bursting, she said, "My mother is gone. I haven't heard from my brother, and we both know my father will never return. Their promises will leave with them. Give me something to hold on to."

She spun on her uninjured leg, dreading the walk up the stairs.

"You," Rhys called after her. "I promised you."

Isla Belle sighed, wishing the battle inside her would stop. He was kind but cruel—she hung her head and took another step. She heard him mount the horse behind her. Rhys circled around to her front. He grasped the horse's reins with one hand, then held out his other hand to her. Isla Belle looked at it, hesitating.

"Isla Belle, I did make promises to your mother. And father. But nothing matters more than the promise I made to you at the age of ten. Come with me so I may be free of it."

She kept her gaze low so he couldn't read her mood or thoughts. Isla Belle searched her memories, wishing she could remember what promise she had forced. And then it came, his bitterness, the resentment. She had imprisoned him. He, being the same, kind man who tenderly healed her, wanted to leave. She had chained him to Wellesley. Isla Belle had made him cold. "You are free, Rhys."

"*Fy annwyl,* I am anything but." He swung a leg over and dismounted in front of her.

Isla Belle searched his softening face.

"You were ten when the earl—"

"Edmund." In an instant, Isla Belle was just a girl running through the grass, tears streaming down her cheeks. Edmund's father had died, leaving him with a title and no discipline. He was older, closer to Rhys in age. Edmund had followed Isla Belle to the rose garden and cornered her, demanding a kiss—and more. She had shrieked and twisted free, running straight to the river and waiting, knowing Rhys would come. He did, he always found her.

"You were huddled against the crossed trees." Rhys' voice dropped low. "I promised you, a frightened girl—"

"I wasn't scared. I was angry."

Rhys gave a rare smile, his eyes crinkling. "I promised you—"

"I would not be married to a cruel man." Isla Belle tucked a loose curl behind her ear. "You can't promise what you can't control."

"Come with me." He held out his hand. "And I will keep that promise."

Without thinking, she dropped the walking stick to the cobbled stone and placed her hand on his. She didn't know where or what lay ahead, only that her fate—and hand—was with Rhys.

He motioned for a groomsmen to stand with her and the horse, disappearing into the castle and returning with a few bags. Isla Belle eyed the packages, wondering if they contained food or documents. Rhys mounted the gelding and boosted Isla Belle up, settling her in front of him in the saddle. He reached around her to take up the reins, holding Isla Belle against his body. Rhys clicked his tongue to the horse and they were off.

Isla Belle turned and with a pang of farewell, took one last glance at her childhood home. Rhys' arms were around her but she tried not to lean against him. The less contact they had, the better. Her pulse raced, and her breath was short. She had not been this physically close to a man, only Rhys. During the annual festivals, she had danced with several young men but her body had never responded like this.

She could not allow herself to think too deeply about Rhys—the way his breath stirred her hair, the way his chest radiated heat against her back, or the way his muscled arms jostled against her as the horse picked its way through the fallen branches along the banks of the River Wye.

Hours passed without stopping, not to eat, not to rest. And not for an aching leg.

The setting sun took refuge behind the trees. Isla Belle's stomach twisted with hunger and for the first time in her life, she wondered when it would be filled. A wolf's howl split the air. Isla Belle shuddered, and Rhys tensed. She had never heard them cry, at least not outside the safety of her home. Another howled—this one much closer.

Isla Belle instinctively grabbed for the reins, wanting to put more distance between her and the predators. Rhys clicked his tongue and flicked the reins. The gelding lurched forward, and Isla Belle to the side. Rhys threw the reins into one hand, his other wrapped fully around Isla Belle, securing her flat against him. Through a narrow slit between the trees, Isla Belle caught a glimpse of a cottage.

"Almost, *fy annwyl.*"

Isla Belle felt, more than heard, his low voice. Her father once regulated the county's hunting, striking a balance of prey and predator. Without his steady hand, the villagers would have left little for the wolves to eat.

Another howl pierced the night, closer still. Rhys' arm tightened further, urging the gelding into a faster gallop. The cottage came into better view as the ground became more uneven. Isla Belle grasped Rhys' thighs to stay seated as they plunged on, the cooling river air streaming through her hair.

The howls multiplied, Isla Belle kept her gaze forward, willing the horse faster still. Feeling every strike of the gelding's hooves, Rhys guided them to an ivy covered gate surrounding the dwelling. He pulled back on the reins—sending Isla Belle forward—Rhys kept his grip strong, arm taut. With a kick of his boot, he unlatched the gate and with practiced ease, the horse spun them inside.

Rhys slid off the gelding, tugging Isla Belle with him. He snapped the gate closed just as another howl reached her ears.

ISLA BELLE THORNE

SACRAMENTO, CALIFORNIA: PRESENT DAY

*T*he sound of a wolf howling woke me with a start, the morning sun piercing my tired eyes. Covering my head with a pillow, I groaned and then sat up. The howling was an ambulance, not a wolf. I'd never owned a dog, but I could picture with uncanny clarity the unmistakeable pitch of a wolf's howl. The strength and power of the howl was more intense than a dog's. Instinctively, I reached for the ring on my necklace. It'd become a comfort when the world felt wobbly.

I stood and stretched, the bandage from yesterday's blood draw catching on the side of my shirt. Rolling up my sleeve, I picked at the adhesive, eventually ripping it off. The exposed skin had purpled horribly. When my blood was drawn last week with the assistant, my skin closed up so quickly after he'd taken the needle out, he hadn't used a cotton swab or bandage. This time around appeared to be the exact opposite. I ran a finger across the insertion point and felt moisture. Sure enough, a dab of blood was on the tip of my finger.

The murmur of voices interrupted my exploration. Ty was up and apparently had company. I showered and dressed without looking in the mirror. I didn't need confirmation that I looked as bad as I felt.

After visiting my mother in the hospital on my way home, I'd spent the night trying to work every angle proving the Exchange's motive for the experiment as altruistic. When the numbers began blurring and my head throbbed, I gave up and battled dreams of Rhys and his blue-eyed woman.

Stumbling in the shared living area, I interrupted Stephen and Ty, the former frowning while Ty laughed—their immediate silence made me cringe.

Stephen was on his feet and at my side in an instant. "You look terrible."

"Thanks," I mumbled. "I have a headache."

"This is more than a mere headache, Isla." The concern in Stephen's voice made my heart constrict. He'd taken me as one of his own when he didn't have to. He slid two fingers to my wrist, his gaze on my face—on my eye color. Guiding me to the sofa, he shed the uncle persona to the doctor he once was. "Does your head throb or is it a dull ache? Have you been feeling feverish? When did you last eat? Have you—?"

"I'm just tired, Stephen." It was the truth. I was exhausted. There hadn't been more than an hour or two of uninterrupted sleep in weeks. I'd taken the semi-honest approach and told my doctor about the insomnia. The dreams were more intense—and that was one tidbit of information I refused to divulge.

Stephen and Ty exchanged a look, ending when Ty gave a slight shake of the head.

"I'm fine. I've been a good girl and have done everything my doctor has asked of me." Shaking my finger, I said, "Whatever you two just said to each other, don't."

Ty clutched his chest and huffed, pretending to be offended. Fear snuck in. Ty became dramatic when things turned dire.

"Something's wrong, Isla," Stephen whispered next to me.

There was only so much I was willing to admit. Rhys was a real person but at the moment, I felt no relief in that fact. His glare from across the lobby had sent me reeling. That was another fact that made me question my state of mind.

My visions would have to wait. At least, until I could get Mom to

Garuda. If they could help curb or even cure her illness, then I could pursue my visions. A rush of guilt came over me. Mom wasn't a to-do list to check off. A dedicated daughter would worry more about her mother, not about herself. "I can't sleep. That's all."

Ty rolled his eyes and threw himself on the armchair across from me. "Liar, liar."

I felt Stephen's gaze and quietly confessed, "I have...nightmares."

Stephen's eyes grew wide and silence filled the room, tension growing second by second. His reaction gave me a chill. He'd grown up with my mother's mind playing tricks on her. Nightmares were something we both feared.

Ty watched his father, the playful cousin gone. "It's just nightmares, Dad, nothing serious."

Dad. Ty never called him Dad. Or Father. He'd called him Stephen since he was a toddler, despite Stephen being the only father Ty had ever known. It was both odd and charming, like their quirky relationship.

Stephen covered my hand on the couch. "How long?"

I felt my face heat. "They're just bad dreams."

He stared at me, his face blank. After a moment, he shook his head. "I want you to start logging your sleep."

"I'm—"

"Not fine," Stephen barked. I winced. He cleared his throat, his face washed in shame. "If you can't sleep, your brain can't function. I will not lose you. Not on my watch."

I will not lose you. His words squeezed the breath from my lungs. His hand was still on mine, but I was alone. I could never tell him about the visions. It would break him.

Nodding my head, I said, "Okay."

"You should stay home tonight," Ty offered gently. Turning to his father, he asked, "She was hoping to talk to Denton about Dottie."

Stephen stiffened. "About what?"

"Getting her to Garuda." Ty gave me a sheepish look. If that was an apology, he was failing.

"What?" Shaking his head, Stephen stood and paced in the small strip of area between Ty's armchair and where I sat on the sofa. "You have no idea what you're asking."

"She needs help." I gripped the edge of the couch. "Nothing works. We've been down this road how many times?"

Stephen paused but said nothing.

"What can Stanford's hospital do this time that they haven't done before?" Waving my arm at Ty, I added, "What if Garuda could help? What if some experimental treatment could reach her?" My voice caught. Experimental treatment. That's what I'd just spent the night reading about. Garuda might save my mother. Or kill her.

Both Stephen and Ty looked at me. Then looked at each other.

Finally, Stephen sat down. "Garuda is not what you think."

Ty arched an eyebrow, his shock apparent. "It's a medical sanctuary."

Nodding slowly, Stephen smiled sadly. "In a way, yes. But people aren't magically cured. They don't come sick and walk out whole."

"She hasn't spoken. Not once. Any improvement would be a win at this point." Squeezing the edge of the couch, I shrugged. My mother needed a miracle, no matter how desperate. "I don't know what else to do."

"Everything they do is an experiment, Isla Belle." Stephen folded his hands together. "There is no guarantee."

"I gathered that much." I'd spent the night swimming in a failed experiment. If anyone knew the risk, it was me.

"Do you think Denton would do it?" Ty leaned forward, his expression hopeful. "She's a ward of the Exchange. That has to mean something."

Stephen's head snapped up.

Ty nodded at me. "She already knows."

The betrayal cut. Stephen had known and never told me. Tucking my chin, I stared at my lap. It shouldn't be this hard. Stephen had the clout and both Ty and I worked for the Exchange. There shouldn't be secrets anymore, and my mother shouldn't have to suffer.

Stephen's mouth hung open, then closed again.

"I don't need to know why or how." It wasn't a total lie. The time would come when I'd want to know everything but right now, I needed Mom to get better. "How can I talk to Denton?"

"Can you talk to him?" Ty faced Stephen. "Would it be better coming from you?"

"It would look like I'm interfering again." Stephen rubbed his forehead with his thumb. "I was pretty vocal when she approached the Exchange the first time around."

"For what?" Both Ty and I asked.

Stephen's eyes flicked between us.

My stomach fluttered. "What else don't I know?"

"Relax, Isla Belle." Stephen covered my hand once more, his smile genuine. "Dottie has been open about her infertility."

"Yes." *Keep going*, was what I meant.

"The Samaritan Exchange ran an ongoing fertility clinic." Stephen's face darkened for a moment before brightening. "Any complications that come from conception through birth are the Exchange's responsibility."

Ty sat back, folding his arms. "How would that make—"

"My birth was the end of her sanity." It was the truth, out in the open. Guilt swam around me, dividing me from Stephen on the couch next to me. I was and forever would be, the reason my mother became crazy.

"We don't know that for sure," Stephen said softly.

"The Exchange seems to think so." Another slice of honesty. It cut just as deep as the earlier admission. "Mom should be in Garuda, Stephen. She's their ward. And she needs help."

"Isla?" Stephen ducked his head, forcing me to meet his gaze. "You are not the reason my sister is sick."

I said nothing. I felt nothing. Only a compulsion to help my mother. I might be the reason for her illness, but I could also help cure her.

"She was sick long before you were born." Stephen squeezed my hand. "Have you read her plays?"

A look of recognition passed over Ty. I shook my head no. "Not in years."

Stephen sighed, his face appearing to have an internal debate. "You should read them. It might clear up any confusion you have about her mental state."

"If she was crazy, she wouldn't have been in the fertility clinic," Ty said, his voice flat.

"My sister has always found a way to get what she wants."

"Her plays had a following," I whispered. He was trying to make me feel better but he was lying. Both Ty and I knew it. "Critics loved her."

Stephen stood and pulled on the ends of the jacket. "This probably isn't the best time for me to bring up her past. Just know that you're not the cause."

"You can't just say that and walk away." Standing, I placed a hand on his arm.

"Read the plays, Isla Belle."

"No." I flinched at the anger in my voice. "Tell me what you know. Now."

Stephen closed his eyes for a brief moment, appearing to brace himself. "I love my sister. I do."

"That's never been up for debate," Ty added, stepping closer.

Stephen nodded, a hand sliding over his face. "There were a handful of critics that she could manipulate. And directors. She made her way in the world by playing people against each other."

"That's not right but that doesn't sound crazy." The woman I knew could be crying one moment, then laughing with a frightening hysteria the next. *That* was crazy.

"She would use her mood to manipulate those around her, especially those who cared for her." Stephen didn't look at me. He kept his gaze on his shoes. "She could find anyone's pressure point."

"But why have a child?" Ty shoved his hands in his pocket. "That doesn't make sense."

"I opposed the idea," Stephen admitted. "She held it against me. Still does."

"Is that why she believes you conspired against her?" I asked.

"She is not wrong." Stephen frowned. He took a step toward the door. "When she was pregnant, she lived on Garuda, away from her little following and critics. When she returned, she'd lost the control she once held. There was a new darling in town, one with less of a bite. She was shunned."

"That's when she moved to the Palo Alto home," Ty said, his shoulders relaxing.

"I still ended her career." My mind raced. Waves of nothing came over me—like I was lost in a sea of nothingness. The room felt too small. *I* felt too small.

Stephen turned to me. "It was a lie, Isla Belle. Your birth forced her to be honest. At least, for a time."

"She's still my mother." Even if she lied. Even if she manipulated people. She raised me. And now, she needed me.

Stephen placed a warm hand on my shoulder. "She's still my sister, too."

Ty tugged on the back of his collar. "So, what's the plan?"

There was only one option for me. "I'll speak with Denton."

LADY ISLA BELLE WELLESLEY

RIVER WYE, WALES: 1535

*T*he evening sun peeked through the foliage of the borrowed cottage. Tucked against a deserted mill, the home was hidden from view. Rhys wiped Lady Isla Belle's sweating forehead, his anger barely contained. He was a fool, an absolute miserable fool. It had been a week since he'd stolen her away—unable to see the hurt in her eyes. He'd hoped for another month or two; it would have given her more time to heal. Rhys and her parents had schemed but were outwitted by the king. He prayed the duke's rank protected them from the tower or at least, the cruel interrogations.

Isla Belle had been warm the night they left. Like the utter fool he was, Rhys thought his touch had brought a blush. Rhys was a healer, yet too distracted to catch the signs of a fever. He'd known she was injured. The blasted woman had hopped from illness to injury since she was a small child. Lady Isla Belle was only one of two children from her family who lived long enough to walk. It was just one of many reasons the duke needed Rhys with Isla Belle. Rhys' noble—and secret—pedigree was as enticing as his healing talent.

Isla Belle's eyes fluttered. Gently, he traced her eyebrows and nose, settling her back into a deeper sleep. This was no place for the daughter of a duke. Wringing a new rag, he wiped her forehead again.

Rhys had taken her to the leaky cottage, a dwelling barely containing one bed, one chair and a pitiful fireplace. The home clung to the border between his country and hers, a land drowning in lawlessness. He'd saved coin and jewels for the journey, but the timing was wrong. He had been rushed by the king's command and Isla Belle's restlessness.

From his perch on the well worn chair, Rhys tenderly spread ointment on her chapped lips and brushed golden curls off her face. The afternoon light gave her skin an ethereal glow. Even in sickness, the lady was beautiful, heart shaped mouth and noble cheeks. Rhys leaned forward and pressed his lips to her forehead. He was cursed with an unnatural life, lonely and long. There would come a day when she would not be within reach. For a moment, she was here, and he would do all that he could to provide for her. He was only a boy when he'd agreed to marry Isla Belle, but he'd given the duke his word. It was a secret held only by her parents and Rhys' steward back in Wales.

Rhys and Isla Belle would now trade places, his station elevated and hers in peril. The only difference, he'd known who she was since her birth. He pulled her close, hoping to keep her safe. There was a piece of him, tucked away in the shadowy parts hidden beneath shame and guilt, that wanted her to need him—that part of him relished in the healing of her injuries. Another piece wished she could have her life of comfort still. Rhys descended from Welsh royalty but Wales was a fickle country—mercurial like England's king.

Isla Belle still smelled of her expensive rose water and lavender oils. She'd never known hunger. Or hunters at her heels.

The sight of her, the soft skin and easy smile—she was the very heart of temptation. Her eyes fluttered. He reached to trace her face. She opened her eyes wide. He froze. The color of her eyes swirled dark then bright and back again before settling on the soft blue of peace. Not pain.

He sighed in relief.

"You have not slept," Isla Belle said, her voice parched.

He reached for a cup, stopping when she placed a hand on his arm.

She made an effort to sit up, giving him another round of relief. If she wanted to move, she was past danger.

"I've been a touch busy." He gave her a smile but inwardly cursed himself, shouldering the blame.

Isla Belle's face fell. "You've been busy for weeks."

"I..." He didn't have the words. Rhys knew her brother was at court, never to return to Wellesley. He knew the king was coming for Isla Belle. Not because she was the king's choice, but because King Henry was a spoiled child and Isla Belle was the unwitting reprimand from the Marcher Lords. It was a fight for control between greedy men. Isla Belle was everything the country needed, young and vibrant. "You're healing nicely."

"Healing nicely," she repeated his words, an eyebrow arched. She looked as regal and irritated as her mother. "Can you do something for me?"

Before Rhys could answer, she plowed ahead.

"Could you find my friend? He's missing." She folded her arms and turned to the window. "He used to sing, not only to me but to the mothers who lost their babies. He used to talk to me—"

"Lady Isla Belle—"

"If you address me as *Lady* anything one more time I swear it, Rhys. It will be the last thing you say. To me or anyone else." Her hands gripped the blankets in white knuckled fists, warming Rhys to the very core.

He stifled a grin.

Her eyes narrowed, storming and swirling to the brightest of blue, the color of anger. Rhys threw back his head and laughed, his shoulders shaking at the abandon of his worries. Isla Belle had returned.

"Have you gone mad?" Her voice crackled with fury.

Rhys leaned forward, his elbows on his knees. "Yes. Absolutely mad."

She bit her lip, a smile growing. Looking away, she cleared her throat, the beginnings of her icy façade cracking.

"What am I to think of you?" Isla Belle asked softly.

"Think of me?" It wasn't just his promise that kept Rhys returning to her, again and again. He'd felt this urge to surround her, protect her since their eyes met.

"Tell me, Rhys. Tell me what you know."

Rhys heard the warning, knowing she would want information he could not divulge. If she knew what or who he was, her life could be in danger. Depending on the man, Glyndwrs were either Britain's last savior or deadliest saboteur. "You need to rest."

"I will ask once, Rhys. Only once." Isla Belle placed a hand on his arm. "And then I will leave."

"Isla—"

"If you cannot trust me, how can I trust you?" She pierced him with those blasted eyes. He was hers. He'd always been hers. "Is my mother safe?"

"Yes." It wasn't the whole truth, but he couldn't break her heart. Not yet.

"Is my brother safe?"

Rhys hesitated. She moved her legs, as if to stand.

He blurted, "For now. Yes, he is safe."

"What did the rider bring you?" Her gaze didn't waver, only her eyes, the colors fighting amongst themselves.

His heart waged the same war within him. Rhys sat up and folded his arms. "The king's soldiers were in route to collect you. They should be at the castle by now."

"That is why you brought me?" Her tone cut him to the quick. "You gave me a pretty speech about a promise. You needed me to trust you. You needed me to come with you and hide away. For my mother, yes? She asked this of you?"

"A pretty speech?" Rhys' mouth slacked at the accusation. He'd spent the week in worry over her fever. "You think I did this for *her*?"

"You're devoted to her and my family."

"Is that a crime?" Despite himself, his voice raised. He stood and wiped his face, pacing at the foot of the rickety bed. "Is it wrong to keep you safe? Wrong to care for you? Blast it, Isla Belle, I'll take the crime. I've already got the punishment."

"Care for me?" Isla Belle swung her legs to the side of the bed and stood. "You left me at Wellesley. You shut me out. Like I was nothing."

Rhys stared at her, realizing the blackening color of her eyes was because of him, not the loss of her family—but him. "I hurt you."

"Gathered that, have you?" Leaning on the bedpost, she scanned the room.

"I…" His mind went blank. *"Fy annwyl,* I am—"

"Don't." Isla Belle pointed at him. "Do not pretend I am your *beloved* and then forget me." She touched her temple, wincing at what he assumed was the memory. "Do not kiss me and disappear."

Rhys cleared his throat and offered weakly, "You were injured."

She blushed, red washing her cheeks and neck. "You kissed me because I broke my leg?"

"No—"

"Then what?"

"I don't, I don't know." Kissing her—attending her, it had felt right when everything else had felt wrong. "You should—"

"Rest?" Isla Belle looked murderous, her hair disheveled and jaw clenched.

"No, not rest." Rhys groaned. "What did I do to earn your ire?"

"Have you listened to a word I've said?" A tear slid down her cheek, the red fading from her skin.

"When have I not?" He motioned to her leg, the bed and where his horse stood outside. "My entire life is devoted to you, how can I not hear what you speak?"

Isla Belle gripped the crooked bed post, her posture slumped. Rhys stepped closer, worried she'd not let him help her back to bed. She gazed up at him through thick lashes. "Devoted to me?"

"The blankets, the powders, this cottage." His horse neighed nervously outside. "It wasn't for me or your mother."

"But you hardly spoke to me." She shook her head, rubbing the bridge of her nose. "And when you did, it wasn't like before. You were—"

The horse complained again, this time ending with a snort. It pawed at the wall. Rhys held a finger to his lips and crept toward the door. The lords were at war with each other and England; Isla Belle and Rhys would be an easy target, her speech noble and accent English.

The gelding tossed his head and danced anxiously as Rhys opened the door. He placed both hands on the horse' neck, cooing softly and listening for predators, both animal and human. The cottage was to be a few days' rest, not a week.

The heavy stillness, the lack of birds and their whisperings, told him a predator was near. With only a shared look of warning they dropped the conversation and readied the horse. The unfinished words amid Rhys and Isla Belle hung between them as they mounted his gelding. His arms wrapped around her, but not as tightly as before. He was more aware of Isla Belle, the softness of her body. Her voice, full of hurt, echoed in his mind.

Rhys guided the horse toward the river, the natural border between his ancestral land of Wales and a nation forever on the brink of war, England. At Wellesley he was nothing more than a simple physician, but when he crossed the river, he was no longer an orphaned Welshman escaping with the king's requested lady. He would no longer be just Rhys Glyndwr but would be *Rhys ap Owain*. He was the son of the late *Owain ap Gruffydd*, Wale's renowned and notorious rebel.

Rhys kept an arm around Isla Belle's waist, her silence oppressive. "It is my fault. All of this."

She straightened but said nothing.

"There's something I need to tell you." The impending night invited his confession. The story belonged more to her than him.

"There's many things you need to tell me."

Rhys wondered how much she truly understood. "I am not who you think I am."

Her head turned. "I've heard the whispers."

"Your parents knew. They've always known." He saw her nod but was lost without being able to look her in the eye. She might know of his ancestry, but she couldn't know the danger it held. "I am sorry, Isla Belle. I am."

"You are not the one I blame for my parents, Rhys," She sounded irritated, confusing him. "Why didn't my mother's family come? Why did no one help us?"

"I do not know." Rhys slowed the gelding to a gentle walk. "But we will soon enough."

"How?" She fidgeted.

Rhys had forgotten how feverish Isla Belle was when they crossed the river. "We're in Wales. We've been this side of River Wye for a week."

"You've taken me to Wales?" She flinched. "Are you mad? They're part of the problem."

"We still do not know where their loyalties lie."

"My mother's ancestors, those same Marcher Lords, *they* gave King Henry's father an English crown. They did this. They want me at his side. Why would they betray him now?" Isla Belle said, her voice rising. "They won't help us, Rhys. No one will. He's won."

Those same Marcher Lords. Rhys felt the weight of her words. Isla Belle didn't know.

"He's afraid, Isla Belle." As if by command, the breeze picked up, distorting sounds around them. "He hasn't forgotten their power. He fears it." *And the myths surrounding us,* Rhys stilled his tongue.

Isla Belle didn't belong here, not on a plain horse or in the encroaching night. "He fears no one."

"Every man has a fear." Rhys urged the gelding around a thick gathering of trees.

"Except you." Her words fell flat, echoing in his mind.

"I have fears like any other." Rhys spoke low, hoping it'd keep her calm.

Isla Belle shook her head. "I am the only thing you fear."

ISLA BELLE THORNE

SACRAMENTO, CALIFORNIA: PRESENT DAY

*T*he cold night air nipped at my skin, the temperature falling as we inched closer to the holidays. Stephen had tried once more to convince me to stay home but I owed my mother—and myself—some answers. An army of silk dresses and black tuxedoes made their way up the two-prong staircase of the Stanford mansion. Earlier, Stephen had told me that Leland Stanford built the mansion in Sacramento years before he built the university in Palo Alto. I'd almost told Stephen that I had no memory of Leland, only his wife, Jane—an impossible idea. The Stanfords were buried a century before my birth.

My birth. That one simple day appeared to be the culprit of my mother's illness. My mother was difficult, that was a fact. But manipulative enough to conjure a career in playwriting? That was too far fetched. Even if everything was true, that still wouldn't explain her bouts of drug abuse and hallucinations. Since I was a child, she'd bounced between diagnosis and medications. Neither lasting more than a few months.

Kindergarten was the first time I remember Stephen picking me up from school, announcing how excited he was that I would be staying with him. I smiled at the memory. His stiff lip and stoic expression worried my teacher. The more Stephen tried to infuse excitement into his voice, the more scared she became.

I learned—and still know—that Stephen was constant, in his affection and in his determination to save his family. Even now, he'd gone ahead to the charity auction at the Stanford mansion to pave the way for me. He'd hope to tell Denton that I was eager to speak with him. But the hesitation in how Stephen spoke about Denton, alluded to a rift between them. There was no doubt it had to do with my mother.

Catching my breath, I took in the Stanford family's magnificent Victorian mansion. The familiar feeling was back. A vision on the cusp of appearing. Visions shouldn't bring peace—but they did and always left me feeling exhausted. The dread I'd been carrying fell from my shoulders. I grabbed the skirt of my tea length dress and placed a hand on the crème handrail, my skin humming with excitement.

Then it happened. The world shifted, the dresses in front of me morphed into an older woman with a dark grey bun, Jane Stanford. She tugged the shawl from around her shoulders and placed it around mine. She smiled sympathetically and spoke of her own child's death. Hugging myself, I felt the loss of an empty womb.

"Isla?"

The woman evaporated, exposing the Stanford mansion once more and a dapper Dr. Euston. His suit didn't quite match him. He tugged on his sleeves. I couldn't decide if they were too short or too tight. His fidgeting made it difficult to tell.

"How are you this evening, Isla Belle?" His smile strained, ever so quickly. Following his gaze, I spotted Stephen's profile at the top of the stairs. Apparently, my mother affected more than just Denton and Stephen's relationship.

"I'm good." It was an absolute and complete lie. "I'm still working on how to spin the alpaca experiment."

His eyebrow furrowed.

"You were trying to identify a longevity gene and transplant it to the alpacas." We started walking up the stairs. He pursed his lips. For him to draw this much of a blank, I worried about the number of experiments Euston had done. I tried again, "Seventeen animals died."

"Ah…" He sighed. "That one."

We reached the foyer, my hands at my side and away from the rail. "I hope you don't mind but I have to ask. Why did you run the experiment? You've never used animals before."

Dr. Euston scanned the foyer, probably looking for Denton. "Because the trees didn't work."

"Trees?"

"Fantastic." He looked past me, frowning. "They invited the news."

Over my shoulder, I saw a petite woman speaking into a handheld microphone in front of a frustrated cameraman.

"That's just great." Dr. Euston rubbed his eye with the palm of his hand. "Wonderful."

He turned to go. I grabbed his arm. "What trees?"

"Oh." Dr. Euston's face brightened. "The so-called immortal tree. We couldn't splice the genetic make up. Well, we could but the human sequence wouldn't accept it."

Before I could ask more, he disappeared into the crowd. I'd have to find another way to get the information.

"Denton knows you want to speak with him." Stephen's voice startled me. He squeezed my shoulder. "I should take off."

"Are you sure?"

He nodded, his gaze on Dr. Euston's retreating back.

"Thank you." *For everything,* I almost added.

His eyes crinkled. We weren't demonstrative, but if he'd reached for me, I would have hugged him. It couldn't have been easy speaking to Denton. But Stephen did it. He'd always come through for me.

"Good luck." Without another word, Stephen left.

I walked between two ushers; black earpieces tucked into their right ears. Gilded mirrors lined the walls, topped with carved moldings reaching the seventeen-foot ceiling. Ty told me each room, except the ballroom and library, held separate silent auctions.

Slipping into the first room on the right, I searched for Denton. Several short rows of chairs were placed in the middle of the room. The walls were a dark crimson with the floors a checkered marble. The oval piano with painted flowers on the wood was wrong. It should've been in the state room. I left, trying to find the blue room and grabbed a pamphlet left on a hallway end table. It gave auction information but nothing about the house. I flipped to the back sheet. The blue room. The information had to be here. I hadn't googled it. I hadn't read it. I'd never been to the Stanford mansion but I knew deep in my bones that everything was off.

From room to room, I walked, the house more foreign and the mission to find Denton less important. The furniture was rearranged in all the wrong places or in the wrong room altogether. I heard Jane Stanford whispering condolences for my loss. I'd miscarried again. *Impossible.* I'd never been pregnant. It was just another dream with the blond man and the blue-eyed woman.

Walking downstairs, I wiped my forehead and grabbed a glass of champagne from a server, and started counting. Anything to keep the vision—and growing headache—at bay.

One...two...three...

With my back against the wall, I raised my glass and shuddered. Another vision. The blue-eyed woman. She burst back into my mind with blonde hair, then transformed into a nervous red-haired beauty. I clenched my fist. She faded into a fiery Spanish girl.

Four...five...

She morphed into a pale, thin young woman on the verge of death.

Six... Seven...

She disappeared, replaced with an anxious toddler. And then— death. The weight of an anvil hit my chest. Gasping at the pain, the champagne flute fell from my hands. I dropped to my knees, the glass shattering as we both hit the floor. Hands ushered me away, placing me on a small white-framed bed.

A presence of authority came in. The hands left the room in a quiet hush. A soft voice cooed in my ear. My face and neck were cooled by a compress. The rush of a migraine twisted my insides.

I closed my eyes, murmuring, "It's all wrong. The furniture. The woman."

"Shhhhh," the man whispered.

Someone peeled the bloody hem off my leg. A needle pricked my thigh. I bit down the nausea. My knee was wiped, the stringent burning my nose. A man hummed, while digging and plucking the small shards of glass from my skin. I felt the calm of the painkiller ease the migraine's grip. Slowly, I opened my eyes.

Dr. Denton cradled my knee with one hand, the other holding medical tweezers. The greatest man of modern medicine had come to my aid. I was a complete stranger. A nobody.

I noticed the droplets of blood on the floor. They were thick, like pudding. The blood stayed wet as if unable to coagulate.

That's not right, I tried to say but my mouth wouldn't work.

He winked at me, catching me off guard. His hair had silvered more since the gallery, if it were possible to do so in so short of time. His eyes twinkled. He watched me study him.

"There's m'girl." He spoke with a slight accent, still American but more formal. More stiff.

He pulled out a thin tube I recognized, glue for the skin. It was used for minor surgeries with animals, ideal when holding down a squirming goat. He smeared it while I winced, the glue burning the cuts on my skin.

"Hopefully, tomorrow you'll be as good as new," he lied.

Denton, a doctor, was promising a faster recovery than possible. Watching my mother, I knew the effects of the painkiller. It would only be another thirty minutes until I'd be completely intoxicated, ten minutes after that, I'd be asleep. Or trapped in another dream.

"Let's get you home."

My stomach lurched. "I'm...okay..." I said between gasps, the pain spiked when I tried to speak.

"Shhhhh." He lifted my arms and pulled me to my feet.

My blood lined the cuffs of his shirt. I couldn't apologize, another word could send me to the floor. He helped me to the foyer with two suit-clad men on either side of us.

"Dr. Denton!" A man exclaimed, rushing forward. His gaze settled on Denton's bloody sleeve, his face losing color. "Are you hurt?" Turning to me, he demanded, "What happened?"

Denton waved away his concern. "Ah, the blood is hers."

Denton's face was slightly sallow, not quite pallid but a shadow of liver irritation. He appeared healthy but anything from a simple infection to a major blood transfusion could bring about hepatitis. I watched him blink, noticing the sclera, the white of his eyes, hadn't yellowed. He was on either side, the beginning or the end of liver trauma.

"You're drunk." The man sniffed at me, turning up his nose. I noticed his official tag. He must've been some sort of supervisor. I'd ruined his evening.

Swaying into Denton, I slurred, "Sorry."

"She has that nasty bug going around." Denton steadied me, his arm across my shoulder. He was lying. "Let's get you home."

The man's face turned to a splotchy red. "I'll take her. You don't have to worry—"

"I worry about them all." Denton looped his arm around mine, patting my hand that lay on top of his forearm.

A chill swept across my neck. Stephen had told him I wanted to talk to him but I was missing something. Denton was too relaxed and too familiar with me. There was a tie between us, some sort of connection. I couldn't explain it. But it was there all the same. And it calmed me. Eased the pain.

I relaxed my grip and straightened. Concentrating on my speech, I said slowly, "Thank you, Dr. Denton. I think I'll be okay."

"You're anything but." Denton's eyes crinkled, appearing genuinely concerned just like Stephen had earlier.

The walls wavered. The lights dimmed. I fought for control of my body.

Denton released me, a look of embarrassment on his face. He retreated, glancing around self-consciously. He pulled a card from his suit jacket and placed it in my hand. He tilted his head to the side, an internal dialogue appeared to be happening.

Denton finally gave a small shake of the head. "I've a few questions regarding your case study."

"My case?" I squeaked. The case could be my mother or the alpaca experiment...I couldn't finish the thought. My mind froze in the muddy haze of medication.

"It's fascinating, isn't it?" He put his hand on the wall, wiping his forehead with the other. "The world has focused on quantity of life, never on quality."

I nodded. At least, I think I did.

"We've erroneously assumed they meant the same thing. If we could have extended the mobility of the older generation, then health care, on a global scale of course, would be forever changed. The entire approach would have worked." Denton's words jumbled together, swirling like the walls of the mansion. "I've only a few more days in the states. I'd love to chat before...."

My head felt like I was swimming underwater. The floor looked oddly comfortable. I just needed to sleep for a minute. Or two.

The wall shifted. The room began to spin. In a quick rush, I felt arms underneath me, my body cradled to a broad chest. I grimaced at the blurry faces. My vision swirled; a man became three shirts with one head. Then a whole man again. Closing my eyes, I envisioned carriages and the click clack of horseshoes on cobbled stones. The street lamp morphed into a never-ending streak of light.

"She needs help," whispered a strained voice.

I whimpered at his words—he wasn't the healer I yearned for.

LADY ISLA BELLE WELLESLEY

RIVER WYE, ENGLAND: 1535

*L*ady Isla Belle welcomed the surrounding darkness, softening Rhys' confession. He blamed himself for her family, she suspected as much. And now Rhys had brought her to Wales, her mother's native country. The Marcher Lords had become suspiciously quiet. Isla Belle might have been sheltered, her life of a lady warranted seclusion from politics, but she knew enough. If the Marcher Lords wanted to help, her father wouldn't be at court and her mother wouldn't be at the mercy of the king.

Her life was a game played by men overcome with fear. Rhys was no different.

Late into the night, he stopped the horse. He unpacked and let the gelding roam. Isla Belle stared at the stars, her back against a fallen log while Rhys was slumped against a boulder. His hunched shoulders rose and fell softly as he slept. How many nights he stood vigil at the cottage Isla Belle didn't know.

Using the log, she inched herself to a stand, the night giving her courage. She limped to him, her hands moving along the rough bark, helping her stay upright. She stepped on a twig. The horse neighed in response.

Rhys' eyes snapped open, locking onto Isla Belle. He swayed to a stand, his hands on her shoulders. "Are you in pain?"

"No." Isla Belle smiled at his sleepy voice. She threw her arms around him, nuzzling his neck. She waited for the rejection, for him to pull away. This was farewell, she would leave once he fell asleep again. Isla Belle would not burden him another day. She wanted to be loved. Cherished. But to Rhys she was nothing more than an obligation.

His body went rigid in her embrace. She stifled the whimper, wishing this wasn't the last memory of him. But then, his arm slid around her and pulled her close. Isla Belle's heart soared, her pulse racing. His body, taut and lithe, against hers. Warm and solid, she wished to stay this way, in his arms, breathing in the scent of him. She felt the impending heartache and drew away.

He released her. Isla Belle kept her gaze on the ground, afraid of what he would see. Even in the dark, she feared he could read the color of her eyes or hear the pounding of her heart.

Rhys touched her chin and lifted it, forcing her to look at him. He gazed down at her, as if absorbing Isla Belle.

"I hurt you, *fy annwyl*." He murmured slowly, tracing a finger along her cheek. The slack of his jaw—he was still drunk with sleep.

Isla Belle held her breath, unable to move.

"I am sorry." His other hand cradled her face.

His warm, smooth hands on her skin made her burn, a fever unlike any other. He couldn't be fully awake but she'd take the touch all the same. Her heart threatened to leap from her chest. She should pull away, she should leave.

Rhys's hand slipped to the back of her neck, his fingers threaded through her hair. He lowered his head. Isla Belle inhaled, frightened at the hurt he could cause. Rhys brushed his lips against hers, warm, inviting. The scruff on his chin chafed her skin, tingling and teasing her. Rhys drew her closer still—his back stiffened. He was awake.

Wide eyed, he retreated, his eyes full of shame. A look of guilt ripped across his face.

"Rhys…" A surge, a need to be close, filled Isla Belle. She pulled him close once more.

He hesitated.

She leaned into him, brushing her lips against his. Slowly, he kissed back—then more urgent. Hunger and confusion of the past few weeks grew inside Isla Belle. Her hands gripped his shirt. Rhys, no longer the childhood friend, was a man, his mouth exploring Isla Belle's. One of his hands stayed entwined in her hair, the other trailed down her back, settling at her waist.

Consumed by Rhys, her mind dizzied, no longer aware of the dangerous world at her heels. His hand at her waist remained firm, yet gentle. She felt the warmth of his body against hers and for a moment she wished—one more day. One more kiss.

The thought snapped her back to where she stood. Isla Belle could set Rhys free. She'd seen it, the resentment. His laugh back at the cottage, the sound deep and rich. It'd been far too long since she'd heard it.

This was wrong, their embrace. Isla Belle stepped back. She would not imprison him. He was good and kind—he was everything to her. But Rhys never had a choice. He did as he was bid from the moment the duchess found him. Isla Belle was forever his charge, not his love.

Rhys arched an eyebrow, barely visible in the moonlight. "Talk to me."

"I won't do it." She clapped a hand over her mouth. Years of trust coupled with his kiss had loosened her tongue.

"What won't you do?" he gently pressed.

"Wales." She bid the rising grief to stay hidden. "Marcher Lords."

Rhys placed a comforting hand on her shoulder. "They will protect you."

"And you?" She brushed off his hand, not missing the confusion in his face. "Who will protect you?"

"The king doesn't want to share his bed with me." Rhys cupped her elbow and grinned.

Isla Belle pushed his chest. He covered her hand with his. She felt the hammering of his heart. He'd returned. This was her Rhys, playful and gentle. She'd missed him back in Wellesley.

Gathering her against his chest, Rhys lay his forehead against hers. "I am sorry for hurting you. But you cannot leave me now."

She started, shocked that he knew what she planned. His laugh rumbled in his chest. "Oh, *fy annwyl*, I've given up. You've stolen a piece of me. I won't be asking for it back."

Her heart melted. Isla Belle wrapped her arms around him and let his concern wash over her. Home, Rhys felt like home.

"You don't have to." She closed her eyes for a moment, speaking to his chest. Her noble blood had given her a lifetime in a gilded cage, but his lowly healer station gave him freedom. "You can choose. You can leave."

The horse fidgeted, neighing like it had at the cottage. The air stilled.

Rhys lifted her chin once more. "I've made my choice."

Isla Belle's skin prickled. She leaned in. A branch snapped. "Did you hear that?"

The low ripple of the river was the only sound. A heavy blanket of silence rolled in. Isla Belle felt the sensation of impending danger, like prey being stalked.

"Shhhh," he whispered.

She turned at the sound of a voice in the distance.

"Down." Rhys dropped to his knees, pulling Isla Belle with him.

Arrows hit the grass and rocks around them, the direction coming from the meadows. The gelding reared and took off with a piercing shriek.

Isla Belle and Rhys were trapped between the river and the hidden army. He grabbed her elbows. "We'll swim to safety."

Mounted soldiers came around the bend—brass guns aimed at him. Rhys dropped her hand. "I kidnapped you. Isla Belle, are you listening? I stole you."

"No." She reached for him.

"We've been betrayed." He backed away. "Only two people knew the route. Your mother and father."

His words chilled her to the bone. Her parents' betrayal had her trembling. She'd heard of torture meant to loosen tongues. People came back broken. And mad.

"Lady Isla Belle." The leader rode through the middle of the soldiers, the royal crest emblazoned on his tunic. He dismounted and bowed with a smirk. He had once visited the castle and kissed her hand. His name escaped her but not the look of hunger. He spoke with the same sing-song accent of a Welshman. It was subtle, just a trace like Rhys once had. Her mother had squashed any evidence of Wales when Queen Anne's favor fell. "I've come to collect you."

"Milford?" Ever observant, Rhys had remembered the man. "You're not English."

The captain straightened and whistled to his men. "We have a Welsh king on the throne. Why not a Welsh army?"

Isla Belle searched Rhys's face, the captain had said what she feared. They were on their own. Wales would not help them.

Captain Milford laughed, the confident sound of a victor. He nodded to Rhys. "What would your family think of this?"

Panic in her chest, Isla Belle hobbled a step from the captain and glanced at the surrounding soldiers. Rhys hesitated under the captain's scrutiny, another mystery. Her heart sank—another secret she was not privy to.

"I've no loyalty to them." Rhys kept his face blank like he'd done for months.

The captain waved at Isla Belle. "Stealing the daughter of a duke. That would land you in their graces. Crafty man, you are."

"I am her healer, nothing more." Rhys' voice was measured, calm and sure.

Isla Belle tucked her head, wishing she'd not heard him. Her leg throbbed with a vengeance.

"—who stole a lady." The captain gave a slight nod to his men. They surrounded both Isla Belle and Rhys.

"I was not taken." Isla Belle would not let Rhys be punished for her sake. He had done enough, cared enough.

"Her leg was broken." Rhys motioned to her injured leg. "She couldn't escape."

"If that is the story you're peddling." The captain rolled his eyes and motioned to the soldiers. They tightened their circle around Isla Belle. Her eyes wide, she flexed her hands at her side.

Holding out his arms in surrender, Rhys dropped to his knees. "Leave her be. I stole—"

Captain Milford raised his hand, cutting off Rhys' words. "If you confess, you'll forfeit your lands and title but keep your head."

Isla Belle spun around, her leg screaming in pain. Rhys held no title. "He's a healer. He holds no lands to forfeit."

Captain Milford smirked and tsked. "She doesn't know, does she?"

Rhys held out his hands. "I confess to the crimes."

The captain leaned over Rhys. "Say the words. And she'll be free."

Isla Belle forced the conviction in her words. "Are you deaf, Captain? He's a servant in my house and bound to obey my family."

The captain scoffed. "He's a Glyndwr—"

"My mother's family will not stand—"

"Your mother cannot help you. Better to be whipped by me than hanged by the bishop."

"Hanged?" Isla Belle's knees weakened.

"You can be loyal to the crown or you can be hanged. Those are your choices." The captain stood and folded his arms. "You've no idea the trouble you've caused."

"Then take me." Isla Belle held out her arms, mimicking Rhys.

"Oh, we intend to." Captain Milford waved to the soldiers. They latched onto Rhys' limbs and shoved his face to the ground.

"Do not touch him." Isla Belle fell to her knees in front of Rhys, cradling his head. Other soldiers came forward and ripped the clothes from his back. Isla Belle pulled on the men's arms. "You will not harm him."

The captain snatched her arm, spinning her around. Her leg screamed with pain. He grabbed a fistful of hair at the base of her neck and pulled her head back. She refused to whimper.

Rhys struggled to free an arm. "Let her go."

Isla Belle's nails scratched at Milford's thick, muscled arm. He clutched her chin with his other hand, his fingers digging into her skin. "You are a fool, woman. You are nothing but a means to an end. A payment for an old debt."

"Your debt? Or the king's?" She snapped, hating that her voice caught. Rhys wouldn't use her. Doubt crept in.

"Your healer is a thief and a liar." The captain tightened his grip.

Rhys' cried out. "The fault was mine."

With a wicked grin, Milford held Isla Belle firm as she struggled in his grip. "Your pretty face can't save him."

He sneered before releasing her. Isla Belle tested her mouth, opening and closing her jaw. She straightened her shoulders and smoothed her skirts. If not for her trembling hands, she'd appear proud. Regal. Instead of frightened.

Isla Belle took a deep breath. "I'm the daughter of a duke."

"You are the daughter of nothing." Milford folded his hands, his face calm except for the ticking of a vein on his neck.

"You will not harm him." Isla Belle needed a threat. Her mother's words filled her mind, *superstitions were weapons used on the weak.* Isla Belle garnered strength with each breath. "He is from the River Wye."

The soldiers hushed, eying their captain. A spark of fear slipped through. Milford would know of the Welsh healers of the river, men able to harness an unending life. They were just bedtime stories but Isla Belle didn't care. She grasped for any tool, anything to stop them from hurting Rhys.

The captain adjusted the cuffs of his military tunic, his smile both wry and bored. "Then it won't hurt, will it?"

Rhys struggled against the soldiers holding his shoulders to the ground. "Milford, name your price."

The soldiers tensed and exchanged nervous glances. Milford kneeled before Rhys and grabbed him by the hair, twisting his face to the sky, a thirsty gleam in his eye. "I can't be bought. And I don't believe in superstitions."

The captain stood, allowing his soldiers to stretch Rhys, face down, along the grass, a man to each arm and leg.

"No!" Isla Belle screamed.

"Take her away," Rhys begged.

Milford snapped his fingers at her. A soldier wrapped his arms around her to shield the view. Isla Belle twisted, catching sight of Rhys' bare back. "Sorry, milady."

"Shall I count your crimes or the lashes?" Not waiting for an answer, the captain cracked the whip twice and sliced into Rhys's skin.

"Nooooo!" Isla Belle howled, her hands trembling.

Rhys gasped for air, blood webbing along his back. His body twitched as another crack cut his back, followed by another. And another.

Isla Belle swallowed the rising bile. Another lash. She heard the call for rags to soak the blood but her eyes remained locked on Rhys' shivering frame. She kicked and screamed.

Another lash.

Arms reached out, carrying her away.

Another lash.

And then Rhys stilled.

ISLA BELLE THORNE

SACRAMENTO, CALIFORNIA: PRESENT DAY

*E*yes. The woman. Blue eyes. Blinking, I squinted at the ceiling. The woman was in my dreams again. Her hair was different but the blond—*Rhys*—was still at her side. I felt a twinge of jealousy. Groaning, I felt every inch of my tired body. Aching from my head down to my feet, I tried sitting—my stomach lurched.

"Whooooooa, easy girl." Ty's head took up my entire view.

With a slow twist of my head, I saw the fabric of the couch. We were in the living room of the suite. A vague memory of Dr. Euston talking to me about trees emerged. And one of Denton asking me questions. Or maybe I was the one asking.

Pain. Rhys. An ache crept into my heart. I missed him. Rhys, a man I didn't know.

"That's one way of getting an introduction." Ty shoved pillows behind my back and helped me sit up, his voice booming. "You needed to open your mouth, not split your knee."

Blinking slowly, I whispered, "Stop shouting."

He chuckled. "I'd say you have a hangover but I'm pretty sure you didn't drink."

"I did talk to Denton, I think." Bending my leg, I flinched. "I kind of remember talking to him."

"You don't know?"

"No, not really." There were bits and pieces of memory but seeing visions made me question everything.

"You were talking to him. Then fell. By the time I got there you were stitched up and were loopy from whatever meds they gave you." Ty stretched on the floor next to me. He was either finishing or beginning a work out.

"Since when does a charity event have emergency care?" As far as I knew, the Exchange never hosted events, only participated.

Ty's face sobered. "Since protestors turned violent."

He grabbed the remote and turned on the television. Clicking through the channels, they echoed the same thing. The newswoman at the event last night was attacked on her way home. She was targeted because she'd interviewed attendees instead of protestors.

I folded my arms around the nearest pillow. "But the people in charge of the auction couldn't have anticipated that."

"This wasn't the first time." With another click, Ty shut off the news. "The governor's ball left three food servers in critical condition."

"Why target them?" I didn't pay attention to politics, but attacking employees didn't sit well. Anger at failed experiments made more sense.

Ty tapped the remote against his leg. "I don't think it matters why or who. People get blinded by their goals. Happens all the time."

"But killing?"

He spun the remote in a tight circle on his palm. "No one's died yet."

"What does the Exchange say about all of it?"

"They hate conflict in all forms."

"All of it?" Mom once told me she had protestors at one of her plays. Decades later, she was still giddy talking about it. The controversy gave her a sold out theatre. She believed conflict helped. If Euston thought the same way, there could be dozens of deadly experiments. "Are they canceling the rest of the events?"

Ty shook his head. "Probably not."

"Why?"

He set the remote on the couch's armrest. He acted like a cooped up dog that hadn't been walked in weeks. "They're kind of in a tight spot."

"What's that supposed to mean?"

Ty stood and grabbed a glass of water from the kitchen. "It means the Samaritan Exchange is already on thin ice. If we pull out of upcoming events, we'll look guilty. Or at least, not friendly."

"*Are* we guilty?" Using the armrest, I pulled myself to a stand.

Ty slowly set the cup of water on the counter. "They're not saints. But they do save lives."

"That doesn't answer my question."

"As of last night, we have protestors at every hospital—the ones affiliated with the Exchange. All because the U.S. government buys vaccines exclusively from us." With his index finger, he pushed the water away from him at the base of the cup. "We're being blamed as the sole reason for the rise in autism."

Not once had Euston or any of the other scientists expressed dismay or regret for the dead animals. I'd read into other experiments where sympathy was lacking. As a scientist, I understood emotions wouldn't be written into reports, but Dr. Euston seemed to be more frustrated than compassionate with the failures.

Ty swallowed hard. "With my own eyes, I've seen polio victims unable to walk. I've taken testimony from parents who've lost child after child to measles or pox. But here, in my native country, that same organization that stopped disease and illness to millions of others is being crucified. It takes time. It takes trial and error before everything works right."

The playful cousin I'd known my entire life was nowhere to be seen. He worked his jaw and braced himself against the counter. The Exchange had ignited a passion in him—for something other than chasing women.

"You trust them." Trust didn't come easily, not for me. There had to be a catch. Back when mom would call, bursting with compliments, there was a reason. She wanted assurance or money—*something*. There was always a motivating factor. Always. "That's why you want my mom to go to Garuda. You believe they'll fix her. You believe in the Exchange and all that they stand for."

"Don't you?" He put the cup in the sink.

"Maybe. Maybe not." Everything felt twisted; not just with the Exchange. Mom was my parent, and I loved her, but I didn't exactly trust her. Stephen had kept secrets from me as well. Part of me wondered what else he knew. I was the result of the fertility clinic and if I'd learned anything in my short time with the Exchange, there was always a price to success. What had my birth cost?

"Do you remember anything from last night?" Ty asked. "Did you ask him about your mom?"

"I honestly don't know." Propping my leg on the couch cushion, I twisted and turned my knee. "The night is kind of a blur."

"I didn't tell him." Ty rolled his eyes when I didn't answer. "Stephen. I didn't tell him you got hurt."

"Has he said anything?" I knew Stephen would be in touch. He refused to stay with us at his own suite, opting for a hotel room a few streets away. I was grateful for him but he was a man who kept his cards close. And yet, he offered his heart freely. He'd made it clear he was concerned about me, and not just because of my mother.

Shrugging, Ty said, "Just that your mom's transfer date is Saturday." Thankfully, he looked away.

I sank back to the couch. If Mom went to the university hospital in Palo Alto again, nothing would ever change. She would never truly heal. But I was growing more wary of Garuda, even if I couldn't articulate why. "Have you read anything about Euston's tree project?"

Ty raised his eyebrows in confusion. "Other than the alpacas, he sticks with humans."

"I could have sworn he said something about a tree study." Not that my memory, or my head in anyway, could be trusted.

"Would it be published?" He tossed his phone to me.

Opening the internet icon, I searched *immortal tree Jeffrey Euston*. Several images appeared, one with Euston front and center of what appeared to be a massive room. Three six-foot-tall trees were behind him with information displays, according to the description at the bottom of the image.

The room looked familiar, and for some reason, I knew the entire wall behind the photographer was made of glass. Zooming in with my fingers, I read *Garuda Observatory* on the wall behind Dr. Euston. Gripping the phone, I felt a wave of nausea. I'd never been to Garuda. But I could have sworn I'd been in that room.

"What'd you find?" Ty's voice was muted. He was rummaging in the fridge. Our kitchen would never hold enough food for Ty. The man was an eating machine.

Scrolling, I read out loud, "Researchers studied and compared each variation of the same tree Euston spliced."

Whoever had written the article didn't outline Euston's objective for the study. It looked more like a high school science report highlighting the differences between the trees. The report was at least savvy enough to include the Latin names of the trees, *Sequoiadendron giganteum, Sequoia sempervirens,* and *Metasequoia glyptostroboides.*

"How many types of trees?" He shut the refrigerator with a pained sigh. He hadn't found whatever he was craving.

"Three." Using my elbows, I shifted to a more comfortable position on the couch. "One's tall, one's wide and one's small."

"And I'm starving." Ty whined like a two year old.

"Dr. Euston disproved the myth of the Immortal Tree, commonly known as a Redwood."

"Fascinating." He pouted and walked to the armchair, covering his eyes with his arm. He should have been in theatre not my mother.

"They quote Euston explaining the differences between biologically immortal and just aging slowly."

Lifting his arm, Ty peeked at me. "One has the ability to regenerate its cells, the other just takes forever to die."

Bringing a hand to my chest, I pretended to cry. "I'm so proud."

He rolled his eyes. "And they say I'm dramatic."

Pointing the phone at him like a microphone, I asked, "Which one can only die through trauma? And which one is susceptible to disease?"

Ty made a face. "Is it bad that I really don't care?"

"Why does Euston care? Why bother with trees in the first place?" Setting the phone down, I tapped the back with my fingers. "The article said Redwood trees can't be killed by fungus, disease or any infestation but when people walk around the tree it dies. Just walking next to it can kill the almighty immortal tree?"

Ty lifted his arm and gave me the side eye. He was past hungry, nearing hangry.

"Come on, Ty. The Exchange has explored the human body from conception to death and pretty much everything in between. Why look into trees?" When Ty didn't answer, I picked up the phone again, scrolling once more. "It says the offshoots of the Redwood tree die at a much more rapid pace."

"Congratulations." He sat up and clapped his hands once. "The kids don't live as long as the parents. Now let's go get food."

"I'm missing something."

"It's called food."

There was more to it. I was missing something that felt obvious but couldn't put my finger on it. An elephant had crept into the room. Part of me wanted to know the truth, part of me wanted to hide.

"What if it worked?" Slowly, an idea stretched inside my head. "If either study worked, what could be gained?"

"We'd be able to transplant a longevity gene into humans." Ty came over and snatched his phone back. "We already know that."

"Would it stop the protestors?"

He paused, his thumb extended as if ready to type. "Say that again?"

"If they could prove they'd solved mortality or at least extend man's expiration date, would that stop people from protesting?"

Ty stared absently at his phone, his eyes narrowing. "I'm not sure. Angry people don't see reason."

"But what if they're worked up over death? What if that's really what's scaring them?"

"They're angry, not scared."

Shaking my head, I said, "There isn't much of a difference. People don't get angry without being scared first. People are scared of dying, whether it's them or their family. They're the same with illness." *Including mental illness.* I swallowed hard. I wasn't angry but I was definitely scared.

"Oh." His eyes lit with understanding. "If autism were no longer an issue—if anything was no longer an issue, they'd have nothing to scream about."

"Technically, we wouldn't even need vaccines." I could almost hear his mind calculating all the scenarios. "Ty, what if Euston solved mortality in all its forms?"

He blinked and in a heartbreakingly soft voice he said, "But Euston didn't. The animals died."

LADY ISLA BELLE WELLESLEY

RIVER WYE, ENGLAND: 1535

*L*ady Isla Belle gritted her teeth, refusing to cry out as she dismounted from Captain Milford's horse, her leg throbbing. The sun had decided to shine. It stepped from behind thick summer clouds, giving light to the small army. The weather was too bright for her heavy heart. The world moved on, the sun still rose and her life was still not her own. By what the captain said, her family was ruined, including Rhys, the last of her loved ones. Isla Belle had nothing. Nothing to lose and nothing to give.

The soldiers kept their heads down and arms at their sides. No one offered help or sympathy, not even the captain who insisted on her riding in his saddle, directly in front of him. She'd felt his thigh behind hers with every stride. His breath on her neck.

She hobbled from the horses and sat near the roaring fire, her stomach grumbling. Soldiers had raced ahead to prepare the camp. One with curly black hair, his face young and humble, offered Isla Belle a boiled egg and burnt toast.

"No, thank you." Her mouth dried as did her appetite. She shivered involuntarily, the weather unseasonably cold.

"Your belly is hungry, milady." He tried again, lowering his eyes like her childhood servants—like how Rhys should have been. "You've not eaten in days."

"Day," she corrected, her voice hollow. It'd only been a day. Yet it felt like an eternity. She wouldn't go to court. She'd escape even if it meant death.

Images of Rhys' bare back covered in a bloody web replayed in her mind, his screams echoing in her ears. They'd left him, his body bloody and broken. He'd rescued her from the king's grasp, only to be whipped. She knew the threat of infection. She'd spent too many years at his heels and under his care. With no one to help him, he would die.

Her Welsh mother had told her of the River Wye myths, the legends of those who couldn't die. Superstition was a weapon the duchess would wield but Isla Belle knew the truth. Rhys was a man like any other, a living, breathing man that could die—that *would* die— he'd sacrificed himself for her.

"Leave her be." The captain appeared at her side and kneeled, the hem of his tunic sweeping the dewy grass. "She'll eat soon enough."

"Why would I eat?" Isla Belle gathered courage. She could—she *would* be strong. She forced herself to relax and slid under a blanket of apathy. Rhys was an abandoned orphan, and yet he rose to prominence in her father's house. She would not yield to the captain or the king. "What more could you possibly do?"

"I'm sure the king can think of something." Milford grinned and appeared to wait, for what she didn't know. "Or our glorious Bishop Lee."

Isla Belle didn't know the bishop, but the look in Milford's eye chilled her. A year earlier her family was elevated, the favorite of the queen and now, her family was broken. Her father had grown impatient with the king's temper but had never shown disrespect. Isla Belle pictured her mother, her tall grace. Isla Belle held her tongue and slowed her breathing, hoping she appeared calm.

Milford's eyes narrowed, only a moment, and then nothing. There was more to his purpose, he was hiding something. "Your mother cares nothing for her neck. Or the lives of her family."

"Then why take me to her?" Rhys' words came to her mind, *we've been betrayed, I told only two people. Your mother and your father.*

Milford ran a thumb along Isla Belle's cheek. "Perhaps I won't."

She lifted her chin from the captain's touch. She needed time. She needed a plan. "My family has done nothing wrong."

"Not according to the queen. And let's not forget the council." Milford waved away a limping soldier offering food. The captain's dismissal gave the rest of the army permission to eat. They smacked their lips, devouring their meager ration.

"I know nothing of a council."

"Or of your healer." Milford appeared to be enjoying Isla Belle's confusion and Rhys' secrets.

There it was again, the doubt creeping in at the captain's words. Isla Belle knew the delicate thread between Wales and England. She'd not been privy to everything but she knew enough that most Welshmen were suspicious of the English, including most of the Marcher lords. But Rhys had never shown caution with her family, the duchess was the daughter of a Marcher lord and the duke was an English nobleman. Her family should have terrified Rhys, not embraced him.

"If I do as I'm bid, will the king release my family?" If Isla Belle couldn't save herself, at least she could help her family. Rhys' sacrifice wouldn't be in vain.

The captain's gaze settled behind Isla Belle. He squinted and uncurled to his full height. "Look."

She turned slowly and stared at the horizon, the direction of her home. Large clouds of thick, grey smoke rose to the sky. Her home, her childhood. Her lungs froze, her heart cracking. Within those stone walls she took her first steps. And fell in love. Rhys. Her family. Her life, her soul was being chipped away, bit by bit.

"Anyone caught defying the king will be stripped of land and title. That includes your healer. And you." He spoke with a low, hungry voice and placed a heavy hand on her shoulder. She was no longer protected by the rights and privilege of nobility. She gritted her teeth and willed herself not to wince or shudder.

He brushed the hair from off her neck and laughed at her grimace. The soldiers began to settle, nodding off one by one. Isla Belle would be surrounded by sleeping men and a greedy captain. The limping soldier was the last moving body. His task still undone, he hobbled around, collecting the bowls.

Isla Belle noticed the nearest soldier's black curly hair ruffle in the wind. Unblinking eyes stared back at her. The soldier next to him slumped over, his legs at an awkward angle. Suspicion came heavy and she stifled a gasp. The captain shifted behind her, she felt the distance grow between them as he moved. An odd mixture of relief and fear came over her.

The limping soldier piled the empty bowls, one on top of the other on the grass. He tossed his cap to the ground and pulled his faded, blood stained chemise over his head, exposing puckered skin and oozing lash marks across his back.

"Rhys." Isla Belle covered her mouth.

The captain spun around.

She braced herself on an oversized rock. Rhys faced them, his chin held high. His eyes in the shadows.

"Rhys?" Isla Belle hugged herself, her fingers digging into her side. Her mother's myths—no, she slammed her mind shut. Impossible. This was a trick. It couldn't be him.

Rhys held her gaze and slowly came closer, flinching at each footfall.

Milford scoffed and turned to her—with a twinge of fear in his eye —and kicked at the limp leg of a soldier. "Nightshade."

Rhys held his tongue, his skin turning ashen. He wasn't as healed as he appeared. Silently, he came closer still. A glint of metal showed in his hand. Isla feared the captain would notice.

"Ah, hemlock." Milford answered himself, his voice belying the confidence in his stance.

Isla Belle watched them both, her mouth dry. They were but two steps from each other, neither looking at his enemy, Milford's focus on his men, Rhys on her.

She retreated, unsure of her mind. Rhys wore the clothes of a tired soldier, world-worn. His eyes, his arms—he was *alive*—she winced, the sound of the whip slicing his skin still fresh.

"Rhys?" she repeated, more for herself than him.

"Yes, hemlock. I knew it." Milford spoke as if he was discussing the weather instead of poisons. He bent, one arm lifting the arm of a soldier, the other deftly pulling a brass gun from the dead man's belt. He smirked at Isla Belle, his hand hiding the weapon. "Do not fear, my—"

The captain froze. A knife in his chest, near his shoulder. He crumpled, the gun falling with a thud. Isla Belle scrambled to the top of the rock, Rhys' hand still extended from throwing the weapon. Blood spread across Milford's shoulder. The captain, wide eyed and mouth hung open in shock, looked down at the knife, disbelief carved in his face.

"Isla Belle."

A hand touched her. She jumped.

"Isla Belle." Rhys held up both his arms, his breathing heavy and uneven. "It's me, *fy annwyl.*"

"No." She recoiled, her gaze gathering in the sight. Milford's bleeding body. The limp soldiers surrounding them. Rhys's impossible recovery. "You were—were—were whipped. *Whipped.*"

Red and grey webbing crept up Milford's neck and down his arms, ending with purple marks on his hands.

"You poisoned the knife." Her voice was barely above a whisper. Rhys was a healer. He would not kill—she remembered his darkened eyes in the months leading to her escape. He'd changed once before. The thought twisted her stomach. Her Rhys, the one she loved since childhood, was kind, patient. He would not kill. This was a dream. This wasn't real.

Rhys hooked an arm around her waist and guided her off the rock, his grip firm but gentle. She moved to elbow him, his palm cradled the blow. He didn't grunt. He didn't curse. He kept walking, his arms steady. She twisted from his touch.

He pulled her back against his bare chest. "We need to leave."

She looked at each of the dozens of soldiers, including the captain

—ending with Rhys's pained face. The soldiers' bodies were splayed in awkward poses. "How? How are you alive? How did you find—"

She searched Rhys' face, the perfect mirroring of his body.

He fidgeted under her scrutiny and repeated, "We need to leave."

"I can't." Isla Belle's mind raced, not able to focus on Rhys or the men. Or her own fate.

Her body trembled, so unsure of what she saw. She'd watched the soldiers crumble and the captain die before her eyes. The fire on the horizon. Father. Mother. Brother. Everyone—Rhys.

Quick on his feet, Rhys pricked her finger and dropped the crude needle. "I'm sorry, Isla Belle. Hate me tomorrow. But I need you to be at peace."

"What did you do?"

"Shhhhh." He cradled her face, an apology in his tone. "They're only sleeping."

Her head began to spin. She shook her head and closed her eyes. "You should be dead. The whipping. The fevers from...from the..." She stamped her injured leg, hoping the pain would clear her head, keep her awake.

"Don't, Isla Belle. For once, submit."

She kicked again but found only air. Rhys swept her legs from under her and brought her against his chest. She placed a palm on the smooth skin.

"I thought you were..."

"I know." He cooed in her ear, his breathing strained from her weight. "Tomorrow, *fy annwyl.*"

ISLA BELLE THORNE

SACRAMENTO, CALIFORNIA: PRESENT DAY

Ty had left to get groceries. The alpaca file lay on the table in our living room. My knee ached but the room felt stifling. I hobbled to the window and braced myself against the glass. Slowly, I bent my knee, testing the pain and strength of the stitches. The wound felt tight but not overly painful. From my view, the roof of my mother's hospital was a straight shot but from street level, it was just over a mile. A long drive with traffic but an easy—and cold—walk.

Both Ty and Stephen had offered to drive me later but their care was kind—and stifling. Ty's trip to the grocery store gave me an hour, possibly two. It took fifteen minutes to find the stack of her plays I'd hauled from her apartment. I tucked the first one I saw in my jacket and carefully, slowly made my way downstairs.

Just as my knee started to throb something fierce, the hospital came into view. Each step felt worse and I wondered how I was going to make it home. Entering the building, I winced as I crammed into the elevator, worried about every little bump and nudge from the other passengers.

My pain melted away with one look at my mother. Her skin had turned to a sickening ash. Her face had lost fluid, flattening her eyes and ears. I stood like a stranger in her room, afraid and helpless. A nurse entered behind me, circling me and checking her vitals.

"Is she still being transferred?" I managed to say. The nurse hesitated and checked her watch. Stepping forward, I tried to hide the limp. "Please. She's my mother. Please tell me if she's gong to be transferred like this."

Her face softened, her hand lowering back to her side. "I honestly don't know."

"She doesn't look stable enough."

The nurse frowned, pity in her eyes. "I wish I knew."

Gripping the back of a nearby chair, I sighed. "I'm scared she won't make it."

The woman shifted uncomfortably. "I—"

"—can't tell me anything." This wasn't my first rodeo. Hospitals were sadly part of my childhood. And adulthood. "I know. I'm not trying to be difficult. I just…I just don't know what to do."

"I had a patient once." She hesitated, inching toward me. "And she looked like death warmed over—"

"Don't." I held up a hand. She was trying to be kind but my heart couldn't take it. My mother was rushing toward death like she once chased the spotlight. "Hearing about miracles won't help her. I know what death looks like." My years waiting in the emergency room had educated me more than I cared to admit.

"You might want to listen carefully." She emphasized each word. Clearing her throat, she patted Mom's foot under the blanket. "A patient of mine had come in. Drug overdose."

Dread snuck into the room, a draft of grief followed in its wake. Instead of fear, I felt frustration. I stood in the middle of the same hospital room day after day and I was no closer to helping my mother than when she was first wheeled through the door. Stephen had been promised by the EMT that Mom's stomach would be pumped before the medication could take effect but here she lay, her eyes blank and unfocused. My job was just as confusing. The entire Exchange was one secret after another. I sank into the chair and cradled my head in my hands.

"She coded in the ambulance on the way here. We knew who she was." The nurse came closer. "She's what we call a frequent flyer."

My head snapped up. "What does that mean?"

"It means we know the drill." She glanced at my mother and gave a subtle shake. "We don't know how or why they do this. We don't know how it starts. We only know how it ends."

I waited for the anger at how callous she spoke of my mother's impending death. None came. "She could still pull through."

"True." She smiled sadly and whispered, "How many times have you been here?" She put up a hand to stop my reply. "Not today or this week. How many times have you been in a hospital waiting for her?"

"Does it matter?" Placing a protective hand over my knee, I gingerly stood. My mother's play slipped from its snug position under my jacket, sliding across the hospital floor.

The nurse picked up the play. "Do you want her to pull through or do you want her healed?"

"It's the same thing." It wasn't but I wouldn't admit that yet.

She held out the play. "I don't know the particulars of your mother, but I do know what addiction looks like. And I know what mental illness looks like as well."

"That doesn't mean we brush her aside." I took my mother's play from her hands, not able to look her in the eye. "You don't give up on family." Stephen had taught me that.

"You're young." There was regret in her voice. "If you weren't here, what would you be doing?"

"Working." Or at least trying to. Work made me feel just as frustrated. Problems chased me like Ty pursued women.

"I'm a mother." She waited for me to look up. "I wouldn't want my daughter at my bedside."

"You wouldn't be here."

She nodded. "Not by choice."

"My mother didn't choose this," I lied. My mother might not have signed up for a hospital bed when she swallowed the pills but she did want my uncle's reaction. She wanted him to feel pain.

"Not directly." The nurse checked her watch. "But don't we all wind up where we truly want to be?"

A snort escaped. "No. We don't." There was nothing that made me want to be in the room. I hadn't wanted the Exchange job, at least not with Stephen's influence.

"You don't want to be here?" She touched my shoulder. "I don't think there's anywhere you'd rather be than at your mother's side."

I flinched at her words. They were cold. And true. "I didn't want to watch my mother die."

She let her hand fall. "That's the tricky part. We end up where *we* want to be but everyone else ends up where *they* want to be."

There—in the middle of downtown Sacramento—came the final blow. *Everyone else ends up where they want to be.* Mom could flip from tears to teasing in seconds. She could corral the waiter of our table to serve us free appetizers, charm rolling off her in waves. Mom would call in the middle of the night, her sobs loud and terrifying—only to be cheerful the next morning when Stephen drove me over to check on her.

Mom was where she always strived to be—the center of our lives. Stephen accused her of playing people like a chess game, manipulating everyone to her advantage. Ty had hinted as well. Every spare moment I had, brought me to her bedside.

The nurse watched me, her emotions flicking from pity, regret and back again. "You're worth more than a roller coaster."

"I can't abandon her."

"And you can't fix her either."

"Then what *exactly* am I supposed to do?" I flinched at my tone but didn't care. My mother's play was in my hand. That was the only thing I knew for certain. I had dreams of a stranger and hadn't slept in weeks. And now a nurse had come to give me the worst pep talk of the century. "She's an addict, I get it. I'm not blind. I'm not stupid. But I have nowhere to turn. She is going to be transferred. That's a death sentence. Look at her. She won't make it. She might not even make it staying here."

"I'm sorry—"

"I don't want *sorry*." Shaking the play in the air, my voice kept rising. "I want answers. I want something to hold onto. If I help her, I'm enabling. If I don't, she's hospitalized. I'm damned if I do and damned if I don't."

"If you were to do nothing. Absolutely nothing. What would change?"

Her words sent me back. I retreated until my calves hit the chair. No one had asked me that before. *What would change?* Everything. That's what I wanted to say. "Nothing."

She blinked and nodded her head.

I covered my mouth as if the gesture could take back the word. *Nothing.* Shaking my head, I grabbed the nurse. "That's not what I meant. Everything would change. I would be nothing without my mother." Stephen's face appeared in my mind. He was the one who'd taken me to get immunizations. He's the one who dropped me off at college and helped me fill out the paperwork. *Nothing.* That's what I would have become without Stephen.

With a great force, I pulled back and faced my mother's hollow features. For all her faults, that's who she still was, my mother. Limping to her side, I reached for her hand. "I'm sorry."

I heard the nurse slip out before I could apologize for my behavior —or thank her for taking the time. My mother's immediate future looked bleak but somehow, peace had crept in the room. The nurse had given terrible news, diagnosing her as a complete waste of time. She shattered the promise I hadn't realized I was keeping—that I would be here, waiting and helping—no matter what. If this was truly my mother's choice, direct or indirect, who was I to change her course?

My mind dizzied, unable to grasp what was happening. I felt both helpless and hopeful. The noose I'd felt around my neck loosened. Even if I could somehow convince Denton to transfer my mother— would Garuda even help her? If this is where she wanted to be, where did that leave me?

Climbing onto my mother's bed, I sat on the edge. The play in my hand had three acts. Scanning the first page, I paused. She'd written about a woman who lived for centuries, unable to die. She mourned the loss of her husband, the grief taking its toll on her mind. An hour later, I stared at the last page. There was no happy ending. It ended abruptly with the woman in a modern day hospital. She had tried— and failed—to get polio, HIV...a whole slew of fatal diseases. Instead, her body had created vaccines. The play was odd but not insane. It definitely wasn't worth the accolades she received but neither did it solicit concern about her mental state.

Remembering the nurse's words, I reached for my mother's hand. The plot was choppy and the overall play was a bit odd but it was charming in its own way. Possibly because the idea was very much my mother. The impossible was always alluring.

With a single tear down my face, I accepted that my mother's life was written by her. If this was her final scene, Dottie Thorne was the only one who could rewrite the ending.

ISLA BELLE THORNE

SACRAMENTO, CALIFORNIA: PRESENT DAY

I'd felt numb walking back to the suite and only gave one word answers to Ty when he'd come home with food. I wasn't devastated—that would have been a normal response—the idea of my mother dying should throw me off kilter. I should be on my knees, tears streaming down my face. And yet, like a spectator of my own life, I kept going, one foot in front of the other.

Ty went to shower for tonight's event. I'd debated going at all. There seemed to be little point. My mother was dying. But in the shower I went, as if nothing had happened. As if my mother was fine.

I plucked the last of the rollers from my hair and combed my fingers through the large waves. There wasn't enough concealer in the world to hide the dark circles under my eyes. The headaches kept coming and going, their rhythm circular but not at all predictable. If I could just sleep, the pain would go away. Maybe that's how my mother had felt. If she could just sleep a little or take another pill, the pain would go away.

The more intense headaches had started when the visions became more frequent. Tonight of all nights, my mind should be sharp. This would be my last chance to talk to Denton before he'd return to Garuda. And yet, I felt nothing. The compulsion to seek him or even

163

Rhys had disappeared. Maybe this was grief. Or maybe I was too exhausted to care.

Pinning the first few wavy strands of my hair, I glanced at my blue eyed, red lipped reflection. The reflection shifted, a woman with red wavy hair glanced back at me, her head tilted to the side. *Another vision.* I grasped the armrest of the chair, sucking down short breaths. My nails dug into the fabric. The woman needed to stay in the back of my mind. The thought of Ty barging in and watching me have an episode churned my stomach.

This wasn't how it was supposed to be. The headaches were increasing whether or not I had a vision. It wasn't lining up. Stephen might be right—this was more than simple headaches. Something could be wrong.

I forced myself to look away from the mirror. Stephen had already left a voicemail asking how I was doing. Ty swore up and down that Stephen didn't know about the fall at the Stanford mansion. But did he know Mom was inching toward death?

Twisting and tugging at the dress, another rush of frustration came. I'd lost weight since I bought my dress, a Southern portrait style designed to hug a woman's silhouette. I clenched my hands into tight fists. There had to be a way to regain control—of my mother's care, my headaches...of *something.* And then the feeling was gone. I was numb once more.

I glared at the mirror, daring the reflection to change. Nothing.

Giving one last look, I took off the necklace with the gold band from my mother's apartment. For being so small and simple, it provided a great deal of comfort; even if Ty said I fiddled with it too much.

I sent Ty a text that I'd meet him at the theatre. The event wasn't publicized, soliciting privacy over marketing. It was only three blocks and the sun hadn't set. I would be cold but not freezing. My knee felt better than when I'd walked to the hospital earlier. I'd catch a ride home with Ty afterward but the idea of being outside and alone tempted me.

Walking through security, I entered the 19th century theatre.

Flanked by guards on either side, an electronic safe stood on the center of a gilded table. The screen displayed a thermometer image, signifying the rising donations. I slipped past the waiting donors and climbed the stairs to the upper level. On the far side balcony, away from any familiar faces, I quietly found an empty seat.

As a kid, Mom had taken me to several daytime practices of local plays. One by one the orchestra would tune each instrument. The cacophony was as soothing then as it was now. An image pulled at my heart. Mom was running her hands along the tops of the seats. Even with Garuda's help, she wouldn't be entering a theatre anytime soon. Until Stephen had accused her of coercing critics, I'd thought Mom secretly resented me for killing her career. But the nurse painted a different story. Right here, alone with my thoughts, there was a bit of relief and I wasn't sure why.

The lights dimmed, and I shrugged out of my coat. Before I could save the seat next to me a couple took the last of the empty chairs. Earlier, Ty had come up with a plan. Whoever saw Denton first was to monopolize his time until the other could join. Between the two of us, we would find Denton and ask about my mother. My stomach twisted, no longer sure if we should be convincing Denton. I couldn't admit it to Ty yet. He hadn't seen my mother. To be fair, I didn't fully understand what I was feeling or what had transpired at the hospital. The only thing I knew for certain was my mother was dying.

Without a master of ceremonies, the curtain rose, revealing two empty seats on the stage. A raven-haired man in jeans walked in, holding a small banjo, immediately followed by a blonde man in a tuxedo carrying a violin. The banjo player plucked a few notes and walked toward his seat. Just as he was about to sit, the violinist ran the bow across his instrument and mimicked the same notes. The banjo player nearly missed his seat, much to the delight of the audience. Like a soothing breeze, joy caressed each audience member, gaining strength row by row.

The banjo player began again, this time with a longer rendition.

With a toss of his hair, the violinist smiled. My heart leapt.

"Rhys," I whispered. A spark lit inside me. Leaning in, I felt the fire spread.

Rhys matched the banjo player note for note. Four more times, they bantered back and forth. Rhys deftly stroked the violin into the cheerful fiddle song of cowboys. The banjo joined in mid-measure, and the audience clapped along. Faster and faster they dueled, each man furiously and happily dancing along with his instrument until they collapsed simultaneously with dramatic flair into their respective chairs to grateful applause.

While the men retreated to the shadows, a young girl in a white satin dress waltzed and spun to a silent dance in the center of the stage. With the help of a hidden orchestra, she sang *O Holy Night* in a polished, unexpectedly mature voice. She was followed by a blind woman, her cane thin and covered in twinkling crystals. She played a piano medley of David Lanz, Bach, and George Winston. The confidence she carried, the accuracy of her fingers. The audience—including me, watched in wonder.

Rhys entered the stage once more. He had visited me in my dreams, this fair boy named Rhys. The thought of his soft, golden hair and sky-blue eyes warmed my cheeks. *Soft hair?* I'd never touched it, but I knew it was smooth, fine. His laugh was airy and easily provoked—I had never heard him laugh. Nor had I ever touched him.

A small orchestra composed of several elementary-aged children appeared behind Rhys. With respectful silence, he began to play Partita for Violin Solo No. 2 in the appropriate D Minor.

My hands wrestled in my lap, tangling the silky folds of my dress. I had loved this song when my mother played it. She'd close her eyes and sway with the music. Even as a child, the emotions and the story resonated with me. It was a four-part tribute to Johann S. Bach's first wife and her death. Rhys played the low hum to the youngsters' accompaniment.

The loss of Bach's wife was tangible, held in every note, the pain etched in Rhys' face. I felt the unbreakable pull, the moth to the light, the lion to its prey, as I watched.

The mood of the music seemed to flow through his body, consuming him. Genuine.

I glanced around. Every man and woman sat frozen. They appeared engrossed in their own painful memory of loss.

I rose from my seat and kept to the shadows, inching along the balcony, closer to the side of the stage below. No one should feel this strongly about a stranger—at least no sane person. Unable to maintain my composure, I wrapped my arms around my waist and fled the auditorium.

With a hand on the rail, I ran down the stairs gripping the skirt of my dress. Someone called my name. Refusing to answer, I turned to another round of stairs, hoping it led to a back entrance. The light dimmed as I descended into the belly of the theatre. There was a feeling of comfort in the stairwell, urging me to keep going. My phone vibrated, pulling me back to my senses. With the back of my hand I wiped my wet cheek. Only an idiot would cry like this.

My phone vibrated again. Leaning against the rail, I pulled my phone from my bodice.

It was Ty. *Sitting next to Denton. Where are you going?*

Of course he'd found Denton. Ty was forever in the right place at the right time.

Another text. *Get. Over. Here.*

Looking around, I wondered where I was. The floor was cement. Ty didn't need to worry, not tonight. I texted back, *Bathroom.*

The lights were turned down as if I was behind or under the stage. The sound of a door opening startled me. I half expected Ty to appear but I kept quiet. Whoever it was would scurry to get whatever prop and then disappear again. A man sighed, the sound echoing to where I stood on the stairs. I felt a pull, the warmth of an impending embrace tugged at me. It didn't make sense—I stood frozen, unsure if I should give into the feeling or run up the stairs to my cousin.

The unmistakable sound of an instrument case opening pulled at my heart. Late at night, when my mother thought I was sleeping—when *she* should be sleeping—Mom would open her cello case and play. I'd wait for the sound and sneak to my bedroom door. Some melodies were sad, others were peaceful but with my back against the door, I'd feel as if all was right in the world.

And then she stopped.

Sinking to the cold, cement stairs, I wrapped my arms around my knees, the memory too strong to bare standing up. Stephen had come, threatening to take me from her if she didn't clean up her act. I'd hid under my bed and heard every word. I was only twelve but wished with all my heart I could make them stop arguing. I'd never loved and hated two people with such intensity at the same time. Stephen had left in a huff and my mother began drinking and playing. Her hand slipped and the bow slammed into the floor, breaking in two pieces. In the drunken rage, she kicked the cello. The evidence and instrument were gone the next morning—as was my mother. For the next few months, I would visit her on *Family Night* at the high-end rehab facility where she'd hob nob with celebrities eager for my mother to put their lives on the stage. At least, according to her. Like an idiot, I hung on her every word, devouring each lie.

Closing my eyes, I took a deep breath and stood on the stairs. A thought nagged me. Stephen had mentioned my mother's plays. What if everything my uncle had said was true?

"I'm not doing interviews no matter how sneaky you people are." The voice was familiar. And a man's.

Shocked, I opened my eyes. Rhys stood before me, his tuxedo jacket gone and the first few buttons on his white shirt undone. He motioned upstairs, indicating where I should go.

Gripping the rail, I stood. "I'm not a reporter."

He stepped closer, narrowing his eyes. I ducked my chin, wondering if he could see the changing color of my eyes in the darkened stairwell.

A door opened at the top of the stairs. "Isla Belle?" Ty called from above.

Rhys flinched. With wide eyes he retreated, his back against the wall. He shook his head and disappeared around the corner in the dark, taking my breath with him.

RHYS GLYNDWR

RIVER WYE, WALES: 1535

A breeze caressed the leaves, ruffling the stolen tunic on Rhys' raw back. The pain seared through him, setting Rhys' nerves on edge. The wind carried the sound of rope stretching. The borrowed horse neighed, fidgeting under the saddle and shying away from the line of trees. Rhys held the reins firm but the horse nervously backed away. Searching for the culprit, Rhys froze.

Twirling at the end of a rope, swung four dead men. Rhys tucked a sleeping Isla Belle tighter against his chest and pushed the horse to a gallop. They rode for hours, long past sunset and on into the night. The image of the hung men followed him, pounding in his head in rhythm with the horse's hooves. It's why he drugged Milford's small army instead of killing them despite the temptation. The temptation to kill was very real—even now. With his back ripped to shreds, he wondered if he'd made the correct choice. He shook the thought. He would not become like the captain or the king. This wasn't the country he'd hope to return to. He'd spent his life fighting death, not inviting it.

The moon sent unnatural shadows across the ground, the air thick with impending moisture. Rhys held his elbows at his side, arms straight ahead to keep Isla Belle centered. She fidgeted quietly. Soon she would be fully awake and question him. He had endured the whipping and he would again, but if Isla Belle rejected Wales, he didn't know what he'd do. He'd spent his life protecting her but if she knew the truth—if given the choice, would she choose him?

Isla Belle stiffened, signaling the fading grip of the tonic. The look she'd given Rhys, the accusation that he'd killed the men and captain. Rhys knew the shock of death. The unblinking stare of a person gone was rarely forgotten. Isla Belle had accompanied him to the village, but he had always sent her away when death was near. He would not kill, not in front of her. The thought made Rhys pause. Was Isla Belle's presence the only thing keeping him from killing; was he truly no better than the king—or the lords?

Shame filled him. All he ever wanted was Isla Belle. What had begun as a silent contract from the duke had grown to honest affection. Her sharp tongue and stubborn streak, the vices the duchess had failed to cure Isla Belle of were the very things he loved most. Isla Belle had been honest, her devotion pure while Rhys had given her nothing but secrets.

He didn't know what his future held. His country consisted of lordships independent of the crown. Each Marcher lord built his own castle, established his own laws. But Rhys' father had defied both Marcher and English law. He'd established himself as not only the savior of Wales but the country's one true heir, rendering Rhys a threat to King Henry at birth.

Rhys slowed the stolen horse to a walk. He listened to Isla Belle's breathing and felt—not for the first time—a surge of jealousy. Her body would accept the potions, unlike his. His pain could never be dulled; and he would never feel the ache of growing old. The duke had warned him, told him to guard his secret or Rhys' fate would mirror his parents, full of loss and heartache.

His back throbbed; his skin tore afresh yesterday when he lifted Isla Belle to the horse. The captain had placed rough, unworthy hands on her. His jaw clenched at the memory.

Her stomach grumbled, reminding him of his own hunger. Rhys sidled up to a fallen log, grateful for the cover of night and stared at the thick brush on the ground. He would feel the full force of his dismount. Rhys inhaled as he swung his leg over. He held his breath and dropped, keeping his hand on the horse to steady him.

Pushing his offered hand aside, Isla Belle slid down, landing beside him in silence. She didn't glance at him or meet his gaze. A part of him was relieved at not helping her; a part of him hurt because of her distance.

Rhys pulled the tie, releasing the medical bag and set it on an overturned log. He unfolded the stale bread and boiled eggs from a dirty linen cloth. It was enough food to cross the river but not a day more. They'd lost precious time with the whipping and her rescue.

Isla Belle, her face lit by the moon, stared at him, eyes swirling between shades of blue—fear to anger and back to fear. She didn't reach for him nor did she rebuke him. Her indifference was deafening. Isla stood between Rhys and the horse, the silence growing heavy. He broke their gaze, lying to himself that it didn't bother him.

"Eat." Rhys offered a chunk of the bread, his hands shaking from the pain creeping up his back and down his arm. He'd kept ripping his wounds open. He needed only a few days more of rest to allow his body to fully heal. Reprieve was a comfort he couldn't take. Not with a vengeful king on the throne. He needed to tend to his back or beg Isla Belle for help. Her blank expression squashed the thought.

"Isla, eat. Please."

She blinked and turned her head, cutting off his view of her torn heart and splintered mind. He'd watched it in others, the soul cracking under pain.

Her stomach growled. Isla Belle wrapped her arms around her middle, most likely to dim the sound. She took a tentative step forward, keeping the overturned log as a buffer. The scent of rain grew.

Thunder cracked, drowning his words. Rhys peered at the sky and thanked his fate. Rain would wash any trace of their escape. Blinking at the raindrops falling on his face, he slipped under the cover of trees lining the riverbank, closer to Isla Belle.

Her arms tightened around her. "What does it mean to be a Glyndwr?"

"If you're English, it's my family's name." Rhys raised an eyebrow. He'd expected questions about the men or even how he was still alive but not about his ancestry. Not yet. "If you're from my village, it's a shortened version of Glyndyfrdwy."

She scoffed, her hands dropping to her side. "What a revelation, Rhys. I hadn't gathered that on my own."

He smiled to himself. He'd sparked her ire and despite himself, he felt hope. "Is that all, then?"

"Do not lie to me." Her hands gripped her skirt. "Tell me what you're hiding. All of it."

He set the bread down on the log and kept his eyes on the rain falling to the grass. She was finally speaking. He should be relieved. "Will you eat first?"

She shook her head. "What title? What lands?"

"The Glyndwr—"

"If you even think of saying the Glyndwr lands, I swear to you, Rhys—"

"Will you let me finish?" Rhys let out a haggard breath. He'd raised his voice and the effort made him feel every inch of his injury. "Your family—your *mother's* ancestral lands border my own. The Glyndwr lands are directly east of your grandfather's."

Narrowing her eyes, she opened her mouth to speak but this time, Rhys cut her off.

"Your parents knew who I was." He looked to the west but felt no pull or kinship with his native country. His loyalty was to her, only her. "Or rather, *what* I am."

"And you are?"

"I am Rhys Glyndwr. My father was *Owain ab Gruffydd,* lord of Glyndyfrdwy." His voice remained steady but his mind recalled with vivid clarity the last moment he saw his father. His father had paid a dear price for his rebellion against the English. His mother too.

"Owen Glendower?" Isla Belle furrowed her brow. Rhys tried not to flinch at the slaughter of his father's name. The English pronunciation didn't sit well, even from Isla Belle. "Prince of Wales?"

"There is no Prince of Wales," Rhys added darkly. "Just as there are no true Marcher Lords."

She lifted her chin, a defiant gleam in her eye. "Tell that to my grandfather."

"He and Captain Milford are the new Marcher Lords. Men who've abandoned their country and given their allegiance to England."

Isla Belle's gaze dropped to the grass. "Or married their children to English noblemen."

"The Welsh want the same voice and freedoms as their English neighbors. Either united or separate, that's what my father fought for." Rhys was only a boy when he left, but he'd seen the desperation of his countrymen. England wasn't the only land torn apart by war. The memories were still fresh, to King Henry and to Britain. The king needed an heir—at any cost. "That is who I am, Isla Belle. I am *Rhys ap Owain* of Glyndyfrdwy. The title. The lands. And the myths."

"Rhys Glyndwr is easier."

"How very English of you." Rhys opened his medical bag, untying the ends. He risked a glance and saw half her face covered in shadows. The sky had darkened. He couldn't read her eyes, or her mood. He braced himself against the fallen trunk, a hand on either side of his bag and waited, knowing what was to come.

"Owen Glendower? The man who ruled Wales?" Isla Belle folded her arms. "He died in 1415."

"He did not."

"I am not a fool, Rhys." She mirrored him, her hands on the log. "I am not a man, but I have been taught. Your supposed father was born over a hundred years ago."

"The fall of 1359." He dug his fingers into the log, willing her to believe.

She stared at him, her blonde curls framing the challenge in her eyes. The duke had given her freedom, allowing her the luxury of speaking her mind. But her wit would not save her. The future had come, demanding her family and then herself. She'd been raised to wear a title and bear noble heirs, not deny a dangerous king or marry a rebel's son.

"The leader of the Welsh revolt. That is your father?" She fidgeted. "The revolt that happened a century ago? Tell me, Rhys. *This* is how you—"

"Yes," he snapped, instantly regretting his tone. "It is all true. The whole of it, Isla Belle."

Her eyes widened; she said nothing.

As a peace offering, he changed the subject and sat on the log. "The soldiers…the sleeping tonic bought us some time."

It had given half a day at most. Milford had sent a message to the king the day Rhys was whipped, the announcement of Lady Isla Belle's capture. It was the last conscious thought Rhys had remembered before succumbing to the pain. Milford wasn't dumb enough to return empty handed.

"Whether it's true or not, this…it's not over, is it?" Desperation filled her voice.

"Far from it." Rhys pulled out the thread and needle.

He focused on the task at hand. It kept him grounded, kept him firmly in *today*, away from the sorrow of *tomorrow* and *yesterday*. The soft pitter-patter of rain drops on leaves filled the air, the smell of fresh grass and clean surrounding them. Holding up the needle, Rhys waited for lightning to thread the string. He held the needle in one hand and pulled his shirt over his head with the other. Rhys wouldn't be able to reach most of the marks, but he would try lower cuts, anything to hurry the healing along.

Lightning lit the sky. Isla Belle gasped.

Rhys glanced back to find she was looking at him. At his back. She quickly turned her head, sorrow in her eyes.

"I'm sorry," she whispered. "I don't understand it all. Your father. The captain. You saved me and…I don't know what to say."

"I'm a stubborn man, Isla Belle. I didn't do anything I didn't want to." He leaned onto the trunk for support. The movement from taking off his shirt sent tremors of pain, his muscles twinging under the raw skin.

"Can I help?" She circled to face him, her palm extended. She swallowed hard as if summoning courage. "I can sew."

"You do not have to, *fy annwyl*."

"I'm a stubborn woman, Rhys. I won't do anything I don't want to." She smiled, her eyes crinkling. He warmed—realizing how much he missed his Isla Belle. "Turn around."

Rhys obediently sat on a nearby rock to give her a better angle with the moon's gentle light.

"No tonic?"

He shook his head once. "It won't take. Not for me."

"Your tonics never fail. I've seen you still a horse."

"If only I were a horse."

She placed a cool hand on his shoulder. "I can't promise I'll be gentle."

Rhys covered her hand with his and squeezed before letting go. She pierced his skin with the needle. He inhaled and squeezed. He felt her hesitate and begged, "The quicker you sew, the quicker you'll finish."

Her fingers shook on his shoulders as she tugged and pulled his skin. Rhys clenched his free hand, pumping it open and closed with each of her strokes.

"Midnight slumber close surround thee," she murmured his lullaby.

Rhys smiled despite the pain and cocked his head to the side. "All through the night."

"Angels watching, e'er around thee..." her voice wavered. She more spoke than sang. Music, in any form, was not her talent.

"All through the night. O'er thy spirit gently stealing." He'd sung while tending her—more times than he could count. "Visions of delight revealing, breathes a pure and holy feeling."

Her hair spilled over his shoulder as she wrapped a thin linen cloth around his torso, securing a balm to the wound. She paused, whispering, "You came for me."

"I had to."

"No." She tucked the needled into the extra linen, her hands trembling. "You didn't."

He gently pulled the bundle from her hand, replacing it with his, then looked up at her shadowed face. "I'd not leave you to them."

"Who are you, Rhys?" She stared at his hand. "Tell me. Not who your father is but who you are."

"Ask what you're wanting."

"I don't understand." Her eyes flitting about, everywhere but on his. "How are you alive? You should be dead. Or nearly."

"I should be, but I can't." Rhys waited, the understanding would come. "Death won't come for me. At least, not very easily."

"And why?" Isla Belle laughed nervously at herself, taking a step back.

"Like my father, I can't do a lot of things." He spoke slowly so she'd have to hear each word and understand precisely what was said. "I can't stop the pain with a tonic. Nor can I explain why."

She scanned his bare chest before looking away. His skin warmed under her attention. Rhys stood and took a slow step toward her. He should hand her the bread and keep his distance—he no longer had Wellesley's protection or Glyndwr lands. He shouldn't notice the way she reacted to him. He swallowed. He shouldn't do a lot of things.

She offered a half-smile. "You're a healer who can't heal his own body."

"Look at me, Isla Belle." He'd heard the whispers, the odd look of his face, the exactness of his features. It was the mark of immortality. "Do not pretend you don't know."

"Rhys, don't."

"I've not been truly sick. Not once. I can't get that close to death."

She bit her lip, her gaze on the ground. "But I saw you. The blood."

"Ay, I bleed. There's a way for me to die, but I don't know how." His arms dropped to his side. "It took centuries for my father to die—and even then, it took a dozen men. I don't know how any of it works. I just know I'm different. That my father was different."

"And my father knew?" She didn't look up.

"Yes." He cupped her shoulder.

Isla Belle closed her eyes. "What will happen to him? To my family?"

Rhys gingerly wrapped an arm around her shoulders, bringing her to his chest. "I'm sorry."

Isla Belle relaxed in his grip and lay her head against his chest. "Do not leave me."

"Isla Belle, I've never—"

"No more secrets" She pulled away, her eyes shadowed. "No more shutting me out."

The temptation to kiss her pumped through his veins. "Ay."

"Promise." She furrowed her brow, her gaze intense. "I have lost my family and my home. I will not lose you."

"Never, *fy annwyl.*"

ISLA BELLE THORNE

SACRAMENTO, CALIFORNIA: PRESENT DAY

*S*taring at the wall in the darkened stairwell of the theatre, I willed Rhys to reappear. Or maybe he hadn't been there at all. He'd disappeared when Ty had opened the door.

Descending the steps, Ty swatted my shoulder. "What are you doing?"

Without looking at him, I could lie. "Looking for Denton."

"What—why? I told you I'm sitting next to him." He turned me around. "What's going on?"

"I thought I saw Rhys." *Thought* being the operative word. I wasn't sure. Part of me believed it was true, the other part wanted to run. He'd left me. Rhys had heard my name and left. At least, I thought.

"Did you talk to him?" Even in the dim stairwell I could see, I could *feel* Ty's hope for my mother. I wanted to shrink from him. Ty hadn't seen my mother reading in the hospital. The nurse had not sat him down to drive the point home—my mother was exactly where she wanted to be. "What'd he say?"

A divide had erupted between Ty and me. I wanted to cling to my secrets a little longer. Tossing a look over my shoulder, I shrugged. "He freaked out when you called my name."

"Yeah, that's not weird." He frowned. "Did he say anything?"

"Did you not hear me? He disappeared."

"Perfect." Bending over, he offered his arm and with a dramatic flair only Ty could get away with, he said, "My lady."

"Not so fast."

He rolled his eyes and dropped his arm. "We'll use Staverton to get to Denton."

"I'm not telling Denton that I scared Rhys."

"Why do you call him Rhys?" Ty held out his arm, waiting for me to accompany him. "Everyone else calls him Staverton."

My cheeks warmed. "I...don't know."

"Please tell me you didn't say *Rhys* to his face." He shook his head. "The guy is kind of a big deal. You can't just call him Rhys."

"That's his name."

"Thomas is Denton's first name, but you won't see anyone calling him that."

"Says the guy who only calls his father Stephen. Not Dad. Not father—"

Ty poked my rib. "And you wonder why he ran away."

"He was scared of you, not me." It was a lie. The moment Ty said my name, Rhys had fled.

Ty poked me again. I yelped and swatted his hand away. We approached the main floor, both of us squinting in the bright lights. Following Ty, I met Denton standing in the aisle. Denton looked ready to leave, not at all eager to sit back down. I desperately wanted to turn around and find Rhys. It didn't make sense but every step away from the darkened stairwell felt sad, a weird type of grief.

"What's wrong?" Ty had caught the look.

"Nothing. Just tired."

Before he could say anything Denton stepped forward. "Miss Thorne?"

"Dr. Denton." I shook his offered hand.

"How are you feeling?" Denton motioned to my leg. The two men surrounding him retreated back a step. "You seem to be healing nicely."

I blinked—reminded of my injury at the Stanford mansion I'd

completely forgotten. That night felt like a lifetime ago. "I am, thank you."

Denton grinned. "Good, good."

With Ty next to me, I felt a little bolder. "I just saw Rh—Mr. Staverton. Although, I might have scared him."

Denton arched an eyebrow. "You spoke to him?"

Ty smirked and I fought the temptation to kick him. "No, not really. I was hoping to but he left. He seemed in a hurry."

Denton scratched his neck and waited a beat. "He is...yeah, he can be in a hurry sometimes. But you spoke to him?"

I risked a glance at Ty. He appeared just as confused as I was. "No. He wondered why I was there and then he was gone."

Nodding, Denton pursed his lips. "That's a shame."

"I was hoping to speak to him." My face went hot and I didn't miss the curiosity in Ty's eyes. "Or you."

Denton held out his arm. "Oh?"

Ty gave an encouraging nod. He wanted to help my mother but that had nothing to do with Rhys. My stomach twisted. That was something else entirely. My hand went to where the ring should have been dangling on a necklace. Apparently, I didn't need the ring to distract me. Only Rhys.

Ty raised his eyebrows, as if to say *keep going*.

"My mother, Dottie—Dorothea Thorne is a ward of the Samaritan Exchange." Denton's eyes widened. He'd not expected that. I pressed on. "Because she's a ward, I don't have a say in where she'll be transferred." Or if she should be transferred at all.

Denton's face softened. "And you'd like to become her guardian?"

With Ty's expectant face, I was compelled to ask—my own desire no longer here. "No. I mean, that would be nice but I was wondering if she could be transferred to Garuda instead of Stanford."

Denton's slack-mouthed expression killed the last of my resolve. The weight of my mother, her years of drug abuse and hysteria hung in his unspoken response. The three of us, Ty, Denton and myself stood in silence.

Gripping the top of the seat, I wished I could disappear, not just from the theatre but from this world. Ty and Stephen had each other and their health. I had visions and a mother who once danced along the border of crazy and insane—and now walked a thin line between life and death.

With a nod, I excused myself. "Thank you for your time, Dr. Denton."

Ty gave a slight shake of his head. He hadn't given up yet. But he was Tyler Cael; winning was in his DNA.

"Miss Thorne?" Denton's face had recovered, worry instead of disbelief lined his face. He looked every inch the man burdened with an international organization. I felt a tug of pity. My mother was just one of millions. The Samaritan Exchange worked tirelessly to better everyone's health. I'd come begging for a favor from an overdrawn well.

"I shouldn't have asked." It wasn't an apology and I wasn't sorry. Ty and Stephen were family but neither man was my parent. I never knew my father, that was the beauty of a fertility clinic. I hadn't been rejected by a dead-beat-dad, but if my mother never recovered, I was as good as an orphan.

No. That couldn't be a possibility.

"Never stop asking. Never stop advocating. For your mother or anyone else unable to speak for themselves." Denton smiled sadly.

Glancing at the floor, I half expected to be floating. I felt untethered, unattached to the people and world around me. The temptation to give in, to live only in that fictional world my mind imagined was growing more attractive. Maybe I was more like my mother than Stephen or Ty realized.

"Miss Thorne?" Denton asked, pulling me from my thoughts. The lights began to dim, signaling the end of the intermission. He motioned toward the doors. "Would you mind if we skipped the rest of the performance and step out to the lobby?"

"Really?" I glanced at Ty—I couldn't trust that we'd heard the same thing.

Ty cracked a dimpled smile and returned to his seat. I'd expected him to come, to be a part of the conversation. I waited, but Ty didn't turn around. I was on my own.

Joining Denton, I stepped in line up the aisle against the incoming flow of the audience, his two bodyguards flanking us. At the entrance, near the fundraising table stood two cameramen from opposing television channels.

"It seems plans have changed," Denton said with a sigh.

I should hesitate. He wanted to keep something hidden; what other reason would he avoid the news? I should turn around but the pull was back, the feeling of compulsion toward Rhys. The empty stairwell was just a few yards in front of me.

Without thinking, I blurted, "The basement was dark and abandoned."

"That sounds like the beginning of a bad movie." Denton arched an eyebrow, amusement tugging at his lips. There was something familiar about the way he cocked his head to the side. "I think *a dark and stormy night* sounds better, don't you?"

"I'd take a dark and stormy night over protestors any day." My joke fell flat, ending with a rush of awkward silence. Waiting a beat, I asked, "Too soon?"

With a twinkle in his eye, Denton said, "Anything to do with protestors is too soon."

Counting Denton's guards, I was about to descend into darkness with three strangers to search for Rhys, a man I dreamed about. Crazy most definitely ran in my family—maybe I needed to be in Garuda as well.

Denton's bodyguards entered first. With every step down, the pull became stronger. I followed the guards and Denton to a small alcove just off the stage, my eyes adjusting to the dim light. Music vibrated the ceiling above us. The walls were painted a dark green, almost black and two discarded sofas lined two of the walls. Denton sat on the nearest sofa, leaning back as if he'd done it a thousand times before. The guards searched the room and left with a silent nod.

"They're a lively bunch." Denton smiled at his own sarcasm. "Thank you for accommodating an old man, Miss Thorne."

There it was again, the familiar look. My mind and gut started arguing, one thought I should run, the other wanted me to stay.

"When is your mother to be transferred?" Denton crossed a leg over the other, his accent tugged at a memory. No, a vision. A memory would be impossible. I was not my mother.

"Soon." If she was transferred at all.

"You seem confused." He leaned forward. Even in the shadowy room, his eagerness was apparent.

"My mother's situation has never *not* been confusing." Shrugging, I debated on whether to sit.

"I wasn't talking about Dottie." Rubbing the bridge of his nose, he now appeared to be struggling with a decision. "I was talking about you."

"What about me?" The pull grew, but it didn't make sense. I'd only ever felt it when I'd had a vision of Rhys or saw him in person.

"Your mother might be, well, honestly, she might be beyond help."

I blanched, remembering the nurse's words. She believed my mother was exactly where she wanted to be. The way Denton spoke, he appeared to know more about Mom than even her attending nurse.

Denton held out his hands in surrender. "But you are not."

But you are not. Denton's words implied an eerie familiarity.

A chill swept up my spine. "How well do you know my mother?"

Fidgeting, he pulled at his collar. "More than she'd ever admit."

"That doesn't tell me much." My pulse quickened. The little he confessed made me leery of being in a dark room with his minions standing guard just outside the door. "How involved were you?"

I didn't say it but we both knew I was asking about the fertility clinic.

"Very." He wasn't looking at me. His shoulders slumped a little, aging him by decades. The silver in his hair seemed to grow. In fact, the more I looked, the more I realized he'd aged an incredible amount since his portrait hanging in the conference room. Had he looked like this at the Stanford mansion?

"Why did you say..." Grateful for the darkened room, I blinked. I touched my cheek, surprised by the threat of tears. Crying didn't make sense and it wasn't going to help anyone. "Why did you say my mother was beyond help?" *But I'm not.*

"She was offered help before." His voice came rough with bitter undertones. "And she refused."

"You sound like my uncle." Except Stephen would have forced the issue. She'd accuse him of conspiracy with colorful insults—but ultimately, she'd go.

"He's a good man…"

"But?"

Denton laughed, a sad and hollow sound. "He's a better man than I."

"He can't help himself." The chill left, replaced with the warmth of my family. "He feels this need to save her. To save us all."

"I know the feeling."

"Then why is he a better man than you?" *What else do you know* was on the tip of my tongue.

"Because he knows when to walk away."

"We are talking about the same man, as in, Stephen Cael? The geneticist?" My uncle didn't know the first thing about walking away. He should have left my mother to her own devices decades ago. I wasn't his daughter but somehow a scholarship or grant would suddenly appear when I needed it. He knew I wanted to earn my own way, but he never, not ever, walked away. "I'm fairly certain he doesn't know what that means."

"He does. And he has." Denton didn't meet my gaze. "And he's all the better for it."

"Who is?" A familiar voice barked.

My heart flipped in my chest. Rhys entered the room, his arms folded. A vision.

Denton waved his hand toward me. "We were talking about her uncle, Stephen Cael."

This wasn't a dream. A lump formed in my throat.

Rhys stepped closer, his brow furrowed. He blinked, his eyes adjusting. "Cael?"

184

"That's my uncle," I whispered.

"You?" His face lit with recognition. He must have remembered me from the stairs earlier.

An energy snapped alive in the space between us. Like an electric current, it crackled and hissed along my skin, both cooling and warming. The room seemed to melt away. The music vibrating from above muted to nothing. Rhys' face, once hard and accusing, softened. His lips stretched to a whisper of a smile. The gesture so small, felt like a caress.

A loud boom shook the room.

"Denton!" The guard's voice threw me back to reality.

Like a sucker punch, air rushed from my lungs, reality ripping the moment from me. The walls blurred. I waited for him to disappear.

Rhys came to me, a war waging in his eyes. He was torn but I didn't know why. Another boom from above. He hesitated. The guards shouted.

Rhys hooked an arm around my waist and pulled me forward. I stiffened—this was the same man who'd run from me just an hour earlier.

With his lips against my temple, he whispered, "Trust me, *fy annwyl.*"

RHYS GLYNDWR

RIVER WYE, WALES: 1535

For three days, Rhys and Isla Belle traveled by night, the howling of the wolves guiding them forward. When the wolves quieted, Rhys would hide Isla Belle and the horse until the howls began again. The once frightening sound had become a comfort, warning them against other predators—the army just one of many lurking along River Wye's woodlands.

Rhys didn't know who was carrying out the hangings. The Marcher Lords were tasked with judging capital crimes but hanging was traditionally an English punishment, ushered in by the king's mandate for Welsh councils. Rhys felt more like a foreigner than a native with each passing mile.

As they rode, the knot came loose on their shared blanket, the edges slipping from his shoulders. His back was nearly healed but Isla Belle's subdued demeanor had brought another injury. His body could heal unnaturally fast but his soul was a different matter. For most of her life, Isla Belle had never kept her thoughts inside. She'd speak or act without thinking, her eyes betraying her emotions as well. She'd lost her family, future, and all that was familiar. Rhys had hoped he'd be enough to soothe her.

He reached around Isla Belle and tightened the knot. She slipped her hand under his, bringing his arms closer around her. Her words, *I will not lose you,* echoed in Rhys' mind.

He was the Glyndwr heir by birth, but his absence wouldn't be looked on kindly, not by the suspicious lords. If he wasn't accepted, he might not live long enough to keep his promise to Isla Belle—if his body would allow him to die.

If Rhys *was* accepted as the Welsh heir, England would come calling for a pledge of loyalty. Neither would come easy. King Henry hadn't looked twice at Rhys when he had accompanied the duke. But would the king recognize Rhys as the healer now that Owain's son returned?

In a few hours' time, Rhys would know his fate. He'd fled to England for protection from the surrounding Marcher Lords. They feared his father's growing restlessness. Owain had wanted a Welshman as King of Britain, not a cowed man pretending to be English. The Marcher Lords wanted peace, not the fairy tale of King Arthur—the legend that a Welshman would rule Britain. The idea had warmed Rhys' father on fireless nights and cooled his temper during his bloody campaign. Rhys hadn't cared for Britain's legacy or who was English or Welsh. He'd wanted a home, a family.

"The wolves are growing quiet." Isla Belle nestled against Rhys' neck.

"They won't leave the river. Not on this side." Several new cottages dotted the path. There were barely enough for a hamlet, too few for a proper village. It'd been a dozen years since he'd been this far west. Sneaking back to his home would be more difficult with the growth. To these people, he was nothing but a stranger.

"Rhys?" She sat up, more than likely noticing the stretch of homes. "What happens now?"

"I take you to my home."

"That's not what I meant." She tucked her head and dropped her hand from his arm. "You'll receive your lands. Your inheritance. But my family defied the king. What happens to me?"

"I defied the king as well."

Isla Belle leaned forward and pulled back on the reins, slowing the horse to a stop. "Then why go back?"

"Wales wants to be a partner, not a slave to England." Rhys had hoped to make it to the east gate of his property before first light. Urging his gelding forward, he slid the reins from her hand. "You're the daughter of an English duke and the granddaughter of a Welsh lord. If anyone can elevate their cause, it's you."

"Captain Milford said my father was stripped of land and title."

"King Henry could strip your father of the title but he can't pull your grandfather's border lands. Or Marcher lordship. He might be the King of England but his father was Welsh. The king can't take a Welshman's land or title without causing another rebellion."

"But the captain said you'd lose yours as well."

Rhys shrugged, his back tight with freshly healed skin. "Milford is a traitor to his country." The captain would bear the mark of Rhys' poison. Rhys had hoped it'd be a warning against retaliating.

"You left your country as a boy."

Isla Belle was right, but Rhys wouldn't give in. He'd left Wales to save his neck and only returned to save hers. The days of little food and even less sleep wrapped around his shoulders, pulling his spirit low. With pinched faces men and women stopped, buckets and tools in their hands and suspicion in their eyes.

"I don't know what lies ahead, *fy annwyl*," Rhys said, his lips against her temple.

"If you leave me, I swear I will hunt you down."

He grinned, feeling a burst of hope. This was his Isla Belle, her wit and fire always at the ready. The men and women seemed to collectively narrow their gaze. He nodded in greeting, but they kept their gaze steady.

Isla Belle *tsked*. "Do they think we've come to pillage?"

"I'd keep your voice down. They'll hear England." His own accent had slipped over the years. Rhys wondered if he'd still pass for a native.

She tossed a conspiratorial grin at him. "And they'll hear your confusion."

"Woman—"

Rolling her eyes, Isla Belle mimicked his sing-song accent. "You'll be the death of me."

"Don't test me." Rhys pinched her arm—she squirmed—he tightened his grip.

Giggling, she wrapped her arms over his. "I'm fine, Rhys."

"Your history says different." His voice caught. "You break over nothing."

She shifted, turning to face him. "Are you alright?"

He could only nod. The simple question had awakened the fear in him. He'd spent every moment over the past few months worried over Isla Belle and her family. He'd thought of little else, including his own fate. The nearer he came to his homeland, the closer his heart pushed to the surface.

She brushed his hair off his face. Rhys shouldn't warm under her touch. He should focus on hanged men and Milford.

"It'll work out. I don't know how. But it will." The eagerness in Isla Belle's voice squeezed Rhys' chest.

Her hopefulness underlined the severity of the situation. If Rhys wasn't accepted...he forced himself to stop. Worrying wouldn't change a thing.

"Rhys?"

"I know. It'll work out."

"No." Isla Belle's eyes flickered to near black; the color of fear. "Look."

Halting the gelding, he turned to several neighbors standing together at the town's border. Arms folded, they made their position clear. They didn't trust the strangers. If an English army came looking, Rhys and Isla Belle would be handed over.

Urging the tired horse forward, they covered the last few miles to Hereford. For most of Rhys' life, he'd felt Wales was half a world away from Wellesley but now, with the edge of the castle on the horizon, home felt too close to England.

One last bend of the river and Glyndwr Castle stood before them, perched on the motte Rhys' ancestors built, the Black Mountains a striking background. The keep was five levels tall, the stone white and the brick gatehouse guarding the castle's entrance washed orange and red with the rising sun. Rhys' father had begun remodeling with modern red brick. The clay was cheaper than stone but required more labor. Building the castle had brought the county together but earned the ire of neighboring lords. Workers came from several counties, staying long after the castle was done. As a moment of temporary truce with his neighbors, Owain shifted to stone for the large keep standing watch. For most of his unnaturally long life, Rhys' father had never stopped fortifying Glyndwr Castle.

The town surrounding the castle had grown past the old wooden fencepost and the stamped road Rhys' father had insisted on building. Owain believed if the road and castle were impenetrable, his family and country would live forever. That, and the legend of King Arthur would finally take hold.

"*This* is your home?" The wonder in Isla Belle's voice settled Rhys' nerves.

"Ay."

"Ay?" Isla Belle giggled. "That is all you have to say?"

The smell of fresh bread danced in the early morning air. Rhys allowed himself to take a deep breath of his home, the sweet grass and hawkweed. Home. Rhys was home.

Waving him onward was the Glyndwr flag flapping on the gatehouse towers, the four red and gold dragons in a square. Rhys dismounted and helped Isla Belle do the same. He didn't dare look any of the townspeople in the eye. Not yet. He needed to visit his steward and see for himself that his letters were received—and obeyed.

With sapphire eyes of eager curiosity, Isla Belle watched his home. She'd lost her family and was catapulted to another world. Rhys glanced heavenward, wondering if the fates would give them reprieve.

"*Cymru am byth,*" Rhys murmured with a shake of his head.

Beside him, Isla Belle cast a long look at Rhys. "Long live Wales?"

"Something like that." Rhys' father had repeated the phrase at the beginning and end of every council meeting. Men of rank and power had filled the great hall nestled in the belly of Glyndwr's walls.

"So it's done then?" She hugged herself but kept walking. "England never happened. You're Welsh and nothing else."

"Those were the first words your mother said to me." And the last.

ISLA BELLE THORNE

SACRAMENTO, CALIFORNIA: PRESENT DAY

*D*enton's guards burst into the darkened basement of the theatre, shouting at both Denton and Rhys. Time stopped. The room seemed to shrink. Fireworks went off. The smell of sulphur wafted downstairs.

Three more guards ran into the room, forming a wall around Denton, Rhys and me. Rhys tucked me against him, his touch like a burn on my skin. And then the smell of fresh paint. This wasn't real. It was a vision like so many before. I would wake with a pounding head and an ache in my chest.

We reached the stairwell. Another round of fireworks. The sound echoed in my head. I covered my ears. Through a crack in the human wall, I saw the silhouette of a gunman. He turned to face us, the gun aimed at us.

Pieces fell together. The fireworks were bullets. This wasn't a dream. Ty was on the main floor.

Two more men joined the first. One held a can of spray paint, the other pointed a gun at us. In a blur, the guards shoved us out the side door. Pushing against Rhys, I reached for the door. Arms pulled me back.

"Ty!" I screamed, my nails scraping the metal door. A loud bang shook the walls of the building, the door trembling under my hands. Pounding the metal, I shouted, "Ty! Ty!"

"What do you have in the car?" Rhys yelled at Denton and wrapped his arms around me, his scent causing me to pause. "Chlordiazepoxide?"

I froze. *Chlordiazepoxide.* My mother had been given that drug. If I struggled, Denton would inject me. I'd be of no use to Ty. Reality sank in. Rhys was a stranger, not someone I should trust.

"Please..." my voice caught. "My cousin. Please."

Rhys' arms relaxed. He turned me toward a waiting car, the door open with an anxious guard. "We have to leave."

"I'm not leaving without Ty."

Rhys and the guard exchanged a look—the same one Ty and Stephen had exchanged just a day before. They thought I was losing control.

"Look at me." I held out my arms. "My voice is steady. My sentences are complete. I am in complete control of my faculties." Pointing a shaking hand to the theatre, I took a step back. "My cousin is in that building. I am not, I am not leaving without him."

Rhys held out his arms—like he'd done a million times before in my mind—and with the same soft murmur I'd heard in my dreams, he said, "I'll go in. Get in the car, and I'll go in."

"You'll find him?"

"I'll find him." He seemed closer.

Alarm rang in my ears. How'd he come so close without moving? He had an arm around my waist. Doubt rose in my throat. With a soft push, I was in the car. Rhys behind me. He'd lied. The door shut. Panic shot me in the chest. Betrayal. They'd lied.

I scrambled over Rhys, my hand on the door. My sleeve was pushed up. The prick of a needle, the burn of medication. And then nothing.

Blinking, I saw the familiar ceiling tiles of a hospital room. *Hospital room?* Panic set in. In a rush, I remembered the theatre. The gunman.

"Ty..." My throat was dry. I'd failed him and felt the shame. I should have gone back inside.

"He's here, Isla Belle." Stephen's voice was faraway. I struggled to sit up. "Wait, Isla. Let them help you."

My breath came shallow. He'd used the same tone of voice with my mother. Tears pricked my eyes. I blinked them back. Crying wouldn't help me. I'd watched my mother struggle and argue with nurses. With Stephen. The more she tried, the less they'd believe her. Fear pumped in my veins. My heart raced.

"Her blood pressure is skyrocketing," a voice said above my head.

"Isla…" Stephen cooed, a hand on my shoulder. The bed groaned, my torso was raised to a sitting position. Worry lined Stephen's face, his tired eyes red with lack of sleep. "I need you to breathe with me."

"Where's Ty?"

Squeezing my shoulder, he hesitated. "He's here."

"In the hospital?"

Looking over my head—I assumed to a nurse—he nodded. "There was…an incident."

"Don't lie to me." There was a gunman. I remembered a vague smell of paint. That's more than a mere *incident*.

"She needs to rest." The woman sounded frustrated.

"I'm fine." It wasn't a lie. For the first time in months, I didn't have a headache. I had no doubt they'd loaded me with enough meds to level a tank. It was standard protocol for panic attacks. I'd watched it a dozen times before. My mother would go from hysterical to zombie in mere minutes. And here I was. There was no turning back. I'd been hospitalized like her. For the rest of my life, I'd be labeled crazy. Tranquilizers would be the first line of defense. Forever.

"I'm fine." My voice shook.

"You are still being evaluated." Stephen pulled a chair close, the sound of the legs scraping the floor made me flinch. I hadn't remembered a fire or any smoke. Stephen cleared his throat. "Denton wants you monitored for twenty-four hours."

"Of course, he does." It shouldn't have come out bitter. But the betrayal was deep. I'd believed Rhys. He promised he'd go in for Ty. He'd lied. Denton was the only doctor in the car. He'd given the shot. I hated them both. And now Stephen; he'd either bought the lie of smoke or was eager to sell the con. He'd done the same with Mom. He'd promise her the world, offering mountains of diamonds and sold out theaters.

"Isla?" Stephen narrowed his gaze. "What is going on?"

"Am I going to be transferred to Stanford as well?" Each word drenched in anger. "Am I a ward now too?"

Stephen sat up, an eyebrow arched. "What are you talking about?"

I glanced at the nurse. She fiddled with the machine above my head, but I knew she'd heard every word.

"Isla?" Stephen covered my hand in his. "You've had a traumatic—"

"Don't." Recoiling, I ripped my hand away, tucking it under the blanket. "I know how this works."

His eyes lit with recognition. My heart sank. Everything was now on the table. He smiled—making me pause. "You think you're here... because of your mom?"

"Not because of her." I wasn't that dumb. I was here because I had a meltdown in front of Denton. And it wasn't the first time. He was there when I fell from a vision at the Stanford mansion. Two strikes— not to mention Denton was well aware of who my mother was. He'd already admitted that she was beyond help.

Stephen reached for my folded hands. "You are not your mother."

"So you've said." But we weren't that different.

"You are one of a hundred people being evaluated at the hospital." He waited, continuing after I met his gaze. "Denton said you witnessed a possible gunman."

A sliver of comfort came—Denton trusted me as a possible witness. People didn't want an insane witness, I couldn't be crazy. "Just his profile."

"But you witnessed something." Stephen's face relaxed. "Denton wants to make sure you are healthy enough to testify should the need arise."

"Testify? I barely saw the guy."

A flicker of color pulled at my periphery. A muted television on the wall with an image of the theater front and center. Stephen pulled the remote from the side table. Placing a hand on his, I shook my head. A short black and white video appeared—the security camera from the side exit of the theatre. The quality was poor, the picture grainy. I glanced at Stephen but his focus was on me, not the news. The clip showed two guards ushering Denton to a waiting car, and then a struggle of arms. I swallowed hard, waiting for me to appear on the green. The video cut to another clip, this one showing me banging against the door. With a click of the remote, Stephen turned off the t.v.

"You are not crazy, Isla Belle." He lay the remote back on the table. "No one would ever think that."

The security footage proved I was at the theatre but not Rhys. Only me. Stephen hadn't mentioned him either. An eerie chill swept up my neck. I'd had a vision in front of Denton—it was the only explanation. Stephen didn't need to know, he would never look at me the same. I could only nod, my vision blurring. "Denton gave me a shot."

Stephen nodded. "He said you wouldn't leave without Ty."

"Where is he?" I should have been with Ty. Not in the basement with Denton. Or Rhys. Ty would never have left me. He was devoted. Kind.

"He's in surgery—"

"No!" I cried. *Not Ty.*

"For a broken arm."

"She needs rest," the nurse warned.

Stephen shook his head at her. "She's fine."

A broken arm was a far cry from the bullet wound I'd imagined. "Broken arm?"

"I'm sure he'll be bragging about the metal in his arm soon enough." Stephen gave a lopsided grin. "Prepare yourself for an avalanche of stupid Superman jokes."

"Superman?"

"Before surgery he told the doctor he couldn't wait to be," Stephen made air quotes, "a man of steel."

Peace warmed me. "That sounds like Ty."

"He's okay, Isla Belle."

"They wouldn't let me find him." It came out like a pout, but I didn't care.

"You couldn't have done anything if you had."

"If something would have—"

"Isla Belle." Stephen's voice caught. "Don't you ever blame yourself for what you can't control. Ty is a grown man who makes his own choices. You cannot blame yourself for anything he does or does not do. Just like you cannot—you *will not* blame yourself for what your mother does."

"A little pot kettle-ly, don't you think?"

Stephen furrowed his brow, clearly confused.

"Pot calling the kettle black."

He smirked—and just like that, all was right in the world. "Touché, Isla Belle. Touché."

Shrugging, I said, "I'll be here all week."

"Nope. Just until four this afternoon." With that, Stephen gave me a nod. "I'm going to check on Ty. I'll be back."

"He's been back and forth for hours." The nurse pulled out a flashlight and checked my eyes. "Sorry, I needed to wait for him to leave before I could do the rest of the checklist."

"Check for what?"

"Your doctor wanted a verbal concussion check when you were awake. All reports and workups will be sent over as soon as I'm done." She tapped on the keyboard to her right. "Any feelings of nausea?"

"No." Aside from my recent appointments, Stephen had been to nearly every one since I was little. It felt odd not having him there for this one. "Why couldn't you do anything when he was here?"

"HIPPA guidelines." The nurse kept typing.

"But this was an emergency."

She pursed her lips. "On a scale from one to ten, how is your pain?"

"Zero."

She clicked away on the keyboard. "And feelings of panic?"

"Why?" I tried for a neutral tone—and failed.

She shot me a quizzical look over her shoulder. "There's a note to check for signs of stress or trauma. It's routine procedure for disaster victims."

"What happened? Do you know?"

The nurse paled, realizing her mistake. "Whenever there's an earthquake or a flood, or a bomb."

"There was a bomb?"

"Sorry." She shook her head and bit her lip. "The investigation is ongoing. No one is quite sure what happened." She offered a weak smile. "You should rest."

"I'm fine."

"Yes, you are." Pity filled her eyes.

She viewed me as just another confused victim. But I hadn't seen anything, other than the silhouettes of the gunmen. Whether they were criminals or guards, I didn't know. The only thing I knew for sure was last night was not a dream. The smell of the bullets, the feel of Rhys' hand on my back. My face flushed at the memory. His protective arm around my waist had felt natural. And familiar.

RHYS GLYNDWR

HEREFORDSHIRE, WALES: 1535

*F*our groomsmen stood in front of the gatehouse, three of them leaning against the wall with folded arms, their focus on Rhys and Isla Belle.

"*Beth ydych chi eisiau?*" The larger of the three jutted his chin, revealing scars down his neck. Either from wolf or from battle, they gave him a powerful aura. He stepped forward, repeating, "*Beth ydych chi eisiau?*"

It took a moment for Rhys to translate the thick Welsh accent. *What do you want* finally rang in his head. He'd have to become quicker to prove his ancestry. For years, he'd continued his native tongue in the privacy of the duchess' quarters but her words came choppy. Slowly, Rhys' time in England had stripped bits of Welsh from his mind, replacing the words in English.

"I've come to see the steward." Rhys held onto the vowels, soaking each English word with the sing-song accent of his childhood.

"*Saesneg?*" The guard elbowed his neighbor. "He's an Englishman."

"Or Welsh. I've been accused of both." Rhys shrugged, hoping he'd come across unaffected. "Either way, I've come to see my steward."

The guard's eyes widened at *my*. Rhys held his breath. The guard could imprison him before letting Rhys inside. The man grunted, looking both Rhys and Isla Belle over before giving a nod to his fellow guard. The smaller man disappeared without a word.

Rhys kept his breathing steady. Before his father was captured, guests were welcomed inside before interviews were done. The guard grunted again, unaware of former customs. The homecoming of Owain's son and heir could be bloody or welcoming. Isla Belle fidgeted next to him. He needed to hurry before she spoke her mind with her English tongue.

The guard rubbed his jaw and began circling them. Isla Belle's eye color flickered. She'd be labeled a witch if she wasn't careful. Only men were able to be peculiar.

"I'd not get too close to the horse." Rhys warned, although he doubted the animal had enough energy to kick.

The guard scoffed but turned back to face Rhys and Isla Belle. "*Argylwyddes?*"

A lady? Rhys pictured the duchess and her regal posture. She could silence warriors with one withering look. Isla Belle was no different. He straightened his back and arched an eyebrow. "Yes. She's a lady."

"*Merch dug.*" *Daughter of a duke.* Isla Belle gave the guard an icy stare. Her pronunciation was horrid but the words were correct.

Rhys reached for her. The woman didn't know when to stop her mouth.

The guard threw back his head and laughed, a hand slapping his thigh. "*Mam y ddreigion.*"

Rhys cracked a smile. *Mother of dragons.* He wrapped an arm around a fuming Isla Belle. She probably didn't understand the idiom but knew the teasing tone. "It's not a bad thing, *fy annwyl.*"

"According to who?" Her fist was still clenched at her side, but her face had softened at the endearment. She eyed Rhys before asking, "What does it mean?"

"Mother of dragons." He held her firm when she started toward the guard—igniting another round of laughter from the man. "You're proving his point."

Isla Belle glared at both of them. Rhys held up his hands in surrender.

"Poor dab." Chuckling, the guard came to Rhys' side and clapped him on the back. "Come inside before she strikes you down where you stand."

Isla Belle spun toward the guard, fire in her eyes. Rhys gave a subtle shake of the head. She narrowed her eyes but said nothing. Following the guard, they handed the tired horse to a groomsmen and walked through the overhanging arch. Rhys glanced up through the kill holes used during a siege. Memories begged to come alive; he shut them down and forced himself to look forward, his life depended on it. As did Isla Belle's.

She fell silent, her gaze taking in the enormity of the castle. The walls were thicker than the length of a horse. Owain had wanted the castle to stand long after he was buried; even though Owain believed he'd never die. A pang of grief pierced Rhys. He'd never cried over his family or his fate. He'd plowed ahead, arriving at Wellesley with parchment in his bag, the last order from his father. The duchess knew before reading what had happened. She was Welsh to her core.

Past the wall, the courtyard was busy with horses, vendors and servants. The village outside had tripled in size but internal workings of the castle seemed to have stayed the same. Rhys glanced back at the gatehouse tower half-expecting his father to appear in a window. Owain claimed the top left tower as his own quarters while Rhys's mother was kept in the keep, the square the size of a mountain in the center of the courtyard. Should the castle fall, she would be protected. That was Owain's first mistake.

Rhys pulled Isla Belle to his side, his hand reaching for hers. She would never live in the separate tower. They would be together, in death and in life. He would not repeat history.

Just before the keep, a man toggled toward them, a cane bearing the brunt of his small frame. The grey beard covered most of his face but Rhys knew him in an instant. *Mathias.*

The guard jabbed a thumb over his shoulder to Rhys and Isla Belle, nodding a greeting to Mathias.

"Thank you, Tobias." A smile broke out on the steward's face, changing the landscape from pained to joy. Shaking his head, he said, *"Beth wnaeth I ti ddod? Mae eisiau berwi dy ben."*

Isla Belle turned to Rhys, the question in her eyes. He smiled and said, "It's an old saying."

"You should probably keep me in the dark then." The narrowing of her eyes suggested otherwise.

"I'm only teasing." Rhys held her close. "It means *what made you come? You need your head boiled.*"

She wrinkled her nose. "You're right. It doesn't make sense."

Tobias rolled his eyes. "I'll give my head for breaking."

Rhys bit back a laugh. He was home.

"Don't even try to explain that one." Isla Belle held up her hand. "Even in English you sound mad."

The weight on Rhys' shoulders lifted. He stood on native soil with Isla Belle in his arms. All was well.

"It means *they should be married*, my dear." The steward's eyes twinkled. His English held barely a trace of a Welsh accent, not a tapping of an *r* or stringing out of a vowel.

"Oh." Isla Belle's face washed pink, then red. The longer the silence stretched, the deeper her blush.

Rhys dropped his arm around her and embraced his old friend. Other than the beard, the man hadn't changed. He'd struggled with his leg since Owain's last campaign. Loyal to the end, Mathias never abandoned his station. Shame tugged at Rhys' heart. He'd doubted the old man over the past week, wondering who was trustworthy in the mercurial nation.

"Come." Mathias retreated, motioning toward the keep. To the guard, he said with a firm voice, "Sound the banns, we've a feast to celebrate. The duke is home."

"Duke?" Isla Belle whispered behind him. Rhys had been careful, divulging only the necessary details. But the betrayal in her voice pierced him.

Rhys joined her side, an apology in his throat. Without a word, they followed Mathias to the holy rooms in the back of the chapel.

The library, the desk—nothing had changed in the years since Rhys had left.

Emotions came alive in the darkened room. This room held the last memory of Owain as the Prince of Wales. Here Rhys' father had read the king's edict, demoting *Owain ap Gruffydd* to Owain Glendower, a mere English duke, punishment for rebellion. The arms and flag displayed behind the desk were in Welsh, instead of English. The inscription in the mantle was *Owain ap Gruffydd* of Glyndyfrwy instead of Owen Glendower. At Rhys' birth, the English king bestowed the title of Earl and heir of the duchy to Rhys. The supposed generosity had chafed Owain; he'd refused to acknowledge the title. He'd insisted the neighboring lords call Rhys *Etifedd Cymraeg*, the Welsh Heir.

Mathias pulled the chair at the head of the oversized desk and dipped his head. Rhys swallowed the rising emotion, unsure if it was guilt, grief or fear. Once he sat, Mathias pulled the chair to his right for Isla Belle. She'd kept her chin down, guarding her emotions from both Rhys and the steward. Under the table, Rhys reached for her, covering her hand. She didn't look at him nor did she turn her palm to welcome his touch.

Fanning the documents on the table in front of Rhys, Mathias pulled a small wooden box from his coat, his gaze flicking to Isla Belle. A wheezing cough escaped as he sat. "The council meets in three days' time. We'll need to be ready. And precise."

Isla Belle fidgeted, her hand slipping from under Rhys's. He looked at her, wishing she'd return his gaze. Without the color of her eyes, he couldn't gauge her mind.

When she didn't look, Rhys turned to Mathias. "Do you have the betrothal contract?"

Isla Belle's head snapped up. Her eyes flashed; anger and fear swirled. He reached for her; she recoiled.

"Here." Mathias cleared his throat, his index finger pushing it toward Isla Belle.

Rhys was grateful. The words would be better read than heard.

"Just tell me what it says." Blinking furiously, she shoved the paper from her. "Milford said you were using me to pay a debt."

Before Rhys could answer, Mathias extended a handkerchief. "No, milady. There is no debt. Only a betrothal."

She took it, her tremulous smile sad. The expression tugged at Rhys' heart. She'd lost her family, her home—and now would learn her fate.

"I'll not force you, *fy annwyl*." He willed her to look at him. She gave a subtle shake of her head.

Mathias tapped the date on the corner of the document. "I know your journey has been hard but this was made before Rhys had left for England."

Isla Belle's gaze flicked from Mathias to Rhys. Then back again. She pulled the parchment back. "Why was I not told?"

"Your father was concerned about your safety." Mathias leaned over the table, his voice soft and consoling. "Owain had led two rebellions when this contract was signed. Fate could go either way. He could regain his throne or be hanged for treason."

"How long have you known?" She spoke to the table, not looking either man in the eye.

"Since I was a boy." Rhys felt Isla Belle retreat into herself.

She nodded. "I see."

Mathias held out a hand. "Both Glyndwr and Wellesley were to combine houses. Only when you were born did they know how."

"And if I were a man?" She sounded eerily similar to her father.

"Then you would be wed to Glyndwr's daughter, had she lived past infancy," Matthias said calmly.

Isla Belle folded her hands in her lap. "That is why you came to Wellesley?"

"England was safer than Wales." Rhys pushed back his chair and kneeled at Isla Belle's. He felt the weight of Mathias's stare. Glyndwr men were proud and never wrong. Owain never admitted defeat or error. But Rhys's father had never known Isla Belle. Rhys had wiped her tears and cared for her like no other. She had been the only woman he'd ever loved. "Your parents welcomed me."

"With open arms, I'm sure," Isla Belle murmured. Still not meeting Rhys' gaze she whispered, "You lied—"

"Isla Belle." He gripped the armrest of her chair. If she walked away, both their lives were in danger. "Please—"

"You said you always had a choice." She shook her head, her lips trembling. "You never had a choice. None of us did."

ISLA BELLE THORNE

SACRAMENTO, CALIFORNIA: PRESENT DAY

There were too many questions regarding Rhys and the theatre. An hour after I was released from the hospital, I slipped my lock picking tools in my jacket and stood at the foot of the Samaritan Exchange's building. I knew their security was state of the art but having my tools made me feel more in control. Unfortunately, they'd tripled security, adding a full body scan before entry. I felt both foolish and panicked.

I needed a reason to enter. Stephen had made it very clear I was not to be back at work, not for the rest of the week.

Pulling out my phone, I called the lab. A woman answered and after a series of identifying questions, I was placed on hold to wait for my lab results.

"This is John Taylor, who am I speaking with?"

Smiling at his serious tone, I said, "This is Isla Belle Thorne, I was wondering if my results were in."

"Your results?" The tapping of a keyboard came through the phone. "We didn't give them to you?"

The same chill, the whisper of something not quite right, washed over me. "No, why?"

"It says—" He cut himself off. "Let me call you back."

The line went dead.

Cradling my phone, I felt unsteady. My world was shifting even if I didn't understand what was happening. I stepped forward, unsure of my next move. Denton, my mom and even Stephen were somehow connected.

Pulling my phone out once more, I called the receptionist on my floor. She answered on the first ring.

"This is Isla Belle Thorne. I'm still being evaluated but I'd like to come by and pick up some files to work from home."

Without skipping a beat, she chirped, "Absolutely. Which files were you needing?"

This was too easy. "I need the fertility clinic files and the longevity projects."

Silence. She cleared her throat. "I'm not sure if we can get the fertility clinic files. Those projects were in Garuda. And with HIPPA, I don't—"

"I don't need the names of the patients. Just the findings." I now understood my uncle's frustration with the HIPPA guidelines.

She hesitated. "I'll see what I can do."

"Is Euston around today?" He was known for being absent minded and I'd hope to siphon any information I could out of him. "Maybe he could help fill in the blanks?"

"No." Her voice came firm. Something was off. "I'll see what I can do. I'll send you an email when I have everything."

"Thank—" The line ended. I waited across the street for my phone to ping, either from the lab or the receptionist. Twenty minutes later, a brief email came, *The files are in the conference room.* No salutation or greeting.

Handing over my badge, my hands trembled. I didn't look the security guard in the eye. There were too many unanswered questions, both with the protestors and with Denton. I needed answers and I needed them now.

The receptionist nodded, talking to someone on the phone. She pointed to the conference room. I was grateful I didn't have a designated office.

The receptionist's posture was stiff and her brow furrowed. She must not be used to random orders—the thought didn't ease my concerns. There was too much mystery, too many hidden secrets for an organization that supposedly existed only to better humanity. Protestors couldn't be this angry, or this tenacious unless something was grotesquely wrong.

Walking past the receptionist's desk, I double checked that she was on the phone and kept going down the hall. The receptionist had compiled the files in only twenty minutes which meant the files were stored close by. Two steps in and I froze—a security guard was posted at the end, another at the opposite end. Deflated, I turned back around to the conference room.

Half a dozen cardboard boxes were stacked in the corner. I lifted the first one—and fell back. I was expecting the weight of files and papers. It was empty. I tossed the empty box and opened the next. Empty. And the next. All were empty.

Either the boxes were never filled or someone had taken the files before I came. Sinking into the nearest chair, I held my head in my hands and groaned. Something crinkled under my shoe. Peeking under the table, I spotted files splayed like they'd fallen and a flash drive a few feet from the pages. Ducking under, I gathered everything, clutching them to my chest. It wasn't much but I'd take it. I didn't know if employees had tried to take the files or if it was a possible protestor. All I knew for sure was I was close to something worth hiding.

This was the organization that helped my mother conceive. This was the organization that provided vaccines to the nation—no, to the world. *Why so many secrets?* Ty believed in the Exchange. My mother trusted them, at least, enough to use their facilities. Why would Denton and Euston bury information? The smoke and mirrors painted the entire organization in horrible light.

Unlike Ty, I hadn't been given a company laptop, but now I wondered if that was good or bad. I gathered the materials and slipped out of the building. My college computer was pitifully slow but also isolated and never connected to the Exchange's online portal.

Ty bragged that tech support helped him three out of every five days. They'd log in and take over his computer until whatever issue was resolved. What should be a benefit, I viewed as suspicious.

Stepping from the building, the December air nipped at my ears and neck, scratching at my exposed skin. Four blocks to my left was the hospital and five blocks to my right was my home. A devoted daughter would check on her mother.

But I stood there, not knowing which way to turn. Tucked under my arm was paperwork and in my pocket was the flash drive. Ty and I had stored everything my mother owned with Stephen, aside from a dozen of her plays. Both the paperwork from the Exchange and my mother's plays were somewhat of a starting point. But for what? I was blinded by secrets and reaching in the dark for answers. The hard, tangible facts I did know were few. I knew my mother utilized the Exchange's fertility clinic—my birth was evidence enough. Rhys and Denton were still active in the Exchange, although I didn't yet know if my experience with Rhys at the theatre was real or a vision. Stephen was on the board and pivotal during the fertility clinics but he was no longer privy to my mother's care. A question wriggled in. The Exchange's mission was to better humanity, whether through preventative—like vaccines—or innovative, like genetic healing. How did a fertility clinic fit into that mission? And why was the fertility clinic shut down?

At the theatre, I could have sworn Rhys pulled me to his side and helped me escape, along with Denton and his security team. Stephen had never mentioned Rhys. Nor was he in the security video. Fear squeezed my lungs. The nagging thought—the same idea that dominated my mind for the past few days—reared back to life. *What if my Rhys isn't real?* The portrait of Rhys Staverton in the conference room; *he* was real. But the man who'd pushed me to safety, the one who appeared in visions day after day—was he real?

The flash drive in my pocket felt heavy. The information it contained wouldn't answer that question. Neither would the papers under my arm. Even the plays waiting for me in my room wouldn't solve my visions of Rhys. If Rhys wasn't real—I swallowed the rising panic—if he wasn't, there was little hope my future wouldn't mirror my mother's. Her grip on reality slipped around my age.

Suddenly, nothing else mattered—only the blond in my dreams. Guilt washed over me. And shame. I should be overwhelmed with concern, for both Mom and Ty but slowly, my feet turned toward the suite. As selfish as it sounded, I needed to know about Rhys. The closest access was through the Exchange.

With frightening numbness, I entered my room and turned on the computer. I took over the dining room table and organized the paper-work with exact movements. It made me feel less crazy, as if making deliberate decisions dug a trench between my mother's mind and mine. The box with her plays sat untouched by the couch. It pulled my gaze as I sat waiting for my computer to come alive. I plugged in the flash drive and clicked on the first file, *projected delivery dates.* The patient names were coded, a mixture of letters and numbers but what was the most impressive was that the doctors appeared to want a specific delivery date.

I searched for a high risk pregnancy. According to Stephen, I had a twin brother that was a stillborn. My mother rarely spoke of him. She'd shrug and say she knew the entire pregnancy that he wouldn't live. Stephen had verified that they knew early on that we had a lethal form of a twin-to-twin transfusion. From the looks of it, there were only two sets of twins, a set of boys a year before my birth and myself —at least, I assumed it was me. The file marked the female living and the male as dead. And then nothing. Three weeks after my birth, the clinic folded.

Scrolling back to the top, the first pregnancy was a year before Ty's birth. He was eight years older than me, nine years total for the clinic to be open. Euston's entire career was built on genetic healing and Stephen was a geneticist but they'd not even lasted a generation. How could they study genes and their responses in only nine years?

I sat back, a thought pummeling me. Ty was born in the span of the clinic. His mother was five years younger than mine. She was eighteen when Ty was born and quickly married Stephen. She divorced him several years later, long before I was born. I did a quick search, finding a boy born on his birthday. I copied the code for the mother and did another search—and froze. Ty's mother matched mine.

I stood and backed away from the computer. This wasn't happening. Too many secrets.

Scrambling back to the keyboard, I copied the code for his father and did another search. Our father's were different. I took a screen shot of both, sending them to my phone. Shaking my head, I paced the living room, flipping between the pictures on my phone.

There was a chance I was wrong. I didn't have definite, infallible proof that I was the twin girl and that he was the boy. My mother was open about the fertility clinic but was Diana? I gripped the back of the chair. If my mother birthed Ty, it would have been just before her first play. And six months before her failed marriage.

How did Stephen wind up with Ty—the answer came with a punch to my gut. He'd tried to take custody of me and was listed as co-guardian since I was in kindergarten. Of course Stephen took Ty. He would never walk away from family. Steadying myself with the back of the chair, I braced for the waves of emotion—anger, suspicion…hurt—but nothing came. Not a tear. It was just another secret in a pile of lies.

There was only one thing I knew—even if it hurt—Stephen loved his family, even when we were wrong. My mother should never have had children. The thought pierced me. My mother was in a hospital and I was damning her.

ISLA BELLE THORNE

SACRAMENTO, CALIFORNIA: PRESENT DAY

*M*y eyes were blurry and my shoulders ached from hunching over the table. I glanced at the time. It was four in the morning. I'd stayed up through the night. I dragged myself to bed but I woke in a panic every few hours with a reoccurring nightmare, the blond who looked like Rhys and his bloody back, left for dead. A man I'd never really met. The names and faces circled in my mind, one continual round. Again and again.

I should have dreamed of my mother. Or Ty. Not of a stranger that didn't know I existed.

My watch beeped. Eight in the morning. Giving up on sleep, I went back to the living room. One look at the table and I felt my heart sink. Ty was my half brother and I didn't know how to tell him. I needed to know for certain before I could shatter his foundation. I'd spent my life wondering if my future would mirror my mother's—what would this do to him? He'd idolized Stephen, a man who'd adopted him without hesitation. Would Ty feel the same if Stephen had kept his parentage secret?

The door swung open. I jumped from the chair, fear in my throat. I'd been caught.

Ty stepped in, Stephen close behind. I took a deep breath. Ty shuffled in. He opted for the couch, his arm in a sling while Stephen sighed and came to me. I gripped the top of the chair, the guilt pricked my heart. Not till Stephen squeezed my shoulder did I take an uneasy breath.

"Careful, Ty." Stephen's voice pierced my thoughts. He sounded tired. Exhausted. He might have lied to Ty but he was a good man. A good father.

If they noticed my bizarre behavior, neither spoke of it. Flexing my fingers open and closed, I prayed the trembling would stop.

"I need to pick up his pain meds." Stephen squeezed my shoulder once more and then turned to Ty. "Stay put."

Ty saluted him with a smirk, holding the position until the door closed. His left arm dropped to his chest, hugging his injured right arm in the sling.

"You look awful." I sat stiffly back in the chair.

With a lopsided smile, he said, "As bad as you?"

"Worse."

Ty laughed, drunk with whatever medication he'd been given at the hospital. "I doubt that."

"How are you feeling?"

He stared at me. It took a moment to realize he was reading my eye color. "Better than you."

"I'm serious."

"So am I." Ty sobered and stood, walking slowly toward me.

Papers were strewn over the dining room table. Squinting, he peered at the stacks of paper. The computer beeped. I should close the laptop but knew that'd invite suspicion. I felt vulnerable enough.

"Is this the alpaca thing?" His words came slow. He was working through the haze.

"Stephen is going to kill us both if he sees you up and about." It wasn't a complete lie. He would never stop caring. Just like my mother couldn't stop the highs and lows, Stephen couldn't stop helping and worrying. I swallowed hard. *My* mother could very well be *our* mother.

"Does he know you're working?" Ty nodded at the paperwork

before giving me a pointed look. He wasn't the only one Stephen was worried about.

"I'm not really working. Just organizing." The lie came easy.

With his left hand, Ty pulled the closest file to him. "What're you organizing?"

"I'm not sure." That was only part of the truth. I'd not yet moved on from the fertility clinic to the rest of the longevity files.

"Do you know what you're looking for?" He held my gaze. There was more to his question. After all, this was my cousin—possibly my half-brother—who'd known me my entire life. He'd seen me through the continual pendulum of my childhood. "Because that's really what you're doing, right? You're looking for answers."

Stephen could walk through the door any minute. The combination of Ty and his father was too much. I wasn't sure who knew what. I for sure no longer trusted Denton and a little bit of me no longer trusted Stephen. I loved him for the wonderful man he was but I couldn't trust that he'd tell me the truth. And I certainly couldn't tell Stephen about my visions. And the worst of it, the horrible truth was I only got the files because I'd spent more time thinking about the fictional Rhys and than I did worrying about my mother. The guilt gnawed at me, nipping at the edges of the visions. Mom might have been manipulative and completely insane, but at least she'd never been this selfish.

Ty tucked his left arm around the sling, cushioning his injured arm. "You want to tell me what's going on?"

"Not really." I couldn't tell him. Not yet.

His chuckle shouldn't sound this nice. Ty would never abandon Stephen. He'd inherited the best of our genes, down to the soul. He cleared his throat and glanced at the door. "Would it help if I sent him a text?" Stephen would rush even faster if Ty texted him.

"Don't you dare."

"For food, *Issla*." He searched his pockets, grunted either from annoyance or pain. Fishing out his phone, he tapped out a text. The phone vibrated a second later. "You care what kind?"

I shook my head.

"He's asking if we want pizza, Mexican or Chinese." Ty chuckled and set the phone on the table. "I told him yes."

"As in, yes to everything?" I pictured Ty shoveling pizza, tacos and chow mien down his throat. The man was a garbage disposal.

"What in our relationship makes you think I turn down food?" His broad, dimpled smile melted the last of my resolve. With his index finger, he flipped the top of a folder open. "Should I start reading or do you want to start talking?"

"Will you tell me what happened?" Gathering my knees, I folded my arms around them. My question wasn't just to distract. Everything online about the theatre was vague, citing the pending investigation. No victims reported, only damages to the building. "What did you see?"

Ty shrugged sheepishly. "Nothing, really."

"You broke your arm."

"I asked you first. You're the one who needs to talk."

"Why?" I dropped my knees. "You're acting suspicious."

Ty scoffed. "Oh, *I'm* acting suspicious?"

I balked but couldn't think of a retort. We were both right. "Fine. But I'm not wrong."

"Neither am I."

We stared at each other. Ty winked. I looked away, biting my lip to keep from smiling.

He playfully shoved my chair with his foot. "I'll tell you mine if you tell me yours."

"Tell you what?" I wasn't the one in the sling.

"Your little secret." Ty flicked his eyes to the table. "I'll even pinky swear if it'll make you feel better."

"We're not five, Ty."

He clicked his tongue and pointed a finger at me. "Nothing gets past you."

I closed my laptop. "You're ridiculous."

"I'm not wrong." He covered my hand with his, waiting until I met his gaze. "I tripped and fell."

"That's how you broke your arm?"

"I broke it and passed out." He gave a nervous laugh. "Didn't see a thing."

"Why the secrecy?"

"Because I followed you." Ty swallowed hard, an apology in his eyes. "I probably shouldn't have, but I've been worried about you. You've been acting kind of strange and then you looked, I don't know. Just weird when you left with Denton."

"You followed me." The numb feeling returned, the same odd feeling when I'd left the Exchange earlier today.

"And then I saw Staverton go down the stairs."

"Rhys?" I didn't miss Ty's flinch at *Rhys*. "You saw Rhys—Staverton? You saw him with your own eyes?"

"Yes..." Ty stretched out the word, concern written on his face. The furrowed brow, the wide eyes—the worry was everywhere. "You didn't?"

"You saw him." Hugging myself, I felt a wave of relief. I couldn't tell Ty about what I'd found but there was a sweet relief in knowing Ty saw him.

"Why does it matter?"

Closing my eyes, I squeezed my arms tighter. "I thought I imagined him."

"Isla?" Ty's voice dropped. "Isla Belle, look at me."

I opened my eyes. He leaned over, favoring his right side. I shook my head. "Don't. Whatever you're going to do or say just listen."

He wiped his face, hurt swimming in his eyes. "What do you think I'm going to do?"

"Put me in a hospital? I don't know." I couldn't look at him. The air turned thick, the room shrinking minute by minute. It was time. "I dream of him. Of Rhys. I have these visions. They feel real. And last night I didn't know if it was a vision or if it was him."

Ty said nothing. His silence stifled the room.

"Sometimes Denton's there. In the dreams."

Ty held out his hand. "Do you think maybe it's because you work with them? It's not uncommon."

"I've had these visions since I was a kid." There it was, the truth out for him to see. I felt small, vulnerable. Naked.

"You've always done that." There was optimism in his voice. Childhood had a way of painting memories prettier than they were.

"Ty—"

"Faith. Do you remember Faith?" When I didn't answer, he continued, "You and Stephen were dropping me off my freshman year. We were walking through the oval. You kept looking around asking for Faith."

His words tugged a memory from my mind. "Faith was a statue. It used to be in the oval."

Ty nodded. "You kept saying that. Do you remember what Stephen asked?" He didn't wait for me to respond. "He asked you, he thought you were teasing, but he finally asked, *really, Isla, when was it in the oval?*"

The moment I had stepped onto the campus, the entire landscape felt off. It wasn't the Stanford I thought it was, despite never visiting the campus. But somehow, I knew it had changed. "I don't know. I just remember it being there."

"1914." Ty picked at the seam of his sling. "I looked it up that semester. It was removed December 2, 1914. Even though you swore up and down it was there the day before."

"Why are you telling me this?"

"Because I need you..." He grabbed my hand and squeezed it. With a shaking voice, he begged, "I need you to know you're not crazy. I think your mom has screwed up your head so badly that no matter where or how you turn, you see evidence of an illness. A disease that isn't there. Not for you."

Your mom. I swallowed the confession. "You just told me—"

"Nobody researches like you, Isla. Nobody." Blinking, he cleared his throat. The sight of him fighting emotions formed a lump in my throat. "Who knows where you got that information about the statue. But it's fact. Not fiction."

He dropped from off his chair and kneeled next to me. "Fact, Isla.

You live and breathe the facts. Dottie never did. You'll find what you're looking for, even if it's false. Don't search for the crazy. Search for the truth."

RHYS GYNDWR

HEREFORDSHIRE, WALES: 1535

*M*atthias froze, his hands on the table in front of him, his back rigid. Rhys watched the man look at the walls, the table—everywhere but Isla Belle and Rhys.

Isla Belle slumped in her chair, her words echoing in Rhys' mind. *You lied. You never had a choice. None of us did.* Her lips trembled and Rhys' heart broke.

"I've always had a choice, Isla Belle." He needed her to believe him. "Three people signed the document. Myself included. No one forced my hand."

"You didn't know me, Rhys. You can't make a choice if you didn't know what you were choosing." The words came too easily. Her mind was made up.

"I could have left Wellesley years ago but I stayed."

The steward stood. "I should leave."

"By devil, Mathias, sit down," Rhys barked, regretting his tone. "I'm sorry."

He felt the pity in his steward's gaze. Mathias nodded and sat. "It's been a trying day, Glyndwr."

"I shouldn't have bellowed like that." Rhys rubbed his eyes with his palms. "I don't know what to do. Don't know how to make it right."

"Why didn't you tell me?" Isla Belle whispered. "I would have gone anywhere with you. All you had to do was ask."

"There was nowhere to go." Rhys let his hands fall to his lap. His back was tight from the healed skin, and he'd slept but a few hours here and there. His soul was stretched but nothing hurt like the midnight color of Isla Belle's eyes—pain. "I promised you, Isla Belle."

"No more—"

"I know. No more pretty words." Rhys had lost. He'd might as well confess. "You won't believe me, but I'll tell you just the same. I was promised. Yes. That is the truth of it. But I fell for you."

Isla Belle's head shot up.

"I became a giant of a man when you looked at me, trust in your eyes. Like only I could help you." Rhys loved her. And yet, he was terrified he'd now lost her. "What's not written on the parchment is what I promised your father the day I left him at court. I told him I'd not just protect you. But that I'd love you. Mark my words, Isla Belle, I'll not stop loving you."

She brushed a tear off her cheek but stayed silent. Hope took seed in Rhys' mind. Isla Belle wouldn't cry if she didn't care. Gently, he held her hand and raised her to a stand. He lifted her chin with his finger.

"I'm sorry, *fy annwyl* for the pain I've caused." She tried to look away. He cupped her jaw, directing her gaze back to him. "I can't promise you a secure future. But everything I have, everything I am—it's yours."

"You said no more pretty words." The midnight color melted to a softer blue.

"I'll not force you."

"I know." A tremulous smile appeared.

"If you had a choice, what would it be?" Rhys tried to focus on anything but her mouth.

Mathias fidgeted. Both men knew Rhys couldn't grant Isla Belle freedom; the king had declared his intentions weeks before. Her only protection was by marriage. But in his heart, Rhys knew he couldn't cage Isla Belle. She was born with a wild tongue and an untamable mind, infuriating the duchess and capturing Rhys' soul.

"Isla Belle?" He needed to hear her answer. "What do you want? What would you choose? Forget the king—"

"Forget the king?" She backed away. "Just like that? Forget the king and the mess we're in?"

And there it was—the truth of it. Isla Belle could only see the gravestone of her future. Not Rhys.

He braced himself on the back of the chair. "You will be restored. Somehow or someway."

"*Eich Uchelder,*" Mathias hissed. "That's not possible."

Your Highness. The formal address made Rhys pause. His father was addressed as *Your Highness.* Being stripped of the Welsh throne wouldn't alter the royal blood coursing through Owain's veins. Not in Wales. Poor or proud, this country claimed Owain as their king—and Rhys the heir. "I'll do whatever I can to protect you. Whether or not you marry me."

"Is that your way of asking?" The blue of her eyes brightened. Hope fell like rain in the room, bringing in the seeds of joy. Rhys doubted that she'd forgiven him yet but the pain wasn't as sharp.

"No." Rhys wracked his knuckles against the back of the chair. "I won't ask. And I won't force."

"You're going back on your word, then?" She asked a bit too innocently.

Mathias's mouth fell open at the sudden change in Isla Belle. She'd gone from tears to teasing in a moment. The steward pulled at his collar and glanced between them both. "King Henry is at our throat and the council at our heels. If you don't marry, she'll be handed over to the king and you, Rhys—you'll be hanged faster than they can tie the rope."

"Tell me everything." Gathering her skirts, Isla Belle threw back her shoulders and straightened her back. She looked every inch a lady, the promised daughter of a duke. "I'm at the center of this. I deserve to know the truth. All of it."

Mathias slid the small wooden box toward Rhys. "Speak fast. Time's not our friend."

"I told you Owain was my father. He led two rebellions and became a legend. No matter how many times he'd been to battle, he'd never die. The years came and went but he kept living. His mother and father were normal. Yet his great grandfather lives on in France."

"Lives on?" Isla Belle furrowed her brow, questions in her eyes. "I'm supposed to believe this?"

"You asked for the truth," Mathias gently added. "It's not a story, milady.

"It's a bit hard to believe."

"Doesn't make it any less real." The steward's gaze fell from Isla Belle to the small wooden box he'd put on the table when they entered. "Owain was hanged. And then burned. Rhys was rushed to Wellesley. We had to keep the heir safe. Wales has no future without a Glyndwr."

"And now?" Isla Belle's eyes flicked from Mathias to the box. "Rhys is back. All should be well now?"

"The lords killed my father. Took a dozen—"

"We don't know who killed him." Mathias refused to look at Rhys. The painful dance emerged, the boy blaming the neighbors and the steward blaming the English. "We don't know who to trust."

"Hanging is a capital offense. Only a council's court could issue that punishment." Rhys knew the laws; they'd been grilled into him since infancy. The years had come and gone, the wording a bit dusty in his head but Rhys knew Welsh law.

"Not anymore." Mathias looked around, as if someone could over-hear. "Six months ago, King Henry appointed a new bishop, Bishop Rowland Lee. Made him the new president of the council. He's been given the authority to carry out capital punishment."

"He's a man of the cloth." Isla Belle didn't hide the doubt. "An old friend of Queen Anne."

"He's no friend to the Welsh." Mathias tapped his fingers against his cane leaning on the table. "He's loyal to Henry and none other."

"Why did we come then? What..." Isla Belle sank to her chair. "What are we doing here, Rhys?"

"The lords are eager for a leader." The conviction in Mathias's voice warmed the room. "They'd hoped Henry's father would be the one. A Welsh king to redeem our people. But instead, King Henry is nothing but a spoiled child. He's handed over Wales to a sinister bishop. A man who hates us. Wants to see every one of us hanging from a tree." The steward's Welsh accent became thicker with each word. He rose from the chair, favoring his injured leg. "The lords will come to your aid, Glydnwr."

"My grandfather is a Marcher Lord." Isla Belle matched Mathias's passion, her temper flaring. "He's not lifted a finger to help us. He'd rather I marry the king than help your country."

"My country?" The steward straightened. "You've Welsh in your blood. This is your land as well."

"A Welsh king wasn't enough. Your grandfather wanted a Welsh queen on the throne. Hedge their bets." Rhys kept his voice steady. "Your grandfather didn't know about me. King Henry still doesn't."

"And now you're supposed to rise from the ashes like a phoenix?" Isla Belle scoffed. "Another myth. Another legend to scare people."

"Owain's life was not a legend or a myth." Mathias smacked the table. "He lived and died for us."

"A regular King Arthur." Her voice dripped in sarcasm. Her disbelief apparent. She didn't trust Matthias the steward and more than likely didn't believe Rhys.

"You've seen me care for the sick. Helping those near death and never succumbing." He felt the cavern widening between them. "I was whipped and left in the mud. There should have been infection. A fever. *Something.*"

Isla Belle warned him, fire in her eyes, "Rhys, what you say—"

"I am Glyndwr's son." He palmed the wooden box. Holding it out, he cracked it open. "Your father hoped you'd be my bride. That your strength of mind and my strength of body would cure this country."

"If I were but a man," she whispered her father's words.

Rhys pulled a gold band from the box, the ring forged in Welsh gold. Every queen since the country's birth had worn the ring. The triskele symbol, the spirals hooked together were etched around the band. The English believed it represented the past, present and future, but Rhys' ancestors believed each spiral represented a different world; the present world around them, the supernatural world for Gods and those passed on—and the celestial world of sun, moon and stars.

Rhys held the ring up, offering it on his palm to Isla Belle. "This belonged to my mother."

Isla Belle softened at *mother.*

His father had buried generations. Wives. Sons. Each person snatching a piece of Owain's heart with them to the grave. He'd become more reckless by the time Rhys was born. Owain cared more for Wales than his own life. "This was his mother's ring as well."

"I've nothing of my family left." Isla Belle's eyes swirled, her emotions overwhelming her.

"Your grandfather." Rhys took a step closer. "And me."

"My grandfather wants to marry me off."

"He's a Marcher Lord, milady." Mathias's conviction was back. He sounded more like a preaching bishop than a loyal steward. "A Welsh Duke is preferable to an English king. There's not a father in Wales who'd not want you wed to Glyndwr."

Rhys winced. It was only a half-truth. The lords loyal to Wales would embrace him—so long as Rhys championed their interests. The other lords would hang him in an instant, or turn Rhys in for treason.

"How soon would we wed?" Isla Belle's gaze turned to the ring.

"As soon as a witness and a priest are gathered." Mathias didn't hide his eagerness.

She nodded. "Do it."

Mathias grabbed his cane and hobbled quickly to the door. Rhys came to her, sliding an arm under hers. "You don't have to, *fy annwyl.*"

She didn't look at him but didn't pull away. "Did you mean it?"

Risking her ire, he tucked a strand of hair behind her ear. "Mean what?"

"All of it." Isla Belle lifted her head, her eyes full of questions. "That you fell for me. All of it."

"Ay." He slid it on her finger. "I meant it."

"I don't know what to believe." She kept her fingers straight, the uncertainty still written on her face. "You're all I've ever known, Rhys."

"I know." His spirit sank. She was giving in because she had no other choice. He would not trap her. This was farewell. He would find another way for her to be free.

"I've trusted you more than anyone."

He wrapped her against his chest. "I'll protect you without a wedding."

"Rhys—"

"No, *fy annwyl*." His voice was unsteady. "I'll not cage you. Think of me when you wear the ring."

"I've thought of you long before the ring." Her hand gripped his shirt. "I don't know what to think about all of this. I don't know who to trust or what to do." She tightened her hold, her hand clenching the fabric. "But you're my home, Rhys. It's cold when you're not around."

Relief warmed him. He kissed her forehead. "I'll never leave you."

"I don't know about Wales. I don't know about the blasted king or my family…"

"Shhh," he cooed and gently swayed with her in his arms.

"I'm scared. And I'm mad that I'm scared." She trembled—and then stopped. Looking at Rhys, she said, "But with you. With you I'm strong. I'm bold…I'm home."

ISLA BELLE THORNE

SACRAMENTO, CALIFORNIA: PRESENT DAY

earch for the truth. Ty's words replayed in my head. I had found a nugget of truth—or at least it appeared to be. When Stephen delivered food, I waited for Ty to drift off. Stephen stood and gave an exhausted sigh, clenching my heart. I couldn't question him tonight. He mumbled a farewell and left. I stood, Ty snoring softly on the couch and my uncle walking down the hallway. I felt horribly alone with the weight on my shoulders.

I went to my room and opened the fertility clinic files on my computer. I knew from the alpaca project that Euston liked to keep the variables low in the experimental group, using one—no more than two—fathers. The mothers were a higher variable. The only way around the problem was if the experiment had a single pregnancy each time. It would make for a more expensive and impossibly long project. Instead, Euston—and every other scientist—opted for parallel experiences, or pregnancies, at the same time. Although, the fertility clinic had a shockingly high mortality rate, only a handful of babies were born out of what seemed like thirty or more.

My head and heart hurt. I needed to switch topics. Ironically, the protestors at the theatre seemed like a safer subject but there was little evidence anything in the fertility or longevity files triggered protestors. Both of these projects were decades ago. The alpaca project was much more recent but the protestors hadn't hinted to animals being the victims.

A few clicks and there was a little information in the fertility clinic on biological immortality but they must have been misfiled. The fertility clinic appeared to be more concerned with dominant and recessive genes, not immortality. There had to be something more, something that would trigger protestors to attack a theatre or any other fundraising event. At the very least, I'd hoped to find some link between Denton, Mom and Stephen—and Rhys. Not even the fertility clinic could achieve that.

Opening and closing each file, I felt even more hopeless. Ty had asked me to search for the truth—not evidence of Mom's insanity. Granted, he'd thought of my mother as mine, not *ours*. Her mental illness was a question still lurking in my mind, but the visions had taken center stage. If Ty was my half-brother and we shared the same mother, why didn't he have visions?

Logic and facts. That's what I had been trained to follow during my undergraduate work. Ty swore that my mind found facts. They might get twisted into dreams but the start of every vision was a fact. If that were true, I must have known Rhys before college. Before high school, before—the logic ended there.

I stared at the dresser and pulled out my necklace with the ring from my mother still attached. Maybe I needed a new starting point. A new fact to follow—the ring.

A calm settled on my shoulders. I slipped the ring on my finger and felt an electric hum. The exhaustion from my impromptu all nighter faded away. Peace. I felt peace.

I refocused my search and typed *Celtic wedding bands* but added *Wales*. I'd never visited the country but had dreamed of it countless times.

Thirteen separate websites gave me nothing but questions. The delicate hope I'd felt earlier was not frayed. All I found was an appraisal for a ring similar to mine listed on a public auction site, dated roughly five years ago. No owner—or buyer—was listed but the auction house was in Palo Alto. There was a digital restoration picture on the appraisal confirming the nicks were Celtic symbols, more specifically a wedding symbol for eternity. The band had the same triangular, circular etching. The color was a mixture of gold and brass —according to the description, the shade was an authentic trait of Welsh gold. My mother had pawned most of her jewelry when I was in high school. She could very well have listed this but it still didn't tell me how she got it. Or why the ring comforted me.

I typed *Rhys Staverton* in the search engine but couldn't press enter. I deleted the name and typed *Rhys Samaritan Exchange.* Just before I hit the return button, I added, *Wales.*

Rhys ap Owain, Marcher Lord of Gruffydd

Rhys Glyndwr, 16th century Welsh lyricist, Ar Hyd y Nos

Rhys Glyndwr, healer

Rhys Amati, English landowner

Rhys Amati, violinist

Rhys, Wellesley County

Rhys Hollander, USS Mayfair

Rhys Staverton Jr and Sr, Garuda founder.

I clicked on *Ar Hyd y Nos,* the words of the melody in my head. It took several minutes before I found the English translation, *Midnight slumber close surround thee...all through the night.* This was the song Rhys had played at the event weeks earlier. Closing my eyes, I heard the words in a sing-song Welsh accent.

In my gut, I knew all of this was tangled together, the ring, my mother, Denton—even Garuda. Denton had sent get well flowers to the suite and some of the daisies were starting to wilt. It was now almost midnight but I sat and picked at the dying bits. My hand scraped the card buried deep in the front on a plastic fork. Pulling it out, I read *Would love to continue our conversation—Denton.* A phone number was scribbled below his name. At first, I thought it was the office line but noticed the +12 at the beginning, indicating a foreign number. When Stephen traveled to England for the Exchange, he'd always include his hotel line, each time it had +44 before the rest of the number.

Sitting on the bed, I had the card in one hand, the necklace in the other. I left the card on my thigh and unhooked the necklace. The band fell to the comforter on the bed. My pulse slowed. Warmth filled me. I slid the band on my finger. My skin prickled. I felt the nudge, the familiar tug of a vision coming. A whisper of an image appeared in my mind, the blond. Rhys. His face was torn between affection and despair. The woman was sad but loved. Much like my mother.

My head began to pound. I needed sleep. Ty had said the ring was a distraction, but I didn't want to take it off. Slipping the empty necklace back in the dresser, I laid on the bed, my hand on the pillow.

The ring was the last thing I saw before drifting to sleep—and the first thing I saw when I woke hours later. The headache was now screaming. I swallowed a dose of painkillers and in a fit of bravery, called the number on the card.

After four rings, a generic voicemail message answered, *Leave a message after the beep.* I hesitated; should I leave a message? Did Denton really mean to continue our conversation—what *was* our conversation? The night was blurry at best.

"Thank you for the flowers," I blurted before ending the call.

I showered and dressed but didn't want to leave the room. Ty or even Stephen would be in the shared living room area by now. I'd purposely avoided looking in the mirror. I'd slept in fits and knew I looked horrible.

The phone on my bed rang, a blocked number. *Denton.* "Hello?"

"Is this Isla Belle Thorne?" The man sounded irritated and younger then Denton.

"Yes, can I help you?"

"This is Detective Williams." He waited a beat. "I know you're still recovering, but we'd like to sit down and confirm some information about the theatre incident."

"Oh…" I felt deflated. "Over the phone or in person?"

"Preferably in person but I understand you were just released from the hospital. We can come to you if that's more convenient." There was something about his voice that made me feel on edge. He'd not warned or threatened but the message was clear, *you will talk to us.* "There's a few inconsistencies we need to clear up."

"I'm not sure I can help but I'm willing." I closed my eyes, wishing the medicine would hurry and kick in. "Not sure if I'm the person you should interview. I didn't see much."

"Any information is a benefit." The detective's voice came clipped as if he were really saying *that's for me to decide.*

"I promise, I barely saw anything."

"But you were seen." He warned.

"What do you mean?" The security footage. A chill crept up my neck. The image was poor, horrible. No one could recognize me. "You were seen leaving with a Dr. Thomas Denton, the highest officer for the Samaritan Exchange." The detective didn't hide his annoyance. "I don't have a dog in this fight, Miss Thorne and it took me all of five minutes to connect your employment, your image and the Exchange. How long before the protestors do the same?"

"Ty…" What if he became a target? "Was Ty Cael in any of the footage?"

"Tyler Cael?" The detective sounded frustrated.

"My cousin." The moment I spoke, I regretted handing over the detective more information. I was grateful I'd at least managed to say *cousin* instead of *brother.*

"Tyler Stephen Cael is your cousin?"

My door cracked open, Ty came in and laid on the bed, his feet dangling off the edge. "Yes, Tyler Cael is my cousin."

Ty sat up, his left arm cradling his right. He'd not put it back in the sling. His brow furrowed. I grabbed a pen and pad from the night stand.

Before I could write anything, Detective Williams asked, "You're telling me that you're related to the Exchange's legal council?"

"Both Ty and I work for them." I dropped the pen. "I thought you wanted information about the theatre."

Ty nodded. He grabbed the pen and wrote *police?* I nodded. He wrote, *Det asked Stephen to talk to you. Said no.*

That's why the man was frustrated with me. "Detective Williams, I'm more than willing to talk to you."

Ty rolled his eyes and underlined *Said no.*

"Something's just come up, Miss Thorne. We'll be in touch." The detective hung up the phone without another word.

"What was that about?" I tossed the phone on the bed. "One minute he's asking to talk and the next he can't get off the phone fast enough."

Ty shrugged. "Lawyers scare the police."

"Liar. He didn't even know you were here." I grabbed a pillow to throw, but he held up his hurt arm. It seemed cruel to attack a one-armed man, even if it was Ty. "You're lucky you're injured."

"People are generally scared of me." Ty flicked the pen. "Especially now that I'm made of steel."

"How long have you waited to say that?" I held up my hand. "Don't answer that."

He smiled wide, his dimples winking at me. "Seriously, I am kind of a big deal out in the real world."

"I'll believe it when I see it."

Ty grabbed my hand and turned it over. "You're wearing it."

"Yeah. I guess I am." My neck and face flushed.

"Why are you blushing?"

I became hotter. "Not a clue."

"You can't just blush like that without knowing." He poked my ribs. "Spill it."

"I already told you." When he arched an eyebrow, I laid on the bed with a huff. I couldn't tell him of our shared parentage theory but it was time to really tell him about Rhys. "I have these stupid dreams about *him.* And one of them is with this ring."

"You've dreamed about this ring?"

"I swear you're deaf."

Ty pulled my hand over, examining the band. "Have you researched this?"

"It's a Celtic symbol." Pulling away, I grabbed the computer and opened it. "And the ring was almost auctioned five years ago."

"You must have seen it before." The conviction in Ty's voice made me pause. "We just have to figure out when and where."

The phone rang, another blocked number.

"Don't answer it." Ty reached for it.

Answering the phone, I started pacing. "Hello?"

"Miss Thorne," Denton chirped. His cheerfulness was in stark contrast to the detective. "I received your message."

Feeling Ty's gaze on me, I walked in the tight space between the bed and the bathroom. "Thank you again for the flowers."

Ty settled down. He appeared to be fine with Denton just not the police.

"You're quite welcome." Denton hesitated. "Listen, I'm getting ready to leave for Garuda."

"Oh." I'd missed my window of opportunity.

"But I'd love for you to come visit."

"Oh." This was an entirely different kind of *oh*. "I don't know if I've been given time off."

Denton chuckled. "I'm sure that can be arranged. Visiting Garuda is something every employee should do at one time or another."

I was fairly certain Ty had never been. He'd gone to England with Stephen a handful of times but Garuda? He would have bragged, a joke at the very least.

"That would be great." I glanced at Ty who'd given up on eaves-dropping and was scrolling through his social media accounts. The sight of him reminded me of Mom. She's the one who should be going to Garuda. But I couldn't ask. I wanted to go so badly that I selfishly didn't want to jeopardize the invitation.

"I'll have your formal invite sent over." There was someone else in the background talking but the voice was muffled. "I need to take off, but I look forward to speaking with you, Miss Thorne."

"Me too." My heart raced like I'd run a marathon. It didn't make sense, but I felt the pull, the same feeling I'd felt in the stairwell. It came when Denton mentioned Garuda and again, right now as I thought about packing to go.

Ty looked up from his phone. "How's your buddy Denton?"

"He invited me to Garuda."

Ty dropped his phone, his mouth slack. "He what?"

"He's sending over a formal invitation." I twisted the band on my finger and watched Ty's shock unfold. Softly, I confessed, "I should have asked for Mom to go."

"You've been invited. That's completely different than asking for Dottie's transfer." He held his injured arm close to him. The last dose of pain meds must be wearing off. "You should go. And don't feel guilty."

"Too late."

"You dream of Rhys and the ring." Ty shrugged. "Sounds like you'll finally get the facts."

Twenty-four hours later, I turned off at the California Piedras Negras Lighthouse exit, putting the rising sun and Sacramento behind me. Ty was probably getting up about now. He'd stubbornly helped me pack instead of resting. Last night, after an enormous amount of convincing, he'd finally gone to bed.

Denton's invitation to visit was too tempting to pass up. I wanted —I *needed*— answers. I should be nervous. I had a ring, other than that, nothing to go on.

The ferry's destination was one of the most secure places in the world, Garuda. Nestled in a small bay a half hour south of San Simeon, I filed behind several other cars waiting for the ferry man. He wore a metal tag with his official title Ferry Director pinned on his lapel, but no name underneath. He scanned our license plates and waved me and my fellow passengers aboard.

The formal invitation gave me two choices, a plane ride or a ferry trip. Soon, I'd be surrounded by water on a sovereign island and the freedom of my own vehicle allowed me to breathe a little easier.

Aside from my truck, most of the cars were minivans. I flipped the hood of my sweatshirt over my head, tying the ends. The pain medication eased the headache but dried my mouth and made the dizziness worse. The waves didn't help. My legs shook as the ferry chugged through the harbor. Up the stairs to the deck I went, my pulse racing. I tucked into a corner chair, the other passengers searching for seats. A tired mother offered several books and snacks to her children before staring at the horizon. I watched the California coast shrink. A helicopter flew overhead, a familiar crest on the side. My stomach flipped. I felt the familiar pull and watched the helicopter skip ahead of us, toward Garuda. With each passing minute, I felt the tension ease away.

For the first time in my life, I felt free.

RHYS GLYNDWR

HEREFORDSHIRE, WALES: 1535

*R*hys didn't recognize the priest standing in the garden of the church nor the rest of the gathering crowd standing under the ancient yew tree. A thin table stood next to the priest. Both his eyes were cloudy, his left almost completely white. Surrounding the tree and the priest stood dozens of men and women. Rhys assumed most were servants of the castle but he'd been gone for so long, he didn't know.

The crowd parted with Mathias hobbling in front of a regal Isla Belle. Taller than most of the women, her golden curls shone in the afternoon sun. Her borrowed gown was a touch too short while the shoulders and waist appeared to be pinned in the back. She'd not inherited the curves of her mother, only the duchess' height and formidable aura.

Rhys left the priest's side—stopped only by Tobias, the guard who'd greeted them at the gate. He gave Rhys a shake of the head. "The bride must come to you, Glyndwr."

The reverence in *Glyndwr* made Rhys pause. Tobias dropped his hand and tipped his head. Rhys took in the crowd, eyes on Isla Belle. He'd expected only one witness and hoped Isla Belle wasn't overwhelmed with all the people attending her impromptu wedding. Less than a week ago, she'd been commanded to be the king's prescribed mistress—only now to be wed in Wales.

Isla Belle met his gaze, her eye color swirling from midnight to bright. With one look at Rhys, her face softened. This was who they were—strong together and unsure when separated. Rhys' pulse pounded with each step she took. He loved her. He loved her stubborn will and wicked tongue. He'd often wondered if this day would ever come. She was to be his wife. A lump formed in his throat.

Mathias took Isla Belle's hand and placed it in Rhys'. With a nod, Mathias stood next to the guard.

Rhys squeezed her hand and faced the priest. "Father."

The priest nodded and cleared his throat. With his hands on the table, he centered himself. "We gather on sacred ground…"

Isla Belle's brow furrowed. They were marrying at the root of a yew tree, not the small church a few feet away. Rhys mouthed *Trust me.* She pursed her lips and said nothing. Rhys was a Glyndwr, a legend of the Welsh. Matthias urged Rhys to marry at the same sacred tree of his countrymen instead of inside the church, like his ancestors. His father, and those before him, believed the yew tree couldn't die. Rhys had once thought his father couldn't die as well. A dozen angry lords had cured the belief of true immortality.

The priest patted the table, beckoning them closer. "What is bound on earth will be bound in the hereafter."

Rhys waited for the rites to be read but saw no scripture on the table. He cast a look at Mathias who seemed to avoid his gaze.

"A union doesn't end in death." The priest gathered their hands and pulled a sash from his cloak. "What is sealed on this hallowed ground cannot be undone."

The priest knotted the sash with a rough tug, their hands held together inside the fabric. He muttered what sounded like a Celtic wedding rite, not the Christian ceremony recognized by England. Rhys knew little of the ceremonies, his brief education was on the laws, not legends. He prayed the witnesses would understand Rhys wanted to be a Welshman, and all that came with that ancestry.

The priest wiped his glistening forehead, his hands trembling with the effort of standing. A wide grin spread across his crackled face.

Mathias whispered behind Rhys, "*Yr ydych chi yn waed fy ngwaed.*"

Ye are blood of my blood. The steward had spent hours reciting the vows to Rhys. Mathias had begged Rhys to say the vows in Welsh. But with Rhys' hand still entwined in hers, he lifted Isla Belle's chin and said in English, "Ye are blood of my blood and bone of my bone. I give ye my body that we two might be one."

Isla Belle eyes flicked from their hands to his face, her nerves on display.

Rhys hurried. "I give ye my spirit, till our life shall be done. Shall we part in this life, our reunion shall be sweet and our parting short. I shall serve you in those ways you require and the honeycomb will taste sweeter coming from my hand."

He guided her to repeat the words. The priest unwrapped the cloth and slipped a knife between their hands. Isla Belle's eyes flashed black —fear.

"Trust me, *fy annwyl.*" Rhys slid his free arm under her left, steadying her.

With a jerk, the priest flicked the blade against each of the palms, blood smearing on the metal. Isla Belle's eyes widened, then narrowed. With deceptive ease, the priest wiped both palms with the wrap. He smiled bright and wide, exposing missing teeth. "You are sealed, never to be separated."

The priest offered the ring to Rhys and folded his arms in front of him, waiting for Rhys to adorn the new bride. Isla Belle's face paled. She'd not expected the ceremony—truth be told, Rhys hadn't either. He swallowed the concern and slid the ring on her finger.

"Thank you, Father." Mathias patted the priest's back and shouted in Welsh.

The crowd shouted back but Rhys didn't understand the words, nor did he try. Tobias ushered the newlyweds to the tower. Shouts and chants erupted as Rhys and Isla Belle were led away.

Up the stairs to the gatehouse tower, the crowd followed. Rhys hooked an arm around Isla Belle's waist, easing the weight on her healing leg.

"I'll leave you to your bliss." Mathias gave Rhys a wink and shut the door, waving away the men and women.

Isla Belle stood in the center of the room, her profile to Rhys. Engraved in the ceiling above her was the same triskele symbol carved into the band on her finger. The desk in the corner held no parchment, his father had used only the desk in holy room at the back of the chapel. Owain had claimed his campaign was divine. Every strategy, by sword or by law was born in the holy room.

The windows of the tower were deep, the walls several feet thick. Even with the fire and candles, the room was dark and cold. The castle was built to keep the enemy out, not harbor warmth. From Isla Belle's rigid posture, the night would be cold on both sides of the wall.

"Isla Belle?" Rhys didn't know where to begin. He'd forgotten about the pagan ceremony. It was truly the one secret he'd not purposely kept from her.

Facing the window, she didn't move.

"Are you well?" Quietly, he came to her. The afternoon light washed her face, giving her an otherworldly glow, her hair looking more red than golden. He slid his hand under hers. "Tell me your mind."

Isla Belle looked at him, as if discovering he was there. Her eyes, round and bright, searched his face. Her mouth parted, the same mouth that had railed against him when he'd teased her or sided with her mother. Guilt nagged at him. He'd loved her for as long as he could remember. She was his. And he'd prove his worth for the rest of his life—however unnatural it may be.

"I wish my mother..." she confessed. She dipped her head.

He lifted her chin with his finger. "I'm sorry."

She nodded.

"Please..." With hands on her shoulders, he turned Isla Belle to face him. "You asked me to not shut you out. I'm now asking the same."

"I don't know..." She looked away. "I don't know what to think. Or what to do."

"It's not meant to be like this." Rhys guided her to the couch but she didn't sit. "A wedding isn't normally rushed. There'd be a feast and songs."

Her clever lips smirked. "I've been to weddings, Rhys."

"Right." They'd been to weddings together. No one questioned the duke's inclusion of the healer servant.

"It's not legal yet, is it?" Isla Belle blushed, the pink quickly growing to a red.

Her nerves gave him strength. Rhys twirled a strand of her hair around his finger. "It's already legal, *fy annwyl*. The betrothal and the exchange of the ring is legally binding here."

"He can't undo it?"

"The king?" Rhys watched her blush deepen. "No. He cannot collect you. You are mine."

Her gaze snapped to him, eyes swirling to violet. *Pleasure.* Then to sapphire. *Happy.*

He hooked an arm around her waist and leaned forward. "I'd forgotten about the ceremony but I meant every word."

Her breath hitched, her eyes searching his face. "Me...me too."

"Blood of my blood, Isla Belle." Rhys cradled her neck with his hand, his thumb caressing her jaw. He touched his forehead against hers. "You're mine, *fy annwyl*. For now and forever."

ISLA BELLE THORNE

GARUDA, NICOLEÑO ISLAND: PRESENT DAY

*T*he salty air brought a strong citrus smell, reminding me of my childhood in California. My pulse hummed. A feeling of comfort wrapped around me. The ferry slowed, inching toward a small harbor sandwiched between two enormous cliffs. The ferry officers guided those driving in our vehicles. In a single line, each car after the other, I drove down a road, coming to an abrupt halt at a rough granite wall several stories high, mimicking a medieval fortress. There was an enormous electronic pocket gate that slid out of view. I had spent my life in and out of hospitals with fear in my throat. I never knew what I'd find—or what state my mother would be in. And yet, I was walking into a foreign country hosting the most prestigious hospital in the world. I should be more hesitant. But I felt this pull, this drive toward Garuda.

As I crept over the threshold, the gate closed with an echoing thud, leaving all of the drivers in total darkness. Slowly, fluorescent lights flickered to life in the oversized tunnel. A dozen uniformed men came forward. They quickly discharged the families before me after a brief search and scan of the offered documents. The families appeared to be residents of Garuda, the children unfazed by the uniformed men or the darkened corridor.

The men gathered and moved toward me. My hands became sweaty. Half of them read from an electronic tablet while the others scanned my truck with black, electric sticks humming.

One of the men described my car and read my license into the radio fixed on his shoulder. He walked back to my window, motioning for me to lower it. Rolling the window down, I held my breath, my hands slipping nervously on the knob.

"Identification, Miss."

I handed over the official invitation and passport—a sad book without a single stamp. He opened the door and stepped aside, waiting for me to exit. Denton had explained my car would have to be inspected for contraband and weaponry. Another uniformed man escorted me through a standing x-ray machine and deposited me in a waiting area. Minutes ticked by ever so slowly. I wished I'd taken my phone from the truck or had something to read, instead I stared at the glossy brochures highlighting the Samaritan Exchange's medical contributions. It felt more like a hospital waiting room than customs. It was far too large and empty with only a few plush chairs set out. The comfort I'd felt earlier faded.

"Miss Thorne."

Two stoic men with identical, close-cropped hair and freshly shaved faces flanked a cheerful Denton. He'd lost considerable weight since our last meeting.

Despite his sallow complexion, he smiled warmly. He stepped forward with both hands extended, a familiar pine smell pierced my nose as he moved.

"Thank you for coming." His words came formal and proper like the suit he wore. The vowels were elongated a split second longer than the American accent I'd grown up with, more like the accent my mother adopted when procuring lines from one of her California's Gold Rush era plays.

"Don't be alarmed, my girl." His eyes crinkled as he spoke. If he'd been chubby he could've played the part of Santa Claus.

"I'm fine," I said hesitantly. But I was here for answers, I reminded myself. This was where I was supposed to be. "Thank you for the invitation."

Denton chuckled, nodding his head. He looped my arm through his, as if he'd done it a hundred times, and walked me outside, the two men trailing behind. The contact was wholly unprofessional, and far too personal—and yet, it felt natural. As we exited, the sun highlighted Denton's thinning hair and weathered skin. The dim lights of the Stanford mansion had masked his age. Either that, or he'd aged a decade in a matter of weeks.

"They'll tow your car to the house after the inspection." He nodded at my truck now parked on a vast blacktop in front of hundreds of other cars. He patted my hand as a dark SUV pulled up. "The lab isn't open today but you're more than welcome to use our library."

"Thank you." It'd come out as a question. I wanted to interview Denton, not a library.

He released my arm and waited for me to climb inside the back-seat of the car. "I'm hoping to be available for dinner. My schedule is a little chaotic every time I return from the states."

It was odd, hearing my homeland referred to as the distant *states*. Garuda was never acquired by California but had stayed a separate, sovereign territory.

Denton circled the car and struggled for a moment before stepping up and sliding into the seat next to mine. He waved away the hands of his men. It wasn't his fragility that touched me. It was the look of his men, their faces creased with worry. Denton was admired, respected. Loved.

Ty believed protestors erroneously blamed the Exchange for the rise in autism and sudden increase in animal testing laboratories. Exchange supporters were tied up in the theater with *killer* written in paint on the walls above them. Still no mention of a gunman. Or a specific project.

Where is Rhys? I almost asked. Denton groaned as the car lurched forward, silencing me. I reached for my phone in my hoodie's pocket but remembered it was back in my truck.

The driver turned up a small hill that revealed a miniature airport with a dozen helicopters and small airplanes all boasting the same insignia stamped on my passport. The image looked like an old depiction of a phoenix, but less intimidating. This bird was more feminine, more regal than menacing. Although the eye appeared a bit too large, too human.

We dipped down into a sprawling city nestled in the shallow valley among the rolling hills. From the initial view, the town was large, more wide than dense. The car cruised over worn cobbled stone, an oddly comforting sound. On the right, stores mimicked the Victorian style while on the left a large park stood in what appeared to be the middle of the town. It hosted a white picketed gazebo partially hidden by an old tree. The branches were the size of a normal tree trunk. A boy, roughly twelve years old, lazily swung one leg back and forth on the lowest branch.

A few yards deeper into the park was a gigantic Christmas tree with a gardening team perched on ladders primping the evergreen. The sight of the tree dried my throat. I'd been so consumed with everything that I'd completely forgotten about holidays. Or life in general. Christmas was next month.

My first Christmas without my mom—if she didn't recover.

We circled the park and drove down a street with more modern buildings, a few stories high. The driver parked in front of a building made almost entirely of glass with pale teal accents in the style of the American architecture of the fifties.

Down the street was a thin parking lot, the first slot labeled *Dr. Jeffrey Euston*. He'd never officially invited me. As my boss, would Euston be offended that I'd gone straight to Denton? Decades ago, Denton had plucked Euston from obscurity in England and shipped him to Garuda the day he graduated from Oxford.

Attached to the parking lot stood a tall brownstone building labeled *Samaritan Exchange: Garuda Medical Sanctuary*.

"You're among giants, m'dear." Denton followed my gaze and tipped his head as he got out of the car. "This is my stop but I'll see you at dinner."

The guard standing outside the building nodded at Denton, adoration on his face. The hairs on my neck rose as the surrounding employees stood as well. He smiled, almost embarrassed at their sign of respect. My skin prickled. Power demanded respect. The way he was treated, he wouldn't be questioned. Corruption came from limitless power—corruption was worth protesting.

The car pulled away from the building and wound down and around toward the edge of town, farther into the island. We climbed the rolling hills covered in citrus and nut trees. A few miles up, the orchards shifted to olive trees. I placed my hand on the window, the air cooling significantly in the higher altitude, the rolling hills turning more steep with each bend. Peace filled me.

The driver slowed at the long gravel drive, tall Cyprus trees lining either side. The last turn revealed a boxy, four-story mansion. *Wellesley.* The name popped into my mind. I'd seen this home before. Before the car fully stopped, I opened the door and ran to the front steps. I closed my eyes, this house, I swore I'd seen it before in a vision. I placed a hand on the stone and envisioned gilded railings and exquisite paintings.

"Miss Thorne?" The driver interrupted my thoughts. I opened my eyes. He stood with my luggage in hand. "I'll place these inside. I'll send someone out if you'd like a tour."

"No. I'm okay." I was anything but. Ty made me promise to call him once I arrived but with my phone in the truck, that was out of the question.

"I'm needed back in town but there's plenty of help inside." With that he nodded and left, entering the front door etched with *Glyndwr, 1535.*

I flipped the hood of my sweatshirt over my head and circled the house. It was larger in person—at least, that's what I told myself. If I could be honest, I'd say it looked larger than I remember. I must have seen pictures of this house. It looked like an old English castle and felt misplaced on this secluded island off the Pacific Coast. The Wellesley home I'd imagined was on the edge of a quiet county in a country once wrought with greedy kings. The thought made me smile. Ty wasn't here. Neither was Stephen—not even Denton. I was alone. I could give into the visions.

The back of the house dipped down to a large lawn, a fountain at the edge. In a vision, I'd danced with dozens of other couples along the lawn. I glanced back at the house. If the driver saw me dancing, he'd for sure tell Denton. I made my way past the fountain and leaned against a tree.

I was in the faraway island waiting to have dinner with a virtual stranger. A man who I didn't fully trust. And yet this house gave me a thrill. I rubbed the bridge of my nose. I was absolutely insane.

There was a stillness in the air. Alone, I felt a dream creep in. The music of a dance from another world. I sucked at all things musical, but no one would see me here. Holding out my arm, I tried to twirl. I heard the snap of a twig and froze.

A horse. A man. Both stood looking at me. The man's face was hidden in the shadow, his hands holding the reins. The horse snorted, turning its attention to the ground. The man moved slowly toward me. I felt the familiar pull and before he came closer, I knew who he was.

Rhys tied the reins to a nearby branch. He was so close I could see his entire face. In the dimming sunset, I studied him. He looked around thirty years old. His eyes seemed older but his face was smooth and unblemished, making me wonder if he was closer to my age.

I stiffened, realizing I was staring. My arms were still frozen in an awkward dancer's pose.

His gaze met mine, his kind blue eyes and soft blonde hair. *Rhys.* "What are you doing?"

My arms dropped. "I have no idea."

He grinned and scratched his neck. "Ay. I can attest to that."

"What do you—"

"You've no idea how to dance." He stepped closer. "That I know."

That I know. I teetered as if on stilts. Words escaped me.

In what felt like a dream, Rhys guided me to his fidgeting horse.

The smell of a worn saddle brought a slew of memories—*dreams* not memories.

Ty's voice, his words made me pause, *Facts, Isla. Search for the truth.*

This wasn't a dream. This wasn't a memory. This was life, the here and the now.

I pushed back my hood. Our hands touched by accident. Lightning shot up my arm, into my chest. An image of him stroking my hair flickered, only for second, before fading. Keeping an arm around my back, he took off his hat and tossed it to the ground, never breaking our gaze.

"Who..." My breath caught in my throat.

He reached for an errant strand of hair and tucked it behind my ear, matching the vision from a moment before. I stared, transfixed. His skin glowed from the lights behind him.

He searched my face and read my eyes, whispering, "Is it you?"

"Yes," I lied. He was looking for someone else. Someone he actually knew. I didn't care. His lips curved as he spoke, tempting me, luring me.

Without another word, Rhys helped me into the saddle. Ty and Stephen were hundreds of miles away. They'd cared for me. What would they think, what would they do if I got on the horse with Rhys?

He slid behind me in the saddle, the hesitation dissolving in an instant. With my back to his chest, we rode in silence. The scent of him clouded reason. Leaning against him, I closed my eyes and felt his warmth. Home. He smelled of home.

Turning, I glanced up at him. He stared at me, unabashed. Wisps of blonde hair blew across his forehead, triggering another image. Not of him, but of the woman with golden curls. Rhys gave a half-grin, unlocking something deep within me. We weaved in and out of orchards, my body aware of every movement. Every breath. Every touch.

The horse nickered in front of a barn lit with old fashioned street lamps, two to a door on what seemed like dozens of stalls. Rhys handed me the reins before dismounting. He turned and held out his arms. Swinging my leg over, I hesitated for the second time.

He placed a hand on each hip. "I won't let you fall."

I already have, I almost said.

His arms wrapped around me, catching me before my feet touched the ground. We stared at each other, our faces just inches apart. The late afternoon air whirled around us, crisp with the soothing cool of winter. He leaned in, his forehead touching mine. He inhaled deeply before gently setting me down.

Rhys led me inside the house, through a side door I already knew existed. We walked hand in hand toward the music room as if we'd done it a thousand times before. Trepidation loosened its grip with each step. The silence invited excitement, an electric current between us. A moment later I stood in front of the piano in a darkened room I'd seen hundreds of times before. Tension snapped and crackled as I let my hand fall from his grasp.

The setting sun provided the only light, not enough to show the grandeur of the marble floors and columns nor the soft bench by the large window to my left—all facts I shouldn't know.

I was acutely conscious of him, the citrus of his shampoo, his lithe frame and perfect face. I looked up and watched him, watching me. He held out his hand again; obediently I raised mine to his. He lowered his face to mine. I inhaled sharply. I had to but lean forward and our lips would touch. He swallowed, his Adam's apple bobbing.

The hunger building, I waited for the kiss. His blue eyes traveled slowly over my face: eyes, eyelashes, brows, lips, until I felt curiously exposed, his breath on my skin. I shivered from familiar longing— something my brain told me I shouldn't know. He rested his nose against mine. I placed a hand on his chest. He traced the side of my neck.

Dozens of dreams exploded in my mind, leaping from one to the next.

Tenderly, his lips brushed against mine, a whisper of a kiss.

I stepped back, unable to breathe—alarm crept in.

He followed, not giving up. His hand cradled my jaw and tilted upward, kissing me again, dissolving the fear.

Little fireworks of delight danced on my skin. My hands gripped his shirt. He smiled, his lips parting before kissing once more.

Something seeped into the room, a weight on my chest. Loss and love swirled in the pit of my stomach. An ache, as if I were saying good bye, stole my breath.

He must have felt it too. He hesitated and stepped back, hunger still in his eyes. Doubt filled me.

Everything stopped.

And then nothing but breathing. I felt magnetized. We stared at each other and waited—for what I didn't know.

Alarms rang in my head. *Search for truth.* "Who are you?"

Regret washed over him, the pain in his eyes and the slump of his shoulders. His eyes flicked to the ring on my hand—his face paling. "No. I'm. No."

I reached for him, fear in my chest.

"You don't know me?" He jumped back as if my touch had burned him. "You don't know me," he repeated; his face lost color, his lips nearly gray. He backed up against the wall, his hand raking his hair. He spun around.

And left.

RHYS GLYNDWR

HEREFORDSHIRE, WALES: 1535

*R*hys marched from the holy room, armed men flanking him. He'd been married for a day and already received word Captain Milford was in England at Ludlow Castle, petitioning for the extradition of Lady Isla Belle. With the lords gathering for the council, time wasn't on their side. The castle was in a frenzy, harnessing horses and packing food for the week's journey.

"I've two copies of the betrothal. And the wedding parchment." Mathias struggled to keep up with the pace. "By marriage she is no longer an English citizen."

"You've said." Rhys didn't hide the bite in his voice. Most of his life had been in service to Isla Belle but in only a day, the connection had deepened. There was power in the union, even if he didn't fully understand why.

Falling back, Mathias warned, "Glyndwr."

"Rhys." Isla Belle shouted, her voice piercing him. The men parted, clearing the way for his wife. Her eyes blazed. She walked toward him, fury in every step.

"*Mam y ddreigion.*" Tobias grinned, elbowing Rhys. The guard had taken a liking to her fire. "Tell me she isn't the mother of dragons, Glyndwr."

"She'll be the death of me, dragon or not," Rhys murmured.

Isla Belle arched an eyebrow. She was too far away to hear, but the woman somehow knew everything. "You're crossing the river." Reaching him, she folded her arms. "You're going—you're going back to *England?*"

"Ay."

Tobias shuffled the men about, leaving Rhys and Isla Belle alone in the courtyard.

"Are you mad?" She cried out. "You were whipped."

"I'm aware." He stepped closer, she retreated.

"When were you going to tell me?"

"I was making my way to you." After he'd made the necessary preparations. Rhys knew she'd protest. He'd planned on telling her after every horse was mounted and each man armed.

The look she tossed him made him doubt the decision. "How thoughtful, Rhys. This isn't like Wellesley with my father at your side. *You're* the duke. You're the one who'll be kept at court." Isla Belle's eyes were bright with anger, flicking to black in an instant. *Fear.*

"We're not going to court, *fy annwyl.*" But Rhys knew what she meant. "We're headed to Ludlow for the council. They'll have to use more than a whip to keep me."

"Milford knows." She bit her lip. "He knows what you are. He knows you were the man who poisoned him. He'll be ready; he'll have more than a whip."

"I have a seat in the council, Isla Belle. Whether Milford is there or not, I have to attend." Rumors of a Glyndwr heir had already been lit, spreading from county to county, courtesy of the quick witted Mathias. Formal dictates were largely ignored but a whispering neighbor bursting with gossip traveled faster than a royal edict ever could. "I need to be there in the flesh. Show both the bishop and the king that Wales has a leader, and we've not forgotten what was promised."

Isla Belle moved closer, her limp nearly gone. She placed a hand on his chest. "If you leave me—"

"I will return to you." Rhys covered her hand.

"No." Her lips quirked to a wicked grin. "I'm going with you."

Tobias approached, the reins of Isla Belle's new horse in hand. He didn't shrug or even pretend to be sheepish. With a wink at Isla Belle, he murmured to Rhys, *"Mam y ddreigion."*

"Blast it man." Rhys ran a hand through his hair. "You are not going, Isla Belle."

Quick on her feet, she turned from him and mounted. Tobias tossed the reins over the horse's head, disappearing before Rhys could strangle him.

"You'd better hurry." Isla Belle patted the horse's neck. "The men are restless."

The woman was mad. She'd forsaken everything he'd risked to accompany him. "You have no idea the dangers that lie ahead."

"Did we not cross the river together?" Her horse snorted, appearing to agree with its mistress. "I'm well aware of the risks."

Tobias returned, this time with Rhys' horse. Per tradition, the beast was a magnificent Welsh cob. The only conciliation in Tobias handing over the reins was the look of envy in Isla Belle's eyes as she looked at the cob. Glaring at his wife, Rhys mounted the Welsh stallion. She kept her gaze on the beast but kept silent. Rhys turned his stare on Tobias who rode to his side.

"I'll not war with a woman like that." The guard grinned.

"You'd risk my ire instead?" Rhys groaned. He couldn't show his worth as a leader if he couldn't maintain order in his own household.

"Ay." Tobias laughed, the sound rich and deep. "You're not half as scary."

"I can be scary." Even to his own ears, Rhys heard the whine.

"Just not like the dragon's mother." Tobias threw back his head, his shoulders shaking in laughter. "She'll face the Hanging Bishop and not blink an eye."

"Don't get that in her head." Rhys couldn't fight the smile. He glanced over his shoulder, Isla Belle's focus was on the horizon, her golden hair unwinding from the plait. She was a sight to behold.

For days, they stopped only to eat and give the horses a few hours rest. Isla Belle and Rhys rode side by side, the very picture of what they faced, England and Wales, running together, toward a future of their own making. Messengers would come and go throughout the day, sending word from surrounding counties. Mathias exchanged gossip. Milford and Bishop Lee were seen arguing, leadership was ripe for the taking. The king's latest mistress was pregnant, and Queen Anne's trial had just concluded. England was distracted, but Wales was not. The English had nibbled away, pulling the marshlands into an eternal tug of war between the two countries.

Descending into Shropshire county, Isla Belle slowed her horse. "My grandfather will be here. He'll not be happy to see me."

"Who's your grandfather?" Tobias looked her over—Rhys didn't appreciate the attention. "You're not a Stanley are you?"

"No." Rhys cut in. "She's a Woodville."

"No wonder she's a dragon." Tobias whistled. "You had to snag this one as your wife, Glyndwr?" He groaned, murmuring, *"Medraist di ddimd wyn march ffarmwr."*

"Do I want to know what he said?" Isla Belle asked, watching Tobias circle his horse to a waiting group of men.

"Couldn't you steal a farmer's daughter?" Rhys mimicked Tobias' deep voice. He nodded to an approaching Mathias. "And here we go."

The steward sidled up to Rhys, his hand massaging his troubled leg. "We'll enter on the North side of the River Teme."

"Why?" Isla Belle asked.

From their perch, the easiest way was through the south meadow.

"The bishop has posted warnings that way." Mathias gave Rhys a knowing look. Bishop Lee had begun nailing hanged men on posts throughout the counties. "Our men will lose their hearts if they see the dead."

Rhys nodded. "To the north, then."

"Mathias!" A man in tattered clothes sped toward the steward. He leaned back in the saddle, halting the panting horse. The man flipped open the leather bag and handed a stack of parchment to the steward. Without another word, the messenger spun his mount and galloped away, dirt and grass flying after.

Mathias unrolled the parchment, his eyes scanning. His head snapped up. "This could tip either way, for or against our cause."

With help from surrounding men, Rhys and Mathias dismounted and huddled under a makeshift canopy. With his finger, the steward underlined the elegant writing; each letter beautifully written. "Parliament wants to combine the marshlands, Welsh and English."

"Parliament?" Isla Belle stood over the men, Mathias, Rhys and Tobias kneeling over the document. "Now Wales and the marshes are worthy of representation?"

Tobias snickered.

"If you call me a dragon I will—"

"I've said nothing, *milady*." The guard held up his hands. "You've been a *duges* for less than a week and you've already taken up our cross?"

"She won't be a duchess in either tongue if you don't quit jesting." Narrowing his eyes at Tobias, the steward smacked the parchment. "The king wants to make a deal."

"English law will rule." Rhys tapped the next paragraph. "The Marcher lords will no longer hold court. Their rights and privileges will be revoked. They'll rebel."

"But they'll have a voice." Isla Belle stood and looked to the surrounding men for support. "Welsh gentry will be on equal footing with English nobles. Isn't that what you want?"

"We want Wales to be left alone." A man behind her muttered.

"And peace." Mathias didn't lift his gaze to Isla Belle or his men. "We've been at war for too long."

"Isn't this a solution to both?" Isla Belle turned around. The men seemed to sense her urgency but instead of joining in, they stepped back.

"We'll never be equal, *mam y ddreigion*," Tobias said softly, pointing toward Ludlow Castle. "The almighty bishop has hanged thousands of us. Just for speaking our native tongue. We're met with suspicion and charged with treason. And why? Because we were born on the wrong side of the river."

"Won't this stop the bishop, then?" Isla Belle nodded to the parchment. "Won't it steal the bishop's right to hang? It'll be English law. Welsh nobility will hold privileges a man of the cloth can't touch."

"If you were a man, I'd send you myself." Tobias winked. "But you're a touch too pretty."

Isla Belle gave a sad smile. Rhys stepped to her side, a hand on the small of her back. The Duke of Wellesley had said those same words since Isla Belle's infancy. *If you were but a man.*

"Whatever is decided, we make it together." Rhys met each man's gaze, not moving to the next until Rhys received a nod, or an *ay.* "The king doesn't want a rebellion nor does he want a war. The pope and his enemies on the continent are giving him enough grief. He needs us."

"King Henry has a poor way of showing it." A man behind Isla Belle shifted, fear and bitterness in his tone.

"I've heard the king say it myself." Rhys straightened his posture, hoping the grief was hidden. He'd left the duke in the king's clutches. Wellesley had given Rhys a home, kindness and a wife.

"King's a spoiled child." Tobias muttered. "Nothing but a bloody tyrant."

The murmurs grew.

"Is it true?" Isla Belle stepped from Rhys, turning once more to each of the men. "Did your lot put Henry's father on the throne?"

The murmurs quieted.

"I'm English, but even I know who crowned King Henry." Her eyes flicked from fear to pain, then back again. Rhys watched the men, wondering if they noticed the changing colors. She circled Mathias who stood, rolling the parchment into a tight circle. "The war of the roses—the war for the throne was between two Welshmen."

Tobias eyed Mathias, both men looked at Rhys. Isla Belle was on dangerous ground.

"The English won't be happy." She folded her arms, hiding trembling hands. "Wales put a Welsh on an English throne. And now." She motioned to the parchment. "Welsh nobility are equal to English. Same in parliament."

The circle of men exchanged looks, some bewildered and some tempted by her words.

"Is this the cause for Bishop Lee's hatred?" Isla Belle gave a one shoulder shrug. Rhys caught the color of her eyes. For all the playacting, she was scared. "And now you bring the Glyndwr heir to council." She tsked. With a shake of her head, she added, "If the man was worried about Wales before…" Another shrug.

Tobias winked at her. "Your Welsh is dreadful but we'll take you, dragon." He threw his hand in the air, shouting, "Glyndwr!"

The men joined in. Rhys pulled Isla Belle close. *"Fy annwyl,* you'll—"

"Be the death of me." She smiled to the men but her hands gripped Rhys' tunic. "Pray they accept the king's agreement."

"Ay, *fy annwyl.*" He pressed his lips to her ear. "You should have stayed."

"Rhys—"

"But I'm grateful you came." He tightened his hold. "I'll never forgive myself if something happens to you."

"Ay." She mimicked his accent. "I feel the same."

ISLA BELLE THORNE

GARUDA, NICOLEÑO ISLAND: PRESENT DAY

*R*etreating, Rhys's face drained of color. He turned and ran. My mind raced. Shame mixed with anger. I'd followed a stranger into a house, in a foreign territory. Men had chased my mother just like women hounded Ty. I'd watched dozens of girls do the walk of shame after a night with Ty. There'd never been a boy or a man that had interested me, just Rhys, the same man fleeing like I was contagious.

You don't know me. His words repeated in my mind.

My lips still tingled from the kiss. His footsteps echoed. He was climbing the stairs, headed down the hallway and into the bedroom, fifth door on the left. There'd be a four poster bed and French doors leading to a balcony. With his hair splayed across his forehead, Rhys would lay diagonally on the bed, his feet hanging off the edge.

Cradling my head, I waited for the image to leave. I touched the smooth finish of the piano. It was real, but the notes in my head weren't. The song, the lullaby was there in the room. Both inaudible and tangible. My dress. The muted light from the moon darkened the fabric. I gripped the skirt, the fabric in my fingers. It was real. Kicking off my heels, I stood on the stone floors; toes instantly cold.

A nagging thought crept in. Was the kiss real? I touched my lips. *Is Rhys real?*

I'd ridden with Rhys, his chest hugging my back. He'd gently lifted me from the saddle. Goosebumps littered my skin. He'd kissed me—and left.

A tear slipped down my cheek. Confused, I touched it and held it out to the light. It was real, but it couldn't be. *You don't know me.* Rhys was a stranger. I'd never been to the island. Nor had I ever touched Rhys until today. Tears were for broken hearts. Or a grieving daughter. Not for strangers.

The tear couldn't be for Rhys. It had to be for my mom. Spinning around, I realized I was in a house far from everything I knew. Ty was hundreds of miles away. I was alone in someone else's home and no way to contact my family in California.

Barefoot, I glided over the cool floors in search of a phone. According to Ty's theory, I must have studied this mansion. The house was enormous, almost castle-like. The ground floor was an open foyer the size of a not-so-modest hotel, granite columns included.

I held my breath, a brief vision of Rhys lying on a grassy meadow. He smelled faintly of hay and horse. No—I pulled myself from the vision's grasp. This was wrong. All of it. I couldn't—I wouldn't succumb.

A headache speared my thoughts. Raw anger came through. The headaches that wouldn't quit, the visions that stalked my thoughts and the secrets kept from me.

My mother would have demanded an answer from Denton and hooked Rhys like a fish until she had an explanation. She was my mother, and I was her daughter. I would not be weak.

With a snap, a vision crashed down.

Rhys held me close in newly-wedded bliss. We crossed the threshold of the stone mansion. Into his chest, I giggled and clung to him. He knocked my feet against the mahogany coat rack, sending it clattering to the floor. We laughed, our heads tipped, innocence and fresh love. The hem of my dress snagged on the coat rack. Rhys tripped on my dress and dropped me. I brought him down as I fell, my hands still on him. He kissed my nose and rolled over to his back, a soft, content chuckle rumbling.

We lay with hands intertwined, my eyes on the stained glass, his finger tracing my thumb. The foyer was more of a courtyard with stairs, each corner leading up to the second and third floors. Each hallway was decorated the same from the green marble to gold plated crown molding to sparkling chandeliers.

The stone chilled my back. I felt Rhys' hand stiffen. I tamed the terror. This grand house with stone walls and spacious ceilings would never keep me warm. Suppressing a cough, I felt the familiar weight in my lungs. The house he built for me would never let me live.

I gripped the piano bench and breathed through the pain. It wasn't a vision. It was a byproduct of the headaches. They had triggered them. It would explain the frequency and intensity. Never, even as a child, were they ever this strong.

Gingerly, I walked under the hallway, knowing that upstairs I'd just passed six doors. It felt safer, walking underneath instead of next to them. Most were guest bedrooms with a neglected nursery at the end. I paused directly under the room, feeling the ache of an empty womb. Shaking the odd sensation, I kept walking until I reached the double wooden doors at the end of the hallway.

I pushed, the doors squawking open. They revealed an impressive library with the distinct smell of aged books. Home. I was home. My chest went light. Breathing was easier.

The room was complete with small alcoves, with only enough room for one oversized chair. Moonlight entered the room and ricocheted off the entry wall's mirror. The room held an even flow of the night's soft light.

Books. Books upon books. They were everywhere, except for the space reserved for seven portraits occupying two balconies on the open second floor. My hand skimmed the polished wood banister. I rushed up the short stairs. The woman in the first portrait had beautiful blue eyes and blonde hair, complementing the deep blue of her medieval attire. She had the same high cheekbones and petite features of the noble class. Her clothes and hair reminded me of the visions.

At the bottom of the painting, just below the point where the canvas met the wooden frame was a naked, faded patch the size of a small plaque. Every other portrait included a small gold tag in the same spot.

Scooting sideways, I examined the next one. A fiery red-headed woman with a rigid pose stood in the second painting. She was stunning in her own right but lacked the beauty of the first. Her blue eyes were fierce and glittered with intelligence. Her long, tight white satin bodice with paned sleeves was lined in a pink, matching petticoat. I traced the neckline of the dress, almost feeling the coarse fabric, so unlike Lady Isla Belle's silk gowns. Rubbing my finger along her name plate, I stopped. Mary Pearl.

Marching forward, I passed Ava Rose. I was guided by some intangible force to the other balcony, feeling a growing dread in my stomach.

The fourth canvas was of a pale and sickly woman named, Aili. Staring at the her eyes, I chewed the inside of my cheek. The shape and shade of her eyes were recognizable, something I'd seen before. Ty's words begged to be heard, shouting in my head. *Don't search for the crazy. Search for the truth.*

The fifth lady, Charlotte, was more elegant, graceful than the previous. The sixth must have been a daughter, a toddler. These women, and the one child, possessed the same startling set of blue eyes.

Familiar eyes. Almost as if—*no.*

They were not from my dreams; that would be impossible. I stole a glance at the last canvas. An ache crept in my chest. An angelic baby wrapped in a blue flannel cloth, her eyes closed. Unconsciously, my finger traced the name plate. After removing my finger, I gasped.

Isla Belle.

RHYS GLYNDWR

LUDLOW CASTLE, ENGLAND: 1535

*O*rders were given to the groomsmen. Half would take the day shift, the other half the night. Neither the bishop or the king would get the best of Rhys' men. With Mathias and Tobias flanking him, Rhys held the parchment, his heart beating wildly. His childhood was spent healing, not ruling or leading men. A broken bone could be mended within months while countries took years. If they mended at all.

"Oh blast it all." Tobias rubbed his hands down his face.

Rhys followed his gaze. Isla Belle was entering Ludlow Castle. Alone. The foolish woman was entering a council full of Marcher Lords and a hateful bishop.

She slipped from view, men from other counties following her entry. Rhys ran toward the castle.

Tobias cut him off, a hand on Rhys' shoulder. "You cannot rush in there."

Mathias and Tobias exchanged a nod. "You'll need to look in control. That you'd planned for her to go in first."

Rhys shoved Tobias' hand off his shoulder. "That's my wife."

"Her mind is sharp, Glyndwr." The doubt in Mathias's voice underlined his words. "Walk calmly. Walk proud. For her sake."

For her sake. Rhys swallowed the rising panic, his hands clenching at his sides. His willful wife was too headstrong for her own good. She should've stayed in Wales. She would have been surrounded by brick, stone and the Glyndwr name. They walked on English soil now. The same land that whipped his back raw.

Steeling himself, Rhys straightened his posture. Both the duke and duchess carried an air of authority, something Rhys had never mastered. His father could skewer men with a look, Isla Belle as well. Rhys' greatest conquests were against disease and fever, not men.

The men walked together, Rhys in the middle of their small company. Through the portcullis, between English soldiers and into the great hall. Rhys spotted the back of Isla Belle's golden head slipping inside the council. He rushed toward her, stopped again by Tobias' thick arm.

"Mind yourself, *eich uchelder.*" Tobias' voice boomed, emphasizing *Your Highness.*

Men stopped talking, each turning his focus to Rhys. He was used to the second looks and the hard stares. He knew his face was different, striking even. He fought the temptation to find Isla Belle and demand her to leave. Even in the council for his native country, Rhys put Isla Belle above all else.

"What is this?" A man called out, disdain in every word.

Isla Belle stood, her back to the council, her gaze on the bishop. To strangers, her face was bathed in innocence, only the changing colors of her eyes belied her intent. "He is here. I rode beside him, the Glyndwr heir has returned."

The room erupted in whispers, gossip skipping maniacally from one man to the next. Isla Belle had locked the council's attention before the bishop had a chance to take control. She was brilliant— even if Rhys wanted to throttle her.

The men parted in front of Rhys, allowing a direct view of the council table. A man sat, his fingers perched together on the table. He wore the black hat and holy robes, but the sneer on his face was anything but divine.

"Your Excellency." Tobias grimaced at *excellency*. "May I introduce you to *eich uchelder*, Rhys Glyndwr?"

A hush fell on the crowd. The near two hundred men gathered from Wales, the marshes and English border towns. All of them turned to Rhys, the bishop forgotten. Rhys felt the weight of their scrutiny.

"And who is Rhys Glyndwr?" The bishop stood, a severe frown on his lips. He either didn't know the name or didn't care. "As president of this council, I will determine who takes a seat." Bishop Lee could try, but nothing he said or did would fully capture the council's attention now.

Rhys held out the parchment. "As heir of Glyndwr, I bring King Henry's edict."

It wasn't a complete lie. He held the intercepted document. He walked toward the bishop. Isla Belle stepped forward. He didn't turn to her or hesitate. Their hands brushed as he passed.

"He's no heir, Your Excellency." Milford came from the corner of the room.

Rhys heard Isla Belle's gasp. He froze, fighting the urge to turn around and embrace her.

"He's a thief." Milford turned his dark gaze, looking past Rhys where Isla Belle stood. "I whipped him myself."

Rhys laid the parchment on the table and unbuckled his belt. He pulled his tunic over his head, displaying his bare, smooth back. "Show me the lashes?"

Milford nodded to Isla Belle. "Ask the lady, she was there."

Bishop Lee motioned for her to step forward. "And you are?"

Isla Belle stood next to Rhys, her pride at the ready. "I'm Lady Glyndwr, his wife."

Milford scoffed. "You lie."

She held out her hand. "I believe the witnesses to the wedding are present."

Pointing a finger at her, Milford said, "This woman is Lady Isla Belle Wellesley. She was summoned by the king. Her own mother has confessed treason. This woman should be clapped in irons."

"She's a Welsh lady, Your Excellency." Rhys nearly choked on *Your Excellency*. The man was not holy or divine. He was bathed in hate. "The betrothal was decades old, long before the king asked for a mistress."

"Mistress?" The bishop scoffed. "What are you suggesting?"

Rhys held out his arms. "I've not seen the order. Those words came from Captain Milford."

Bishop Lee pursed his lips. "Captain?"

"Don't you twist this." Milford folded his arms, the fingers of his left hand were limp, stained with purple webbing from the poisoned injury. His stare was murderous. His eyes flicking from Rhys to Isla Belle. "You were there, woman. You watched me whip him."

"I believe the evidence is clear." Isla Belle motioned to Rhys' smooth back. She swallowed hard, her gaze fluttering everywhere but on Rhys.

"You've never come to council before." Bishop Lee sat back in his chair, his fingers steepled.

"I've been away, studying English and Welsh laws." There was a sliver of truth in Rhys' statement. The duke had helped enlarge Rhys' knowledge.

"Why would the king entrust his word to you?" The bishop didn't wait for an answer. He gathered the parchment. He scanned the first paragraph, his jaw clenching. "We've no time to discuss this today."

"We're in support of it." Rhys leaned over the table and tapped the document. "We're to be equals."

"In parliament and in rank." Isla Belle stepped forward.

"You will remain silent or you will leave," Bishop Lee snapped.

Tobias sent a look of warning to Rhys. She'd crossed a line.

"We've sent our support to parliament." The lie came easy. Rhys pulled the tunic back over his head and buckled his belt. He needed to keep his hands busy. Confronting and leading, this was not what Rhys had prepared for. In truth, he'd given up on returning to Wales. Though he'd never admitted it out loud. It wasn't until the king called for Isla Belle did Rhys change course.

"You don't know the way of things." The bishop pounded the table and stood. "You are no heir. You are no duke, Welsh or not. You've no seat in this council."

"There is no council." Rhys turned from the man and spoke to the gathered gentry. "This document asks a lot of us but the king knows our worth. The Council of Wales is disbanded, replaced with parliament in London."

Men stood, fists raised and shouts erupting. Tobias pumped his arms in the air, nodding for Rhys to continue.

"We've a Welsh king on the throne—"

"You will be silent." The bishop sneered. "If you value your neck, you'll still that tongue."

"The rights and privileges of the English nobility will be ours." Rhys held an arm out, indicating the bishop. "You'll answer to your peers instead of the cloth."

"It's not my word you cross, boy. It's the king's." Spittle fell from the bishop's lips. "This land has been lawless long enough. I've been tasked with giving order."

"You'd defy your king?" Rhys nodded to Milford. "I know a man willing to carry out the punishment."

"I am the man willing to punish," Bishop Lee whispered. "I'm not the man to cross."

"And I'm the man who cannot die."

The bishop hesitated, looking from Rhys to Milford. The whispers of the Glyndwr myth had reached his ears. Mathias had made sure of it. Bishop Lee narrowed his gaze and gathered strength. "English subjects will speak English. Not Welsh."

The room quieted, suspicion in the air.

Bishop Lee grabbed the shoulder of the man to his left. "The council will send a record to the king. The edict was supported."

Rhys tipped his head. "Thank you—"

"Including the acceptance of English as the official language." The bishop rubbed his temples. "Anything else is considered treason."

"We'll await the king's word." Rhys waited for Bishop Lee to meet his gaze. "I am the heir of Owain ab Gruffydd, lord of Glyndyfrdwy. I am Welsh from my blood to my bones. And so is your king."

A vein on the bishop's neck ticked. "This council is dismissed."

"Ay." Rhys nodded, smirking. "For now and forever."

With that, he gathered Isla Belle, and headed to the door. Men he'd never met stood, tipping their heads in respect. Murmurs of *Eich Uchelder* and *Your Highness* echoed in their wake. Rhys had made his mark, his hand trembling on Isla Belle's back.

Outside, Mathias hobbled next to them. "That's one way to unite Wales."

"I was supporting the king's edict."

"Do you think that's what King Henry will hear?" Mathias pulled on Rhys' elbow. "You've made an enemy."

"He's made friends, too," Tobias whispered. Rhys followed his gaze. The council gathered behind them. "They've heard the rumors, Mathias. And by the looks of it, they believe."

"Bishop Lee will never forget this." Mathias continued his hobbled walk. "He hates us, Glyndwr. He blames us for his miserable life."

"Why?" Isla Belle asked.

"I've no idea." The steward didn't hide his annoyance at her question. "The man says we're scheming to take the throne. But he doesn't believe it. He doesn't think we're worthy of a rebellion."

"Ay, now keep walking." Tobias whispered, "At least out of the bishop's view."

Rhys eyed the great hall. They were a few days ride from the River Wye, the line between countries that were supposed to be separate. At least, according to his father. A man who'd given his life for an idea. A myth.

"What happens now?" Isla Belle's tone was soft.

"We gather the lords," Rhys said. "Bishop Lee will come calling. So will Milford."

"And we'll be ready." Tobias cocked his head to the side, grinning. "Do you think they'll mind?"

Isla Belle rolled her eyes. Rhys mirrored his grin.

"Oh, come on." Tobias' grin stretched. "Ask me."

With a sigh, Isla Belle asked, "What will they mind?"

"That we have a dragon on our side?" Tobias' laughter ate half the sentence. He threw an arm around Mathias's shoulders, not letting go until the steward grinned.

"It's done." Isla Belle stood on her toes and wrapped her arms around Rhys' neck, calming his fears. "For now."

"For now."

ISLA BELLE THORNE

GARUDA, NICOLEÑO ISLAND: PRESENT DAY

*T*he nameplate of the portrait was inscribed with *Isla Belle*. The paintings—I'd seen those same blue-eyed women in my dreams. This wasn't possible. My stomach churned and my head pounded. Gripping the handrail, I forced myself to breathe in. And then out. Slowly, I descended to the library door. One last glance—to make sure they were real—I looked at the portraits. From below, the blonde woman looked the most familiar, but then the baby. The flannel cloth.

I'd seen the fabric before. And the baby. But from where, I didn't know.

I ran down the hall, listening for an employee. Denton would be back soon. My stomach did a flip. I didn't want to talk to him. Or Rhys. I needed facts first. My name was in a stranger's house. Isla Belle wasn't Jane or Ashley or any other ordinary name. I'd been the only Isla Belle—and then I stopped. My mother had changed her wedding album into a scrapbook filled with everything about my birth, but I had no idea where my luggage was.

A hand on the wall, I remembered Mom's words. She'd told me once that her fertility doctor helped name me. What if the doctor was Denton?

My mind flew back to the basement of the theatre.

Your mother might be, well, honestly, she might be beyond help. Denton sat on the couch and held out his hands in surrender. He'd known my mother well. Ty could very well have been her first child.

The air felt thick. Heavy. I needed air. I found the side door—something I shouldn't remember—and burst through to the cold December air. Sitting on the steps, I folded my arms over my knees.

The crunch of tires on gravel pulled me from my hiding spot. The cleanest tow truck I'd ever seen hauled my Chevy up the drive. An emblem with a red dragon facing a purple phoenix was on the door of the tow truck. The dragon seemed familiar. Of course a stupid dragon on a tow truck I'd never seen before would look familiar.

Two women in aprons came up the walk, engrossed in conversation. They looked at me, then at the tow truck. The older one asked, "Can we help you?"

"Do you work here?" I spoke to them but kept my eye on the driver. He began lowering my beat up truck. There couldn't be a bigger difference between the sleek tow truck and my forty something year old Chevy. "I'm a guest but don't know which room. I'd just like to see where I'm staying. Where my luggage is." I rambled, not understanding why I was nervous.

The women turned to each other. The older one smiled warmly. "Guests normally stay in town but I bet we can find your room." She tossed a glance over her shoulder at my truck. "Come get us after you're done."

The driver of the tow truck worked silently, coming to me with my keys. I signed his form and before I could thank him, read the listed address, *Staverton, Glyndwr Hill.* I'd thought this was Denton's home. He'd invited me, not Rhys.

I opened my truck and there on the seat was my phone. Seven missed phone calls from Ty. Instead of reading his texts to me, I quickly typed out, *Can't talk. Found something interesting.*

I wanted to send the picture of the portraits before calling. I'd not yet spoken, at least not really, to Denton. And I was not going to admit I'd kissed Rhys. Ty might kill me for that one.

The women were in the kitchen just off the entry. They guided me upstairs to the second door to the left. The layout would be a bed in the corner with the bathroom along the north wall.

The older woman opened the door with a smile. "Let us know if we can do anything else."

"Thanks." My luggage was just inside the door, the handle still up. As soon as the door clicked shut, I threw the luggage on the bed and unzipped it. My mother's scrapbook was on top, along with a few of my mother's plays. I'd only taken the oldest, leaving the rest for Ty to read. The last one I'd read had to do with biological immortality. Mom must have grasped some information from Stephen but she'd butchered the concept horribly in her book. She'd treated it like a fairytale without the science or rules. There was always a cause and effect, always a price for playing with nature. I grabbed the scrapbook; there had to be answers in it.

My phone chirped with a text. I turned the phone over, not wanting the distraction. Flipping to the beginning of the book, I tugged my picture from the first page. Twin babies. My mother said it was common in fertility patients to expect multiples. I'd found the same thing during my artificial insemination rounds with animals. My mother never seemed bothered by the fact she'd lost my stillborn brother. For a woman bathed in the dramatic arts, Mom was constantly stoic about my twin's death. But holding the picture, I wondered if it broke her. The birth changed her. Even if Stephen would never admit it.

Both babies were swaddled in the faded flannel from the hospital, both with their eyes closed. And there it was. I held my breath. The painting in the library—same blanket, same baby. Same picture.

No. It wasn't possible. Ty's voice in my head, *Facts, Isla.*

I flipped to the next page. A yellowed note with my name. My lungs seized. An impression of a ring. A band was once pressed against the aged paper.

Rhys' handwriting. It was him—he'd written *Isla Belle.* I knew it. I knew it like I knew the ring on my hand was mine. Grabbing the picture, I made my way back to the library, Ty's insistence in my head, *search for the truth.*

Just outside the library, the sounds of a piano being played, echoing over the marbled floors. It was a song Rhys had sung in my dreams.

Midnight slumber close surround thee, all through the night. I mouthed the words. *Angels watching e'er around thee, all through the night.*

A pull wrapped around my waist and guided me to the music room. Rhys sat on the piano, his back to me. He stopped playing and propped his head with his left hand, his right fiddling with the keys.

"Though I roam a minstrel lonely, all through the night," I whispered. Singing was my mother's gift, not mine. But I knew the words. I knew this song. "My true harp shall praise sing only, all through the night."

Rhys' hand missed a note. He'd heard me. I spoke louder, "Love's young dream."

He turned, his profile to me. The afternoon light glowed around him and the piano.

I took two steps in. "Yet my strains of love."

Rhys stood and leaned against the piano, a thumb scratching his jaw. In a soothing tenor, he sang, "Shall hover near the presence of my lover."

"Why did you leave?" I leaned into the doorframe, the picture tucked into my palm. "Earlier. Why did you leave?"

"What's your name?" He threw his hands into his pockets and came closer, suspicion in his voice.

"Isla Belle."

He flinched and asked in a clipped one, "What's your real name?"

"My real name is Isla Belle Thorne." The sound of a door opening and closing came from the front of the house, far behind me.

"That's not possible. You would know me." He rocked on his heels. "I was there when Isla Belle Thorne was born."

"You what?" The walls blurred. *I was there.* The man didn't look a day over thirty. Even if he was there, he'd have been too young to remember. "And just how old were you when I was born?"

He looked away. "I was there when she was born. And when she died."

"Right." The man was insane. This whole time I thought *I* was crazy but Rhys, he was the very definition. "I'm fairly certain I'd know if I died."

"You aren't her." Doubt had crept into his voice. "I thought you were...but you aren't."

"And how would you know?" I held up my hand to stop him from answering. "I am Isla Belle Thorne. The one thing I don't know is who you really are. It doesn't make sense. I know your last name isn't Staverton. It's Glyndwr." He flinched. I scowled. "Just because I can't say it the way you do doesn't mean it isn't true."

Rhys' face softened. "You sound like her."

"If *her* means *me*. Then, yeah. I do sound like her because I *am* her. Isla Belle." This was getting ridiculous. "I came here for answers. Not to prove who I am."

"Answers to what?" Something in him changed. The look in his eye, both gentle and intense.

"My mother. The fertility clinic. Me. The dreams." Another door opened and closed somewhere in the house. Everything echoed—and then I felt my face flush. If I could hear the door that meant everyone else in the house could hear us. "I've got a laundry list of questions."

Rhys circled me and shut the music room door. His entire aura had softened, like earlier when we'd kissed. "What dreams?"

"I'm not crazy." It was too defensive. He raised his eyebrows but said nothing. I retreated, backing away from him. The kiss didn't need to be repeated.

"I didn't say you were."

"But you will."

"Try me." A challenge lit in his eyes. He was a stranger. There was no reason to trust him. And yet he held my gaze. "What dreams?"

No. I couldn't. My head throbbed. I'd never called Ty back. A million other things I should be doing flew through my mind—telling Rhys about the visions was not on that list. Shaking my head, I said, "I should go."

"There. Right, there." Rhys pointed at me. "Your eyes changed color."

I ducked my head. My face and neck flushed.

"I've known only one person with eyes like that." Rhys stepped closer. "And I've been around a long time."

The piano bench was against my calves. I had nowhere to go. "It's a family trait."

"And these dreams." His voice was soothing, luring. Confidence oozed from him. He came closer still. "What did you dream exactly?"

"Nothing, really." Alarms rang in my head. He'd tell Denton. I'd be committed, declared insane by midnight.

He was inches from me, his scent wrapping around me. "Are you saying you *don't* dream of me?"

Closing my eyes shut, I said, "If I did, you'd think I was—"

"No." He waited. I opened my eyes. He smiled sadly, grief etched in his striking face. "I'd think you were mine."

My knees weakened. There was too much warmth in his voice. He'd kissed me—and left, only to suddenly become kind. Almost intimate.

I held out the picture. "Why is there a picture of me in the library?"

"Why don't you ask the real question?"

"And what is the real question?" My voice was rising. Ty would kill me if he knew I was interrogating Rhys.

With a breathy whisper, Rhys asked, "Are you not curious? Ask me why there's pictures of you."

Pictures. Shaking my head, I flinched, my head spinning. The visions—the blue-eyed woman was me? *No.* I shook the thought.

The door swung open. Denton burst in, a smile on his face. One look at us and he froze. "You've…uh, met."

"Imagine that." Rhys smiled ruefully. His gaze flicked to the ring on my hand. I felt the rush of warmth on my cheeks. He blinked before giving a subtle shake of his head.

I looked between the two of them. Rhys's shoulders tensed and Denton was wary and wide-eyed.

"Please don't tell him about the dreams," I whispered, placing a pleading hand on Rhys' arm.

Rhys swallowed, his focus back on the ring. "Trust me. He already knows."

Sliding from him, I wished for some way out of an awkward conversation. I was Denton's guest after begging him to transfer my mother here. Yet I'd come and kissed Rhys. Nothing could be worse.

"So, you know?" Denton's shoulders sagged.

I waited for Rhys to answer but then realized Denton was asking me. This was my opportunity. "I know? I've found out a lot of things. Ty is one of them."

Rhys's eyebrows shot up. He'd not expected that. "Stephen's kid?"

"He's not." Folding my arms, I shot them both a curious look. We weren't on the same page. We weren't even in the same book. "He's my brother, isn't he?"

Denton frowned. "I can confirm that Dorothea Thorne gave birth to that boy. As far as Stephen's adoption, well." He pursed his lips. "That was a complicated family matter. The details I'm not privy to."

Disappointment fell on my shoulders. I was missing something but I would ask as many questions as they'd let me. "Why are protestors targeting the Exchange?"

Denton stepped forward. "That's a complicated question. There's a lot of anger. And fear. But the protesting is not what you think."

"What I think?" He hadn't a clue what I thought. I held up a hand when Denton opened his mouth. "I once thought the Exchange existed solely to benefit human life. But what I've found is secrets and skeletons."

Rhys scoffed, his eyes darkening. "The Samaritan Exchange was founded to better one life. Not lives."

"One life? What does that even mean?"

Denton gave a curt shake of his head. "That's not entirely true."

Rhys squared his stance, defiance in his eye. "I've been nothing but truthful."

No. The hope—the foundation I had clung to since I was a child, no. The belief that my uncle and that even myself as a patient for inoculations was a fairytale. And a false one at that. They cared about one person—apparently Rhys was that one person.

"You can't be serious." I glanced between them. "The vaccines. The cures—"

"Were to solve mortality. *One* person's mortality. Not the world's." Rhys ran a hand through his hair, his face screwed up in frustration. He pointed at Denton. "How long have you known?"

"Known what?" I'd come for answers but Rhys had shifted the entire conversation, shoving me to the sidelines.

Denton rubbed his neck. "When you left the hospital, we revived her."

"I gathered that." Rhys spat. "Why didn't you tell me?" He held out his hand, motioning to me. "She doesn't know who I am."

"I'm right here." Neither man appeared to hear me.

"Her memories are just dreams." Rhys sat on the piano bench, defeat in his voice. "She doesn't know."

"Again. I'm right here." Stephen and Ty did the same thing with my mother in the room. They'd exchange a knowing glance, the conversation in their eyes. "And my dreams aren't memories."

"Oh, but they are." Rhys held up the picture to Denton. "Look familiar?"

"Please, don't." I felt myself shrinking, the embarrassment too real.

"I can explain." Denton came forward. "That's why she's here."

I froze. Embarrassment replaced with suspicion. "What are you talking about?"

"When—*why* didn't you tell me?" The picture shook in Rhys' hand. He appeared to be on the edge—of what I didn't know. The trembling of his hand matched the emotion in his voice.

Denton opened his mouth to speak, his gaze searching Rhys' face. "I didn't know if she'd live. I had to be sure."

I had to be sure. Exhaustion wrapped around me, energy draining from me. "What am I missing?"

Clenching his jaw, Rhys tossed the picture at Denton. The photo fluttered to the marble floor. "You lied to me."

A chill swept up my neck. Not only was I missing vital information but Rhys, the man I'd dreamed about my entire life was losing control. He'd been the constant in a mercurial upbringing. But this Rhys was endearing one moment, then angry in the next—so unlike the Rhys in my visions. I felt a pang of homesickness, yearning for the man who'd comforted me through my mother's moods.

"She's here now, Rhys." Denton held out his arm, indicating me. "She's here. She's alive."

Images of the blue-eyed woman flickered in my head, the hair and face changing but the eyes were always the same. And Rhys. He was there. Always.

"What…" I swallowed the fear—and the pain from my head—and whispered, "What are you saying?"

Picking up the picture, Denton offered it back to Rhys. "It's true."

Rhys hesitated before taking it. "She doesn't know me."

Denton cast an apologetic look my way. "Then tell her."

"Stop." Shaking my head, I begged, "Just stop. Whatever you're doing. Just don't."

Rhys kneeled in front of me and laid the picture on the bench. "My name is Rhys Glyndwr." He relaxed his mouth and the Welsh accent from my dreams came through. "And you are Lady Isla Belle, my wife."

RHYS GLYNDWR

RIVER WYE, WALES: 1535

*R*hys divided his men, sending smaller companies to each county. With only a days' ride left, Rhys sent Matthias ahead to Glyndwr. Tobias and a few of his men would stay with Isla Belle and Rhys on the outskirts of Herefordshire. He felt the weight of responsibility; to the men and women tilling the land on these small farms and to the gentry stitching the broken country back together.

Tobias halted his horse in front of Isla Belle and Rhys. "There's a cottage just up the road. It's not much to look at but it'll keep the rain out."

"Where will you be?" Isla Belle asked, dismounting and stretching her legs.

"Ah, have you a tender spot in that dragon heart of yours?" The guard winked at her, a mischievous glint in his eye.

"How can I drive a dagger through your heart if I don't know where you sleep?" She asked a touch too sweet.

"Ay, you're a devilish one." Tobias threw back his head, laughing. "I'll be checking the outpost. I heard rumors of Milford creeping behind us."

Isla Belle's head snapped to Rhys. "We crossed the river though."

"We're safe," Rhys lied. "Go on, I'll be there soon."

She hesitated before leading her horse up the road, followed by two guards.

"What are the rumors?" Rhys dismounted and patted the horse's neck.

"That he's joined forces with the bishop." The mischief was gone from Tobias, his face washed in concern. "Milford wants to help with the hangings."

"Any word from our messenger?" Rhys had sent a man to parliament, accepting the terms before the bishop could send an inflammatory version of the council meeting. It was a dangerous game. By royal decree, Bishop Lee *was* the president of the council—and Wales' greatest threat.

"Not yet." Tobias' horse snorted. "But all will be well, Glyndwr."

"I'll hold you to it."

Tobias winked at him. "So will your dragon."

Despite himself, Rhys smiled, his attention pulled to his wife up the road. "That she will."

They departed with a nod, and Rhys followed Isla Belle, dismissing the guards to help Tobias. Entering the crooked cottage, Rhys leaned into the doorframe, his wife rubbing her sore leg. Although healed, it bothered her still.

Isla Belle turned to him, a clever smile on her lips. "I might kill him."

"I have no doubt." Rhys chuckled. "You're my dragon, *fy annwyl.*"

She tried mimicking his accent. "Ay, and you, mine."

He lifted her by the waist, bringing their bodies closer. He kissed her temple and her neck. Gooseflesh spread across her skin, inviting him, tempting him. She tightened her grasp. He broke their kiss, relishing the sound of her breathless sigh. They held each other, letting the comfort of privacy fall on them. This was the first moment of rest. Rhys hoped their future held more.

Dogs barked, followed by angry shouts. They froze in their embrace. Rhys grabbed Isla Belle's hand and flew to the window. His men were shouting and horses were shrieking.

A rush of footsteps and then a bang on the door. Rhys pushed the door. It didn't budge. Isla Belle's eyes darkened. *Fear.* She scrambled about the room while Rhys shoved his body against the door. Nothing.

"There's not a sword or tool in sight," Isla Belle whispered.

Tobias would be at the outpost. They were on their own. Peeking through a crack in the wooden door, he spied an overturned wagon wedged against the door.

"We're trapped." Her voice was eerily calm.

Rhys pulled her to his chest. "We'll find a way."

Flamed arrows flew through the broken windows, piercing the wooden floor. Fire erupted and danced along the carved root floor, smoke burning Rhys' eyes. Isla Belle covered her mouth in horror as another pack of arrows rained through the thin ceiling. Rhys wrapped his arms over Isla Belle's head, sheltering her.

Another round of arrows, some with only smoke trailing their course, the fire snuffed out by the shifting wind.

Isla Belle whimpered, ducking out from under Rhys' arms. He grabbed her hand, pulling Isla toward the back of the room.

Rhys felt a tug, glancing back he saw an arrow pierced Isla Belle's chest. He froze, his arm still outstretched. Another arrow landed at Isla's feet, the flame weak. Her hands grasped frantically at the arrow in her chest. Her face froze in a terrified grimace.

Rhys' vision blurred as another arrow pierced the makeshift bed, igniting the sheets. Two more arrows pierced Isla Belle's chest, another landed in her thigh, her skin dousing the flame. She fell slowly, almost frozen in time. He threw himself under her, the arrows breaking at the ends, tearing at her skin. Isla fell, heavy and limp. Blood crept across her chest, crimson rivers soaking into the fabric. Carefully, he turned her face to his. Tears fell from her unblinking blue eyes.

The world stilled to only Rhys and Isla Belle. His mind refused to think, his heart rejecting what he saw.

The smell of smoke returned Rhys to his senses. He lifted Isla Belle. A fire had eaten part of the back wall, sending wood crashing to the ground.

He ignored the searing pain and found the strength to cradle Isla Belle, keeping to the shadows in the house. Through a hole in the wall, Rhys saw soldiers surround Tobias in front of the garden. The guard, defiant and loyal, spat at the ground. The soldiers appeared to be waiting for the house to burn to the ground.

A breeze carried Tobias' bold words. "You won't kill him. He's a Glyndwr. You could burn every house to the ground and he'll live. So will Wales. " He threw a fist in the air and shouted, "*Cymru am byth!*" *Long live Wales.*

The fire roared, drowning out the soldiers and their commands. Tucked in an alcove, Rhys cradled Isla Belle's blood-soaked body, stroking her golden hair—her beautiful golden hair. He snapped the arrow's feathered ends and pulled her against his chest. "I'm so sorry."

Isla's eyes fluttered as her limbs convulsed erratically. Rhys leaned his forehead against hers, rocking her to the words of their lullaby in a soft tenor.

"Midnight slumber close surround thee, all through the night. Angels watching e'er around thee, all through the night..."

Her blood warmed his chest. Flashes of memory shot through his mind. The stolen moments at her sickbed. The look of trust she'd given him, time after time.

"Though I roam a minstrel lonely, all through the night. My true harp shall praise sing only, all through the night. Love's young dream, alas, is over. Yet my strains of love shall hover, near the presence of my lover. All through the night..." he sang as another memory overcame him.

Isla Belle was nearly twelve the first time Rhys hummed her the lullaby. Her eyes were dark, nearly black with fear. It was the first time she'd broken a bone. The fever had left her breathless.

"Hark a solemn bell is ringing, clear through the night. Thou, my love, art heavenward winging, home through the night..."

A few months later, he'd found her on the floor of the former nursery, vulnerable despite her regal attire. She'd disobeyed her mother once again, her will too wild to be kept in a castle. Rhys had grabbed an old blanket from the cradle, covered her and sang.

"Earthly dust from off thee shaken…"

The memory slipped as her shaking slowed. Rhys clenched tighter, trying to force life into her body. He rocked more forcefully. The movement would somehow save her. It had to. He needed her, the realization coming too late.

"Soul immortal shalt thou awaken…"

Images rushed through his mind, reminding him of how she'd cut through the harvest grain on horseback with nothing but her undergarments, all to win a wager. She'd dress as a maid to tend the suckling lambs. Rhys shook his head, feeling the picture fade. He fought the growing hoarseness in his voice and buried himself in her neck.

"With thy last dim journey taken…"

His voice broke, his throat tightened. He squeezed her tightly. She would wake from the force. He rocked furiously becoming angrier with each word. His body pounded against the floor.

"Home through the night!"

She stilled.

Rhys lay her down, arranging her hair as a golden halo and closed her eyes. His world went numb. She was gone.

"You were mine." Bending down, Rhys kissed her lips gently. He quickly wiped his tears from her cheeks, alarmed at the warmth still left in the lifeless body.

Rhys lay next to her, his mind blank and his heart numb. Men shouting and the smell of smoke could not raise him. The fired died and the soldiers disappeared, assuming both were dead—no man could live through a fire that hot, that long. Rhys stared at Isla Belle as the sun dipped below the horizon and the moon whispered an ethereal farewell. The gentle caress of night air pulled Rhys back from the emptiness.

Without a word or a tear, Rhys carried her to the roots of a yew tree and slowly—painfully, dug her grave.

ISLA BELLE THORNE

GARUDA, NICOLEÑO ISLAND: PRESENT DAY

*R*hys spoke softly, his words blending together. He spoke of a wedding and then of death. Of returning to him. I shook my head. He was lying, or insane. Like my mother.

He squeezed my hand. "I don't understand all of it. I just know that you and I are sealed. Bonded."

Scooting to the side of the piano bench, I slipped from his grasp and circled the piano, the instrument a buffer between Rhys and me. Denton shot me a wide-eyed look of surprise. As if *I* was the irrational one. I'd spent my life around crazy and these two were the very epitome.

Rhys stood, his arms outstretched. He'd done the same thing in my dreams. Maybe crazy liked company—particularly my company. "Isla Belle, you've nothing to be scared of."

"You just told me you're five hundred years old." There were only two ways out. Both on the other side of the room. "And let's not forget that I'm supposed to have married you. Oh wait, how could I have married you five centuries ago when I was born in *this* century?"

"Ay." Rhys rubbed the back of his head. "For this life."

"Are you listening to yourself?" I wanted to balk but there was something about the way he said it that made me question. I couldn't put my finger on it nor could I understand it.

"It rings true, doesn't it?" Searching my face, Rhys smirked. "There's something about it that feels right."

"I've said nothing remotely close to that." But he was right. Long before the kiss, the dreams felt real. "Why the pictures?"

"Because he thought you'd died. He's kept a portrait of each life." Denton tugged on his collar. He unbuttoned his sleeves, uncovering a bandage. The lines in his face seemed to deepen. The exhaustion aged him and yet, his coloring had improved since I'd met him this morning. "That moment, that picture of you as a baby, was the hardest. We'd exhausted modern medicine to give you the greatest chance of survival. But we failed. You'd died as a baby. It was a miracle that you were revived. I didn't think you'd last long and couldn't risk telling Rhys. He'd..." Denton cast long look at Rhys. "He'd become worse. The grieving took its toll. When he thought the bond was finally broken, I didn't correct him. Not until I could be certain you were like us. Or healthy at the very least."

"What do you mean like *us*?" It came out of my mouth before I could stop myself.

Rhys' face softened. "Like me."

"Not like him." Denton hesitated, an internal debate appeared to be happening. "Subsequent generations live shorter. The gene becomes diluted. That is why I am younger than Rhys."

My eyes must have been the size of saucers. They were serious. Denton just admitted to being biologically immortal. And yet, the alpaca experiment had proved Denton's theory, the younger generations living shorter. The theory had also been proven with the tree project Euston had looked into. "The longevity gene, that's what this is all about?"

Rhys made a circle with his finger, indicating the house. "If by *this* you mean the Exchange, then yes."

"But they died." Seventeen animals had died. I'd read and reread every inch of that project.

Rhys' brow furrowed. He didn't know. Suspicion crept in. What else didn't he know—and why would he be kept in the dark?

Denton stepped forward. "The Exchange has done a lot of good." He sighed, sounding infinitely older than he looked. "But we are not saints. There's been a great cost to our accomplishments." There was truth in his statement. Nature had a way of adjusting, taking just as much as it gave.

I rubbed the bridge of my nose. "I shouldn't ask. I really shouldn't. But here I am, what *bond* are you talking about?"

"We're sealed." Rhys arched an eyebrow, his patience running out. "But every time you return, you remember less."

"Right." They believed the words. I didn't. It'd been years since I'd worked in a laboratory but the scientist in me rejected everything they said. I'd chased a scientific education because facts were something I could hold, something that could be explained. My mother was never steady, never reliable, but science had rules and laws that the world around me had to obey. "You're suggesting I'm reincarnated? Denton, you're a doctor. How can you believe this?"

"My tenure as a doctor has proved your case." He folded his hands behind his back.

"You've got to be kidding me?" A laugh came out, sounding more like a sigh. "You're in charge of the Samaritan Exchange and you're telling me you believe in reincarnation—no, you believe *I'm* reincarnated? That I magically skipped from one life to the next?"

"You're the scientist. You tell us." Denton rocked on his heels. "You have visions of the women in the library and the man in front of you. Nothing we say will convince you of your own memories. When you're ready, we can go over the facts."

"What facts?" I still had questions. "I came here to find out about my mom. About all the little secrets that don't add up."

"Nothing else?" Rhys spoke, his eyes earnest. "You felt no other compulsion?"

And there it was—the truth of it. I *had* felt this strange pull, toward Rhys not Garuda. I'd felt it in the theatre the first time I heard him play the violin. The feeling reappeared with a vengeance the next time I heard him. And then in the stairwell.

My breath hitched. There was comfort in Rhys even if I didn't want to admit it.

A knowing smile appeared on Denton's face. "You've a sound mind, Isla Belle. Don't dismiss your visions as craziness. You're not your mother."

"I'm not sure who is crazy and who isn't." It fell out before I could stop myself. "My mother..." I took a deep breath. "She would say something like this. And she'd believe it."

"She did believe it," Denton said softly.

"What?" The air seemed too still. The room stifling. "What did you say?"

"She knew." Denton nodded.

The play—my mother had modeled the immortal story after Rhys and me.

"And Stephen?" Had my entire family kept secrets from me? Stephen had tenderly cared for me, he wouldn't lie to me, keep me in the dark. Not, not Stephen. And yet—he'd kept Ty's true parentage from us. "Does he know?"

"He's your mother's brother." Denton shrugged, like that answered the question.

"That doesn't mean much." Stepping from the piano, I felt detached. I didn't know who I could trust. "They're not exactly close."

My phone rang, the sound blaring in the cold room. Pulling it from my pocket, my finger slipped, answering it.

Before I could bring it to my ear, Ty shouted, "Where. Are. You?"

Rhys' eyes narrowed. I could feel his protectiveness from across the piano. That was something I shouldn't know.

"Hi, Ty." My voice sounded foreign.

"Seven missed calls, Isla Belle." Ty's voice was near desperate. Something was wrong. "Did you even read the texts?"

"I'm sorry."

"Dottie's—" He stopped himself. My heart sank, my hand gripping the phone. He whispered, his voice breaking, "She's not going to be transferred. She's not okay. It's not going to be okay. They're waiting until you get here."

"I'm coming." I watched my hand end the call—as if it belonged to someone else. This wasn't happening.

"Are you alright?" Denton's low voice carried.

"My mother..." The words wouldn't come. I simply stared at my phone.

"We'll take the helicopter," Denton said turning for the door.

"You don't have to come." In truth, I didn't want them to come. Their recent revelation needed more scrutiny but I couldn't analyze their words in front of them. And not with my mother dying. I needed to be alone with my thoughts.

"I do a lot of things I don't have to." Denton left without another word.

Their sudden camaraderie didn't sit well. They felt as if I was one of them but I wasn't. I was still the girl with a sick mother and the girl who dreamed of the same man all her life. None of that bound us together. If anything, it set us apart.

Rhys watched Denton go adding softly, "I saw you, didn't I?"

"The stairwell," I whispered. He was there until Ty showed up. "Why did you run?"

"He said your name. I thought a protestor had found out and was using the information against me. A cruel joke." He smiled ruefully. "I'd thought it was over. You'd died as a baby. It was done."

"So you ran?"

"You're not the only one who questions your sanity." Rhys nodded at the door where Denton left. "I've not been well. When you leave, when you die, it takes a piece of me. But you're here. And healthy this time." He held up my hand, his thumb rolling the band over my finger. "Ye are blood of my blood and bone of my bone. I give ye my body that we two might be one."

The feeling came, the pull from somewhere else. The marble floors faded to the vibrant green of a lush meadow. We stood under the yew tree, the priest reaching for our hands. I winced at the flick of the knife. And then it was gone—the vision draining from me.

Rhys searched my face. Tucking my chin, I cut off his view. I hated that he could see my emotions. It was all too familiar. Too real.

"It wasn't always this hard, *fy annwyl*." He lifted my chin. An electric current hummed under my skin. "Once you had memories not dreams. We don't know how it all works. But I was hoping we could figure it out together."

"I can't say yes." The temptation was there. I should leave, but that suddenly felt wrong. And Rhys felt right. "But I can't say no."

"I'd expect nothing less."

"Why hold on?" Tugging at his wrist, I stepped back. "If I'm your wife and keep leaving, why wait?"

It was his turn to look away. "I like to pretend I have a choice."

"You have a choice, Rhys. I release you."

He smirked. "You've released me before and I've always come back. I choose you. I'll not waver now."

"Are you hearing what—"

"That's not what I meant." Rhys scowled. "I like to pretend. Pretend that I could chose to not love you. But there was never any choice." He stepped forward and touched my hair. "It was your spirit that trapped me. Even as a child, you'd not submit. You'd not back down. And yet, you'd look at me with those eyes of yours." He smiled with a faraway look in his eye. "I became more than a man when you looked at me. You'd love and fight with the same passion. And I loved you for it."

The spark was lit, the warmth spreading through my chest. A creature stirred inside of me. It believed him—a part of me did, too.

He dropped his hand, his smile falling. "Even when the world wanted you to sit pretty, you refused. And now, when I've presented our history you have to fight me on it. That's who you are, Isla Belle. It's in your soul. And I can't stop."

"I'm not sure my mother would agree." Peace coursed through me. He spoke of a childhood I'd only dreamed of. He spoke of a person I'd always wanted to be. The blue-eyed woman had always felt more free, more brave than me. The weight of my mother felt instantly lighter.

"When have you taken no as an answer?" He tipped his head, a challenge in his eye. He held out his hand.

I stood there, feeling the weight of what he was offering. Rhys had been the constant in an unsteady life. He'd visited me in visions and dreams. Here he was in the flesh, extending help and support, the very things I craved from my mother. I didn't believe—not fully, not yet—but there was something between us. I stepped closer and raised my hand, touching his face. The pull, familiar and comforting, wrapped around me, guiding my heart to his. He hooked an arm around me, his lips curling to a mischievous smile. Home. Rhys was home—*I* was home.

He kissed my temple, whispering, "We'll figure this out, *fy annwyl.*"

RHYS GLYNDWR

LONDON, ENGLAND: 1645

*C*hildren scurried in front of Rhys, their clothes tattered and faces gaunt. All of London was touched in some way by the dreaded plague and the aftermath of the civil war. The rain had ceased, but the air was still chilled from the moisture. Rhys meandered around a small courtyard, with little more than a thin, worn shirt.

He'd felt a pull on the anniversary of Isla Belle's death. He dreamed of her, her death burned in his memory. He'd followed the feeling, landing him in the city where he'd given her a proper burial in a gravesite, closer to her family's land.

Several unaged years came and went, just like his father. No one knew how. Decades swirled past Rhys while he remained young, untouched by time.

Two small children chased a matted dog, passing Rhys in their dingy brown and gray clothes. They slipped and tumbled over the wet street. He sniffed at the mortality in the air and prayed for death. Isla Belle had left an ache in his soul. She'd snuck into his heart despite his efforts. His loneliness threatened to consume him.

A modest black carriage, curtains drawn, drove up the street toward Rhys. A woman in a blue shawl draped along thin shoulders darted from Rhys' side to the street, standing in front of the approaching horses. She waved frantically, her shawl falling to the dirty street.

"Stop!" Rhys ran to her and pulled her aside. He was a healer, a savior to the core. The horses reared, pawing their hooves in the air. The carriage swayed to a stop. The door swung open, exposing a smartly dressed man, his hair black and his frame slender. A violent cough escaped as he stomped down the steps of the carriage, his face red with righteous anger.

"Doctor!" The woman scrambled to the carriage. "Help!"

The doctor brushed her off with a wave of his hand and barked at the driver. "Get on with it or you'll not be paid."

"Please, I need your help," she begged.

The doctor climbed back in and slammed the door with such force it snapped back open. An attractive woman with thick, dark red hair peeked through the opening. She leaned forward, almost standing. Her skin was fair but her body lacked healthy curves.

"Close the door, Mary."

She bowed in submission to the frowning doctor, her gaze never leaving Rhys. Her eyes—the color flickering—pierced him to the core. He knew those eyes. They flashed to a dark blue. He had watched them lose their light over a century ago.

"Isla?" He stepped forward. A burning warmed his chest. He noticed the ring on her wedding hand. He felt the ring on his own pinky. He'd stolen it from Isla's finger before leaving her to the grave.

The woman could not be his. She belonged to another. Her brow furrowed, her mouth opened. They stared without blinking before she tucked her chin, her eyes brightening to a brilliant sapphire, a happy shade. A blush crept up her neck, pinking her freckled cheeks.

The doctor's face darkened. "Close the door, *love*."

"Isla!" Rhys called after the departing carriage, standing alone in the wet street. Images of Isla Belle teasing him filled his mind. *She is gone.* The thought circled in his head, over and over. He rubbed his temples and approached the dilapidated St. Paul church. If he was beyond saving, at least he could light a candle for the red-headed woman.

"You cannot find salvation in there." A thin woman glided down the steps of the church, her dress and manner fine but her accent hard to place.

Rhys looked around for whom the woman addressed.

"Yes, you." She smiled warmly, her face striking. Each side mirrored the other. Her skin smooth, unblemished. "Nothing you do, or say in there will change your life."

He took a step back and said wryly, "Did you not come from worshipping?"

"I leave the worshipping to the believers." Her eyes sparkled, her teeth perfectly white and aligned. "But I do love the quiet."

"Why are you so familiar with me?"

"You are a young one, aren't you?" She smiled and bowed slightly to an approaching family. "I'd wager you're one, maybe two hundred years?"

Rhys glanced around feeling vulnerable and exposed. He had longed for answers and held the image of Isla Belle in his mind. "You know what I am?"

Carriages busied themselves while hungry children played. No one paid him any heed, except the woman, stepping uncomfortably close. He'd not been in the intimate company of others in ages, no more than a moment or two. He stepped back, unsure of what to do.

"Hush, child." She tsked, her eyebrow arched. She cocked her head to the side, examining him. "We all look the same, don't we?"

"Child?" He scoffed, then checked himself. His face didn't look a day past twenty. He climbed a step towards her.

She covered half her face with one hand, then the other to show the exactness of her features. "We stand out. You'll need to learn to blend in or you'll spend an eternity in hiding."

"I'll not live forever." It was possible to die. At least, he hoped. His father had died, so too could Rhys.

She curtsied as a group of merchants passed, their hats wider and waists more fitted than in Isla Belle's time. "I don't think you have a choice."

"You're at peace with it?" Rhys nodded as a merchant eyed them, brow furrowed with suspicion. She had curtsied as if she were below the merchant class yet her language was that of a gently bred woman.

She ignored the merchant's attention and looked just past Rhys, her mind elsewhere. With an inaudible sigh, she placed a hand on his arm. "You're alone, then? No children of your own."

He shrank from her touch, aghast that she would reach for him. "I've a wife."

"A wife?" Her brow furrowed, her voice low. The stairs of the church became crowded, filling with beggars and worshippers alike. "You married one of us?"

"No." He retreated, nearly tripping on the steps.

"You're from the River Wye, aren't you?" The woman followed Rhys, dismissing a beggar with a flick of her wrist. "Your accent is still there. You're not even trying to mask it."

He retreated again. She was too forward, too comfortable. "She wasn't one of us. Whatever it is that we are."

She smiled sadly and straightened. "Ah, then. I shall take my leave."

Her sudden withdrawal gave him pause. Loneliness pricked him, taking him by surprise. Guilt had kept him warm at night, that and Isla Belle's eyes. The color of pleasure, pain—even fear, found him.

"Do you wish to die?" He'd spoken too loudly. A mother ushered her children away from them. Rhys nodded in apology.

"No, not die." The woman turned to go, saying over her shoulder. "But I'd give anything to see my family again despite what they say."

"They?"

"Others like us." She shrugged and shook her head at the church. "They say it's a tender mercy, our families dying."

"A blessing?" he asked, no longer caring who heard.

"A blessing that they die instead of live forever with the pain of losing loved ones. Their children. Their parents. Their families." Lifting her chin, she didn't wait for an answer and descended the steps. "Would you rather she return, only to die again?"

"Return?" Rhys scrambled after her.

The myths surrounding his family never spoke of the dead returning. His mother had never come to find him. Neither had his father.

The red haired woman in the carriage; she had Isla Belle's eyes.

"Please," Rhys begged, circling the woman, her features, exact.

"Could you survive her death again?" She squared her stance, facing him. Her eyes focused on the church behind them. "It'll drive you mad."

Rhys motioned to an approaching young couple with hands intertwined, exchanging adoring glances. "Is it possible?"

"It's a myth. Another Welsh story. One I wish were true." With longing in her eyes, she looked at the ground. "It is as I said, only a myth."

"So is our immortality." If there was a sliver of chance he could hold Isla Belle once more, he'd take it. He'd embrace her. He would never hesitate to hold her again. He'd rush toward her, beg her to marry him all over again.

"We can die. Just not for many centuries. But yes, we *can* die."

"And yet we are both here."

She arched an eyebrow. "Do you find it cruel, till death us part?"

He brushed her off. "Our priest never said those words. We wed under a yew tree, not a church."

"Do you know nothing of your people?" She mimicked his Welsh accent with eyes wide, a mixture of fear and frustration. "The yew tree is the tree of life. What is bound on earth is bound in the hereafter."

The words fell on him, sinking into his being. The hair on his neck stood on end. He gave a stiff nod and said, "I wish you well."

"Your souls are sealed." She lifted her chin, aware of the dismissal. "She'll move onto the next world but only for a moment. She's chained to you in this one. As long as you're here, she will come to you."

The woman in the carriage—was she Isla Belle? "She'll come to me?"

"You do not know what you're playing with." She looked to heaven with a sigh.

"Then tell me, woman."

"I cannot decide if it's a blessing or a curse." She leveled him eyes round and wide. "You've seen her, haven't you?"

"I thought—for a moment—but it's not possible." He'd loved Isla for only a fraction of his life, yet her memory still held its grip. "The woman, her hair was different. Voice, too." But the eyes.

She glanced at Rhys' ringed finger. "It has begun then."

ISLA BELLE THORNE

SACRAMENTO, CALIFORNIA: PRESENT DAY

*T*he helicopter ride was a blur as was the ride to my mother's hospital. Stephen gave a stiff nod to Denton and Rhys when they accompanied me into the room. Rhys entered his phone number into my phone, asking me to call him. Without a word, everyone—including the nurses—left me to speak to my mother alone. Cradling her hand in mine, I sat on the edge of her bed. Most of her face was covered by medical equipment. Her skin had grayed and her face, the little I could see, had sunken. More than anything, I could feel the death in the air.

Gathering both her hands, I laid them across her stomach and braced myself for the grief. The seconds ticked by but only comfort came over me.

Her breathing was labored, pulling at my heart. It wasn't right to keep her here, not when she so desperately hurt. I still didn't know if my birth was her downfall, that was one of a few questions that I no longer wanted to know the answer. She was plagued with a mental illness I didn't understand. I combed her hair with my fingers, wishing I had taken the time to do her make up and nails. She could have gone out in style, a homecoming worthy of Dottie Thorne.

Slowly, the nurse entered, along with Stephen and Ty. The

machines were quieted—the only sound was her labored breathing. Ty reached for my hand. We clung to each other like the orphans we were—even if Ty didn't know it yet.

Of all the visions and memories I'd had, watching my mother pass was the most surreal. One moment she was there and the next, like a draft in a room, she was gone.

In a daze, I walked from the hospital without a destination. My phone kept beeping but I didn't want to check it. I didn't want life to move on. It didn't feel right.

My feet took me to the steps of the Exchange. Pulling my phone out, I wondered if Rhys was inside. There were several missed phone calls from the detective. His questions could wait. A news station pulled up, a cameraman and newswoman began setting up on the courtyard. The threat of protestors was still very much alive but today—no, today they just didn't matter. Scrolling down, I saw a missed phone call from the Exchange laboratory. I called back but like an idiot, I realized it was Saturday, no one was in. Saturday—my mother was supposed to be transferred to Stanford today. There would be a funeral, a casket...I sank to the grass, feeling massively overwhelmed.

Checking my texts, I could feel Ty's rising panic when I hadn't answered earlier. I had to tell him about who his mother was. The weight on my shoulders doubled.

Not today. I could only do one hard thing today. Two police cruisers pulled up on either side of the news station. One officer walked inside while the other sat on the hood.

If there was going to be a protest, I wanted to be far away from here. I debated on calling Ty to pick me up but felt the weight of the ring on my finger. My heart lifted. No, I would contact Rhys. I sent a quick text, *Wound up walking to Xchange. On the front lawn.*

Turning back to my phone I checked my email, only two were sent. One was from the detective and one from the medical assistant. An image was attached to the detective's email, a cemetery littered with gravestones. My throat went dry, my gaze drifting to the police cruisers.

The detective had written, *Have you seen this? This was posted on a protestor's site.*

I'd never seen the cemetery but I felt a strong connection. And then I knew—the fertility clinic. Using my fingers, I zoomed in. Many of the gravestones had a baby carved into the headstone. *No.* I had to be wrong.

The dull pain of my headache spread. I'd left my prescription back in Garuda. I checked the email from the medical assistant, hoping I could email them for a refill. With my mother's impending funeral, I would be in California for the time being.

Miss Thorne,

Here is a copy of your records, your father requested a copy last week—his signature was included in the file. We would like to schedule a consultation as soon as possible.

Clicking the image, I gripped my phone. There, on the first scanned page was printed *Thomas Denton* with his signature immediately below his name. He was a damned liar. He wasn't my father. And yet the pieces started falling into place. Denton had said he wanted to make sure I was like *us*, that I could live longer. He'd corrected Rhys, telling me I wasn't like Rhys but like Denton. Had he given me the longevity gene?

I scrolled down to my blood panel—it showed my white count dangerously high, indicative of a serious illness and the chronic indicator also high. Whatever was wrong with me, I've had for months, if not years. My kidney and liver functions were off as well. This wasn't right. This had to be someone else's blood. I wasn't sick, only headaches and if Denton *had* given me the longevity gene, I wouldn't be sick—not even remotely unwell—for several decades. This wasn't adding up.

Denton had signed for this. He'd bypassed the HIPPA guidelines—and then the answer came. My mother was a ward of the Exchange. Denton wouldn't have to prove much for me to be another ward.

Another news station pulled up as did another police cruiser. People began crossing the street, clogging the traffic. Within a matter of minutes, chants erupted across the courtyard.

"Isla Belle!" Rhys yelled from across the grass. Denton was behind him, nodding along to what a police officer was saying. Rhys began walking, only to stop and turn his head.

I followed his gaze. An engine revved. Two motorcycles burst onto the courtyard, aiming for the front doors of the Exchange. The police officer pulled Denton to the side. Rhys ran toward me.

Sirens wailed. The motorcycles crashed into the front of the building. Another set of motorcycles popped over the sidewalk onto the grass, followed by a brown SUV. *Killer* was spray painted in white across the side.

With sirens on, the police cruisers pulled forward, forming a semi circle around the front of the building. A white SUV honked at the police car and jumped the curb, honking at the protestors to move. It kept going, aiming toward the building. Rhys slipped passed the cruisers.

A truck jumped the curb, colliding into a police car, spinning the cruiser around to smash into its neighboring police car. The motorcycles rode in circles, popping wheelies and shouting, the words drowned in the sound of the engines.

I stood frozen as a truck rushed passed me, plowing toward the spinning police cruiser. Rhys raced toward me. The truck caught the edge of the police car and flipped—on top of Rhys.

The world stopped. In an instant, the women from my dreams flashed in my mind, their deaths flickering in quick succession. Grief, and all its crushing weight tossed me about. I struggled to breath. The images faded, and once again I was at the Exchange—and Rhys was trapped under the truck.

I ran to him, a policeman pulling me back. An ache opened in my heart, the pain deep, piercing. Wrestling in the policeman's arms, I fought. Rhys needed me. And I needed him.

Images of him laughing flickered in my mind. His teasing. His voice. This was not happening. This was not—could not be real. Rhys had to be okay.

In a blur, medics arrived. They put Rhys on a stretcher. I fought against the policeman's grip. They rushed Rhys away. Covering my ears, I fell to the ground, not realizing the screaming was mine.

Denton came to me, regret in his eyes. I couldn't hear. I couldn't speak.

Time was distorted. Feeling both rushed and agonizingly slow, I was transported to Rhys' bedside. I couldn't look at him. He groaned and fidgeted. He'd returned to California because of me, because of my mother.

Denton entered the hospital room. Unable to hide the anger, I turned from him. He'd not shed a tear. Rhys was his longtime business partner and he'd been too calm, too collected.

And he'd lied to me. He'd taken a copy of my records.

The protestors had proudly taken responsibility for attacking the Exchange, saying they'd come to *kill the killer,* blaming the Exchange for fatal experiments. Denton had yet to accept responsibility for anything.

"You've not changed, Isla Belle." Denton's voice was gentle, angering me further. "It's not just your eye color that gives away your thoughts."

"You signed my records as my father."

His eyes widened for a fraction of a second. "That I did."

"Are you saying, you're—"

"We needed to cure your mortality or at least slow it down." He didn't meet my gaze. "The..." he hesitated. "The doctors thought they could use my DNA."

"By doctors, do you mean Stephen?" I flinched at my tone.

"I think you already know the answer to that." Denton sat opposite me, on the other side of the bed. "When you're done being angry, check his vitals, Isla Belle."

He'd easily switched subjects. I wanted to scream at him. He sat there so calm while Rhys was dying.

"He has thirteen broken bones and three ruptured organs." I glared at the nurse entering the room. Rhys needed pain meds hours ago. She should have been here, doing her job. Why Rhys wasn't in the intensive care unit was beyond me.

"For someone who doesn't believe in Rhys' story, you seem to care an awful lot." Again, his calm, smooth voice. It grated on my nerves. "He'll be glad to know you care. Just don't break on him. He doesn't know about the headaches or the dizziness. Rhys can't handle another loss."

"Are you out of your mind?"

"I'm serious, Isla Belle. He doesn't know you're sick."

"I'm not sick. I'm not the one in a hospital bed. I'm not the one who needs your help." The nurse flinched. I hadn't realized I was yelling. Turning to her, I said, "He needs something. Anything."

Denton broke our gaze, turning his attention to the machine. Rhys' blood pressure and pulse rose during his twisting, only to sink back to normal levels when he stopped. That wasn't right. They should be all over the place. His temperature was stable as well. On the whiteboard above the machine, the pain medication slot was empty.

"What can you give him?" I asked the nurse, purposely not looking at Denton. Rhys began twisting and turning again.

The nurse furrowed her brow, looking between us. "Nothing."

Denton held up his hands. "It's not what you think, Isla Belle."

"And just what am I thinking?" I seethed, my hands clenching at my sides. The man was a sadist. "How could you? He's your partner. Your friend. You're denying him pain relief?"

"Could you leave us for a moment?" Denton asked the nurse, polite as always. He waited for her to go. "Rhys has lived for nearly five hundred years. He's what you would call biologically immortal. That's the part we can explain."

"What does that have to do with him right now? Look at him!" Rhys clenched his eyes. The machine beeped, his blood pressure was rising again. I begged, "Give him something, Denton."

"Look at his chest." He stood and pulled back the hospital blanket.

Despite myself, I looked. The car had pinned Rhys. Fragmented pieces of the car's frame had stabbed him in the chest, puncturing a lung. Several ribs were broken. His entire chest should be red and swollen but all I saw was the yellow and brown; the bruises were already healing. It'd been ten hours at most since the car rolled onto him, not the one—or even two weeks—of healing. No one could heal this fast. It wasn't possible.

A thought nagged at the edge of my mind. There was more to Rhys' healing than what I saw. There was more to all of it. The pieces slid into place. Memories flooded my mind. The images flickered, my hair sometimes blonde, then red...and now black. I sat back, my breath coming hard.

"The dreams or visions that you've had." Denton placed the blanket back over Rhys, tucking the ends. "Those were real. You've returned to him. That's the part we can't quite figure out."

"People with the longevity gene live for a hundred maybe a hundred and twenty years. Not *five* hundred." My words lost their fight. "It's not supposed to be possible."

"And yet part of you knows it's true."

"Why didn't you tell me? Or Rhys?" The images still ran through my mind, each moment bringing warmth instead of fear.

"Rhys was actively trying to die, Isla Belle. Do you understand me?" Denton didn't wait for me to answer. "I watched him. He'd inject himself with disease, only for his cells to produce the antibody. Instead of dying, he manufactured a vaccine."

Ty had mentioned the Exchange was on the forefront for vaccinations. What Denton said made sense. I didn't want it to, but it did.

Denton sighed and wiped his face with both hands. "He needs *you*, not medication."

"I shouldn't believe you." But I did.

Denton tapped his temple. *He doesn't know you're sick.* The room grew cold—I shivered. When I was recovering in the hospital, the nurse ran reports and sent them to Denton. His view was a front row seat to my mortality. I'd naively assumed the headaches were a result of the visions—but the dreams had always been a part of my life, including childhood. "You knew about my health. You weren't planning on telling him, were you?"

"I was still on the fence." His eyes held a piercing sorrow. "I was hoping we could figure it out together. You're a bright girl, we could have used your brain."

"Does he have any idea? Any hint that I'm sick?"

"Not yet." Denton shook his head. He smiled sadly and reached over, a hand over mine.

"Biological immortality or any gene modification can't be forced. That's what happened with the alpacas." I stared at his hand, the warmth growing. Death awaited me, that was my future.

He squeezed my hand. "I am not ready to give up, are you?"

Here was where I belonged. There was still so much left to do but I wasn't alone. In truth, I never was.

Rhys relaxed, his pulse settling down. He groaned once more and opened his eyes. Squinting, he said, *"Dim hwyl fawr?"*

I sent a questioning look to Denton.

"I'm afraid I don't speak Welsh. That's your department, m'dear." Denton nodded, leaving me with a confused Rhys. "I'll be back."

I forced a smile. "What does *dim howl—*"

Rhys flinched, saying in a thick accent, "Your Welsh is awful."

"Good morning to you, too."

Rhys smirked. The pain in his eyes melted my heart, Denton's words not yet forgotten. Rhys' lips spread to a teasing smile. The electric current snapped back to life.

"I'm sorry, Rhys. You shouldn't be here. Not like this."

Grimacing, he shook his head and scooted over, patting the side of the bed. "Come here, *fy annwyl.*"

"I'll hurt you." I still came to his side and held his hand. This was where I would always end up, next to him.

"You'll hurt me more if you don't let me hold you."

"That makes zero sense." But his words felt like a caress all the same.

He smiled, the pain in his eyes dimming, replaced with mischief. "When have you and I ever made sense?"

I let him pull me to the bed. Gingerly, I lay next to him.

"I'm not made of glass, Isla Belle." He chuckled, his breathing shallow. He wasn't as painfree as he pretended. "You're the one who breaks."

"Tell that to your face." Curling into him, the ache in my chest shriveled. Home. Rhys was home.

Rhys's thumb rolled the band on my finger. "I've missed you."

"I'm here now." Listening to his heart beat, I relished the feeling of safety, of comfort. Rhys' life and our bond didn't make sense but it was real. Everything between us was real. And alive.

"Forever. You're here forever." Rhys sighed with a contented smile, cracking my heart.

The few facts I could string together didn't paint a future worth smiling about. Rhys had lived for centuries, saddled with our bond and my reincarnation. I was sick—with what or how severe I didn't know for sure. Rhys wrongly believed all was well this time, that I was healthy.

I'd spent enough time with the alpaca experiment to know one thing. I had an uphill battle on my hands, but I wasn't alone.

Rhys tightened his grip and kissed my head. He was blissfully ignorant—and I'd keep him that way. He'd spent hundreds of years mourning me, I wouldn't take this moment from him.

My headaches were a sign of mortality but hope elbowed its way in. If I believed Garuda could cure my mother, why not me? There were more questions in my life than answers but with Rhys by my side, we could face them. Together.

Rhys tipped my chin, brushing his lips against mine. Peace filled my veins. Warmth settled inside me. Nothing else mattered. Tomorrow we could worry.

Detective Williams believed there were more protestors ready to do more damage. We would figure it out, that I knew. But right here, in Rhys' arms, nothing else mattered. I was home.

ALSO BY CLARISSA KAE

Prince of Death

Reign of Mercy

Reign of Chaos (Winter 2026)

Time Slip Novels

Of Ink And Sea

Women's Fiction

Pieces To Mend

Once And Future Wife Series

Once And Future Wife

Victorian Retellings

A Dark Beauty, Beauty & the Beast

Cinders Like Glass , Cinderella

A Stolen Heart, Robin Hood

Taming Christmas, Taming of the Shrew (standalone)

A Light So Fleeting, Rapunzel (novella)

The Wolf of Heathclove Manor (novella)

ABOUT THE AUTHOR

Clarissa Kae is a preeminent voice whose professional career began as a freelance editor in 2007. She's the former president of her local California Writers Club after spending several years as the Critique Director.

Since her first novel, she's explored different writing genres and created a loyal group of fans who eagerly await her upcoming release. With numerous awards to her name, Clarissa continues to honor the role of storyteller.

Aside from the writing community, she and her daughters founded Kind Girls Make Strong Women to help undervalued nonprofit organizations—from reuniting children with families to giving Junior Olympic athletes their shot at success.

She lives in the agricultural belly of California with her family and farm of horses, chickens, dogs and kittens aplenty.

Discover more...
    www.clarissakae.com
    Insta (@clarissa__kae)
    Facebook (@authorclarissakae)

www.ingramcontent.com/pod-product-compliance
Lightning Source LLC
Chambersburg PA
CBHW030421180626
46812CB00005B/2119